Fool's Gold

Rene

ALSO BY ZANA BELL
FROM CLIPPER LARGE PRINT

Close to the Wind

Fool's Gold

Zana Bell

W F HOWES LTD

This large print edition published in 2015 by
W F Howes Ltd
Unit 4, Rearsby Business Park, Gaddesby Lane,
Rearsby, Leicester LE7 4YH

1 3 5 7 9 10 8 6 4 2

First published in the United Kingdom in 2014
by Choc Lit Limited

A CIP catalogue record for this book is available
from the British Library

ISBN 978 1 47129 460 0

Typeset by Palimpsest Book Production Limited,
Falkirk, Stirlingshire

Printed and bound in Great Britain
by TJ International Ltd, Padstow, Cornwall

CHAPTER 1

1866, West Coast Forests, New Zealand.

Guinevere scarcely dared breathe. The small cluster of weka scratched amongst the leaves, gradually shifting from the dark shadow of the trees to the sun-splashed clearing. *Go on* she urged the flightless birds silently. *Another foot and I've got you.*

A thread of perspiration ran down her face. It was stifling under the black cloth but she was not to be distracted now as the largest weka strayed into the late afternoon sun, its mottled brown plumage glinting in the light.

Now see it.

He did. The wink of her grandmother's locket caught his attention and he went to inspect it. *Ha!* Guinevere felt a surge of triumph. She'd heard weka could not resist glittering objects. The locket was secured to a large stone. That should hold his attention for a minute, surely. Timing was essential, the wet plate would be drying fast. Silently she slid out from under the shroud, then, holding her breath, she removed the lens cap. The almighty

1

explosion shattered the silence and reverberated around the mountains. The family fled in squawking alarm while Guinevere stared dumbfounded at the weka now lying headless in the grass.

Then she saw him, rifle held loosely in one hand, as he sauntered across the clearing towards the weka – her weka.

Those long, long hours of preparation and now all for nothing. Fury, white hot and brighter than any magnesium flash, ignited. Without pausing to think, Guinevere erupted out of the bushes.

'How dare you.'

The man spun on his heel, his rifle coming up in reflex.

'You *ruined* my shot! I took hours setting it all up.'

He fell back a step, lowering his gun. 'What the—?'

He was very tall, his shoulders broad. She couldn't see his face, covered as it was in beard and with his hat pulled low. His clothes were battered and shabby. Dried mud coated his boots and trouser cuffs. His shirtsleeves were rolled up and his arms were as brown as a farm labourer's. *Murderer*. Bubbling rage engulfed her.

'You bumbling *idiot*. Do you have *any* idea how much the Royal Geographical Society would have paid for a photograph like that? Well, do you?'

'Photograph? Jaysus, woman! What the hell are you talking about?' His Irish voice was low and curt with incredulity. At the same time there was something very still, very watchful about him. He'd taken the bird in a single shot.

A cloud came over the sun and the shadows of the forest all around them deepened, making Guinevere shiver. The huge, jagged spine of snow-capped mountains seemed to lean in, more forbidding than ever. She was suddenly conscious that the two of them were all alone in this huge, untamed land and that he had a gun. Then her family's motto flashed across her mind: *courage jusqu'à la mort*. Her chin came up and she swept the branch aside to reveal the tripod and black shroud.

'Look, simpleton! I've been preparing this past hour for the perfect shot and then, just as I was about to take it, you had to go and ruin it all.'

His jaw clenched under the thick beard. 'Simpleton yourself! What man would ever expect to find some silly English girl with a camera squatting under the bushes out here, a day's walk from the nearest town?'

A tiny voice of reason whispered that he had a point, but in his tone was that dismissive note of male superiority she'd come to hate over the past month.

'How like a man to take one look at a family of birds and immediately wish to annihilate it!'

'What? Like the way the English annihilate Irish families?' His contempt seared. 'I was hungry, dammit. A lady like yourself wouldn't know how that feels.'

'Oh, wouldn't I?' She smiled grimly. 'Why else would I be squatting under a bush a day's walk from anywhere?'

That seemed to give him pause for thought. He scratched his neck, then pushed the brim of his hat back with the barrel of his rifle.

Guinevere found herself looking up into cool grey eyes that surveyed her with as much curiosity as hostility.

'Where's your husband?'

'I'm not married.'

'Your father or brother then?'

'My father died two months ago.' She glared, defying sympathy. 'Not that it is any of your business.'

They might be in the middle of the forest at the bottom of the world, but she was not going to tolerate the presumptuous behaviour of strange men. The Irishman, however, continued unabashed in his impertinence.

'What? So you are here all alone?' Her silence answered his question. 'Oh, for the love of Jaysus, have you no sense? You cannot be going about alone in this country.' His gun made a sweeping motion towards the forest that stretched impenetrably about them. ''Tis riddled with adventurers and gold seekers. Finding a woman alone they could—'

He broke off but she knew what he meant and her shoulders stiffened though she couldn't meet his eyes.

'Cerberus will protect me. He won't let anyone near,' she said grandly.

His lip curled. 'Guardian of the underworld? And where is this fine hound?'

'Tied up at my camp.'

'Let me guess. So as not to spoil your pretty picture?'

Her chin came up again. 'Don't you *dare* condescend to me you, you . . .' She searched for a suitable insult and his brows drew together, his lips compressed as he waited for it. 'You *man!*' She spat the word.

The man laughed, surprise and humour chasing away the shadows in his face. 'Yes, I'm a man. I've heard many worse insults from English lips.'

He spoke without his previous curtness, but she'd had her fill of men and was in no mood to acknowledge the lilt of laughter in his deep voice. She tossed her head.

'And now you'll tell me that I've no business doing a man's work in a man's country and that I should go back to my needlework and be a good girl.'

Understanding dawned in his eyes and he smiled. 'Been meeting a bit of opposition here, have you?'

His smile was lopsided and very disarming.

'A fair bit,' she admitted and almost smiled back before suspicion forestalled her. Now she was fatherless, every man she met took it as his God-given right to tell her what to do. Her eyes narrowed. 'So are you going to start in too?'

He raised his hands, one still holding the gun, in surrender. 'Not I! I haven't lived this long without learning never to pick a fight I know I cannot be winning.'

It must have been the release of tension but this time Guinevere couldn't help smiling.

The man lowered his hands and said, 'Look, as I ruined your shot, the least I can do is share the bird with you.' Guinevere hesitated and the man's eyes cooled again. 'That is, if an English lady like yourself will accept the help of a common Irishman.'

'Oh, don't be ridiculous. It's just that . . .' Guinevere bit her lip, not knowing how to continue.

The man seemed to realise what was troubling her. 'I'm sorry, I haven't introduced myself. Quinn O'Donnell.' He extended his hand and gave her another lopsided smile. 'Ready to cook you the best meal for miles around. But if you'd rather not, say the word and I'll be on my way and not disturbing you again.'

She took his hand. It was lean, warm and calloused. 'Pleased to meet you, Mr O'Donnell. I'm Guinevere Stanhope and I freely admit I'm starving. I never thought I'd be away from civilisation for so long and didn't bring nearly enough provisions.'

He released her hand and cocked his head. 'Just how long have you been out here?'

'It'll be my third night. I'd only expected to be out for one but these weka proved more difficult to photograph than I'd first imagined. They tend to only come out near dusk so it's been hard to get them in the sunlight.'

'And then I came along to ruin it.' The Irishman's tone was almost apologetic as he stooped to pick up the bird. Then he spied her locket and squatted down. The sideways look he cast her was amused, but also more attentive. 'This here to attract the bird?'

She nodded, watching as his fingers deftly undid the lace knotted around the stone. 'I needed to keep him in the sun and reasonably still for the exposure.'

'Clever.' He held out the locket to her and straightened, lifting the bird as he did so. His movements were fluid and economical. 'Should I cook this here?'

He was giving her the opportunity to keep her camp private. As Guinevere pocketed her locket, her thoughts raced. Men intent on harm did not usually introduce themselves, did they? She wasn't very conversant with the ways of robbers and rapists – another gap in her upbringing and education. New Zealand, she was discovering, was most adept in presenting her with hitherto unknown situations.

She looked at Mr O'Donnell. He stood quietly, not rushing her. Was that sympathy in his eyes for her predicament? There was a wary stillness about him but deep down she felt she could trust him. Her instincts were all she had to go on these days, and she made her decision.

'No, I'm camped just up the river and I'd like to get back to Cerberus. He's been tied up for hours. I'll lead the way but must get my equipment first. There'll be no photographs today. The plate will have dried by now and that was the last of the light.'

The Irishman watched as she took several minutes dismantling her equipment.

'Sorry for spoiling your shot.' He sounded genuinely remorseful. 'Must've taken some time setting it all up.'

She glanced up and smiled. 'You weren't to know I was there. Sorry for attacking you. My temper is my besetting sin – well, one of them at any rate. There, I'm ready.'

'Fine, I'll be carrying that for you,' he said, stepping forward but she forestalled him with a shake of her head.

'Oh, no! My father always taught me that only a photographer has any business carrying a camera. I never let anyone touch my equipment. Besides,' she added candidly, 'I'd rather carry it than a dead bird.'

'I'll just get my clobber, then.'

He strode back to a tree where he stooped to swing a battered pack onto his back and she noted the wide shallow pan strapped to the outside. Definitely a miner. The hotelier had told her that the area had been in the grip of madness since the first sighting of gold a year earlier, with men pouring into it from all over the world.

When Mr O'Donnell came back towards her, he nodded and wordlessly she turned to lead the way. As she threaded through the foliage, bushes snagged the skirts of her dark green riding habit, which she twitched impatiently to free herself. Was it her imagination or did she feel his eyes following her movements? Had she made a mistake in encouraging friendliness?

She kept her voice steady as she said, 'It's just around this rock. Oh, there's Cerberus now.'

She took some comfort in the volley of barks and growls that greeted their arrival. Cerberus, large and ungainly, was straining at the rope that tethered him to a tree and she went immediately to free him. Though she felt she could trust Mr O'Donnell, it didn't hurt to have her faithful hound at her side. The dog was clearly unhappy at having a stranger in the camp and as soon as the last knot was untied, he leapt at the interloper.

'Cerberus!' she shouted.

The dog paused in his assault but continued to snarl, lip curled back from long teeth. The Irishman, having held his ground, now proffered an open palm which Cerberus sniffed and considered. The growling ceased and the tail began wagging. Quinn stroked the dog's head, whereupon the dog promptly rolled on his back so that Quinn might scratch his stomach too. Using the toe of his boot to rub the spot Cerberus wanted, Quinn looked up at his companion.

'Well now, 'tis relieved I am, ma'am, to know

9

you have this hell hound to protect you. Where did you find him?'

Hands on hips, torn between amusement and exasperation, Guinevere had to laugh. 'Hopeless animal! On the wharf at Hokitika. He just adopted me – followed me everywhere.'

'Given encouragement no doubt. And the . . . er . . . horse? 'Tis a horse, I take it.' He gestured to her mount, tethered to nearby bushes.

'Pegasus? Yes, I think so, though judging from his temperament there must be mule in there too.'

'Pegasus, is it?' His tone was distinctly ironic as he eyed the horse with its knobbed back, knock-knees and moth-eaten pelt. 'Was he also on the wharf?'

'Not exactly,' Guinevere said evasively. The Irishman's eyebrow rose and feeling slightly goaded, she added, 'He was in the knacker's yard, if you must know.' The man's continuing silence reinforced her defensiveness. 'He was looking at me with beseeching eyes and I simply couldn't let him die. You'd have felt the same!'

Mr O'Donnell shook his head. 'Oh no, I'm not one to be held hostage by a pair of eyes, no matter how beseeching. Besides, a woman alone shouldn't be burdening herself with a pack of useless animals.'

'They are not useless!' she declared, then saw his sceptical glance at her horse. 'Well, Pegasus was perhaps a bit of a mistake,' she conceded, 'but Cerberus wasn't. Why, only last week he bit the most provoking bank manager I have ever met in my life.'

The corner of his mouth lifted. 'And just how many bank managers have you met, might I ask?'

She felt herself flush but remained defiant. 'Well, only one, but that was still one too many!'

He forbore making further comment, though she saw amusement glimmer in his eyes before he turned to look around her camp. No, she had nothing to fear from him, she decided. Yet he was a strange man, alternately grim then amused. She wasn't sure which was more infuriating.

They were standing quite close together now and she saw a scar curled up from his cheekbone to the corner of his left eye. His nose was slightly angled as though it had been broken and not set quite straight. His smoke-grey eyes were surprisingly light in contrast to his tanned skin, his gaze intent. He had the Celts' brooding intensity and a strong, somewhat autocratic face above his beard. Arthurian, she thought fancifully, with a hint of Viking about the cheekbones. He'd make a marvellous study for a photograph.

'An unusual set-up you have here,' he remarked and as he glanced down, he caught her scrutinising him. Again he went uncannily still, his eyes unreadable.

Feeling self-conscious, Guinevere spoke quickly. 'I know. Now, can I get you a knife or plate?'

'No, don't trouble yourself. I have it all right here.'

To her relief, he let the moment pass and swung his pack down onto the ground. It was little more than a blanket rolled about a few belongings, amongst which were a sharp knife and a large tin plate.

'You just relax,' he told her as he tossed his hat to one side and, picking up the bird, made his way to the river's edge where he set about plucking it.

Relieved that her assistance was not required for this grisly task, Guinevere tucked her equipment away in the tent, then sat on a nearby log and watched his quick fingers at work. His hair was dark, thick, straight and rather long. It, like his beard, must measure the number of weeks he'd been up here in the mountains, panning for gold. Did he ever get lonely, too?

Mr O'Donnell was like no man of her acquaintance. Squatting on his haunches, he seemed completely at home in the forest, yet he was clearly conversant with Greek mythology. He was swift to take offence over the strangest things, but he was also quick to laugh. Did this indicate a passionate nature? Yet there was that untouchable stillness about him. Was it only the siren song of gold that had drawn this man to these vast, empty forests?

Quinn too was curious as his fingers tore at the feathers. What in the hell did she think she was playing at, camped here all alone at the bottom of the world? Quinn shook his head at himself. What in the hell did he think *he* was playing at, cooking for an Englishwoman who, to judge by her manner

12

of speaking, was clearly of the class he most loathed? It had been over five years since he'd sworn never to tug a forelock at the English ever again. Even now, that damnable English imperiousness he detected in her voice set his teeth on edge. And yet . . .

He stole a glance at her now and saw her hand go to her head. At the time she'd been too furious to notice her hair half tumble from its pins as she'd launched like a spitting wild cat from the bushes. He smiled inwardly at the memory. Then she'd seen his gun and though fear had flashed in her brown eyes, her chin had jerked up.

Her dress was the same dark green as the forest, and the white oval of her face stood out in contrast, with its striking cheekbones and wide eyes. She was not beautiful, but there was something delicate yet strong about her – like a tree sprite. This absurd thought made him shake his head at himself again. He remembered how she'd twitched her skirt free from the bushes and in one long slash he sliced open the belly of the weka. It had been far too long since he'd been with a woman.

She gasped at the sight of blood, then laughed as though embarrassed by her shock. 'You look like you've done that before.'

He threw the entrails to Cerberus who wolfed them down. 'I grew up on a farm and 'twas my job to prepare the birds for the family when I was a child. I hated it then, but it's proved handy over the years.'

He found it hard not to pause to watch the feminine, almost intimate gestures of the English girl as she wound her abundant hair back up into a knot, which she then skewered into place. It pleased him that one lock had escaped her notice, falling untamed down her back.

'I never learned anything half so useful when I was young. Which part of Ireland are you from?'

'Cork,' he said. 'Have you been to Ireland?'

She shook her head. 'No. I'd never been out of England until Father decided to come to New Zealand.'

'And why did he come?' asked Quinn, pausing for a second to look at her.

'To photograph the moa. Have you heard of it, Mr O'Donnell?'

He frowned. 'What, that bird that looks like an overgrown ostrich?'

She nodded, leaning forward eagerly, her fore-arms on her knees. 'Yes, that's it. Some grow to over nine feet tall, you know.'

'Grew, you mean,' he corrected her. 'Sure, but it's extinct now. The Maori ate them all, long ago.'

'There's no proof of that! There have been recent sightings, you know.'

Quinn shook his head. 'By men either bored or witless from going too many days without civilisation. 'Tis a wild-goose chase you are on.'

'Oh, you can scoff, but my father was certain it still exists. A photograph of one would be worth a fortune; both financially and scientifically.'

14

'Is that a fact? And just how much would it be worth?' Quinn neatly split the bird into smaller cuts that would cook quicker over the fire.

She sat back, her voice less confident now, though she was clearly not going to back down. Of course she wouldn't. She was bloody English.

'Well, I'm not exactly sure, but Father was convinced it would be a considerable sum.'

Quinn began piling twigs to make a fire and Guinevere passed him some from around her feet. 'Ah, so your father's interest was more financial than scientific?'

Her manner assumed a touch of ice. 'That,' she said for the second time in their brief acquaintance, 'is none of your business.'

Quinn struck the match with more force than strictly necessary to control his sudden flare of fury – arrogant, hoity-toity that she was! He wished suddenly that he hadn't taken pity on her. Irish had no business feeding the English – even in the middle of nowhere. But as he grimly blew on the flame to fan it, she added, 'I'm sorry, I prefer not to talk of my father, although I intend continuing with his work. Surely you can understand that?'

Damnable female. He didn't like the way she could pull that lady-of-the-manor act and he didn't like the way she could disconcert him by promptly dropping it. She didn't wait for him to reply though, as she changed the subject.

'And why are *you* in New Zealand, Mr O'Donnell?'

The way she asked the question with genuine

15

interest, the walls of the forest might have melted away and they could have been in some fancy house sipping tea and he not a servant but a valued guest. He rocked back on his heels and looked at her. 'The gold.'

'And you say *I'm* on a wild-goose chase!'

He bristled, then saw teasing gold lights in her eyes. 'True,' he acknowledged with a slow smile. ''Tis a hard call to say which of us is the greater fool.'

She laughed but almost immediately fell silent, staring into the flames.

Quinn noted the anxious frown between her eyes and felt an unexpected twinge of guilt. 'I'm probably wrong,' he said as he skewered the weka onto a stick. ''Tis a huge country and the forests are very deep. There is every chance there are still some of those birdies about.'

'Yes,' she said as she prodded the fire, but her bright tone sounded forced. 'Yes indeed!'

She watched in silence as he fashioned a makeshift spit out of stout sticks. When the meat was cooking over the flames, Quinn relaxed back against a tree. 'And what photographs have you taken thus far in New Zealand, Miss Stanhope?'

The girl began talking of some of the sights she had photographed since her arrival in Hokitika a few weeks earlier. Quinn knew the town well, for it offered miners respite from the loneliness of the mountains and many diverse ways of losing all their hard-won gold. Like all ports and gold-mining towns, it was a rough and rowdy place and he wondered what the locals had made of this slip of a girl setting up her tripod in the main street. He wouldn't have thought there was anything worth photographing, but it was clear she had a different way of looking at things – in all sorts of ways. Animation lit her face as she described her shots and the developing processes, revealing a passion surprisingly deep for an Englishwoman.

Quinn watched the small, vivid face under its weight of hair and as he listened to her lively explanations, he realised, with surprise, that he was experiencing an almost forgotten emotion – contentment. The forest about them darkened and the smell of roasting bird spiralled with the white smoke. When he rose to add another branch to the fire and turn the spit, Guinevere's stomach rumbled. She blushed.

'Oh, I do beg your pardon, Mr O'Donnell.'

Even as she spoke the words his own stomach complained loudly and they both laughed.

'We'll have some water. That'll take the edge off,' Quinn said, and went to the river where he filled their cups.

'Thank you,' she said, accepting her tin mug from him. 'Have you noticed how delicious the water is here?'

'I have. You can't beat water straight down from the snow,' he said, indicating with a jerk of his chin the mountain peaks which glowed ghostly against the black night. 'Plus the constant topping up from the rain, of course.'

'Isn't it amazing just how much it rains? I don't think I've ever been anywhere that's as wet as New Zealand.'

'That's because we're on the West Coast. The east has far less rain,' Quinn told her. 'Fewer impossibly dense forests and fewer sandflies,' he added with feeling as he slapped at the tiny insects that were the bane of all new settlers.

'Fewer moa also, I suppose.'

The corner of his mouth lifted. 'I fear so. Not so much gold around Christchurch either come to that.'

She heaved a theatrical sigh and leaned forward to stir the flames. 'Then we are stuck here, are we not, Mr O'Donnell?'

''Twould seem so.' He watched the glow of the flames warm her face, catching the lights in her eyes and suddenly this did not seem quite such a hardship. As she looked up, their looks tangled. Somewhere nearby, an owl hooted.

'Right! Let's see if that bird is ready now.' He knew he'd sounded abrupt.

Guinevere turned away as though the fire was suddenly too hot and said, 'I do hope so. I'm famished.'

The slight tension dissolved as they devoured the weka and Quinn was surprised at how much a little thing like her could put away.

'That was heaven,' said Guinevere at last, licking her fingers and leaning back against a log with a satiated sigh, while he washed his knife and plate and rolled up his pack again. 'Mr O'Donnell, that was the best meal I've ever eaten.'

''Tis just hunger.' He laughed dismissively but was pleased.

'Oh, no, it is not! I was very hungry last night too but I still noticed the bread was stale and the cheese mouldy.'

She was clearly not used to or prepared for the outdoors. Well, she wouldn't be, would she? Her camp was crude. There was a strange black tent, but she had also strung up a fly, which was not set right and couldn't have stopped much of the morning dew. Some bracken had been piled up but it looked ragged and uninviting, even to a man used to sleeping on the hard ground. Worst of all, she didn't understand the country she was in.

'You mustn't be sleeping here tonight, Miss Stanhope,' he said.

'Mustn't?'

He didn't heed her tone. 'No. 'Tis coming on to rain.'

She looked purposefully up at the clear, star-studded sky. 'Indeed?'

Still he did not pay sufficient attention to the underlying edge. 'These rivers come up to a flood quick as a flash and this morning I saw a dam on the upper reaches of this river − not much is holding it up, just a fallen tree and some bushes. 'Twon't take much to dislodge them and then all the waters will be pouring down and you'll be swept away.'

She looked at the wide but shallow river flowing over the stones in the light of the half moon. 'Hmm.'

'Best move you up onto higher ground. I'll camp nearby to see you are safe.'

She tilted her head and looked at him down the length of her small, straight nose. 'Thank you, Mr O'Donnell, but it simply isn't necessary or possible. I cannot move my equipment at night. That tent there is the mobile darkroom that my father designed. It's one of a kind and irreplaceable. What if it should get damaged in the dark? And if I should stumble when carrying the plates or camera, they would break because they are very fragile.'

'They'll be a lot more broken if the flood comes.'

'What makes you so sure it will rain?'

He hesitated for the night was clear. 'There's a smell when rain is about to come.'

'I cannot detect anything beyond the usual smells of the forest.'

He was tempted to tell her that was because she was a pampered young woman, raised in a big house where maids shut the windows at the first hint of rain. However, he was reluctant to destroy the amicable feeling that had grown between them.

'You haven't had any experience,' he said, then tried to placate. ''Tis not your fault. I've just done more of this sort of thing. Your life has been sheltered and you wouldn't know . . .' he faltered as he saw quite another type of storm gathering in

20

her face. 'If you'd just listen to reason,' he added, reasonably enough.

Her eyes flashed gold in the firelight. 'Listen to reason! If you only knew how much I *loathe* that expression and loathe the men who have applied it to me these past two months since my father died. "Lady Guinevere, you cannot remain alone in New Zealand, listen to reason. You cannot seek the moa alone, listen to reason. Go home and find a nice husband, listen to reason!" It's eighteen hundred and sixty six for goodness sake, not the Dark Ages! I've had my fill of men telling me what to do and where to go and I *refuse* to have some man laying down the law to me in the middle of nowhere.'

Quinn's own temper ignited. Hell, she was a *real* lady. The English were bad; the aristocracy even worse. No wonder she was such a haughty little piece. He rose, damned if he was going to stay for any more insults. 'I can see you're quite beyond reasoning with—' he began with dignity, but she cut in.

'You aren't reasoning with me, you're telling me!'

'I'm trying to help you for your own good, woman.'

'That's what all men say. It's quite insufferable.'

'Well, I'll be on my way then.' Quinn knew he sounded like an aggrieved child, but Guinevere was just as bad.

'That's fine. I can manage perfectly well on my own, thank you.'

Quinn swung his pack on his back and glowered down at her. She glowered back. 'In that case, *m'lady*,' he said, larding the word with contempt, 'I'll wish you a good night.'

He gave a little bow that mocked and saw with pleasure her flinch before he turned and disappeared into the trees.

CHAPTER 2

Guinevere watched Quinn disappear into the trees, dismay extinguishing the fury that had consumed her just seconds before. Part of her longed to run after him, catch him by his arm and swing him around to explain that of course she hadn't meant to offend, she was just so tired of fighting men with their infuriating, smiling condescension. She wanted to tell him how wonderful the evening had been. It had been so long since she had had anyone to talk and laugh with and she had felt as comfortable with him as if he had been an old friend.

She didn't like to admit it, but she had even felt reassured to think there would be someone nearby tonight. She had barely slept the previous two nights, despite the comforting bulk of Cerberus by her side. Every strange sound had made her start and the moon had shed just enough light to fill her glade, so picturesque by daylight, with terrifying shapes and shadows.

Now it was too late; the Irishman had been swallowed up by the dark trees. She tried to rekindle her indignation. Horrid man! So opinionated! All that nonsense about rain when the sky was perfectly clear. Yet even as she tried to laugh at the notion, it seemed that the temperature had already dropped a degree and a wind was beginning to stir.

Disconsolate, she sat down again by the fire, prodding it to make the flames more cheerful but she did even this wrong and the fire guttered. She was such a failure. She hadn't had a fire the previous nights, not being able to encourage flames out of the green branches, and had given up in disgust, blaming the lack of dry tinder.

Tonight, Mr O'Donnell – curse the man – had had a comforting blaze going in no time. He was right, she had lived a sheltered life. Fires belonged to the province of maids. They were something she'd accepted as part of life, just as she'd taken food, warmth and security for granted. All of which had been stripped away these past few months.

She immediately thrust these thoughts aside. It was not her father's fault she was in this predicament and she knew he would have been appalled and disbelieving even to imagine his only child stranded alone at the bottom of the world, with only a few guineas to her name. He hadn't intended to die, had simply complained of a rather bad headache and had gone to bed early, never to wake up again.

'Cerebral haemorrhage most likely,' the ship's doctor had said. 'We could do an examination to confirm it if you like.'

Gwen had not been able to bear the thought of her father's head, with its high, intelligent brow and eyes once alight with enthusiasm, being cut open. Instead, he had been stitched into a shroud and consigned to the ocean – a romantic burial that Gwen couldn't help but think he would have approved of.

'Come, Cerberus,' she said. 'You at least are reliable – the only male who is not entirely stubborn and controlling.' She put her arms around the huge mutt and gave him a hug. He licked her ear, which made her laugh and feel better.

Where would Mr O'Donnell be now? She had never met anyone like him; so watchful and wary. She'd felt that one wrong move from her and he would be off – like a wild animal coming into her camp, but only on his terms. Once in a lull in the conversation, he'd returned to his own thoughts and she'd watched shadows gather in his face and his mouth twist. Yet as soon as she'd made a comment pulling him back to the moment, the shadows had disappeared and she'd startled a laugh from him. She'd amused him often over the evening, sometimes deliberately and sometimes, infuriatingly, quite unconsciously. She'd enjoyed watching that reluctant, lopsided grin spreading across his face. He reminded her of one of Rossetti's paintings depicting an older, battle-hardened Lancelot, who despite obvious fatigue still carried his sword in readiness.

Lancelot. The name went through her like a jolt

25

and she giggled. Just as well no one was around to say that to! They might have thought that she—

Guinevere nipped any further notions firmly in the bud as she stood up, shaking out her skirts. Time for bed, but first a visit to the shelter of a bush. She found these outdoor ablutions exquisitely embarrassing even though she knew she was alone. Mr O'Donnell, judging by his temper, would be far away by now. Yet, as she squatted in the deep shadows, she still felt vulnerable.

The heap of branches she had gathered in an attempt to soften the forest floor was uncomfortable and it took a lot of wriggling to try to get a hollow she could sleep in. Cerberus curled up beside her and she welcomed his reassuring bulk leaning against her legs. As she had done every night since her father's death, Guinevere closed her eyes, willing herself to relax by conjuring up the image of Maidenhurst. Though it was midsummer here in this strange, upside-down world, in England January snow would still be swaddling the manor house where she'd lived all her life. She could picture it vividly; the bare tracery of ivy covering the red bricks, awaiting summer to transform the house into a living mass of green. The leaded windows would be latched and the downstairs parlour would have wooden shutters closed tight to keep in the warmth from the generous hearth. Maidenhurst was not beautiful in the normal sense for it had been built in Elizabethan times and then been added to over the centuries, not always with sensitivity but always with verve.

Guinevere began her nightly tour of each room, beginning with the large hall with its dark panelling and progressing through to the dining room where fifty years earlier the sixth Lord Stanhope had had the happy notion of installing French windows which opened out onto lawns sprawling down to the lake beyond. She visited her father's study and, even deep in the New Zealand forest, she would swear she could smell the pungent smoke of his cigars mixed with the leather of the tooled books lining the walls. Up the wide, welcoming staircase, where Pre-Raphaelite paintings alternated with the portraits of her forefathers. Along the passage, past her old nursery with its scuffed furniture and battered toys, and on to her bedroom whose windows looked out past a three hundred year old oak and into the walled garden, which had first been planted four centuries earlier. And on the walls, more paintings.

She began to catalogue them in her mind: *St Joan*, an early work of Rossetti's; a drawing by Lizzie Siddal of Guinevere's spaniel which had died when she was fifteen. Then there was – but now the pictures blurred and became confused as lulled by this familiar litany, Guinevere was finally able to slip sideways into the blessed oblivion of sleep, where fear did not knot her stomach as it did each day in this foreign world.

★   ★   ★

Guinevere awoke several hours later with the first heavy drops of rain presaging a storm, and then the heavens split open as though the skies had been unable to support the weight of water any more.

'No!' she cried out, feeling bitterly the injustice of the weather for proving that insufferable man right. Was he right too, then, about the river flooding? The river was so shallow. But then she thought of the steep banks further downstream where the river narrowed and her heart clenched. Fierce waters must have carved that course in the past. Scrambling up, she hastily collected her scattered belongings together then tried to saddle Pegasus. It was well nigh impossible for the rain was already driving down with blinding intensity and the clouds had long since buried any welcome gleam from moon or stars. The fire still gave off a faint glow, which helped her a little, but within minutes even that had been swiftly extinguished by the falling torrents.

'Oh God. Oh God.' She could not find the words for any further prayers as fear clutched her belly and terror clouded her mind. Her hands were slippery and shaking as she tried to secure the buckles and fit the bridle.

'There, boy, there, it'll be all right,' she whispered as much to reassure herself as to comfort the frightened horse that skittered and flinched under the raindrops that stung, such was the ferocity with which they fell.

Guinevere's hair had escaped from the mooring hairpins and hung about her face in wet curtains which she swept impatiently back with her hands as she fought to get the precious tripod and camera box into the straps on the saddle. The roar of the storm was distracting, the wind whipping the trees so that branches cracked and rattled and thunder rolled about the hills. Even so, she suddenly caught the sound of a new roaring and her heart nearly stopped. It was like nothing she had ever heard before, save for once when she'd visited some large waterfalls when she had been a child. Then she'd laughed at the roar and fury of rushing water as she clutched her father's hand. Now she leapt into the saddle, gathering the reins, determined to escape.

The trees hemming her glade, however, were as stout as fortress walls in the dark and Pegasus shied away from the dense foliage. During the day it had been hard to see paths to press through and on a stormy night it was virtually impossible. Despairing, Guinevere urged the horse forward but this was no well-bred mare raised to follow commands under trying circumstances. Wishing desperately that she had a whip, she kicked the sides of her mount. The terrified horse took off down the bank of the river where it could see slightly more open ground as she clung to the saddle, as well as the reins, Cerberus bounding beside her. Perhaps Pegasus was right. Just beyond the clearing where she'd met Quinn there had been a steep bank where the trees did not crowd so close together. If they could make it there, they would be safe.

But even as she gave a cry of relief to see the clearing, it was drowned in the explosion of water that swept down the riverbed, completely engulfing her and the horse. Pegasus, swept off his feet, fought to swim and just managed to get his head free of the water's surface as he gave a terrified whinny. Guinevere, choking, could feel her grasp slipping.

'Oh, no, you don't!' she told herself fiercely. 'You *have* to hold on. Don't you *dare* let go.'

That was easier said than done. The skirts of her riding habit strained backwards, her hair caught in stifling waves about her face. The water was icy and she could feel her hands grow numb. Dimly she was aware of Cerberus's frantic barking growing faint as the flood swirled her away. Great shivers wracked her body as she lay on Pegasus's neck, wrapping her arms around him to gain further purchase. Her legs gripped his heaving sides. Pegasus ploughed forward as best he could, but he was an old horse and this exertion was too much for him. Guinevere felt him go limp under her as his heart gave out, just as they were entering the narrowest part of the river where the sides were steep and overhung by branches.

Kicking herself free from the stirrups, Guinevere bobbed away from the sinking horse only to find her skirts and petticoats pulling her down and her

30

boots like weights upon her feet. Gasping and fighting to keep her head up, she tried to strike out for the branches which only hours earlier had been feet above the river but were now tangled in the savage waters.

Time and again water washed over her head, causing her to choke and a log bashed into her side, winding her. Still she fought towards the branches but her ragged breaths swallowed more water than air, each gasp drowning her further. Her head filled with exploding lights and flashes of black and even as she kicked and reached for shore, she could feel her strength failing. It would be so much easier to just surrender, finish it quickly.

Then she thought she heard a shout, faint above the deafening roar of water but a shout nevertheless. Was she dreaming? There it was again.

'Miss Stanhope! I'm here. Grab my hand.'

She couldn't see anything but struck out blindly and a strong hand grasped hers, fingers closing onto her wrist just as there was a last explosion of light in her head. As darkness engulfed her, she heard an Irish voice say, 'You're safe, now. I won't let you go.'

Quinn grasped the fragile wrist, feeling Guinevere go limp.

'Come on, m'lady,' he urged between gritted teeth. ''Tis not the time to be swooning. Wake up, damn you.'

But her hair tossed like a dark stain on the frothing white water, her face nothing more than a pale oval. The heaviness of her clothes made it almost impossible but inch by slow inch he began pulling her in, fighting the drag of the water, muscles strained to screaming point. Then, just as he began hauling her up to the branch to which he clung – just as he thought he might indeed be able to save her – there was a sickening crack and it gave way, tumbling Quinn into the river.

The cold stopped the breath in his chest as the river closed over his head. Water filled his ears and he was violently buffeted and tossed by the force of the flood. His lungs seemed to swell as though to break free of his ribs but still he somehow maintained his grip on the girl. Having vowed he would never let her go, he would go to a watery grave first. Then suddenly, miraculously, his head broke the river's surface, with her clutched to his chest. It was pointless to try swimming. Quinn managed to get onto his back, the girl awkwardly across his body, her head bouncing on his shoulder, her hair filling his nose and mouth. He feared she was already dead but the thought of her lifeless body bouncing down the river to decay alone in some remote place only strengthened his hold upon her. If they were to die, they would die together.

He did not fight the flood except to keep their heads above it as he angled his feet so they were pointing downstream. It was impossible to see anything with the water in his eyes, impossible to hear anything above the roar of the river as the water kept breaking over his head, choking him. A branch thumped into his shoulder sending shards of pain ripping through his body and he had to fight the impulse to loosen his grip on the unconscious woman. It all seemed impossible, yet a tiny part of his brain was still working. He had camped further downstream, in a bend where the river was shallow. Jutting out into the river was a tree, tethered by its roots to the bank. If it were there – if by some miracle it hadn't been swept away – that would be their lifeline. They just had to stay afloat a few more minutes. A few minutes! It already felt like hours. Men drowned swiftly in these floods. And if he missed . . . He shut off his thoughts. There was that faint spark of hope and on that he focused.

They were buffeted and pummelled in the careening waters as Quinn tried to point his feet closer to shore and then they were sweeping around the bend, luck spinning him closer to the bank. Then an enormous collision jarred his whole body and Quinn clutched at the branches, almost sobbing in his relief as he began pulling them both in along the trunk, the force of the river now deflected by the tree. Branches and twigs scraped his face but all his concentration was on the shore. It was not, after all, so very far away, he told himself, shifting his grasp on the unconscious woman whom he still held tight despite his shaking

33

muscles. When he felt the river floor under his boots, he thanked God, then half-falling, half-crawling, he had them both out of the water and on the sodden safety of the river's bank. He shook his head, the thunderous sound of the water mercifully lessened now. However, there was no time to collapse, as he craved, in panting relief. He still had work to do.

'Right, Lady Guinevere,' he said, his voice coming out as a croak. 'You'll not be dying on me now – understand?'

She had taken in a lot of water so he turned her onto her side, dealing several swift blows to her back. She gave a little moan and Quinn had never welcomed a sound more in his entire life. He hit her back again and this time there was a cough, Guinevere vomited river water and then opened her eyes.

She was completely disorientated for a second then whispered hoarsely, 'The river.'

He had to lean over her to catch her words. 'Hush, you're safe now.'

'Pegasus – I think he . . .' But she couldn't bring herself to say the words.

'Don't think about it. Don't think about anything,' said Quinn softly into her ear as he wiped her mouth with a wet handkerchief pulled from his pocket. 'We just have to wait out the storm. Now, how are you? Any broken bones?'

She was dazed. 'Broken bones? No, I don't think so. My side hurts though.'

She squeaked as he ran his hands down her sides though he was not sure if it was from pain or outraged modesty.

'I don't think any ribs are broken,' he said. 'Maybe these corset things do some good after all.'

He squatted back on his heels, the rain plastering his hair to his scalp. 'We've got to get out of this rain. My camp's nearby. Come on.'

She tried to rise but seemed to have lost all her strength so Quinn, also drained, half-supported her, half-dragged her to his camp, mercifully only yards away. He'd found an overhanging rock under which to shelter, knowing from experience a tent would be useless in a storm. They crawled under its meagre but blessed sanctuary, a very cramped space which barely accommodated them both.

'We need to get warm,' he told her unnecessarily, for she was shaking convulsively and he could scarcely talk through his own shivers. Somehow he managed to get a blanket about his shoulders then, scooping her up into the cradle of his arms, he wriggled back against the rock so they were both out of the rain. He adjusted the blanket so that it covered them both as his shoulders curved round her body. She was still violently shuddering but as he began to feel warmth steal back into his body, she seemed to become aware of their situation.

'Mr O'Donnell,' she said, but her voice was muffled now by his shirt and perhaps by shyness too. 'I don't think—'

'Hush, don't think. 'Twill all pass presently, you'll see,' he said, pressing her closer still. 'It always does. No talking for now. We'll just wait out the storm.'

Gently he rocked back and forth as if she were a child, and stroked her hair. Gradually her shaking quietened and her breathing began to smooth out until finally he felt her go limp. Whether she slept or had passed out he didn't know but after fighting for her life she needed rest.

'The storm will pass,' he told himself. 'It always does.'

He tried to ease his muscles but did not want to disturb Guinevere, so instead breathed steadily into the discomfort of cramped limbs. 'This too will pass,' he murmured, trying to filter out the cold, the rain and his burning joints but while he'd been calm and reassuring with her, his thoughts were nothing like as charitable.

As he hunched his head into his shoulders against the cold, he wondered what the hell he, Quinn O'Donnell, was doing sitting in the middle of a thunderstorm with a half-dead, intolerably arrogant Englishwoman clutched to his chest. He should have just kept walking as he'd intended on leaving her camp.

In fact his temper had carried him a good mile down the track but some strange impulse had made him stop and swear under his breath. She was absolutely none of his business and getting involved would just lead to trouble. Having convinced himself, he'd started once more down the track. She was courting trouble, with her disregard of any sensible advice. What she needed was a firm hand to guide her. Of course, her father had died. That was bad luck. Must have been on the ship coming out. That couldn't be easy but even so, it wasn't his business. She'd made it quite clear she didn't want any help – though she clearly needed it. Still, it wasn't his place to get involved. Quinn had taken a few more paces, then wheeled about, swearing vigorously and calling on several saints to preserve him from his insanity even as he did so. Still he'd returned to a point downstream from her camp where, if the river did flood, he might just be able to help.

And it had all come to pass just as he'd predicted, he thought bitterly as the rain drove down around them, the blanket providing only a modicum of warmth. If she'd only bloody listened to him, they wouldn't be in this position right now. Served him right for getting involved with an Englishwoman against his every instinct. Yet despite these thoughts, Quinn's hold on Guinevere unconsciously tightened as he closed his eyes.

The night was long with the rain pelting against the overhang above and his shoulders curled about Guinevere's limp body but in the end he must have nodded off, for when he opened his eyes, the rain had stopped and misty dawn swathed the surrounding mountains. His legs were completely numb, his arms leaden but he hadn't relinquished his hold on the Englishwoman, even in sleep.

In exhausted bemusement he looked down at her, noting her flushed face and her hoarse breathing. Her dress was hitched up, revealing a leg to the knee, her boot looking absurdly heavy as it dangled from a slender ankle. She had been wearing silk stockings but they were shredded now and he shook his head over this unlikely article of clothing. He had seen silk stockings before, and on an English leg – but this memory he immediately cast aside as he adjusted her dress to cover the limb. In doing so his arm shifted under her shoulders and she stirred, opening her eyes and looking straight up into his.

For a minute she simply looked at him before realising where she was. Her eyes flew wide open and she struggled against his chest, pushing away so that she tumbled out of his lap into a heap. He immediately released her and dropped the sodden blanket from his shoulder; relieved to be able to stretch again, yet sorry to lose the warmth of her body.

'Mr O'Donnell!'

'Good morning to you too, Lady Guinevere,' he replied, rising stiffly, flexing limbs and moving his neck again in delicious agony as feeling returned.

She shook her head as though to clear it, lifted one arm to sweep back the weight of her hair and groaned in pain.

'Oh, my goodness.'

He nodded. ''Tis no surprise if you are hurting and aching all over. That was quite a battering you took last night.'

'I remember now – and poor Pegasus. He died you know.' Her voice rasped.

'I know, I saw it. Heard him neigh which was a good thing as it made me look out and there you were, bobbing along like a stick in a ditch once you'd kicked free of him. I lost sight of him immediately.'

He would never tell her that the moment the rain had started, he'd leapt from his safe bivouac to make his way to the riverbank and that when he'd glimpsed the horse in the flooding river his heart had constricted.

'Poor horse. I only gave him a few more weeks of life, after all. And you pulled me out of the river. I was so sure I was going to die.' Her voice was little more than a whisper.

Quinn wondered if she expected him to say something gallant but he wasn't about to play those games, so he merely shrugged and leaned a shoulder against a tree, looking down at her.

'And then you—' She stopped abruptly and he guessed she was remembering the way he'd held her all night and felt a stirring of grim amusement to see how an English lady would cope with such an interesting social situation. Her shoulders went back as she drew herself up, wincing at some twinge of pain. She straightened her skirt, smoothing a fold thoughtfully as though it were mildly creased, rather than torn and filthy and sodden. Then she brushed a matted lock of hair from her cheek, leaving a smear of mud as she looked up.

'Mr O'Donnell,' she said, not quite meeting his eye. 'You—'

'Kept you warm, yes,' he interrupted matter-of-fact, wondering at the same time why he was rescuing her when surely it did an English lady good to feel acute embarrassment on occasion. 'You kept me warm too, which was good. 'Tis the only way to survive these things.'

'Indeed.' She still looked uncertain, then stricken as she asked, 'And Cerberus? I lost him when I was swept away.'

Quinn shook his head. 'Never saw hide nor hair of him.' As her face fell he added, 'But dogs have the damnedest way of surviving – if you'll pardon the expression, m'lady.'

'Oh, don't! Please just call me Miss Stanhope,' Guinevere said. 'I never meant to let that slip. It does nothing but provoke the strangest extremes in people – like you, for instance.'

Quinn heard the spirit beginning to kindle in her voice and couldn't resist.

'I'm sure I cannot be thinking what you mean, m'lady,' he replied in a respectful tone designed to rile and sure enough, she rose to the bait. Though she was still clearly weak, her eyes flashed gold.

'That awful politeness and underlying obsequiousness – oh, not *you*. You aren't obsequious but you become all defensive and high-handed as though expecting me to start ordering you around. You are *not* to do that.'

40

'No, m'lady,' he murmured and her eyes narrowed.

'Mr O'Donnell,' she said, snipping each word with deliberate care, 'you are, without doubt, the most infuriating man who has ever—'

'Saved your life?' he suggested.

'No! Well, yes, I suppose so but . . . oh, not that I'm not very grateful, of course, but—' she broke off at the sudden sound of hysterical barking. 'Cerberus!'

The dog burst through the bushes and launched himself at his mistress, knocking her flat and covering her with licks. Quinn had to haul him off and help Guinevere to sit up again.

'See, I told you he'd be fine.'

Guinevere laughed and sighed, putting both arms around Cerberus and embracing him. 'So you did, Mr O'Donnell, but I hope you are not going to develop the aggravating habit of always pointing out when you are right.'

'Never. Sure, I wouldn't dream of mentioning the rain nor flooding either,' he added, before hastily ducking as a wet wad of leaves whistled past his ear. 'I see you are none the worse for your dunking, then. I thought you didn't have any brothers.'

'I don't. Why?'

'Young ladies do not usually throw things at gentlemen – or so I've been led to believe at any rate – especially those they've barely met.'

She laughed, but blushed too. 'My father was a

patron to a number of artists – the Pre-Raphaelites, have you heard of them? – so I grew up with males coming and going in our house all the time, rather like brothers, I suppose.'

Quinn's eyebrow rose. 'An unorthodox upbringing.'

'An interesting one!' she retorted. 'I grew up with considerably more freedom than is usually granted to women, for my father was a most enlightened man. I'm quite sure an orthodox upbringing would have been a terrible bore.'

Quinn did not venture his views on the privileges of having a boring upbringing. Instead, he squatted down next to her so his face was on a level with hers and asked, 'So how are you feeling this morning?'

'Fine,' she said, but watching her flushed face he knew she'd never admit to anything else. Jaysus, the English were astonishing in their ease of telling lies.

'What about the ribs?'

'My ribs? How did you – oh . . .' A faint blush stained her cheek and she glanced away. 'I remember now.'

'Yes, I checked your ribs. Purely professionally, of course.'

She turned back and eyed him dubiously. 'Are you a doctor?'

'Almost. I never completed my training, but I was a sawbones in the war.'

His tone was brusque but she didn't heed the note of dismissal, asking instead, 'Which war?'

'The civil war in America. 'Tis not important. You still haven't told me how your ribs are – truthfully, now.'

She smiled and pressed her hand to her side gingerly. 'Painful, but nothing broken, I'm sure.'

'Good. I'm afraid 'tis a long walk to Hokitika. Are you up to it?'

'Of course. I'll miss poor Pegasus, though.' Her eyes suddenly widened. 'My camera! How could I have not thought about it before! It was my father's and now it's—'

'Gone.' He would not show sympathy, but it surprised him how something twinged inside to see her expression and he added, 'You're alive, that's all that counts. Was it your only camera?'

'No, I have my own back at the hotel. It's not as good as my father's, but that's not the point. You don't understand, it was all I had left of him.'

'Now that's not true. You'll always carry what he was with you everywhere.' Again he surprised himself for trying to offer a crumb of comfort.

She opened her mouth to argue but must have seen something in his face because she asked instead, 'What about your parents?'

'They died, but a long time ago. I don't need any sympathetic noises.' He straightened up, an unobtrusive way of making distance between them.

'I wasn't going to make any,' she said, but still he flinched at the look in her eyes, which seemed somehow more intimate than his clasp around her all night. But whatever it was she thought she saw in his face, it stopped her from going on about the camera. Instead, she began struggling to get to her feet.

'I should be going now.'

He caught her arm and steadied her as she swayed upright.

'Where to?'

'Hokitika, of course.'

'I thought we'd have breakfast first.'

'We? Are you going there too?' Her voice was politely surprised but the hope that lit her face betrayed her and quenched any reservations he might have had about saddling himself with an Englishwoman for yet another twenty-four hours.

'I was on my way down when we met last night. Makes sense that we travel together now.'

She shook her head. 'No, you are very kind but you've already done too much. I'll just slow you down. I'll be fine – I have Cerberus.'

'Lady Guinevere, I do hope that *you* are not going to develop the aggravating habit of arguing with me over every small thing. I'm coming with you and that's final. Will you not accept help from an Irishman?'

For a second they stood, their gazes locked in determination, but she was the first to look away and she laughed a little self-consciously. 'Being Irish has nothing in the world to do with it. It's just that I've already accepted so much. But yes, if our paths lie in the same direction, I'd be grateful for your company.'

'Good. Now how about breakfast?'

'Breakfast? Here? Are you mocking me?'

'Never more serious in my life,' he assured her as he reached under the overhang of rock where his meagre belongings were stashed and triumphantly produced a tin of sardines. 'There you are, breakfast!'

As it turned out, Guinevere did not have much appetite but he forced her to eat to build up her strength, wishing at the same time he had some dry tinder to make a fire and give her a cup of tea. He mistrusted the flush overlying her pallor and noticed her hand shook when she accepted the oily fish.

'Ready?' he asked, when Cerberus had finished licking out the last of the fish they'd left in the tin for him.

She nodded. 'Absolutely.'

As Quinn helped her to rise, he saw she was a bit unsteady. It worried him but nothing could be done except to get her to Hokitika as quickly as possible.

They began walking along the trail with Quinn, pack on back and gun in hand, leading the way and Cerberus bringing up the rear, constantly distracted by all the tantalising smells. While Quinn made it clear to himself he was only escorting her to Hokitika and no more than that, there was no harm in asking a few questions.

He called over his shoulder, 'Why Cerberus and Pegasus?'

She laughed. 'A bit much I know, but I grew up with Greek mythology. Eccy taught me all the stories.'

'Eccy?'

'Miss Eccleston, my governess. She was like one of the family for years until she got sick and had to leave – some stomach complaint, I think. Broke my heart saying goodbye to her. She cried too.'

'Did she?' His voice remained neutral but his fingers tightened on his gun.

Guinevere continued, 'I had a couple more after that but they didn't stay long. That's the problem with pretty, young governesses Father always used to say.'

'Did he now? And were they all young?'

'Yes. Father said a young pretty woman could be just as clever as an old ugly one, but easier on the eye first thing in the morning. More fun too.'

'For whom?'

She sounded puzzled. 'Me, of course! You've no idea how dreary it would be to be taught by a dull governess. I expect you went to a school – that always sounded much more fun. Did you enjoy it?'

Quinn thought back to the tiny village schoolroom where the students' breath had hung in mists as they scratched words on cracked and broken slates. The schoolmaster, Mr Briant, had been a thin scarecrow of a fellow – probably no more than twenty-two or twenty-three, Quinn now realised – struggling to instil a love of learning into children who shuffled frozen feet and couldn't

46

concentrate for the hunger that gnawed in their bellies.

Yet Mr Briant must have seen something in the scrawny boy, for after Quinn's parents died he persuaded the priests in the monastery to take him in so that he could continue his education. Quinn's three sisters had already been parcelled out to various relatives. Two priests had taken charge of Quinn's learning, pressing him to study six out of seven days all through the winter months when work at the neighbouring manor slowed.

''Twas not fun exactly,' he said, 'but I did have a couple of grand teachers. Father O'Reilly loved stories and language and Father Sullivan was a man of science. I owe them both a lot – not that I've much need of their teaching these days.'

'As a miner? No, I suppose not. What about your medical training? Why didn't you complete it?'

He gave a harsh laugh. 'I had enough of doctoring during the war.'

'Yes, of course. I can understand that. But what took you to America in the first place?'

There was a silence, then Quinn said abruptly, 'I had to leave Ireland.'

'Really? Why?'

'The English drove me out.'

The words hung in the morning air and now it was her turn to be silenced. Quinn wondered what he would see in her face if he turned around. Mistrust? Fear? His mouth tightened but after a minute or so she spoke again in a voice that rasped a little but remained friendly.

'I hear the Irish have a wonderful folklore. Did Father O'Reilly teach you the stories?'

His shoulders suddenly eased, though Quinn did not know why it should matter to him what an Englishwoman thought. 'He did. And though he was a man of God, I think he believed as much in the leprechauns and giants as he did in the Holy Trinity.'

Guinevere laughed. 'Tell me about the leprechauns.'

'Why? Are you planning to photograph them after you've made your fortune with the moa?'

'Mr O'Donnell!' Her voice was reproving but he could hear the underlying laughter and the corner of his mouth lifted despite himself.

'Well now, a leprechaun is generally found in forests, all alone, for he's a solitary creature and a surly one. There's not much fun to be had with him – the clurichaun are the lively ones. The leprechaun works hard and saves his gold, hoarding it in pots at the end of a rainbow.'

'Oh, I've always heard of gold at the end of a rainbow.' He heard the mischief in her voice as she added, 'Well, that's a fair description of yourself you've just given, Mr O'Donnell.'

'What?' For a second he was indignant but then the truth of it struck him. 'Well, they are hard to hold too. Try to catch one and they just slip away. And never trust one either, especially if you are after his pot of gold.'

She laughed. 'I'll bear that in mind – but for the moment your gold is quite safe from me.'

'And me!' he said feelingly. 'Damned if I can find where it's hidden.'

'What are the other ones you mentioned. Clar—?'

'Clurichauns. They're nothing but wastrels. They dress in dandy clothes and are drunken, merry folk with little interest in anything serious. Some say they are just leprechauns when they forget their dour natures for a bit and have some fun.'

'Like the miners in Hokitika?'

Now it was Quinn's turn to laugh as he stopped walking and turned around to look at her. 'I suppose so. You have an interesting way of viewing the world, Lady Guinevere.'

She blushed but smiled back. 'Miss Stanhope,' she corrected him. 'Now, I'm not going to take that as a compliment for I've been in New Zealand long enough to know that criticism comes obliquely wrapped here. How did the leprechauns come to Ireland?'

Quinn suppressed a smile at her observation. Clearly Miss Stanhope had raised eyebrows in Hokitika and people had been hard pushed to find a way to moderate her mad impulses.

Turning to lead the way once more he warned, ''Tis a long tale you will get if you are wanting to know the history of the little people.'

'We have got all day,' she pointed out.

'True. Well . . .' and so Quinn went on to tell her stories as they fought their way along the

49

poorly defined track through the dense bush and the sun struggled to rise above the thick canopy of forest to throw patches of light and shadow over the path.

The Irishman could feel his thin shirt and worn moleskins drying out and he raised his face to the warmth of the New Zealand sun even as he spoke of the mists of Ireland. It was only after a few stories that Quinn realised Guinevere had not spoken for a while and he turned around.

'Miss Stanhope, are you all right?' His voice sounded sharper than he meant but he could see she was unwell.

'I'm fine,' she said.

Quinn strode back to her and put a large palm over her forehead. 'You're not! You've been cooking up a fine fever while I've just been blathering on. Jaysus, woman. Why did you not tell me?'

She smiled wanly. 'What's the point? I have no medicine and all I need is a bed. The sooner we get to Hokitika, the sooner I get one.'

'You look like hell.'

Summoning a thread of energy, she dropped him a curtsy. 'How kind of you to mention that, sir.'

'This is no laughing matter. You are sick.'

'Again, thank you for pointing out the obvious. Now, please, let us continue. It is only the thought of a nice warm bed that is keeping me going.' She shivered as she spoke.

'Of course, I should have thought before. 'Tis all those cursed layers of clothing of yours. See,

I'm dry as a bone again but those petticoat things must still be wet under your dress.'

'They are not that bad,' she assured him, then gave a squeak of indignation. 'Mr O'Donnell, what on *earth* do you think you are doing?'

'Checking 'em,' he said, down on his knees, his hand up her skirt to knee-height, feeling the wet petticoats. 'They are still sodden. You must take them off.'

'I will not.'

'There's only me here and I can assure you I'll neither peep nor take advantage.'

'This is absurd.'

'You'll get consumption if you walk around in them much longer. See reason, woman.'

He thought she was going to argue some more but she must have been feeling worse than he thought for the fight seemed to go out of her.

'Very well,' she said. 'But turn around.'

'I'll do better than that. I'll go around that rock down the way there – see. You'll have all the privacy you need.'

Quinn made his way down the path where he settled himself, back against the rock, eyes half-closed against the bright light. New Zealand was a strange country, no denying it. Four seasons in a day the saying went. No one would have believed there'd been a tempestuous storm only hours earlier. Steam rose gently from the trees and bushes, which were patterned in luscious shades of green against the deep blue of the sky.

The stiffness had left his muscles now and as he relaxed, breathing in the rich smell of damp earth and the light perfume of some wild flower nearby, he felt himself begin to drift off.

'Well! I thought it was my welfare you were concerned with but I see now it was all a ruse to slip away and have a sleep, Mr O'Donnell.'

He opened his eyes at this tart observation and for a minute just let his gaze rest upon her. She looked slighter than ever without the voluminous petticoats and her battered dress clung to her. Her hair fell in wild ringlets down to her hips and the breeze lifted the tendrils which framed her face, all mock severity.

'You look like one of the little people yourself,' he said without thinking.

She laughed and started to admonish him but was clearly nonplussed so said instead, 'Shall we get moving again?'

'Wouldn't you like to rest first?'

She shook her head. 'If I sit down now I'm not sure I'd ever get up again.' Her tone was light but despite the removal of her wet clothes, the flush remained.

'Right, let's start moving again then.'

Once more they began following a faint trail back down the mountains, but now Quinn turned around often to check on his companion. She was game, he had to admit, as she doggedly negotiated the stones and rocks, the bushes and low-hanging branches. But when he saw her beginning to stumble, he felt it time to intervene. Determination was one thing, pig-headedness quite another.

'That's enough,' he said. 'I'll be carrying you from now on.'

'You can't. Your pack.'

'The hell with that,' Quinn said as he swung his pack down and stashed it under bushes by the path. 'I'll come back for it later.' He then lashed his gun to the high branches of a tree back from the track. 'No one ever looks up when they are walking,' he explained. 'Now, onto my back, pig-a-back style. Don't argue, just do it.'

Guinevere was remarkably light but he could feel shivers shake her slight frame. She no longer tried to talk, just laid her head against his shoulder as he supported her slim thighs in his hands.

Quinn was silent too, cursing himself inwardly for his stupidity in not getting those wet clothes off her many hours earlier. While he was used to being wet and dry and wet again, she'd probably never been soaked like that in her life. Plus she'd have been feeling weak still from her near drowning. He just hadn't thought. Of course he shouldn't have burdened himself with her in the first place but having done so, it was up to him to ensure she reached Hokitika safely.

He calculated as he walked; though it was still a very long way to the town, he could cover ground more swiftly than most and she wasn't very much heavier than the pack he carried. If he just kept on going, he might get there some time during the night. The sooner the better.

The hours piling one onto another seemed endless, however. The trail threaded down mountain slopes, along valleys, back up small hills and down again. Quinn jumped streams and waded across rivers, the faithful Cerberus always at his side. Sometimes Quinn stopped for water and each time he lay Guinevere down it seemed that she was worse, though she never complained. She was glad to drink from his cupped hand and her thirst worried him more. In the early afternoon he ripped a sleeve from his shirt and used this to bathe her hot face as he pondered upon the unpredictability of life.

'If someone had told me yesterday that I'd land up playing nursemaid to an Englishwoman, I would have laughed in his face.' Then he realised it was not life but Guinevere who was unpredictable, insinuating herself into his life.

Cerberus whined and Quinn gave him a pat. The dog licked his hand then nudged at Guinevere with his muzzle. She smiled wanly at this and tried to apologise for being a nuisance, but Quinn brushed her words aside.

'Don't talk,' he told her. 'Just focus on keeping your strength up.'

At length, the sun sank and stars were just beginning to fill the sky when the ground miraculously began flattening out towards the coastline. It was an enormous relief for the track was easier now but still Quinn sometimes stumbled, cursing because it jolted Guinevere, cursing because it was a sign of his own strength beginning to falter. She seemed to sleep for most of the time, her body folded over his in a deadweight and to keep himself going he began reciting poetry again under his breath; not English poetry but the old Irish songs that Father O'Reilly had loved so well. He had taught Quinn French and Latin but had made sure he was literate in his own tongue as well.

'We will never be truly conquered,' the priest told him, 'while just one man still speaks in the Irish tongue.'

Now the wonderful music of the words wove through his mind, lifting him from this new land and carrying him back centuries to the land of his forefathers, long before the English had ever set foot in Ireland. A feeling of homesickness rose but he knew this too would pass. He could not return to Ireland – that English witch had seen to that – but he would make a new life here in New Zealand. Find gold, buy land and finally build a house that no man could ever again take from him. This dream, this determination for a place to call home, was what had driven him across the world and now buoyed him through the back-break and heartache of prospecting.

After what felt like an eternity, Quinn saw a faint tremble of lights in the distance, mere pinpricks in the dark but lights nevertheless. At the sight he found new heart and quickened his pace, half-walking, half awkwardly jogging the final half-mile. Guinevere remained a deadweight, bumping against his back. Cerberus, limping now on sore paws, stayed by his heels. Never, Quinn thought, had he ever been so happy to see such a ragged little town.

Hokitika, no more than a handful of buildings a year earlier, had been suddenly swamped by thousands upon thousands of men from all over the world at the first whisper of gold. Overnight calico shops and wooden shacks had been flung up, as well as hotels and taverns of various makeshift designs to accommodate not only miners but the attendant flourishing trades in alcohol, gambling and coarse entertainment.

Though the hour was late, still many crude buildings were lively with the sounds of revelry and as Quinn picked his way down the muddy main street he wondered which disreputable hostelry Lady Guinevere Stanhope had chosen to reside in and what she'd made of it.

'Lady Guinevere,' he called softly to rouse her. 'We're here. Hokitika.'

She stirred and he was glad to hear her voice faint and hoarse ask, 'Already?'

Already! He thought of the last endless hours but now was not the time.

'Where are you staying?'

'The Royal. You can't miss it. It's the biggest building at the end of Revell Street.'

Drunken laughter spilled out of the various

taverns and Quinn had his work cut out negotiating the rough road with its ruts and drunkards, but at the far end of the street he saw a two storey building. This must be the Royal though its name would mislead the unwary. Thrown up in haste, the Royal sagged at the knees and seemed to lean to one side. Even from the street, the smell of beer and boiled cabbage leaking from it was clearly discernible.

Quinn eased Guinevere around and into his arms, grateful for the shift of weight off his back, and smiled down at her.

'Here we are,' and in the glimmer he saw her smile back as he carried her into the hotel.

'Oh, so *you've* got our fine lady then, 'ave you?' The woman at the counter was a slatternly individual with yellow hair and a blowsy manner.

Disliking her lewd inference, Quinn was curt. 'Where's her room?'

'Up the stairs on your right at the back, but no gentlemen callers, mind,' she added, with a coarse laugh.

'Lucky I'm no gentleman, then,' retorted Quinn, taking the stairs two at a time. He kicked open the door and making out the bed through the gloom, laid Guinevere upon it, while Cerberus collapsed into the corner.

Taking matches wrapped in oilskin from his pocket, Quinn struck a light and saw a lamp, which he lit and lifted to look about him. What he saw made him pause in blank amazement.

The room itself was as he had expected. The walls were of brown scrim, the floor was of rough-sawn boards. Limp drapes straddled the windows. Camera equipment was stowed in one corner. What astonished Quinn, however, was that the bed had a beautiful silk cover and the walls were alive with colour from a collection of paintings which adorned them. For a second he just stood and stared, then sniffed and gave a low laugh. Perfume? In Hokitika?

'And what are you laughing at?' Guinevere's voice was little more than a croak but still managed to contain some spirit.

'You! Lady Guinevere, you never fail to amaze me.'

CHAPTER 3

Guinevere smiled back but even the lamp-light couldn't warm the pallor of her face. 'You need to sleep,' Quinn told her unnecessarily. 'Here, I'll help you get into the sheets. But first we need to be getting you out of that dress. It's filthy. Where can I find something else for you to put on?'

'In the trunk over by the window.'

There were in fact several trunks by the window. Quinn could not imagine how anyone could travel with so much luggage. The first, however, contained men's clothes and he remembered her father. Clearly she had not decided yet what to do with his possessions. Quietly closing the lid, Quinn tried the next one. It was like opening Pandora's box for inside it was a jumbled froth of lace, cotton and silk; stays, petticoats, stockings, long-legged drawers, all tossed higgledy-piggledy. Jaysus. She had so much of everything. His fingers suddenly seemed very large and coarse and he noted ruefully in the flickering lamplight that dirt rimmed every fingernail. It was not surprising as he'd been grub-bing for gold these past three weeks, but still it made him feel like a peasant again, illicitly fingering the lady of the manor's intimate clothing.

He pulled out one garment, a soft, filmy white thing which must surely be a nightdress and took it over to the bed. Guinevere's eyes were closed and her breathing rasped. He thought maybe she'd fallen asleep already, but then she opened her eyes though clearly with an effort.

'Here's something. Now, we'll just get you to sit up. I'll undo your dress, then I'll turn my back so you can take it off, right?'

Obediently she leaned forward, pulling her mass of hair over her shoulders so he could reach the fastenings at the back. His fingers were clumsy as they tried to work the row of tiny buttons.

'How the hell did you get into this dress in the first place?'

'Mary helped me.'

'Your maid?'

'No, I didn't have money to keep her on. Fortunately she found another family on the ship. Mary's just a girl who comes to help me for the moment.'

The buttons finally came undone and the back of the dress fell open. He saw a fine shift, muddied now but which once must have been snowy white. Her neck was long and slender and through the fine material, he could see the line of her spine before it disappeared into the clutch of her corsets.

'Can you get those damned corset things off?

What on earth made you think you had to wear such nonsense, especially out in the bush?'

She tried to smile. 'To be seemly, I suppose.' Her fingers struggled with the ribbons but they were too tangled and knotted.

'Here,' said Quinn impatiently and he pulled a small knife from his pocket to slit the ribbons, averting his eyes as the corsets fell open. 'That's good. Now, get yourself into clean clothes and then we'll get you into bed.'

He crossed again to the window where he drew the curtains closed. They were only of calico but still they lent this barren room a little softness. He heard the rustle of garments and tried not to picture what was happening behind him; it was not right to entertain such visions when she was so trusting. Besides, thoughts like that led to trouble – serious trouble. He knew better than anyone that English ladies and Irish peasants did not go together.

To distract his unruly thoughts, Quinn tried to make out the painting in the gloom beside the window. Seemed like a woman of some sort with masses of hair – not unlike Guinevere's – and in her hands she carried flowers. Jaysus, didn't these fellows have anything better to do with their time than paint such stuff? There was the soft thud of clothes falling to the floor.

'Mr O'Donnell, I'm ready.'

Quinn turned and for the briefest second was checked by the sight of white nightdress and the

61

tumble of hair, but this really was *not* the time and the way that she had accepted him in her room and in her state of undress, showed that she saw him as a doctor or footman or some such damned thing but certainly not as a man. So he moved back to the bed, turned down the covers and helped her in. She looked very young against the white pillow.

'Thank you.' She tried to smile but looked exhausted.

''Twas nothing. Now sleep.'

Her eyes fluttered closed then opened again. 'You won't leave me?'

'No, I won't leave you. I'll be watching over you.'

She fell asleep almost immediately and he took her pulse. It was far too fast and when he laid a hand on her temple, he knew her temperature was very high. She must be feeling terrible but still didn't complain.

Having promised not to leave, Quinn now looked about for somewhere he could sleep but the room was bare of furnishings save for a table with an ewer and bowl, and a hard chair. With a sigh he lay down on the floor using the riding habit as a pillow and within minutes he too was asleep.

He did not sleep the night through as he was awake a few hours later to check on his patient. Amazing how the doctor in him took over. He fiercely quashed the thought, however, of how right, how natural it felt to tend to the sick. The ewer had some water in it and ripping the other sleeve from his shirt he used this to cool her soaring temperature. She was clearly very hot so he turned her on her side and, lifting the weight of her hair, bathed the back of her neck which was wet with sweat. Then he pushed up the loose sleeves of her nightdress and ran the damp cloth down her arms. They were so slender, the bones of her hand so fine, that even in the darkness he could picture every detail of the intricate anatomy. Her palms were as soft as he'd imagined they'd be. As he was bathing the second hand, her fingers closed over his and he clasped them reassuringly till her breathing smoothed out and her fingers loosened their hold.

At dawn he woke again to find his patient lying with her hand tucked under her cheek, her large eyes looking down at him.

'Mr O'Donnell, have you been here all night?' Her voice rasped but still managed to have a peremptory note to it.

'I have. You asked me to stay.'

He struggled up to a sitting position, wincing at his stiff neck and noticing how cold his bare arms were.

'Did I?' She sounded doubtful. 'You shouldn't still be here, you know.'

He tensed. Here it came. She'd be furious; castigate him for compromising her. There would be scenes, people would come running to throw him out on the street. But instead she continued,

63

'Sleeping on the floor like that, too! I've been nothing but trouble to you since the moment I met you. I do apologise.'

Her words surprised a smile from him.

'No trouble at all,' he lied. 'Now, let's see how you are.'

He rose and took her wrist. 'Your pulse is more normal though still a little fast. Your head is a bit cooler today, too. Judging from your voice, you must have a terribly sore throat. How are you feeling – truly now? None of that "fine" nonsense.'

In the watery light that struggled through the calico drapes he was pleased to see the hectic flush had gone from her face and the smile, though weak, was still a smile.

'I'm much better than yesterday. Yes, my throat is sore but I'll survive. I'm strong as an ox, really. But what about you? Look at the gooseflesh on your arms. You must be freezing from sleeping on the floor. Get a shirt of my father's from his trunk.'

'I can't do that!'

'You must. I feel terrible that you have spent such a wretched night on my behalf.'

He shook his head.

'Please.'

There was more command than entreaty in this word but still Quinn hesitated. 'Are you sure you want another man wearing your father's clothes?'

'He would have liked you to wear one after all your kindness to me.'

'Well then, I thank you.'

The clothes in her father's trunk were neatly folded, unlike the chaos in his daughter's trunk, and Quinn soon located a shirt of very fine cotton. He lifted it out and looked at it. 'I should wash first if you don't mind. It seems a terrible thing for a shirt like this to go on a dirty back.'

'Not at all. I would give anything for a bath, myself.'

Gwen watched as Quinn pulled the ripped shirt over his head and her eyes followed the long lines of his back that tapered from the wide shoulders to his lean waist. He filled the bowl with the last water from the jug and bent to splash himself. As all men in New Zealand, he was bronzed but she noted that the colour faded to pale gold at the belt of his trousers.

Without thinking she said, 'You really do have the most beautiful torso.'

Quinn's head jerked up and he threw her a startled sideways glance. 'Jaysus, Miss Stanhope, I didn't think you'd be watching me.'

'You are in my room,' she pointed out. 'What else can I do?'

'I thought you'd close your eyes or look away. 'Tis not seemly for a young lady to see a man half-naked.'

She laughed, then groaned as her throat rasped.

'Oh, Mr O'Donnell, you need not have any anxieties on that score. I have seen many male torsos. The painters often used Maidenhurst as their

65

setting so I grew up with models, male and female, about the house. My father always said that the human body is not an object of shame but of celebration rather. You could earn a lot of money posing, you know.'

Quinn snorted and continued his ablutions.

'You'd make a marvellous Spartan. I'm quite sure Will Morris would love the opportunity to paint you.'

'Well, I'm equally sure he'll never get it,' said Quinn categorically as he began to dry himself on his old shirt, not seeing a towel nearby. 'I'd feel a right chump standing about while someone painted me into some nonsense. Spartan indeed.' He shook his head in disbelief.

'But your musculature is so well defined. How did you achieve that?'

'Work,' Quinn informed her dryly. 'Lots of it. And generally not enough food.'

He seemed very tall in her room and despite the domestic act of drying himself, he still carried that untamed air about him – quite unlike any other man of her acquaintance. It must be the wild hair, she thought, the unkempt beard. Or perhaps the heavy boots.

Dropping the shirt over his head, Quinn tucked it into his moleskins then surveyed her. In the soft light of dawn she looked more fey than ever with her tangled mass of hair framing her small, white face with its huge eyes.

'Miss Stanhope,' he said, 'this is the most remarkable conversation to be having.'

'Is it? I do apologise if I made you uncomfortable but you must understand I grew up in a house where these things were commonly talked about over the dining table. There really is nothing wrong in it,' Guinevere assured him. 'It's art.'

He smiled at the inflection she gave the final word but raised an eyebrow. She might look fey but in fact she was outrageous with her absurd mix of innate innocence and assumed worldliness.

'Art it may be, it's still not something usually discussed between a man and a woman – well, not where I come from at any rate. The priests would tan the hide from my back just for engaging in this conversation and as for you, you'd be locked in a nunnery soon as they set eyes on you.'

'That certainly would not suit me.'

'No, and I'm quite sure the nuns would find you didn't suit them.' His manner became brisk. 'Now, m'lady, I must leave before the hotel starts stirring. There's already a few up but don't worry, I'll slip out when no one is about.'

'Why should I worry?'

He stared at her. Sure but her father had a lot to answer for, raising a daughter in such a way. Her forward manner could so easily be misinterpreted by men less than honourable.

'*Lady Guinevere*, your reputation! I fear it has been compromised already but . . .'

Her weak laughter which quickly turned into

coughing stopped his words. He looked at her, eyebrow raised in query.

'Oh, Mr O'Donnell. The whole town thinks I'm mad as it is and I don't care at all about anyone's opinion here, anyway. All they think about is gold. Besides, do you think I don't know what sort of women come to this hotel? I'm not a complete innocent.'

'Well, that's as may be, but you don't want to be seen as no better than them.'

Her hand sliced the air dismissively. 'Why? I don't judge the poor creatures.'

Quinn threw her a scathing look. 'You simply have no idea, Lady Guinevere, just how much your title protects you. In this world, it is all that stands between you and ruin – that and your money. If you lost those . . .' Quinn shook his head. 'Well, you just wouldn't know how to survive. Believe me, stay the lady. 'Tis your only defence. Now, I must go, but will return in a few hours. What was the name of your maid?'

'Mary. Why?'

'I'll get her. I can't be looking after you again, not with everyone around. How did you find her in the first place?'

'Her brother Jem works in the kitchens.'

Quinn nodded. 'Don't leave the room. Stay in bed. I'll put the word around that what you have is contagious. Do you understand?'

Clearly she didn't. She was used to having servants around – people who were all but invisible but who would never dream of laying a finger on her. That careless disregard would not work in a hotel of men. He could not decide whether her heedlessness was from arrogance or innocence. Or perhaps she did have some notion and that's why she'd got Cerberus. Quinn looked across at the hell hound snoring in the corner and shook his head. No guard dog, that one.

'Understand?' he said again very firmly, looking back at his patient.

Though he could see she longed to argue the point, after the briefest hesitation she sighed and nodded.

'Good. I'll be seeing you shortly, then.'

Guinevere watched the door close behind Quinn. For all his height and strength, he moved quietly. Had he learnt this on the battlefields of America, moving through the wounded? She could not even begin to imagine the war, though she had read enough about it in the newspapers. Her father had always encouraged her to keep abreast with what was happening in the rest of the world. She could still picture his animated face when he said, 'A well-informed mind is vastly more important than embroidery, Guinevere.'

At this sudden, vivid memory, tears welled up but she squeezed her eyes closed to stop them. She could not afford any weakness. This wretched illness was making her quite feeble. She even had to fight a sense of desolation at having lost the companionship of Mr O'Donnell for the moment. Absurd – and dangerous. She couldn't allow herself to feel anything more than gratitude to a man who would no doubt be moving out of her life this very morning.

He had been most kind – well, more than kind. He had saved her life, after all. Twice actually, for she would have never made it to Hokitika alone. But even so, he would have no reason to linger now. He'd probably returned to drink and gamble away any gold he had found, perhaps reserving some for the services of a woman and then he'd be back to the mountains in just a few days.

That was the pattern she'd noted in the diggers despite her short time in this country. Hard-living, rollicking fellows with no steadiness, no long-term prospects who made even artists look respectable and sensible. It wasn't that they all came from rough backgrounds either. Coming from countries around the world, there were many educated gentlemen among them, even some with titles, like that French duke whom everyone called Mr Le Duck. But however diverse their backgrounds, they were all united by the single, driving passion for gold; a strange form of myopia for almost none got rich but all had tales of someone who had and that was enough to fuel this insanity. Quinn, for all his kindness and care, was no better than the rest of them.

Just as Guinevere came to this conclusion, a

knock interrupted her thoughts, the door opened and a freckled, round face peeped in.

'Mary! So soon.'

'That nice gentleman sent for me. He's says you are wanting a bath and has arranged one for you.'

'What? How?'

Guinevere struggled into a sitting position as Mary entered the room.

The young girl shrugged and grinned. 'Dunno how he did it, m'lady, but somehow he's tracked down a bathtub and it's right outside the door waiting to be brought in. Here, I'll get you a shawl so's you'll be respectable.'

Guinevere felt dazed as Mary wrapped her in one of her shawls then opened the door to two burly fellows who, eyes averted, wrestled a battered tub into the room. They were followed by young Jem, carefully holding two steaming jugs of water.

'There's more on the way,' Mary explained and though it took some ten minutes of Mary and Jem running up and down the stairs with great jugs and bowls of water from the kitchen, where Quinn was overseeing the heating of it, finally the bath was half full.

As Guinevere lowered herself into it, she thought how she'd never welcomed a bath more in her life. Mary helped her to wash her long, tangled hair and it was pure heaven to rinse away all traces of her near drowning, along with the sweat of her fever.

Later, once more tucked into bed, her hair drying

in fluffy ringlets after a vigorous towelling and brushing out by Mary, Guinevere was just finishing a cup of tea when there was another knock on the door.

'It's Dr O'Donnell, Lady Guinevere, come to see how you are.'

His Irish lilt came softly but clearly through the thin panels. She smiled at his determination to protect her name. Did anyone in this hotel care? However, she nodded to Mary, who opened the door and for a second was quite taken aback. She was not the only one who had cleaned up. All traces of her scruffy rescuer, with his dirty clothes and soft beard, were gone. Quinn stood before her now in crumpled but clean moleskins, her father's shirt and a battered jacket.

'Where did you get your clothes?' she asked. 'You left your pack up on the mountain.'

'Bought them off a miner down on his luck,' he said, coming forward. 'My own stuff is filthy.'

His dark hair swept off his brow and the long line of his jaw and strong chin were exposed. He looked down at her with a smile and she saw that the moustache and beard had been hiding a mouth so beautiful that it would have had the Pre-Raphaelites groping for their pencils.

'You're looking better,' he noted.

'I feel it. Thank you for organising the bath.'

He crossed the room and picked up her wrist to take her pulse. Though he'd done this several times over the past twenty-four hours, Guinevere suddenly felt shy. Quinn somehow seemed like a new man and she peeped at him from under the curtain of her hair. In the bush, with his wild hair and hat pulled low over his brow, he had been arresting but now she was acutely aware of his individual features; the wide brow, the scar on his left cheekbone, the strong nose, that lovely mouth. His eyes were clear and grey with faint lines that fanned out from the corners that crinkled when he smiled. He might have a grim air about him now but this was a face that had laughed a lot in the past and she suddenly fancied she glimpsed a light-hearted boy behind the facade of this solitary man.

Oblivious of her regard, Quinn continued to count her heartbeats. Did he detect the sudden skip in its pace?

'Good,' he said, smiling down at her. 'A definite improvement. You've more colour in your cheeks, too.'

'Have I?' Though she kept her tone light, Guinevere could feel herself blush.

'Still that rasp in your throat, however. Luckily I've found a druggist down the road and have something that will help.'

From his jacket pocket he drew out a bottle and tipped a measure into the cup on her bedside table. 'Drink up,' he said, holding the cup to her lips.

Guinevere was tempted to succumb and sip from his hands as she had just the day before, but she was not going to betray any more weakness.

'I can hold it myself,' she said abruptly, and took the cup from him, noting even as she did so his long, lean hands. He fell back a step immediately, that guarded expression of his suddenly hooding his grey eyes. Heavens, had she offended him again? Trying to smooth over the moment, she tasted the medicine and made a face.

'Ugh. What on earth is it?'

The corner of his mouth lifted but the smile did not reach his eyes. ''Tis the druggist's own recipe. I checked the ingredients and it's sound enough, but I did wonder how it would taste.'

'Disgusting.'

'Ah well, as the priests used to say, it seems it is always the unpalatable things that do us the most good and must be endured virtuously without complaint.'

Guinevere couldn't help smiling at his ironic tone, though she grimaced again at the next sip. 'My father was fervently against anything that made one uncomfortable and had no belief in virtue either, saying it was a scourge to unsettle one's natural desires.'

Quinn took the empty cup from her hands and put it on the table before pulling a chair up and sitting beside the bed. 'Did he now?'

Perhaps the illness was making her overly sensitive but Guinevere thought she detected a censorious undertone. 'I don't mean he wasn't honourable,' she said defensively. 'He was the kindest, most generous of men but he just thought differently from most about actively seeking happiness and enjoyment of life.'

'Mm.'

'What do you mean by "mm"?' Guinevere eyed Quinn. He'd ceased being a handsome interloper in her bedroom and was back to being infuriating. His eyes were more guarded than ever, but those beautifully moulded lips had definitely folded into lines of disapproval. 'Why do you look like that?'

'Just seems to me 'tis easier to seek happiness and enjoyment when you don't have to be spending time seeking food, warmth and safety instead.'

'Well, of course.'

'There's no "of course" about it, where I come from.'

'But that was not my father's fault. Don't make it seem as though it was. And don't sit in judgement of him either when you never met him. Your life has had nothing to do with his.'

'No, but I know his sort. If one is born into luxury, ten must be born into poverty to support it.'

'That's not true.'

'No? Then just how many servants did you have, Lady Guinevere, to look after you and your father?'

Guinevere was outraged but also thrown. 'I don't know,' she stammered. 'I've never thought about it.'

'No,' he agreed. 'I'm quite sure you haven't.'

'Don't you use that tone on me. How dare you be so condescending.'

'Don't be absurd. How can a penniless Irishman condescend to an English lady?'

'I don't know but you do!'

For a second they glared at each other but to Guinevere's surprise, Quinn was the first to break. A rueful smile tugged at his lips and this time it did soften that horrid coolness in his eyes.

'A fine doctor I am, to be getting my patient's temperature soaring again. Lady Guinevere, I apologise. I shouldn't have said anything about your daddy.'

'Thank you,' she said gruffly. 'He was a good man, you know.'

'I'm sure he was.'

'He supported lots of artists.'

'Looked after artists, did he? Ah well, there you go then. And a very fine job he did of it too, I'm sure.'

Guinevere threw him a suspicious sideways glance but his expression was bland. Her eyes narrowed. 'Mr O'Donnell,' she began then paused.

'Lady Guinevere?' Again, his tone was politely neutral but she did not trust him at all.

'You're laughing at me.'

'Sure, now would I do that?'

'Sure, yes you would.'

There was no denying the mischief in his eyes and he laughed. 'I'm sorry, I truly am. I shouldn't be teasing you.'

'No you shouldn't!' But Guinevere could feel herself weakening and despite being still very ruffled, she couldn't help smiling back. 'You are quite insufferable, you know.'

'So I've been told before – two nights ago, in fact.'

Guinevere laughed. 'It seems such a long time ago now. I feel like I've known you for much longer.'

'Do you?' he asked, and as he smiled down into her eyes, there was something in his tone that suddenly made her feel shy again. For a second their eyes locked and Guinevere's heart skipped though she hardly knew why.

Then Quinn shoved the chair back so hard that the legs squeaked on the wooden floor as he rose to his feet. His voice was brisk. 'Well, having riled my patient thoroughly, I'll be leaving now so you can sleep. You were quite right, Lady Guinevere, it would appear you are as strong as an ox, judging by how quickly you are rallying. However, you still look peaky so I'll ensure that no one disturbs you. Shall I take Cerberus with me? I'll find him some food.'

'That would be wonderful but Cerberus never leaves me you know, he's very loyal. He won't go with you.'

'Oh, I think he will.'

Guinevere found his confidence a little annoying but sure enough as soon as Quinn snapped his fingers, Cerberus immediately rose to his feet and came over, tail wagging. Quinn crossed to the door.

'Come boy.' Cerberus followed then paused, looked back at Guinevere and whined.

'Go on,' she urged.

Quinn clicked his long fingers again as he stepped out of the room and the dog, with a final whine, followed. The door closed behind them. So much for loyalty. How aggravating that that man seemed always to be right. Suddenly she realised that she was after all, very exhausted. Infuriatingly, it seemed that Mr O'Donnell was quite right again. She did need rest and closing her eyes, Guinevere was sound asleep in minutes.

CHAPTER 4

Guinevere recovered her strength over the following days and during this time Quinn visited twice daily. Every night, before going to sleep, he vowed to say goodbye in the morning but each time he visited in his role of doctor, he found it strangely difficult to leave her. He couldn't in all fairness, he explained to himself repeatedly, abandon his patient until she was completely recovered.

The town accepted his medical background, especially as the druggist said that the Irishman knew his stuff all right. Bet, the hotel proprietor, always addressed him as Dr O'Donnell, but with an ironical emphasis on the title and a quizzical look in her eye.

''Ere to examine 'er ladyship again?' she would greet him each day with a grin, as Quinn continued to ignore the lewd undertone. However, Bet responded well to the tips he left to ensure her ladyship received a good dinner each night, though once she winked and said, 'I'm not sure 'er ladyship'll be wanting to make a recovery with a doctor like you dancing attendance.'

'Our relationship is purely professional,' Quinn said icily.

'Oh, don't go telling me that! I 'ear the two of you laughing there – nothing professional in the length of time you spend with 'er either. But don't you worry, doc, I won't be telling no one your secret – not that the 'ole town isn't talking about it anyway.'

Quinn made his way up the stairs cursing. He knew he shouldn't linger so long during his visits for in truth it was astonishing just how quickly such a fragile-looking little thing had flung off her fever. But she was lonely and there was something in the way her face lit up when he walked into her room that was strangely warming, though as often as not they would be scrapping within the half hour.

Quinn had brought her a couple of books he'd managed to find and she'd fallen on these with cries of joy. He'd also rustled up some paper and drawing pencils and though she said she was an indifferent artist, he thought her sketches of the thin-ribbed cats, limp lines of washing, and scrawny hens in the backyard of the hotel far preferable to the paintings that adorned her walls.

'Rubbish!' she said, when he ventured this opinion as he leaned over her shoulder to see her work on the table in front of her. She was still in her nightgown but with a shawl wrapped about her, her hair carelessly caught up in a knot on top of her head. He still could not tell if her disregard for conventions came from a casual innocence or a deep-seated arrogance where an Irishman was not worth the effort of dressing properly for. Of course it did not matter how an Englishwoman viewed him; her opinion mattered not a toss. Yet the not knowing irked like an itch.

'Your doodles are real while these . . .' Quinn waved a deprecatory hand at the walls, 'are some rich fellows' fancies of what they think real life is like.'

Guinevere turned to face him earnestly. 'But the whole point of the Pre-Raphaelites is that they do show life as it really is.'

'Then they've missed the point.'

Her head went up. 'You have no idea what you are talking about.'

'And they had no idea about what they were painting. All this nonsense about love and suffering. What would they know about it anyway?'

Moving to the window, Quinn leaned a shoulder against it and crossed his arms.

'Don't you look so dismissive. They've loved. They've suffered,' said Guinevere with passion.

He raised one eyebrow.

'They have,' cried Guinevere. 'They continue to do their art no matter how damning the critics are. And they love with passion – even when the girls come from very poor homes. Why, Gabriel Rossetti sacrificed everything to marry his model, Lizzie, though her father just owned a small shop. He suffered with their unhappy marriage and was grief-stricken when she killed herself. So they *do* know life.'

'No, that proves *my* point! They know nothing of life. Of course a marriage between people of different classes never works. And what do you mean *they've* suffered? What about the models these artists didn't marry, for God's sake? Did these fine artists leave fatherless children in their wake?'

Pushing back her chair, Guinevere rose and leaned forward both hands on the table to say emphatically. 'And if they did, I am quite sure they always provided well for the baby.'

Quinn's lip curled. 'I'd like to hear from the mother how satisfactory she might find that arrangement.' Then seeing her flush in fury and draw breath to battle further, Quinn threw up a hand to stem her words. 'Sure, I only said I like your drawings more, that's all.'

Looking taken aback by this aggressive compliment, Guinevere nodded. 'Thank you. Perhaps I shouldn't sound so churlish but it's just you simply do not understand anything about *art*,' she said in that tone of hers that made his toes curl in fury. Yet still he returned to see her each day.

While Quinn knew that under her delicate looks ran a vein of determination, he hadn't realised quite how irrational and uncompromising she really was until nearly a week had elapsed.

The voice that called, 'Come in,' to his knock

one morning was cheerful and when he went into the room he was pleased and a little surprised to see his patient fully dressed and sitting on the floor with two unpacked trunks about her. Clothes collected in drifts across the floorboards interspersed with piles of drawings and photographs.

Cerberus, who had been watching his mistress's activities with interest, now bounded across the floor in greeting.

'Good morning to you. 'Tis good to see you're up,' said Quinn, fending off the dog's lavish welcome.

Guinevere smiled up at him from the drawings she was sorting. 'Good morning to you too, Mr O'Donnell.'

He looked around at the chaos. 'What are you doing?'

'Getting my affairs in order. I need to see if I can condense my belongings into one trunk. It's easier to travel that way.'

He nodded. 'Good idea.'

Though he would be sorry to see his fair patient go, it was time for her to return to England. New Zealand was no place for a lady, especially not one on her own. Especially not in Hokitika.

He squatted down next to her and asked, 'When do you sail?'

'Sail?' She turned an astonished face to him. 'Who said anything about sailing? I'm talking about when I go after the moa. I'm leaving tomorrow. I took all my money out of the bank today and Bet has introduced me to a Maori man

83

who knows all the forests like the back of his hand. She says if anyone can find the bird, he can. We leave at first light.'

Disbelief drove Quinn to his feet again. 'Oh my God! Not that again! Jaysus, woman. Have you not one sensible bone in your whole body? For a start, you cannot be having money about you in this town – 'tis not safe.'

'It is! I've hidden it here in my box of chemicals which has a false bottom – another of my father's inventions. No one would think to look there.' She indicated a stout wooden box stashed in one corner next to her camera and tripod.

'Any thief worth his salt would smell that out in a trice. But money aside, after all that has happened to you, surely you cannot still be intent on pursuing such a daft scheme?'

Her chin came up. 'If you mean do I intend fulfilling my father's dream, then yes I do.'

'But your father – lovely man though I'm sure he was – was clearly—' He broke off but Guinevere guessed what he was about to say.

'My father was not mad.'

'No, no,' Quinn assured her. 'Just maybe – you know . . .' and his finger tapped his temple lightly. 'In the nicest possible way, of course. Perhaps it was a fever of the brain that he died from.'

Guinevere dropped the photographs she was holding into her lap and glowered up at him. 'My father was *not* touched in the head!'

'All right, maybe not. But surely he would never

have intended for you to go off on such a dangerous venture all alone. What a man can do and a woman can do are two very different things.'

'I will manage.'

Quinn closed his eyes in the face of this stubbornness and exhorted the heavens to provide him with patience.

'M'lady,' he began, but she immediately interrupted him with a bright, brittle smile.

'Oh, wait, I know how this one goes, but you should say, "My *dear* Lady Guinevere, I do implore you . . ."'

Quinn shook his head. 'I never implore.'

'You really should,' continued Guinevere, ignoring him.

'Not should, *must*!'

Guinevere quelled him with an imperious look, even from her position on the floor. '*Should*,' she repeated firmly. 'I'm a lady. You cannot use must on me.'

'I can and I will again. You *must*—'

'Listen to reason!' they both chimed in unison. Despite his frustration Quinn couldn't help smiling and Guinevere laughed.

'Don't be so pompous,' she begged, 'and look at these pictures, instead. Don't you think they are beautiful?'

Quinn however was not about to be deterred. 'Lady Guinevere—'

'I've told you before, I don't want you to use my title.'

'Lady Guinevere,' he continued, 'you don't seem to fully realise the dangers out there. Men are dying all the time. There're floods, ravines, the cold . . . 'Tis a rough country. And then not all men in the mountains are gentlemen, either.'

Unmoved, Guinevere replied, 'There is no point in continuing with this conversation, Mr O'Donnell. My mind is quite made up,' and she returned to her job of sifting the photographs into different piles.

Stony-faced, Quinn surveyed her then squatted down again so that he was only inches from her. 'Did your father ever beat you, m'lady?' he asked in a soft voice.

Guinevere's eyes flew to his face, half-startled, half-laughing. 'Never!'

'Well, he should have!' said Quinn. 'You need some sense knocked into you.'

'Why is it men always call it sense when it is their notion, and whim when it is a woman's?' Guinevere asked as though expressing a curious thought.

A reluctant grin tugged the corners of Quinn's mouth. 'Why is it a woman can be deaf, even with two perfectly good, God-given ears in her head?'

'Probably because men talk such a lot of nonsense. Now, what do you think of these photographs by Margaret Cameron?'

'There's a woman amongst these artists of your father's?' asked Quinn as he took the pile she offered him.

'Oh, yes. There are several; Christina Rossetti combines art and writing, while Lizzie did some wonderful work before she died. But Margaret is the one I'm closest to – she's almost like an aunt to me. I've learned a lot about photography from her.'

Quinn straightened and took the photographs over to the window where the rectangle of sun lit dancing dust motes. Like the paintings on the wall, the pictures were of beautiful women with wild hair and mournful expressions.

'And these are my father's,' said Guinevere, rising and handing him another pile.

As Quinn flicked through them he recognised several myths and stories behind the pictures. This woman must surely be Persephone with a painted wintry landscape behind her and a posy of spring flowers in her hand. Here was an agonised Lady Macbeth washing her hands. Quinn shook his head at all this play-acting but held his tongue. Joan of Arc, some knight – Galahad presumably. And Eve. Quinn paused, shocked. She was dressed in little but cunningly draped foliage, proffering an apple to an even more scantily dressed Adam.

'Did your father take this one too?' he demanded.

Guinevere leaned over to see which one he was talking about. 'The Garden of Eden, yes, do you like it? He let me help with the lighting in that one and I had some say in the posing of the models, too.' She tilted her head and considered the work. 'I think now it would have been better to put the light a little more to the left. What do you think?'

Quinn did not care a toss about the lighting.

'You saw people wearing as little as this?' His scandalised voice made her smile.

'I told you, these things were acceptable in my house. It's art. The human body is nothing to be ashamed of.'

'No, but a young female ought not—'

'Mr O'Donnell, now you are sounding dangerously like my tedious neighbours,' warned Guinevere. 'Do not presume to tell me what a young woman ought and ought not do. I will not be judged.'

He swallowed his next words and, with lips compressed, flicked through the rest of the pictures. They were beautiful, he readily agreed, but some were shocking with diaphanous materials wreathing, but not always concealing, luscious bodies. No wonder she had seen nothing strange in meeting him dressed in little more than a nightdress. The Englishwoman really was from a completely different world from him.

Still, he saw how he could use this to his advantage and turning to her said in a gentler voice, 'Lady Guinevere what are you doing here? Truly, you should be going home. Surely you can see how different your world is to this,' and his hand gestured to the barren little room with its bleak walls, alight only with the colours of her paintings and the silk cover on the bed. 'You belong back there. You must miss it sorely.'

For a second Guinevere looked at him, her wide eyes suddenly vulnerable.

'I do. I miss it horribly,' she said softly.

'Then why not return to it. Go back home. There's nothing for you here.'

She dropped her eyes. 'I cannot.'

'What do you mean?'

'My father—' she broke off and eyed him as though weighing how much to say. Then with a slight shrug of resignation she sat down on the chair as though all fight had at this moment left her. 'My father was a good man, you must understand,' she continued, her voice jerking over difficult sentences as her eyes fixed on her fingers interlaced tightly in her lap. 'He supported artists all his life but he was not . . . wise with money. He spent lavishly and loaned money to the wrong people, then borrowed from worse.' She shrugged. 'I don't really know all that happened. All I do know is that we came here because he had to find money urgently.'

For a second she paused. Then drawing in a breath she looked squarely up at him. 'You see, he mortgaged our house to our neighbour. A gentleman's agreement. He gave us a very generous loan according to my father and all we had to do was repay it in three years . . . no interest even. But if my father didn't, the house would go to Mr Ramsay.'

'And?'

She shrugged. 'Father was given very bad advice about an investment. He was assured that it was a venture that couldn't fail. But it did. It took almost everything, leaving us with only our skills to fall back on and with just a year now to repay the loan. That's when my father came up with the plan to photograph the moa.'

Quinn turned away to look out of the window so that she would not see his face as he shook his head. He simply could find nothing to say to this extraordinary story of folly and foolhardiness. How could any man so carelessly, so heedlessly lose his home? Guinevere may not want to face the fact but clearly her father was a wastrel and Quinn felt white-hot anger rising up against the man who lay safely in his grave, while his daughter was left all alone to fend for herself in this wild country.

Her problems were not, of course, Quinn's problem. He had already done far more than enough for her. He didn't need to feel responsible for her any more. But Jaysus, what a mess! He should have just walked away, leaving her on the side of that river when he'd had the chance.

'Have you any money?'

'Some. Not a lot. That is why I must find the moa.'

He moved to the table where he hitched his hip on the corner next to her. 'No, that is why you must go home to England. There is no alternative because I can tell you now, you've as much chance of finding a moa as a leprechaun.'

'Well, if I don't, then I will find a job.'

'And what exactly do you think you can do, here?' he asked.

'Photographs, of course.'

'For whom? The diggers?' And though she flinched at the derision in his voice, he continued. 'What else, apart from photographs, do you think you are qualified for?'

Her chin came up. 'Governess!' she flung at him.

He shook his head. 'Not in Hokitika.'

'Then I'll move to a city . . . Christchurch. There will be lots of jobs there. I could even work as a maid.'

'You?' Despite the gravity of Guinevere's situation and his own frustration at being enmeshed in it, the incongruous image of her docilely kitted out in a maid's apparel made him smile.

'Don't you dare laugh at me. I don't see myself as any more important than any other woman.'

'Maybe not. But others might not agree. Besides, you'd never cope. The hours are long and the work is heavy and tedious.'

'There is nobility in any sort of work!'

'Oh, Lady Guinevere. You really have *no* idea at all.'

'Don't be so damned superior.'

Quinn wagged a finger at her. 'And you can't be using those words or that tone with anyone you work for, you know, just because you don't like what they say. You'd be turned out without a character the same day.'

He saw her fingers curl into a fist and continued relentlessly.

'Ah, that temper. You said it was one of your besetting sins the day we met. What are the others? Stubbornness? Refusal to see sense?'

'Oh, you are quite insufferable.'

'So I've been told now, on several occasions.'

'Go on then, Mr O'Donnell with all the answers. What would *you* do in my place?'

She had him there. He thought for a minute, brow furrowed.

'There must be someone who can help you. An uncle perhaps, or a grandparent?'

She shook her head.

'This Ramsay, then. Can you not reason with him? Surely he would not throw a girl alone out of her own home?'

She gave him a humourless smile. 'Oh, no, he has no desire to throw me from my home. In fact, he even offered to tear up the contract my father signed.'

'Well, there you are then.'

'If I marry him.'

'Ah.'

A silence fell between them.

'So your father took a gamble and knew that if it didn't come off, he could still barter you off.'

Stung, Guinevere cried, 'No, it's not like that at all!'

'What is it like then?'

92

'Mr Ramsay is one of my father's close associates. He's a man of many talents, one my father felt sure would make a fine husband. Indeed, he urged me to consider the offer very seriously, quite apart from the issue of our home.'

'And you? What do you think of him?'

Guinevere hesitated. 'He's a man of inestimable qualities.'

'Will you marry him?'

Cornered, she tilted her chin. 'If it comes to that – yes.'

Quinn laughed scornfully. 'Inestimable qualities? Sure, a blind man can tell you don't care for him yet you are willing to marry yourself off.'

'He is a man of fine understanding and a steady temperament. I'm sure I couldn't hope for anything better in a husband.'

'But you don't love him?'

'No, and I don't want to. Having witnessed the havoc it has wrought in the lives of the artists my father supported, it seems to me that love can be a very inconvenient emotion. Fortunately, however, it would appear I am immune to it for I have never experienced the slightest pang.'

'Not at all?'

'Well, I once had a *tendre* for one of the artists – a very dashing young man – but he went away for a month and I quite forgot about him, so I don't think that counts, do you?'

Quinn shook his head. 'If you forgot him so easily, it certainly wasn't love.' His voice was bitter.

'What would you know about it? Have you ever been in love?' she demanded sceptically.

Quinn looked down at his clenched hands for a second. 'Once I thought I was,' he said shortly. 'As you say, it is a very inconvenient emotion and not one I'd recommend to anyone.'

'So you understand how I feel then? That love is best avoided?'

'Well, I've certainly no intention of ever saddling myself with that fancy again, I can assure you. But at the same time nothing in the world would induce me to sell myself into a loveless marriage, either. God, you English are a cold-blooded race.'

Bouncing to her feet, arms rigid at her sides, Guinevere cried, 'Oh, you are impossible! You want me to go back to England but if I do I must marry and you don't like that notion either, do you? What other option is there, Mr O'Donnell?'

Quinn looked away, not knowing what to say. Damn it all, he didn't know why it riled him so to think of her marrying. Fortunately she didn't wait for an answer but continued in an impassioned tone, 'It's my *home* we are talking of here. I would do anything to save Maidenhurst. Have you any idea what it is like to face losing your home and everything you hold dear?'

Something snapped inside Quinn and he too sprang to his feet. 'I know all right. I watched my mother dying in childbirth so weakened was she by the famine. My father died the year after – arrested by fine English soldiers for stealing food to feed his children. He died of gaol fever before they had the chance to hang him, leaving us to be parcelled out. I haven't seen my sisters in over ten years and, if that wasn't enough, because of the bloody English I can never go back to Ireland ever again to see them. So don't talk to me about losing everything. What the hell would you know about it with your fancy title and your arranged marriages to help you out of holes of your own making?'

Quinn stopped, horrified to discover he'd been shouting. Horrified that he had said so much.

Guinevere, her face ashen, touched his arm. 'I had no idea.'

'Well, you wouldn't,' Quinn said gruffly. 'It's past history now. It doesn't matter anymore.'

'But surely there must—'

'Leave it!' Her hand dropped and regretting his harsh tone, Quinn added, 'It's not me we're talking of, it's you. Why do you not just return to England and marry this fine gentleman then, if you are satisfied with the terms of the contract?' He tried to sound reasonable but the bitterness was still there, the contempt.

Gwen smiled wanly. 'I don't have enough money for the ticket back to England,' she said. 'I just have the money that my father had on him at the time of his death. The rest is tied up until the terms of the will are read. The letter has gone to the lawyers in London of course, but it will take some time I imagine to sort everything out. In the meantime, I do have enough to continue with my father's work here and earn money in that way.'

'Why don't you apply to this Ramsay fellow for the fare?'

Guinevere stepped back a pace and set her chin. 'Until the moment I marry him, I prefer not to take his money. I do not accept charity.'

''Tis not charity . . . he's to be your husband, after all.'

She shook her head. 'I will not apply to him.'

'You are the most stubborn—'

Guinevere drew herself up, transforming into the haughty English lady he loathed.

'Of course I cannot expect you to understand, so please do not trouble yourself on the matter any longer, Mr O'Donnell,' she said. 'You have been most kind and I am sorry for all the trouble I have caused you in the past week.'

Crossing the room to her bed, she drew some notes from under her pillow. 'I think this will cover the cost of your services – and your kindness. As I intend leaving tomorrow, I thought it best to pay you now.'

He looked at the money she held out then looked back into her eyes, his face hard and his voice dangerously soft. 'I am not one of your flunkeys to be paid off when I am of no use any longer. I did what I did with no thought to payment at all.'

'I don't doubt that you did but you must accept all the same. I told you, I do not accept charity.'

'And as I will never – till hell itself freezes over – accept one penny from the English, 'twould appear that we have reached an impasse. That being the case, I will take my leave, Lady Guinevere, and I wish you every success with your ventures.'

With a bow, he was gone.

CHAPTER 5

By late afternoon Quinn had not called by and Guinevere was greatly missing his visit. But of course, she would never see him again, having finished on such an ugly note.

Cerberus whined at the door needing to go out. Quinn had seen to all practicalities – feeding the dog, taking him for walks, arranging for her own almost edible meals to be brought to her room.

The argument they'd had that morning played through her mind for the hundredth time, yet still she winced at the contempt in his eyes when she had said she would of course marry Mr Ramsay – and she would. What she didn't tell him was how much the thought of it made her shudder. How much more would he despise her for marrying if he knew the truth of how she really felt?

There was nothing wrong with Mr Ramsay. He was some fifteen years senior to her, with a pleasant face, though a little pinched about the nostrils perhaps, a little narrow about the eyes but these were not defects in themselves. He was, as her father had often mentioned, a most astute man who, though he had made a fortune in trade, had the address and style of a gentleman. His mind was particularly well-informed and her father, who had so many interests of his own, had enjoyed many hours discussing science, philosophy and natural history with his neighbour. He truly believed his daughter could not find a better husband in any county in England.

Yet for some reason, Guinevere had taken against the man. Polite indifference had been replaced by something less congenial after they had visited his house for dinner. While there was nothing she could exactly put her finger on, every aspect of the evening served to increase her antipathy for her host. She found all the furnishings to be in exquisite taste yet somehow the house was cold and lacked personality. The dinner was perfectly cooked but the whole quail served on her plate had looked pathetically vulnerable. The library with its enormous, book-lined walls was chilly, while the drawing room a trifle overheated.

Then her father had jovially suggested that Mr Ramsay show her his private museum.

'Never saw anything more fascinating in my life, my dear. You must see it.'

Guinevere had been led into a room that smelt strongly of formaldehyde. Strange fetuses floated in glass jars; a malformed kitten, two puppies seemingly joined together, a baby. She stopped in front of this last, appalled.

'Incredible, is it not?' said her father. 'A sight not many have ever seen, my dear. It's a three month fetus and see, already perfectly formed.'

The baby lay curled in its jar, perfectly formed and perfectly alone. Guinevere thought she had never seen a more desolate sight.

'What happened to the mother?' she whispered.

'Died of consumption. A friend of mine was the doctor who wrote her death certificate. A bit of luck,' said Mr Ramsay, 'for when he saw her condition, he knew how interested I would be to add the fetus to my collection.'

Unable to find anything to say, Guinevere moved on to the glass doors of a cabinet and peeped in, only to give a little scream and leap back. Staring out from behind the doors were two shrunken heads.

'Are they real?' she asked.

Mr Ramsay smiled. 'Indeed they are and give all my visitors a fright. They are the heads of natives from New Zealand. Notice their very fine tattoos. They are a ferocious tribe, the Maori, and when they killed their enemy in battle they used to eat their hapless victims and preserve the heads if there was anything special about them. I believe it was a way of taunting the survivors. I was extremely fortunate to be able to obtain these two specimens. The custom has virtually stopped now so they are very rare indeed. Quite exceptional, aren't they?'

Bile rose in her throat and she could not speak

but her father rattled on. 'Now, this is what I really wanted to show you, Guinevere. It's also from New Zealand and is the thigh bone of a moa – a type of bird. Have you ever seen the like of it before? It would have stood taller than I! People believed it to be extinct but just recently there have been several sightings. Can you imagine what a coup it would be to find proof there were still specimens to be found alive?'

'A photograph of one would be worth a fortune,' mused Mr Ramsay, unwittingly sparking off this whole disastrous venture.

Unable to bear the memories any longer, Guinevere decided to go out; a walk would do her good. She'd been cooped up since she'd returned to Hokitika and needed some air.

Winding a shawl around her shoulders, she called to Cerberus who was delighted to be going out and together they slipped down the stairs. In the hotel bar they could hear the raucous laughter of men already inebriated and somehow this only served to enhance her loneliness.

Though the end of the day was drawing in, there were still several hours of sunlight left. The road was soft and muddy underfoot from the rain earlier that day, but the air was warm and felt clean on her cheeks after her confinement. There were many people in the streets, popping in and out of the ever-growing number of shops and many of them nodded in greeting to her. There were few women in the town, fewer single ones and none with her background, so most knew her by sight at least and her status in the town remained high. This deference was something she took for granted though it irked at times.

Cerberus tore off down the road, nose to the ground, pursuing any number of enticing smells judging by his erratic progress. With no real destination in mind, she walked the length of both main roads of the town, then idly made her way down to the docks to watch the unloading and loading of ships.

Leaning against the rough boards of one of the sheds, in the shadows where she wouldn't be seen, Guinevere contemplated the boats while Cerberus, puzzled but faithful, settled at her feet. Some of these ships would be going back to England. For a second she entertained wild thoughts of stowing aboard. That abominable Irishman was right. She did not belong here in Hokitika, did not belong in New Zealand.

Sorting the pictures had unsettled her. Memories of the lively dinner parties her father had held swirled in her head – the quick thrust and clash of debate, the sparkle of wit. The discussions that would last late into the night, the candles guttering one by one in the candelabras, while they'd talked about things she cared about; art, the position of women, the plight of the poor, the hypocrisy of the age. Here conversations seemed to centre only on gold, on survival. Such a limited people, intent only on the here and now, with no real thought for the finer things of life.

The familiarity and security of her own world with its rich ideals still existed, but at the far end of the earth from her. If she returned, perhaps she could find help from her father's protégés. They were all fond of her, she knew that. Would they be able to raise sufficient money between them to help save the home that had provided such lavish hospitality over the years? She doubted it. They never seemed to have a feather to fly with, most of them.

What if she just let Mr Ramsay have Maidenhurst Manor? But the memory of her father's face rose in front of her. On his last evening alive, her father's unrelenting optimism had slipped momentarily. She had asked, 'What will we do if we don't find the moa?' and he had looked at her and said with uncharacteristic solemnity, 'Then you must marry Mr Ramsay, you do see that, don't you? He will be a kind husband and you will learn to love him. We simply cannot let Maidenhurst fall out of the family – I could never live with the shame.'

And she had said, 'Yes, I do see that.'

Since her father's death, she had revisited this conversation often. She too could not bear the thought of Maidenhurst passing into Mr Ramsay's meticulously white hands. The casual warmth and openness of the manor would wither, even with her there. He did not love her any more than she loved him, of this she was sure, but as a titled wife she would fit nicely into his collection. And unlike her father, he would not encourage her independence for he would require a socially suitable wife. Like the shrunken heads, she would have to watch life pass by beyond the glass walls of her marriage.

Not if she could help it! Resolutely Guinevere pushed herself off the wall. She would not fail her father and would marry Mr Ramsay if she must, but only as the very last resort. If there was a moa out there, she would find it.

The thought of her stash of money hidden beneath her chemicals comforted her. It gave her the chance to fulfil her father's destiny. Perhaps she should have explained it better to Mr O'Donnell. But once she'd seen his scorn, her temper had flared for she would not be judged in that odious manner. Besides what did it matter anyway what the Irishman thought? Their paths had fallen together only by accident and now they were to part again; each had their own quest. She would not spare him another thought.

Having confirmed her decision, Guinevere felt stronger and although she knew she should return to her hotel, the thought of that barren little room deterred her. There could be no harm in walking a little further. She drifted down onto the beach, away from the wharf, to watch the surf chase up the shore then recede again, in soft movements. Soothed and somewhat hypnotised by this rhythm, Guinevere began walking further away from the town.

★　　★　　★

Quinn was propped in a bar, half-cut. Since he'd walked out on Guinevere he'd been steadily drinking. This was what he'd come to Hokitika for, after all. Supplies, some serious drinking, perhaps the services of some girl and then back to find some more gold. That's what diggers did, that's what he did, though he was more canny than most. He usually divided what little gold he may have found into half. Half to save, half to squander.

Though he'd already sunk quantities of raw spirit, Quinn was still clear-headed enough to know that it was time to stop now. The pockets of his trousers were empty and only the pocket inside his jacket held any money. All the money he had in the world, in fact. On route to this mean tavern he'd gone to the bank and withdrawn everything – which admittedly, was not much at all.

Even after hours of dedicated drinking, he was still torn as to what to do. If he gave her the money, she could sail out of his life forever – go back to her precious home, marry her inestimable husband. His lip curled at the thought. If he didn't give her the money, she would hare off on this mad scheme of hers and no doubt be dead in a week. That was not his problem. He could of course make peace with her. Could even offer to go moa hunting if that was what it took, until she saw reason. Then at least he'd know she'd survive. But he didn't have the time to be wasting on a pig-headed Englishwoman hell-bent on marrying another man. He was a man who travelled alone, who shunned attachments of any sort. He'd already done far more than enough for that pesky woman. And yet . . .

'Are you the cove what looked after the sick lady?' A voice at his elbow made him look down. A grubby boy of about ten was looking hopefully up at him. His face was thin, his ears stuck out and his hair was on end but the eager brightness of his expression overcame all these defects.

'I am,' Quinn said warily.

'Are you a doctor?'

'Of sorts.' Quinn was still cautious but the boy sighed with relief.

'Oh, good. My father's gotta broken leg.'

'There's a proper doctor in the town. Go find him, boy.'

'I already did and he sent me to find you. You see me dad's broke it up the mountain. It's just the two of us. He sent me to get help but the doctor says he's more than enough work here without traipsing up the range for just one man.'

'How far away is he?'

'A couple of days walk.'

'A couple of days? Dammit boy, has he been alone all this time?'

The boy shrugged but Quinn could see the anxiety in his face. 'There was nuffing else to be done. I left him beside a river so he's all the water he needs and I gave him all the supplies too.'

'Have you eaten now?'

The boy nodded impatiently. 'Yup, the doctor's

wife made me a good dinner. You will come, won't you?'

'Where is he?'

'Up the Bennelong track. But off to one side, higher up.'

Well, that was a mercy at any rate; it was the same one that he and Guinevere had come down. He could pick up his pack and gun on the way. The name Bennelong was a joke, a corruption of 'Been a Long Track' because it was steep and difficult. How the hell would they get a man with a broken leg down it? They'd cross that bridge when they came to it, Quinn supposed with an inward sigh. For now, it was essential to get back to the poor devil lying alone and helpless, miles from anywhere. If they left immediately, they'd still have a few hours of light.

'Are you rested enough to set off right now?' he asked.

The boy nodded vigorously. 'Aye, the doctor's wife also gave me a bed for a few hours.'

Quinn smiled. Clearly the doctor's wife had been no more able to resist this ragged urchin than he had. Reaching inside his jacket pocket, he pulled out his money and peeled off a few notes for the boy whose eyes widened.

'You go buy us as many provisions as you can with this. I've some business I must attend to. What's your name?'

'Ben.'

'Ben, I'll see you back here in an hour.'

★　★　★

107

Watching the boy disappear, Quinn wondered what the hell he was doing getting involved in yet another drama. For a man who just wanted to be left alone, he hadn't done well over the past week. His fault, he could see that now. He should have just dropped the lady off when they first got to Hokitika and left her to a proper doctor. Served him right for playing the doctor, as he wouldn't be mining for a few more days now.

Still, at least he was suddenly clear as to what to do. He had to get rid of his other involvement. If he got her out of New Zealand she'd be out of his life for good and he could stop feeling responsible for that arrogant, infuriating and downright impossible woman. It was worth the money to buy back his peace of mind.

He went to the hotel and knocked on Guinevere's door but there was no reply. Frowning, Quinn wondered where the hell she could be. He slipped down to the bar, which was humming with business. A group of diggers with the grime of the fields still clinging to them and a thirst that hadn't been slacked for some weeks were employed in the serious matter of getting drunk as quickly as possible. Their rowdy conversation boomed with bonhomie. Two other miners sprawled against the bar with slumped shoulders and empty eyes. The goldfields did not give out its favours evenhandedly.

Bet was serving four wild-looking individuals sitting around a card table. Quinn did not know them but instinctively mistrusted them. The gold-fields attracted all sorts of adventurers and wastrels but this group had the hot, shifty eyes of scavengers. Men who mined alone were vulnerable to attacks from packs like these and this was one of the main reasons why Quinn carried a gun.

They were laughing and jeering with every turn of the cards but they had looked up as he came in and he felt they were watching him for all that they continued to play. It was as though they could smell the money in his pocket.

Quinn waited till Bet returned to the bar and being careful to keep his voice low, asked where Lady Guinevere might be. Bet unfortunately had no such caution and her piercing voice carried over the noise of the bar.

'Lady Guinevere? Nah, I 'aven't seen 'er ledyship about. Is she better then 'cos you know, I ain't been paid for this week's rent but just let 'er stay from the goodness of me 'eart.'

Quinn suspected that it was more from the hopes of another few weeks' regular payments rather than goodness but didn't have time to dispute the matter now. Instead he took a note from his inside pocket, being careful not to give any indication there was more money there and handed it to her.

'That should cover the past week and the next,' he said. 'But mind you don't go charging her twice.'

'Wotcha tek me for?' Bet demanded, but grinned at the same time. Everyone was fair game in this town and if you were stupid enough to be plucked, plucked you would be.

Quinn smiled back but his eyes held hers until she nodded with a shrug.

'You off then?' she asked, and Quinn wished her voice did not carry so.

'Yes, but not for long,' he lied. Who knew how long it would take to locate and bring the man down.

As he left the bar, the nape of his neck prickled. He didn't trust those men at all but though he checked several times, they didn't follow him. He shook off his unease and wondered where the hell a young woman alone would go in such a poor excuse for a town.

Mary maybe? It did not seem likely but time was running out so he made his way to Mary's cottage, which he'd visited that first morning. It was small, white and trim and as he knocked – a trifle harder than he'd meant – he saw the slanted rays of the sun cast his shadow abnormally long over the meticulous vegetable garden. Dear God, let her be here.

Mary answered the door. Over her shoulder he could see the family at the dinner table all turned around to stare, another reminder the hour was getting late.

'Sorry to bother you,' he said. 'You wouldn't be knowing where Lady Guinevere might be, would you?'

'No, sir. I don't know where she is but she must be feeling better then.'

'Why?'

'She always used to go walking when she first arrived. Said she hated being cooped up.'

'Walking alone? That's inviting trouble.'

'Told her so myself, but you know how she is.'

Quinn's lips compressed into a thin line. 'I do.' He was aware of the moments slipping away. 'Mary, can you give her ladyship a letter.'

'Yes, sir.' The perfect servant. If she felt any surprise, she did not show it.

'Ah, Mary . . . would you be having any paper and a pen with you?'

It was a strange request for he was sure they wouldn't but her resourceful father, having listened to this exchange, left the table and came to the door.

'There's the grocer's bill,' he said, 'and Jem's pencil from his school.'

So Quinn was able to scrawl a brief message to Guinevere. There was not room to say much and no time to choose the words carefully, so he scrawled only what needed to be said, before taking the last of the money from his jacket and folding it into the note.

Mary's eyes stared but still she did not comment.

'Make sure she gets this,' he said.

'I will first thing tomorrow. Are you leaving then, sir?'

'I am. I'm going to help a man with a broken leg up the Bennelong track.'

'D'you want me to give her any other message?'

Quinn hesitated. 'Tell her it's not charity, it's business and good sense.'

'Business and good sense, not charity.' Mary smiled. 'I'm not sure she'll agree, mind.'

He gave a short laugh. 'She's not agreed with me from the moment we met so I'm not expecting miracles. Just make sure she catches a ship back home.'

CHAPTER 6

Guinevere watched the sun slide into the sea on the far horizon, colouring the sky vivid orange in its last minutes. Then as the gold faded, it felt somehow like a death.

With a shiver she gathered her shawl tight around her shoulders and realised that she had strayed further than she'd meant to. Even Cerberus seemed to have finally run himself out and was content now to walk at her heels. His company was a comfort as she felt suddenly lonely and not gloriously alone.

They made their way along the beach and Guinevere was glad to see the almost full moon rising over the ragged spine of mountains that towered above the town. Its white face was welcome though the twilight sat lightly still and the sea was as luminous as stained glass. The beach seemed endless and she marvelled that it could be so beautiful and so bleak at the same time, strewn as it was with large pieces of driftwood that had been tumbled down from the mountains by the myriad of rivers. How much her father would have loved to see this world and how much more she could have enjoyed it all with him beside her.

When she finally reached the docks, they were less hectic but still a number of men were busy. This was a hard-working town for all its rough, unshod ways. The twilight thickened as she hurried back down the street to her hotel, aware that it was not wise to be out alone now. Lanterns outside the numerous hotels splashed pools of invitation onto the crude roads and the hum and roar of thousands of men engaged in the pursuit of pleasure enhanced her isolation even further.

If only she were a man she could enter one of these mean buildings and lean, elbows on the counter, sharing the jokes and conversation of those around her. She did not want to return to her room, there was nothing for her there but her pictures. She was glad now to be leaving the next morning and would finish her packing, settle accounts and banish any thought of the Irishman the minute it arose.

Filled with resolve, she hurried through the doors of the Royal, past the noise of the bar and up the stairs, Cerberus panting at her side.

'Come on, nearly home,' she encouraged him.

At the top of the stairs however, she paused, sniffed. There was a terrible and all too familiar smell coming from her room where the door stood ajar. She moved towards it cautiously. Perhaps the wind? But when she pushed the door wide open she knew no wind could have caused this devastation. By the cold light of the moon that shone through the opened window Guinevere could see the upturned trunks that had been ransacked with discarded garments strewn across the floor. Her paintings had been ripped from their frames and tossed aside though amazingly, her camera and tripod were still in the corner. Her silk bed cover had gone, however, as had the pillows she'd brought from England. She must have made some sound of distress because a miner passing on the landing popped his head around the door.

'Good lord!' he exclaimed and disappeared immediately.

Guinevere barely noticed. Stooping, she picked up one of her father's photographs which had a muddied footprint splattered across it. The foot-print was probably not intentional but somehow it felt as personal as a slap in the face. Bile rose in her mouth and she pressed shaking fingers to her lips.

'Oh my gawd.' Bet entered the room. 'I was jest told as how your room's been done over and it's one fine job they did of it too!' She stood arms akimbo, surveying the scene. 'Wot's that stink?'

Guinevere blinked, trying to gather her thoughts. 'My chemicals,' she said, spinning around to look at the corner where they'd been stored in their custom-made box. Now it was lying on its side amongst empty bottles with the lid smashed open and the false bottom splintered. Despair rooted her to the spot and she was unable to move, unable to think.

Bet, in a fastidious manner strangely at odds with her slatternly appearance, picked her way through the chaos to the corner and lifted one of Guinevere's stays between her finger and thumb and sniffed in disgust.

'They've emptied them all over your duds. That's just mean, they didn't need to go and do that.'

'Who would do such a thing?' Guinevere whispered, finally finding her voice.

Bet shook her head. 'I'll lay odds that it was that pack of mongrels downstairs. Soon as they heard that Irishman of yours say he was leaving, I bet they thought this was their chance. Wot've they stolen? Worked it out yet?'

Guinevere was finding this all too hard to comprehend. 'Mr O'Donnell's gone?'

She hadn't meant to sound so desolate but Bet turned to her and said not unkindly, ''E came by but couldn't find ya. Paid your board for two weeks, mind.'

'Where has he gone? Did he say?'

'Nah. But there was a bunch of layabouts playing cards when 'e was telling me. Best get the constable in, eh. I'll go have one fetched while you work out wot's missing, right?'

Guinevere nodded but as soon as Bet had left the room she sank to her knees. The sense of violation overwhelmed her as she looked at the tattered pictures, the soaking clothes. To steal was one thing, this wanton vandalism was something else. And Mr O'Donnell had abandoned her. She could barely take it in.

Resolutely she drew in a deep, shuddering breath; she would not fall apart. She would not be defeated by this. Though her whole body was by now shaking, she forced her mind to start working. Bet was right; she must see what had been stolen.

She did not even begin to search for the money – the emptied chemical chest spoke for itself. Mr O'Donnell had been right, curse him! She should never have left her room. But what if they'd come when she was here? The thought made her shiver but her more practical side argued that they'd only come because the room was empty.

Feeling numb, she rose and went to her over-turned trunk. It did not seem worth looking for her jewellery box but still she sifted through the jumble, one small part of her thinking that maybe, just maybe they might have missed it. Of course they hadn't. Everything was gone; her necklaces from her mother, the earrings her father had given her for her very first ball, her grandmother's locket that she had used to entice the weka, the brooch that had been in the family for over two hundred years.

It was then that she noticed that it was only her clothes lying strewn about the floor in wet pools of chemicals. Her father's trunk was empty but his clothes were gone. Of course, her clothes were of little use to them but his . . . It was the thought of his shirts, his trousers clothing those thieving dogs that finally unlocked her tears which ran down her cheeks as her actions now became frantic. She tossed aside her own petticoats and shifts trying to find something – anything – that still held his essence. There was nothing.

Sitting back on her heels, it took every ounce of breeding not to howl to the uncaring heavens like an abandoned hound. Instead she buried her face in her hands, pressing the heels of her hands as hard as she could into her eyes, as though to dam her tears and crush out the images in front of her as she rocked backwards and forwards in soundless grief and panic.

A cough behind her caused her to drop her hands and look behind her. A very tall, young man in the blue jacket and trousers of a constable stood awkwardly in the doorway. The constabulary was, on the whole, an intrepid crew with their work cut out for them as they brought law into this wild land. Guinevere had seen them step between fighting men in the street and with some swift blows of their own, quell both parties. Perhaps they could find her belongings.

Wiping her tears away in two brusque movements, Guinevere rose from her knees and forced her voice to remain calm.

'I am so glad to see you, officer. Will you appre-
hend them and recover my belongings?'

'We'll do our best, ma'am,' he said heroically
but, overwhelmed to be in the presence of a 'real
lady', he forgot entirely how to proceed until Bet,
losing patience, prodded him in the back and said,
'Well, don't just stand there like a ninny – ask 'er
ledyship wot's missing.'

He cleared his throat. 'Have you detected any
missing items?' he enquired in a rather more offi-
cial manner.

'My father's clothes, my money and my jewellery
box. Pillows and a bedcover too but they are not
important.'

'And where were you at the time of the crime?'
The routine questions were clearly giving the
constable more confidence.

'I was out walking.'

'And how long would you say you were gone?'

Guinevere shrugged. 'A few hours,' she hazarded.

'A few hours?' Her answer clearly shocked the
young man. 'Where would you go in Hokitika for
a few hours?'

'I was down on the beach.'

'Were you with anyone else?'

'No, I was alone – apart from my dog, of course.'

The young officer shook his head and exchanged
a look with Bet who rolled her eyes heavenwards.

'Surely you must know that it is not safe here
to be out by yourself,' he said.

Guinevere blushed. 'It had been mentioned,' she

muttered, 'but I didn't think anything would really happen.'

The silence which greeted this remark was eloquent. The constable then turned to Bet. 'You said there was a group of men in the bar?'

'Yeah. They've been about town these past few days. They'd have heard about her ledyship.'

Guinevere flushed again, this time in anger. It was insufferable to be the talking point of the town. What had they been saying? Suddenly Mr O'Donnell's attempts to preserve her reputation did not seem quaint and she remembered his words, 'Stay the lady. That, and your money are your only defence.' Perhaps his constant presence had been another defence. Why and where had he gone? There was another tearing emptiness inside her that had nothing to do with her missing possessions.

'You know yourself it's no secret that 'er ledyship came back in a terrible way. The whole town's talking about it and the way that Irishman's been looking after 'er – though 'e's been a proper gent, I'll say that for 'im.'

'But you said he left this afternoon. Could he have been a party to this?'

'No!' Guinevere cried but the constable ignored her, looking to his more reliable witness.

Bet pursed her lips and shook her head. 'Nah, 'e's straight up, that one. Sides, 'e paid for 'er board for two weeks. Wouldn't do that now if 'e was planning to rob 'er blind, now would 'e?'

'He might, if he wanted to throw us off his scent. Where was he going, did he say?'

Bet shook her head again. 'It won't be 'ard to find out, though. Somebody'll know something – they always do.'

'I'll ask around. Now, let's see just how this crime was done.'

It was simple enough to work out. After overhearing the conversation with Quinn, the gang would have waited, hoping against reason that Guinevere would not return before the shelter of darkness. They must have been amazed by their own good fortune when the first candles were lit and still no sign of her. The bar was overflowing by then and their departure would not have been noted. A couple had probably slipped up the stairs while the other two slid round the corner to the back of the hotel and waited until things started falling out of the window. The bedcover was in all likelihood used to carry away all their plunder, simple as that. Mercifully, they must have realised the camera equipment wouldn't survive the fall but in less than ten minutes, Guinevere's world had been entirely annihilated.

Just as they were concluding the final details there was a soft knock on the door and Mary popped her head into the room. 'I've just heard, milady. It's all over town.' Then she noticed the state of the room and gasped. 'It's ever such a mess!'

Guinevere thought she'd never heard a more acute understatement.

'I came immediately, I thought you'd need this,' and from the pocket of her apron Mary produced the letter and money. 'Mr O'Donnell left them.'

She handed them to Guinevere who received them wordlessly while the constable and Bet exchanged looks. It only took a few seconds to read the curt note.

'This money is to purchase ten drawings – but only your own work. Leave them with Bet and I'll pick them up later. There is enough money to purchase a berth back to England. Good luck.'

The constable was watching her face. 'May I ask what it says?'

'You can read it if you like,' said Guinevere in an indifferent tone, and passed him the note.

When the young man had finished scanning it, he scratched the back of his neck.

'This doesn't prove his innocence,' he pointed out. 'He might just be trying to get rid of you. Meet his partners on the mountains somewhere.'

Mary was indignant. 'Mr O'Donnell would do no such thing. Didn't you know he's gone to help a man with a broken leg up the Bennelong?'

'Has he? Well that puts things in a different light if we can verify the story.'

'That's easy. Saw the doctor myself on the way here. He stopped me and said to tell Lady Guinevere that now that Mr O'Donnell has gone to help the digger, he'll be happy to be her physician if she needs it. He knew all about the man – sent the boy himself to ask Mr O'Donnell for his help.'

'That seems to settle the issue of Mr O'Donnell's innocence then, and so now that just leaves the final question of what you are going to do, milady. I must warn you now, the chances of recovering your belongings are very slim. We'll do our best but . . .' and he shrugged.

Guinevere nodded, the tiny spark of hope extinguishing as she said flatly, 'I know. It's a huge country. They could go anywhere. Catch a boat out anywhere.'

'Yes, I'm afraid so. Best thing is to take Mr O'Donnell's money and return to England, just as he says.'

'You've a room paid for the next week, meals included so's you'll be sorted till you leave,' Bet added. 'Best thing's for you to get away. You're nothing but a lamb among wolves, 'ere – a right soft target.'

'That's true enough, miss,' said Mary. 'And it's what Dr O'Donnell thought best. He said to tell you it ain't charity, just business and good sense.'

But despite the shock, the horror of violation and the pain of abandonment, Guinevere was already drawing herself up. In just such a manner had her ancestor Lady Gwynneth faced the Roundheads when they arrived beating on the door of Maidenhurst Manor one night when her husband was away. In just such a manner had Lord Alastair Stanhope walked onto the battlefields in Belgium.

Head held high, Guinevere said now, 'I think not. Tomorrow, I will find a job.'

CHAPTER 7

'It's not far now,' Ben said, his breath coming out in little spurts that matched his dogged steps.

'Good. I'm looking forward to my dinner.'

'Me too!'

Quinn smiled at the heartfelt tone. Ben was quite a lad; having insisted on carrying part of the provisions, he'd now been walking stolidly all day after a rough night in the bush, setting the pace and dictating the length of breaks for meals. Quinn had thought it best to give him the control, having no idea himself of how far or fast a boy could travel and had been impressed by Ben's determination. Part of him even envied the man lying up the track somewhere, to have such a loyal son. Never having given any thought to the idea of children previously, Quinn could now see what made people decide to become parents. They'd not talked much but a feeling of companionship had developed between them.

Ben paused and cupping his hand to his mouth, let fly a strangely piercing whistle then stood with head cocked, listening intently. The late afternoon sun shone red through his extraordinary jug ears and it was hard to see where freckles on his face left off and the dust began but his eyes still held their brightness.

His face lit up. 'Hear that?'

'What?'

'Me dad.'

Quinn shook his head. 'I didn't hear anything.'

'Listen.'

Again Ben whistled and this time very faintly, Quinn heard the response. He and Ben grinned at each other.

'Come on! If we get cracking, the billy'll be going in half an hour,' said Quinn. 'Lead the way.'

The relief of finding the father was short-lived. Just as Ben had said, he was lying next to a stream surrounded by empty tins of sardines. A bottle lay next to him with a string about it and Quinn deduced he must have used this to draw the water from the creek. His pack was within reach but the smell was strong for the man had not been able pull himself far to relieve himself. Sandflies were thick and the man's face and hands were swollen with their bites.

'About bloody time!' was his greeting to his faithful son. 'What took you so bloody long? I've been expecting you back these past few hours. And where's the doctor?'

Ben's bright expression faded and his shoulders slumped.

'Sorry, Dad,' he muttered.

Quinn couldn't bear to see the stricken look in his eyes. 'Young Ben here made damned fine time, you should be proud of your lad. The name's Quinn O'Donnell. I've come to see if I can help.'

The man looked at him. 'You don't look like a doctor.'

'The doctor couldn't come but I've set enough bones in my time, Mr . . .?'

'Hanohan. Burt Hanohan. What bones have you set, then? You're not some animal doctor are you? Oh, hell! Just what I need.'

Quinn slid his pack off and shrugged his shoulders to ease the aching muscles. Despite Ben's help, he'd still been carrying far more provisions than he usually would and was a long way from where he preferred to prospect. Profuse gratitude would have been embarrassing but this sour welcome had his temper rising.

'I know you're in pain, man,' he said, carefully keeping his voice calm. 'It can't have been easy waiting alone these past few days either, but we are here now and as soon as I've brewed the billy, we'll see to your leg. As you can see, I've got some splints lashed to my pack. In an hour or so we'll have you more comfortable.'

'Tea. Aye, well I could do with a cuppa. Sick of bloody water and sardines. You bring anything else a man can eat?'

The tea, liberally laced with whisky, did ease relations but also gave Quinn time to ascertain that the severe lines drawn about the man's forehead and around his mouth owed as much to habitual ill-temper as to current pain.

Ben had changed from an alert, confident child to slinking about the periphery of his father – always keeping some distance between them. The image of the loving father that had buoyed Quinn's journey had dissolved in the first minutes and now he sat furious for having put himself in the situation of being responsible for this man's welfare in the immediate future. He could scarcely set the man's leg and then take off, abandoning Ben to sort things out. Well, there was nothing else for it for the moment. First the bone-setting. That would not be pretty, Quinn reflected.

An examination proved more heartening than he'd expected, however. Though there was appalling swelling to the skinny white leg, the break was below the knee and seemed reasonably clean as far as Quinn could tell; the bones were only slightly out of alignment. He had certainly dealt with far worse and Quinn experienced the kindling of a strange excitement. Much as he felt sorry for the man's predicament, there was the almost forgotten satisfaction of knowing he could help, could make a difference. A feeling not often experienced, he thought wryly, when standing knee-deep in freezing rivers day after day, swilling water in the vain hope of seeing flecks of gold.

He and Ben cleaned Burt up and the yelps and groans this act provoked did not, Quinn felt, bode well for the actual bone-setting itself. He stretched both legs out gently and Burt gave a screech of pain. Quinn squatted back on his heels by Burt's feet and looked up the man's body to his contorted face.

'Now look,' he said. 'I'm here to help you but you have a choice. I can quietly pack my bag right now and be on my way without any more mauling or I can stay and set your leg, in which case you'll just take the pain like a man. Which do you want? I cannot be concentrating with you screaming blue murder, d'you understand? Here's a stick to bite on. That will help.'

Burt nodded, muttering. 'Go on then. Get it over with.'

Quinn knew that speed was the best way to get the job done – it lessened the shock to the system – but no sooner had he touched the leg than Burt began writhing and whipped the stick out of his mouth to scream, 'Stop! You're killing me! You're killing me!'

Quinn was tired. He'd walked long hours to help and had known soldiers who'd shown greater fortitude with far greater wounds than this sullen, pathetic man. His temper snapped.

'Shut up you stupid man or I'll chop your bollocks off, and stuff them in your mouth to silence you!' he shouted, but at that same moment someone strong and furious launched himself onto Quinn's back, knocking him away from Burt.

'What the hell—?' Quinn cried, but a fist to his jaw snapped the last of the words back down his throat and he had a confused image of blazing blue eyes, and strong fingers trying to get purchase around his neck.

Quinn managed to get a hand free and swung a punch at his assailant's nose. It lacked force as Quinn was flat on his back, but it was enough to knock the man sideways so that Quinn could roll on him, and punch again, this time catching a cheek bone which made his own knuckles crunch painfully.

Ben was shouting and Burt swearing but their cries just blurred into the background of the fight.

Both men's attention was entirely focused on the other as they fought for dominance, equally matched it seemed in weight and skills. They struggled and wrestled then became locked in a deadly embrace, each struggling to maintain the upper position as they rolled down the riverbank, hitting the stream with a splash.

The icy water came as a shock and Quinn cracked his skull painfully on a rock in the shallows. Dazed and shivering, he shook his head and was trying to collect his wits when his neck was seized and his assailant shoved him under the water once more.

Quinn realised the stream was not deep – he could feel the floor of it grazing his head – but a man could still be drowned in a few inches of water. His fingers scrabbled at the hands holding him under but just as he could feel himself blacking out, he was pulled up into the air again. Furious blue eyes glowered into his.

'Scum of the earth,' the assailant tried to roar but his words came out in heavy pants instead. 'I know your sort – preying on helpless men!'

'Doctor!' croaked Quinn.

'What?'

Ben's cries now seemed to penetrate their senses.

'Don't kill him. He's helping my dad!'

The attacker hesitated.

'He's a doctor,' Ben shouted. 'He's good.'

The assailant looked doubtfully down at Quinn who was still gulping lungfuls of air and could only nod.

'But you threatened to cut his balls off?'

'Medical option,' Quinn gasped.

The attacker eyed him then suddenly pulled Quinn closer to him, rubbing the Irishman's thick hair in disbelief.

Next second Quinn was seized in a second crushing embrace, this one accompanied by a whoop of joy as his assailant shouted jubilantly, 'The colour! By God, it's the colour! My friends we've struck gold!'

CHAPTER 8

Guinevere was up till the small hours of the morning, tidying, cleaning and washing out her clothes. Mary had wanted to stay and help but Guinevere had sent her away.

'I don't have the money to pay you anymore, Mary,' she explained.

'I don't need no payment – I'll stay to help you because,' here Mary shrugged, not sure how to say it, 'because you're you.'

This declaration touched Guinevere. 'That is one of the nicest things anyone has ever said to me,' she responded with a wry smile. 'But this I must do on my own. I need to. Can you understand that?'

Mary nodded but Guinevere could see the pity in her eyes.

'Oh, I wish Mr O'Donnell hadn't chosen this moment to light out of town!' the girl said. 'Still, he was a right gentleman, trying to help you like that. I hope you weren't being serious about getting a job. It just wouldn't be proper. He's right you know – you should go buy the ticket tomorrow as he bid.'

'We'll see,' was all Guinevere replied.

After Mary had gone, Guinevere filled a large bowl with water from the kitchen below, and placed all the foul-smelling clothing into it to soak. The silver nitrate had stained some items black but she would not throw anything away unless she was sure it could not be used in some way. She must learn to think like this now.

Next she turned her attention to the emptied bottles, restoring them to their rightful slots in the box with shaking fingers. There would be no chasing moa now, even if she did decide to use the money Quinn had left her. It would be impossible to replace some of the chemicals here. Christchurch, she supposed, might be a place where she could buy more but that town was a very long way away.

Sorting the pictures was her next concern. Could it have only been that morning she had sorted them into piles, wondering which she might be able to sell, which she could not bear to part with? Most were creased as if clumsy fists had snatched them up to rifle through them. Some had landed in the chemicals when they'd been flung away and were ruined. Several were ripped and the one series which depicted mythological scenes were torn right through. The ones where the shape of breast and thigh were discernible had gone. The thought of grubby fingers, grubby minds – Guinevere shivered. Though she knew there would be no more intruders, she still went over to the window to double-check it was shut then braced a chair under the handle of her door.

Cerberus, who had been sitting in a corner throughout the evening, whined and this brought a watery smile to Guinevere's face. She patted his head.

'I know you wouldn't let anyone in,' she assured him, 'and I don't expect them back, anyway. But I feel better making sure.'

The final part of the cleanup didn't take long. Her dresses had merely been tossed to one side. There were some petticoats, shifts and drawers that were crumpled but undamaged. Guinevere felt agonised at the thought of those creatures rummaging through her drawers, her stockings. She placed her dresses and shawls carefully back into her trunk and managed a slight smile at how her nurse would have rejoiced to see her untidy charge finally tamed. But that thought brought other memories hard on its heels and the smile faded immediately.

After closing the trunk, Guinevere slowly began taking off her dress and dropping her petticoats, checking the barricaded door and closed windows every few seconds as she did so. Though she knew it was absurd, she could not shake the notion that there were unshaven faces leering in at her. She pulled her nightdress over her head, then tore the lacings of her corset undone and leapt into bed, pulling the blankets over her head. She had forgotten her pillows had been stolen. Even this, her last refuge, had been violated. It also obscenely and personally linked her to these scavengers. Somewhere tonight filthy heads would be resting triumphantly on her linen.

'Don't think of it,' she told herself fiercely. 'It's done now. Don't think.'

She had a sudden flash of memory of being held in a tight embrace, a soft Irish voice saying, 'Hush, don't think. 'Twill all pass presently.' He was right, no point in dwelling on the night's events. Instead she must think to the future, to happy times – to Maidenhurst.

She forced herself to draw in a long breath to relax and fixed the image of her home in her mind. February. The daffodils and crocuses would be stirring under their cold blanket of earth now, preparing themselves for a magnificent display of colours all around the lake in just another few weeks. In her mind's eye, Guinevere made her way up from the lake to the familiar wide French doors and walked in through the dining room and up the stairs to her large airy bedroom. It was all still there waiting for her: the huge casement windows overlooking the walled garden and to the fields beyond, the wallpaper depicting scenes from *Don Quixote*, the generous feather bed which folded about her on winter nights keeping her warm and safe. Determinedly she clung to these images until at last her tight grip on her sheets lessened and she slid into sleep.

★   ★   ★

135

When Guinevere awoke the room was soft with early morning light and she lay in bed, taking stock of the situation. She was not feeling at all refreshed. Her dreams had been disturbed and she had woken often but she did feel resigned and resolved. The waves of panic had subsided. There was nothing she could do but move forward.

She turned over and the rustle in her bed for a minute disconcerted her but then she remembered reaching out her hand in the middle of the night and pulling Quinn's money from the bedside table into bed with her. She was taking no more chances and besides, the notes were somehow comforting. She could, of course, go book her berth today. Quinn had given her the means and last night had certainly given her reasons but still Guinevere could not bear to entertain the notion. She would not return in defeat to a loveless marriage – not until she had completely run out of time and options. She remembered her grandiloquent words 'I will find a job' and the look of cynical amusement in Bet's face and the doubt in the young constable's. Neither believed she had it in her. Well, she would show them. Just how was the problem.

Guinevere rolled onto her side, pillowing her head on her arm and looked at Cerberus who was raising a bleary head.

'How does one find employment?' she asked him.

Cerberus thumped his tail but had no more answers than she did.

'I suppose I must start with Bet,' she continued and sighed.

It would not be easy to approach her now that fate had so suddenly reversed their positions of power, but Guinevere suspected this was just the first in a number of actions she would find hard. The only thought that buoyed her was that none could be quite as difficult as marrying Mr Ramsay.

When she was dressed, Guinevere made her way downstairs to the bar where Bet was scrubbing the counter with a hard brush and lots of suds. Her sleeves were rolled up, showing muscular arms and Guinevere stopped in the doorway, crossing her own arms and feeling their slender weakness. How would she cope? But as her nurse had always noted, the more ridiculous the idea, the more stubbornly her ladyship clung to it.

Straightening up, she drew a deep breath and stepped inside. Bet did not look up but continued her rhythmic scrubbing.

'So you're up, are ya? And with more sense I 'ope than you went to sleep with.'

Guinevere perched on one of the chairs, unconsciously adopting the stance drummed into her since childhood; hands cupped in her lap, spine straight.

Bet glanced up from beneath her brows and smiled grimly. 'You're a strange sight in this bar. So, are you off to pay for your berth now? Best get it sorted out quick.'

'I told you, I'm not going.'

Bet sucked her breath in through her teeth. 'I thought you'd 'ave been thinking more clearly this morning. Seems I was mistaken.'

'I am thinking clearly. If I told you that the situation I would return to in England would be even more intolerable than the one I find myself in here, no doubt you would not believe me.'

'No, you're right, I wouldn't.' Bet laid down her brush and looked at Guinevere. 'So what are you thinking you might do, milady?'

This was the first time she'd ever used the term and Guinevere smiled, despite her irritation, at this cynical dig.

'I was hoping you might be able to help me.' Abandoning her drawing room posture, Guinevere rested her forearms on the table and leaned forward. 'If you were looking for a job, Bet, what would you do?'

Bet snorted. 'There's only two jobs in this town.'

'And they are?'

'Cooking and dancing. The second pays better – even if you don't do the bits on the side.'

Guinevere shook her head at the first suggestion. 'Cooking's out of the question. I wouldn't know where to begin, but dancing . . .' Her voice trailed away and she looked thoughtful. 'I can dance and I used to go to a lot of balls.'

'You might find this a bit different,' Bet noted.

'Yes, but it's basically the same principle, isn't it?'

Bet picked up her brush again. 'You tell me, milady, when you've tried it a few nights. But if you want the best out of a poor bunch, go to Mike Willis at the Prince Albert. He'll see you straight.'

Guinevere walked up and down the road three times before she could summon the courage to enter the door of the Prince Albert. When she did finally step inside, she had to pause for a few moments to let her eyes adjust to the dark interior after the bright sunlight.

The Prince Albert had recently been done up, a sign of the growing prosperity of both proprietor and town. Its calico sides had been replaced with weatherboards and a corrugated roof topped its finery. The room was large with a shallow stage at one end and a bar counter at the other. Benches lined the walls.

A portly man with a cigar sticking out of his mouth sat at a small table underneath one of the few windows, books and papers strewn about his elbows.

Guinevere gave a polite cough and said, 'Mr Willis?'

'What is it?'

The man glanced irritably up from his accounts but when he saw who was standing in the doorway he hastily rose, took the cigar out of his mouth and went to greet his guest.

'Lady Guinevere! To what do I owe this pleasure? Please, won't you sit down?'

He pulled up a chair and dusted it down with a swipe of his hand. 'I wasn't expecting company.'

Guinevere took the proffered seat. 'I am sorry to interrupt you.'

'Not at all, not at all.' He took his chair opposite her.

She had clearly caught him off guard but though his eyes were shrewdly appraising, Guinevere thought she also detected a glint of curious sympathy – news of her misfortune would have spread throughout the town by now. She blushed but at the same time squared her shoulders.

'Bet said I should apply to you for a job.'

It was as well, she thought, that his teeth were clamped once more onto his cigar or his jaw would have dropped in amazement. As it was, his eyes bulged. 'A job?'

'Yes. As a – a dancing companion.'

'Ah.'

The silence that fell seemed interminable to Guinevere. Mr Willis gnawed on the cigar and scratched his ear while he thought.

'I can dance,' she added.

The look he threw her was ironic. 'Dancing skills are not necessarily required, milady.'

'Ah.' It was her turn to look thoughtful and wonder what on earth she was doing here and whether she was indeed as crazy as everyone clearly saw her to be.

'This is not a gentlemen's establishment,' he pointed out.

'No, I didn't think it would be.'

'The miners – they are only interested in . . .'

He paused then continued, '. . . in having a good time.'

'I know. I have heard them.'

He nodded. 'Got any idea what you are letting yourself in for?'

The smile she gave him was direct and rueful. 'Probably not. It is only dancing, I'm sure I hardly need add, that I am applying for.'

He seemed a little taken aback by the directness of her response, but there was an appreciative twinkle in his eye when he said, 'Aye, and you may trust me that I'll ensure that no one is left in any doubt about that.'

Guinevere inclined her head. 'Thank you. I would appreciate that. Bet said you would – er, see me straight.'

'That I will. Right. Well, I pay the girls six pounds a week. You dance from sundown till eleven. The girls usually stay after that and play cards with the diggers – that can go on till sunrise.' He looked sideways at Guinevere. 'I think it would be best if you stayed for dancing only. I'll leave the wage the same. Come early this evening and the girls'll show you the ropes.'

'I'll see you this evening, then,' said Guinevere, rising.

He rose too and bowed. 'It will be my honour to have you in my establishment.'

As he watched her depart, he wondered if his most illustrious employee would indeed make an appearance that evening or whether her courage would fail at the eleventh hour. However, seeing the set of her mouth as they concluded their business with a handshake, he thought it just might be that she'd have the nerve to see it through. If he could keep her even for a few nights she would certainly draw in the crowds and it was only with great self-control that he stopped himself from rubbing his hands in glee.

Guinevere spent the rest of the day washing out clothes and being torn between wild visions of running down to the docks to find a ship and pay over Quinn's money forthwith and wondering prosaically what on earth to wear as a dancing companion. She'd only brought one ball-gown to New Zealand and it was far too grand for a dance hall but the other dresses did not seem appropriate either.

In the late afternoon there was a knock on the door and Bet came in with a black dress over her arm.

'Been asking round the girls and Floss says you can use 'er dress seeing as she's about to have a kid.'

She shook it out and Guinevere saw that it was of shiny satin, cut low in the front and with very flounced skirts.

'That's most kind,' she faltered.

Bet gave a short bark of laughter. 'To be 'onest, I don't know whether it was kindness or curiosity that made 'er give it. None of them believes you're going to go through with it.'

'And what did you say?'

'I said that you'd be there, no doubt at all. Never seen such stubbornness in the face of reason in all my days!'

Guinevere accepted the compliment with a rueful smile. 'Am I being so very rash?'

'Yup. But I'll say this for you – you've got guts.' She paused. 'You ain't taken no advice before so's I don't really think you're going to start now but I'll tell you anyway. Don't take no nonsense, right. You've got that fancy way with you – use it if they gets too friendly. Don't wear slippers, wear boots 'cos they's all 'orrid dancers most of them.'

'Thank you. That does seem sound advice.'

'Right you are then.' With a nod of her head, Bet disappeared.

Guinevere struggled into the dress, which smelt strongly of its previous owner and did it up. It hung on her and the neckline was far too low. She might be a dancing girl, but she was determined that no one would mistake her for anything else and she filled the gaping bodice with lace that reached to her throat.

She did not spend much time on her hair, just winding it into a bun from which errant curls sprang to frame her face. She couldn't stop her hands shaking however, and thought she'd never prepared with such reluctance for an evening of dancing.

When Guinevere was almost ready, Bet returned with a glass of spirit and surveyed her, head to one side.

'That dress looks all right. A bit loose but it'll do well. The men won't like the lace but it's a sensible move. Now, I know you ain't much of a drinker but reckon you might need this tonight.'

Seeing no reason not to grasp at straws at this stage, Guinevere accepted the glass and took a sip. The raw alcohol burned, causing her to choke and her eyes to water.

'Just chuck it down, milady. It ain't no French wine.'

Screwing up her face, Guinevere drained the glass.

'Good. That'll 'elp you. Off you go then.'

There was already a large number of customers thronging the bar and sitting on the benches when Guinevere arrived. Word had spread of the new dancing girl and, as Mike had hoped, the men were flooding in but it was still early and most were reasonably sober. They had obviously spruced up for the evening's activities and moleskins, if shabby, were akin to clean, Crimean shirts buttoned, crimson sashes jaunty and neckerchiefs neatly tied.

There was a buzz of interest as she made her way in and feeling what seemed to be hundreds of eyes upon her, Guinevere faltered, wild thoughts of flight shooting through her mind. Then she drew herself up, surreptitiously rubbing damp palms on the unfamiliar skirts of her dress.

'I can do this,' she told herself. 'I *have* to do this!'

At that moment one of the dancing girls stepped forward with both hands outstretched and took Guinevere's fingers in her own.

'I'm Meg, your ladyship. I'm ever so pleased to meet you. Me and the girls are going to be right here if you need us.'

Guinevere smiled gratefully down into the upturned, painted and powdered face. Meg was diminutive and looked barely more than fifteen or sixteen but there was genuine warmth in her soft brown eyes and her shiny red lips smiled kindly.

'Thank you.'

'Now, you come with me and I'll show you the ropes.'

Guinevere was led to where the other girls were gathered in the corner. The orchestra hadn't arrived yet, she was told, so they didn't have much to do at the moment.

Meg made the introductions: Moll, Alice, Freda, Betty and Liza. They were all painted and ranged in age from Meg up to Alice, who looked forty, and Liza, who was possibly even older. Meg was the only one with a friendly expression. The other women eyed her with varying degrees of curiosity, cynical amusement and hostility.

'Please call me Guinevere.'

The girls exchanged glances.

'Don't feel right somehow,' muttered Moll.

'No, really, you must. I'm just like you now.'

This made them smile and the hostility lightened in several faces.

'You'll never be like us – Guinevere,' Freda said, laughing. 'But 'ere, 'ave a drink.'

Guinevere shook her head. 'I've already had one.'

'Better 'ave another,' and a glass was pressed into her hand. She looked down at it and then at the number of men, which seemed to be increasing every minute. How could six women ever hope to dance with so many? She tossed the drink back and won a cheer from the girls.

'That's the spirit. Helps to make the hours go faster. Don't drink any more, mind. What you do is dance with a digger then take him to the bar and make him buy you a drink – it's our job to make sure they spend as much as they can. But you don't do no more than sip the drink, then put it back on the bar. Joe'll whip it away and replace it with an empty glass, see. Smile and make the digger feel like a prince and then you go off to dance with the next chum. Easy as can be. Oh, here's the orchestra now. Work's about to begin, ladies.'

The members of the small orchestra were dressed very credibly in black suits and immaculate white shirts and when the first notes played, Guinevere realised they were surprisingly good musicians. However, there was not much time to enjoy their playing as the girls, in a swirl of brightly coloured skirts, swept up to the benches where the men

146

were eagerly waiting to be selected. Some miners couldn't wait and had already grabbed another digger to spin in lusty, if not elegant, dance.

Drawing in a deep breath and quaking inwardly, Guinevere made her way towards the miners, but when she tried to smile at one young man he turned a fiery red and cried out in panic, 'Oh, no! I don't want to dance with no lady!'

For a second she was nonplussed but fortunately the next man in line bounded to his feet and bowed gallantly.

'I can think of nothing I'd like more, ma'am, than to dance with a proper fine lady. Folks back home just won't believe it when I tell them. Jeremiah Hawthorne, ma'am, and very pleased to make your acquaintance.'

'You're American.'

He grinned and drawled, 'Clever as well as purty! My lucky night,' and without any further introduction he swept her into a jig which was energetic and lively and nothing like she'd ever danced before. When the music stopped her cheeks were flushed but miraculously she was laughing.

'Can I buy you a drink, ma'am?'

He proffered a brawny arm. Mindful of her duties, she put her hand on his sleeve and allowed herself to be taken to the bar. She wondered what on earth to ask for but the barman merely pushed a small glass towards her.

Bodies pressed in about her and the reek of

healthy men was already noticeable. Jeremiah was an amusing companion who talked nonsense and helped her to relax. She smiled, passed a few comments and was surprised to note out of the corner of her eye the dexterous swap of her full glass for an empty one. Surely, if it happened every night, the miners must catch on to it she thought, but if Jeremiah noticed he made no reference to it at all.

He was well-versed in the social etiquette of the dance floor, however, and as soon as the orchestra began striking up the next tune, he bowed and said, 'Why thank you ma'am for your time. Now I can die a happy man knowing what it is to dance with a real lady all the way from England.'

She laughed but had no time to answer for already there were hopeful faces looking at her, trying to catch her eye.

Her next partner was a very young man who blushingly confided he'd never danced with a real lady before. When she told him she'd never danced with a miner before till this evening, he laughed in relief and swept her off with what he seemed to think was style but which turned out to be a trampling of feet for which he apologised, much abashed.

The first few hours flew by as Guinevere whirled from partner to partner, with a brief pause at the bar at the end of each dance. She became terribly thirsty but there was no drink to be had except alcohol.

Pushing past her feelings of humiliation, initially Guinevere thought that it was as easy as Meg had said it would be, but as the hours wore on the men got drunker, tripped more, slurred their speech more. Guinevere blessed Bet many times for the advice of wearing boots but the precarious confidence she'd felt at the beginning of the evening was evaporating fast. Her feet were sore, her head ached and after the first few partners, she lost interest in the trivial conversation she had with each man. In vain she looked for the entertaining Mr Hawthorne but he had disappeared and she assumed he must have gone to play billiards next door.

There were a number of Irish voices around her and once her heart leapt for there, across the room, was a head taller than the rest with thick springing hair. She caught her breath but then the man turned and it wasn't him at all! Fool that she was to hope he might be back in town already and seeking her.

Swallowing her disappointment, Guinevere looked to see how the other girls were managing. She was amazed to see them still smiling, still lively though closer scrutiny showed their responses were purely mechanical. And to think they repeated this night after night after night. It was a wonder they didn't go screaming mad and Guinevere suddenly understood why drinking was a problem amongst this class of women – she could imagine resorting to it herself to help make the tedium bearable. Then she saw Freda being backed against one wall, the miner fumbling at her bodice and pressing his face into her neck. Freda's face was perfectly blank but Guinevere flushed and shuddered. She certainly could never tolerate such behaviour.

But with the passing hours, the men's awe of her decreased with the amount of alcohol consumed and several times she was obliged to quell an overeager miner with her haughtiest look. This stood her in good stead until late evening when one fellow stepped into her path, demanding a dance. He was pockmarked and reeked of raw spirit. Guinevere shot him a look of disdain designed to wither but he was too drunk to notice. Instead he pulled her into a tight embrace.

'You're not much of an armful,' he said, breathing into her face, 'but you're a pretty one.'

Leaning away from him, she averted her face and pressed her hands hard against his chest to break his hold on her.

'Let me go!' It was the tone she used only when a maid was exceedingly impertinent but somehow it seemed not to carry the same authority in the crush of this smoke-filled, dimly-lit room.

'Oh, no, me lady,' the miner said, pulling her even closer as his large hands pressed against the small of her back above her hoops, forcing her hips to his.

'Let me go, I warn you!'

Outraged and not a little frightened, she began to struggle but he only laughed.

'Warn me, eh? Well, you're spirited, I'll say that for you. Just the way I like them. Never kissed me no lady,' and to Guinevere's horror, his wet mouth descended on hers and she tasted alcohol and raw onion as his other hand tugged at the lace about her bodice, fingers scrabbling to insinuate themselves down the loose dress front. His grasp was tight and she struggled, helpless against his strength.

Forgetting her earlier assurances that she was no different from the other girls, Guinevere was both terrified and appalled. This could not be happening to her. Surely this filthy miner did not really think that she, Lady Guinevere Stanhope, could be pawed at like, like – like some sort of common dancing girl. The inconceivable gall!

Blessed rage surged through her, swamping her fear as fury, fuelled by revulsion, lent her strength and with a wrench she managed to swing one hand free, delivering a sound box on his ears. The miner reeled back, clasping the side of his head.

'Whatcha go and do that for?' he asked sounding aggrieved.

In a ringing voice, Guinevere rounded on him. 'You impertinent little man! How dare you! I will not, repeat, will not, tolerate such insolence.'

Her voice carried even above the noise of the music and the roistering company. The dancing faltered and then, as those about them realised what had happened, loud applause broke out, whistles and catcalls filling the air.

'Good on ya! You show him how to treat a lady.'

'Give 'im another, 'e deserves it.'

'What a tigress!'

Though covered with mortification, Guinevere drew herself to her full height. Sir Reginald had faced the Cromwell tribunal with the same haughty pride. Head held high, she walked swiftly through the parting crowds and it was only with supreme control that as soon as she was out of the door, she did not abandon her dignity and run all the way back to the hotel. The walk was the longest of her life and her fingernails dug into the palms of her hands to stop herself from bursting into humiliated tears.

As Guinevere walked into the hotel, Bet looked up from wiping the bar and saw her face.

'Come in the back,' she ordered. 'You need a cuppa.'

Mutely, Guinevere followed her into the hotel's small, ramshackle kitchen which smelt, as always, of stewed cabbage but nevertheless had a reassuringly cheerful fire. In minutes Guinevere had a cup of tea thrust into her hands and Bet sat down heavily beside her.

'Go on, what 'appened, then?'

So Guinevere told her in halting sentences and tears did flow, but only a few when she came to the part where she hit the man.

Bet laughed. 'Wish I'd been there,' she said wistfully.

'Oh, such shocking behaviour,' moaned Guinevere.

'What yours or 'is?'

'His – oh, mine. I don't know.' She stared down into her tea for a minute and then looked up to meet Bet's not unsympathetic gaze.

'I don't know how those girls can stand it. I thought I could do it but I simply can't go back.'

'Never thought you should go in the first place. Tried to warn you, but you're not one to listen to reason, are you?'

Guinevere shook her head. 'No. But I'm listening now. What should I do?'

'Take the Irishman's money and go to England.'

'I won't go back there. Not yet. What else can I do?'

'Then go to Christchurch. There's fancy folk like you there. It's got to be better for you than this place. I can even give you a contact,' Bet said. 'One of my girls was getting beat up by 'er man all the time so a gent what comes 'ere regular, gave 'er the address of 'is godparents in Christchurch. Said they'd give 'er a job. Moll's a good girl for all that she's got no more sense than a sparrow and will 'elp you out if she can.'

Christchurch. Guinevere had a flash of memory of an Irish brogue. Fewer impossibly dense forests. Fewer sandflies.

'How can I get there?'

'Ship.'

'I don't have any money.'

'You do. You've the doctor's money.'

Guinevere bit her lip. 'I don't want to use that. I'm keeping it only for direst emergencies but I'm not quite at the end of my tether yet. Any other suggestions?'

Bet thought for a second then eyed Guinevere speculatively. 'There's your dresses. Reckon I could get some good prices for them from the girls. What d'ya think? Fancy parting with your fancy duds?'

The next morning the town was still buzzing with the night's delicious gossip when Guinevere, her heart breaking, hugged Cerberus for the last time having bequeathed him to a thrilled Jem.

'Goodbye, Cerberus, you look after Jem now,' she whispered and Cerberus whined and licked her cheek down which tears rolled. This made her laugh in a watery way and she rose to shake hands with Bet. 'You will give Mr O'Donnell the pictures, won't you?'

'Yeah, I'll make sure they aren't stolen.'

Guinevere smiled. She was just beginning to like this sarcastic woman. 'Thank you – and not just for minding the pictures for me.'

Bet shrugged. 'I didn't do nothing but town's going to be one 'eck of a lot quieter without you to talk about no more.' There was something approximating warmth in her voice.

Guinevere smiled. Then, picking up one holdall containing the last of her clothes in one hand and her camera and tripod in the other, Lady Guinevere Stanhope made her way down to the docks where she boarded a small ship to Christchurch. She never looked back.

CHAPTER 9

The run on gold lasted three months – just long enough, Quinn noted, for Burt to lie around doing nothing but fire off barbs and unwanted advice, while his two partners slaved from dawn until evening when they could no longer see by the light of the dying sun, and through the haze of their own exhaustion.

Each night straight after dinner, Quinn and Jack fell into impenetrable sleep not caring, as Burt pointed out daily, that they had a suffering man in their midst. They had fashioned crutches for Burt but he said his leg was not set quite right and that it was agony to be upright, so he spent his days propped against a tree, controlling operations he explained, and guarding their gold against any potential marauders.

'I should never have stopped you,' Jack muttered, 'when you had him at your mercy. If I'd seen the true state of things, I'd have helped you relieve the bastard not only of his balls but of his liver, heart and kidneys at the same time.'

Quinn, up to his knees in icy water, looked up from his panning and grinned. 'Your fault entirely for trying to act the hero. No ladies about to impress either.'

Jack laughed and flipped his hair back out of his eyes. 'Ah, but when we return to Christchurch as a couple of swells, there won't be a female who will be able to resist us – especially not the fair Stella!'

It appeared that much of Jack's time, when not grubbing for gold, was taken up by carousing and Quinn suspected that Jack's blue eyes, thick black hair and merry grin did not meet with much resistance anyway. The Englishman was, Quinn hated to admit, good company. After their lively introduction, there was no room for formalities and besides Jack would never have countenanced any. The younger son of a wealthy landowner, he had all the easy confidence of an Eton education and a cheerful childhood. The world had always treated him well and he in turn treated the world with exceptional bonhomie.

Quinn's loathing of well-heeled Englishmen could not withstand the onslaught of Jack's warmth and good humour and a strong friendship had developed as they achingly panned the stream each day, scrupulously dividing all findings into three.

Burt thought he should have more – he'd found the spot in the first place after all but when Jack suggested that he and Quinn should leave then, and go in search of their own spot, Burt quickly agreed to the three-way split.

Ben was an excellent assistant, tirelessly combing through the finer sand to extract every last golden crumb. Quinn and Jack told him that what he found was his but they noted that Burt each night ensured his son added his findings to what he termed the family share.

Though Burt's gripes and admonitions sawed on their nerves, the camp remained amicable enough apart from one notable outburst. As the gold was beginning to peter out, Jack and Quinn had been on an exploratory trip upstream and were just returning when they heard Burt's voice raised in fury at Ben.

'Useless bloody boy!' There was a thwack and a cry. 'Useless! Just like your bloody mother!' Another thwack and another suppressed cry.

They came around the bend in the river to see Burt had got himself upright and was holding Ben in one hand while the other brandished the crutch with which he was beating the boy. Quinn dropped his shovel and in a bound was in the clearing, wrenching Ben free and hurling the crutch into the far bushes.

'Try that again, you bastard,' he shouted, 'and I swear I'll beat you black and blue and see how you like it.'

'He's my son. Don't you bloody interfere!' Burt's face was contorted with rage, but there was fear too.

'Jaysus, you don't deserve to have a mongrel, much less a son. Lay one finger on him in front of me and I vow to the blessed virgin that I'll break that leg of yours again – and the other for good measure.'

'It's all right, Quinn,' said Ben hanging his head. 'It's my fault. I kicked Dad's tea over.'

'No 'tis not bloody all right!' Quinn informed him. 'Sure, you don't deserve treatment like that – no one does but especially not a good boy like yourself, you hear me?'

Ben flushed and raised his eyes to look at Quinn. 'Really?'

'Really,' Quinn said.

From that moment on, Ben's allegiance to the Irishman was unmistakable, much to his father's impotent fury and Jack's amusement.

But now the gold seemed to have disappeared. The days of backbreaking work became less and less satisfactory – sometimes they'd only find a few flakes. The profits had been very satisfying but dreams of a vast fortune began to dry up and around the campfire one evening they took stock of the situation.

'I think it's over,' said Jack. 'Great fun while it lasted but Mother Earth isn't going to give us any more – not here, at any rate.'

'Agreed. We've combed this area. I doubt there is any more to be had.'

'Well, I don't know about that.' Burt laid his empty cup down. 'You've been a mite casual in your panning at times – seen it myself. There's more there, I'm sure of it. You just need to look more carefully.'

'You look more carefully, you peg-legged bastard, instead of sitting on your arse all day.' Jack raked a hand through his hair and turned to Quinn. 'So, what do you think we should do?'

Quinn stirred the flames with a stick, then looked up and grinned at Burt. 'Well, I don't know if you've been counting, but it's been twelve weeks now since we trussed your leg up. I reckon it's about ready to be used again.'

'Ha!' said Jack triumphantly. 'You'll be able to show us where this gold is that you are so sure of. We'll sit on the bank and watch you pan for a change.'

Burt did not look as thrilled as one might expect a man to be on hearing his leg was mended. 'Still pains me something dreadful. I'm sure you didn't set it straight.'

'Straight as I could what with all your wriggling and writhing. Just as well Jack turned up when he did and could hold you down, else you'd have probably dislocated it with all the fuss you made.'

Quinn's words lacked heat but he could not disguise the contempt he felt. Having amputated limbs and attended to unimaginable wounds of men who'd borne their agony with stoicism, he was still less than impressed by Burt's howls of pain.

'We'll take the splints off tomorrow and then I

think we should head back to Hokitika for a bit,' Quinn said.

Jack nodded. 'Agreed. And if Burt prefers to stay here, he's more than welcome. In fact I urge you Burt, to stay.'

'You two are always ganging up on me,' Burt whined, 'and me just a cripple. Here boy, I need to relieve myself and there'll be no help from these fine partners of mine. Give your father a shoulder.'

He heaved himself up and leaning heavily on the long-suffering Ben, disappeared into the trees, mumbling as he went.

'Thank God that'll get him out of our hair for a while, though damned if I've ever known a man to take as long over his business as that one. So, if we leave here, what do you think you'll do? Set up a fine practice and go back to doctoring?'

'Jaysus, no.'

'Why not?'

Quinn was silent for a moment. The sky was black above them and the flames barely made any impression on the night. He looked at Jack who was lying back against a trunk, legs bent, his pipe glowing red. Quinn had never told anyone.

'Really? You want to know?'

'Really.'

'The last man I attended to in America, I murdered.'

Jack gave a startled laugh. 'Don't talk rot!'

'I'm not.'

'I don't believe it,' Jack said. 'I've worked side

by side with you these past three months and you're no murderer, on that I'd stake my life.'

'Then you'd lose. I tell you, I did. He died because of me.'

'Was he a Confederate?'

'No, a Union man like myself.'

'Then I don't understand.'

'It's not something I want to discuss. I betrayed my profession and I'll never go back to it.'

'So what's with helping Burt, then?'

Quinn gave a short laugh. 'Ah well, that was different. Ben asked.'

'And you couldn't refuse, I know – you never can where that boy's concerned. How did he know to ask you?'

'Word had got out I had some medical knowledge.' Quinn was abrupt, not wanting to say more but Jack was not the sort to let things go.

'How?'

'I helped a woman.'

'Oho! Enter the heroine. Why haven't you spoken of her before? Look at your face –it's gone the colour of a beet.'

''Tis not important, I'll not be seeing her again. She's returned to England.'

'An Englishwoman!' Jack crowed and Quinn grinned reluctantly. 'Capital. That certainly would have got your proud Irish spirit in a twist. Come on, what's her name.'

'Lady Guinevere Stanhope.'

'Lady Guinevere? Oh, it just gets better and

better,' and Jack gave a peal of laughter. 'Poor O'Donnell! With so many Irish colleens to choose from, you lost your heart to a—'

'A passing moment – nothing more. That's it. No more to be said now, Jack. She was not the woman I thought her to be, at any rate, once I got to know her.'

'Oh?' There was a silence so Jack added, 'That, by the way, was an invitation to tell more. Go on man, spill the beans. There's no one to hear and we've talked almost every other subject under the bloody sun to death these past weeks. Tell me about the fair Guinevere. She is fair, I take it.'

Quinn smiled. 'She is, but not in the common way. More like a wild little bird than a bird of paradise. I daresay she could not hold a candle to your Stella.'

Stella was the actress Jack had met when staying with his godparents in Christchurch, a veritable goddess who, he declared, had stolen his heart. Quinn suspected the frivolous Englishman's heart was frequently stolen and at no great personal cost.

Jack laughed. 'Well, that's not to say much. No woman can hold a candle to Stella. Go on, tell me how you met.'

So out came the story of the chance meeting, the flood, the week in Hokitika. At that point Quinn, who had been quite animated in the telling of the story, fell silent, his attention apparently caught by the stick which he was twirling between his fingers.

'Come on, man, there's more still. I can tell.'

'Well, then I discovered that this absurd hunt for a moa was because her cursed father had died leaving her virtually penniless, their house mortgaged and the only way to reclaim the place being to marry the man who possesses the mortgage.'

'Poor girl. What'll she do?'

Quinn gave a bitter laugh. 'Do? Why, what all young English girls of good breeding do – she'll marry him, of course. She doesn't care a rap for him but will have him anyway, if she can't raise the money to pay her father's debt.' The stick snapped with a sound like a pistol shot.

Jack was sympathetic but matter-of-fact. 'Well, she doesn't have much choice otherwise, does she?'

Quinn shrugged. 'No. Now that I've had the chance to cool off, I can see that. At the time, I just saw red. My damnable temper, you know. We argued and I said things—'

'But you said she was on her way back to England. I don't understand. If she has no money . . .'

'I bought some of her drawings before coming up here. Couldn't find her, which was probably just as well, so gave the money to her maid to give to her.'

'You what?' Jack jerked upright in astonishment. 'Why? Do you have so much money that you could throw it about like that? I thought your

164

pockets were pretty well to let before we found the colour?'

'I'd been putting some savings by but that did clean me out.'

'Then why, in God's name, would you do something like that?'

Quinn paused, weighing his words. 'I wanted her out of my hair. I've heard it said that if you save someone's life, you are somehow responsible for them. As a doctor, I laughed when I heard that but now . . .' He shrugged. 'I can't explain but somehow I felt that as long as she was in New Zealand, I'd need to look out for her. She doesn't have anyone else here, you see. But I don't need that responsibility – don't want it. I'm just wanting a simple life, no complications and Lady Guinevere Stanhope carried a world of complications with her – starting with her own stubborn temperament.'

This made Jack laugh as he relaxed back against the tree trunk and tamped more tobacco into his pipe. 'That, of course, you cannot understand at all, being as you are the most tractable of fellows.'

Quinn grinned a bit sheepishly. ''Twas a bit like that, hard to tell who was most pig-headed. Billy goats going head-on, most of the time. She and her damned, high-handed ways.' Then more briskly, he said, 'But it's all in the past, now. She's gone and good riddance. An English lady and an Irish peasant . . . 'Twas a laughable mix.'

'Not such a peasant – not then, and especially

not now. You, my friend, are a man of substance as well as a man of education. Well, if your fair lady has sailed away forever, what will you do with your life?'

Quinn stretched back and groaned at the protesting muscles in his shoulders. 'We've done well but I want to buy land and build a fine, fine house so I'll need more money. To be honest though, I've had enough of this gold-panning nonsense. I've been thinking I might invest in a business – go into supplies.'

'Supplies?'

'Think about it. Who are the ones growing very rich from the gold without grubbing at all?'

Jack's eyes widened. 'The traders.'

'That's right! I think a travelling wagon would reap the most profits – reliable ones. None of this hit-and-miss stuff. Thought if I went up into the mountains over the winter when it's most desperate, I'd make the biggest profits.'

'Damned dangerous if you ask me, especially travelling alone. Fellows die here every week what with this hellishly changeable weather – not to mention getting lost in the mountains or drowning,' Jack noted.

'Well, there is that.' Quinn shrugged it off as a trifling thought. 'Trouble is, I still don't have quite enough capital to set myself up with a decent rig. I'll have to stay with digging a bit longer. Who knows I may hit another lucky streak.' He glanced over to his partner. 'What about you?'

'I need to get back to Christchurch and return to the ravishing Stella's side. There are too many damned men always paying her court and besides, her troupe is due to leave for Wellington in a few months. Still,' he added, looking thoughtful, 'your idea's not a bad one. Not a bad one at all.'

He looked like he was about to say something more but at that moment they heard a crashing in the bushes heralding Burt's return and the subject was dropped.

The next day Burt's leg was liberated and Quinn was gratified to see it was straight as a die, though Burt insisted it had a kink. They then packed up camp and set off, Burt moaning and hobbling along but still managing to muster breath to complain and carp all the way down the track. Jack was unusually quiet and Ben stayed close to Quinn's heels, reminding him of Cerberus. Several times the Irishman glanced down to see the small freckled face screwed up against the threat of tears. Once he put his hand on the boy's head and tousled the sandy hair, earning a look of such devotion that he felt positively wrung. But the boy was not his problem. He'd done what he could but soon they would all be parting. He would miss both Jack and Ben and he felt some frustration with himself for getting into this position. He'd sworn to never put himself through the pain of losing people again and yet here he was about to lose these companions and he'd still not quite recovered from the ache of losing Lady bloody Guinevere.

Though he'd been delighted to find gold, it hadn't been as exciting as he'd thought it would be and the weighty bag in his pocket did not give quite the satisfaction he'd expected. Instead, while swilling the water endlessly in his pan, Quinn had found his thoughts wandering often to Guinevere's elfin features and their past conversations. There were whispers of her everywhere. The way the sunlight glinted on the stream's ripples reminded him of the golden lights in her eyes. Sometimes in the breeze, he could almost hear an echo of her laughter.

Where was she now he wondered? Halfway back to England in all likelihood. Would she be happy in her marriage to Ramsay, learn to love him or was she as immune to that emotion as she claimed to be? Not that it was any of his business, but he'd have liked to know how her story would end.

His thoughts were interrupted by Jack's excited cry from up at the front.

'What ho! Wait up, chums.'

A group of miners with several horses on the track in front of them paused and turned around.

'Hello there!' said Jack. 'Are you headed for Hokitika?'

'We are. And you?'

'Well now, here's the thing. We were but,' and turning to Quinn, Jack said, 'I think we should both go to Christchurch instead. What do you say, Quinn? Partners?'

'Partners?'

'Been thinking about what you said. Makes a lot of sense. I need to return to the ravishing Stella's side and chase away her admirers. Also, my godfather's a big noise in Christchurch and may prove a handy contact – he's always looking for business enterprises. If nothing else, we've a couple of free nights in his very comfortable house and free advice thrown in. Are you game for it?'

Quinn thought for exactly half a second of Hokitika without Guinevere and said, 'Why not? Leaving now?'

'Right this minute, if these men will trade a couple of horses and throw in any left over supplies too.'

The miners were startled at this unexpected suggestion but when they heard the price Jack named, they could barely suppress their smiles. 'Deal,' they said, shaking on it quickly, in case the lanky Englishman changed his mind.

Gold was duly exchanged, the horses loaded with remains of flour, sugar and tea and farewells were said all round. Ben could barely raise his head and when he did, the betrayal that Quinn saw in the boy's eyes smote him. Crouching down, he looked into Ben's freckled face.

'This is life, Ben. People come and go in our lives and there's nothing we can do about it. It'll maybe hurt for a bit but after a while you'll see the pain goes. You just be strong and true to your-self and let no man,' here Quinn scowled at Burt, 'lift a hand against you. Understand?'

'No, I don't. Why do people have to go?'

'That's just the way it is.'

'I don't believe you,' Ben said stubbornly. 'You're choosing to leave me.'

Quinn sighed. 'Jack and I are going over the mountains. You know how dangerous that is. Even if your father wanted to come, he couldn't make it on that leg. I'm sorry, Ben, but we all have to follow our own paths.'

'I want to follow yours.'

'Well, of all the ungrateful—' Burt began, but when Quinn straightened, he broke off.

'You treat this boy well, understand. Make sure he gets his fair share of supplies and findings.'

Burt snorted. 'He's my son and I'll treat him any way I bloody well like.' He gave an evil grin. 'It's not like you'll be around to interfere anymore.'

Ben whitened and Quinn took a threatening step towards Burt. 'Listen, you old bastard.'

The older man fell back a pace but didn't lose his smirk. 'Like I said, 'taint none of your business, now. But if you like him so well, you can buy him.'

'What? That's a terrible thing to say, even in jest.'

'Jest? Who's jesting? I mean it. The boy's no use to me at all. I'd be glad to see the back of him. Always been useless, just like his mother.'

Quinn was outraged but even more appalled when he looked down to see hope flaring in the young face.

So it was that ten minutes later Jack and Quinn, with Ben on the saddle behind him, set off for

Christchurch. They were considerably poorer thanks to Jack's negotiations and Quinn's unexpected purchase. He thought fleetingly of Guinevere's drawings that ought to be waiting in Bet's care for him. It couldn't be helped. Perhaps he'd make his way back to Hokitika some day, but it was probably all for the best. He was determined to put her behind him and the drawings would only have served as a reminder.

'I've lost all sense,' Quinn said. 'What the hell have I done by throwing my lot in with the two of you?'

But Ben just laughed and his skinny arms clung tighter to Quinn, while Jack was unrepentant at the price he'd paid for knock-kneed nags.

'Cheap at the price,' he said cheerfully. 'I know myself. If I'd gone to Hokitika I would have lost the lot on wine, women and song. I would have woken with a hangover and empty pockets. This way, I remain on the straight and narrow – and the very steep I might add. I'm an unsteady bloke, O'Donnell, but I figure if I stick by you we may all just come out of this very well. And face it, man, you need me too. We'll cover more ground and have each other's back if anything untoward happens. With me as your partner – why, the world's our oyster.'

'And I'll work as hard as can be,' added Ben.

Quinn laughed. 'Sure, we'll be an unstoppable force. Christchurch here we come.'

The men nudged their horses forward to begin

the steep ascent into the mountains. The track was rough and they knew many men had already lost their lives in the treacherous crossing of the Southern Alps, but nothing could dim the sense of exhilaration and anticipation they felt as they set off towards their unknown future.

CHAPTER 10

Guinevere peeked at her reflection in the murky slither of mirror that had been provided for her in this tiny attic room. The maid's cap sat demurely enough but her heavy hair, though severely drawn back, still threatened to escape the hairpins. With luck they would hold for the duration of the meal she was to serve tonight.

'You must not fail this time,' she informed her reflection severely. 'If you do, it's back to the dance floor.' The memory of boots, beards and boozy breath still made her shudder. However, the face that looked back at her was nearly four months older, four months wiser. As humiliating as the dance hall had been, Guinevere now knew there were worse fates of homelessness and hunger and, worst of all, loneliness.

She would never have believed, even a few months ago, just how gratefully she would welcome the opportunity to be a housemaid, but circumstances had finally driven her to use Bet's contact. As luck would have it, one of the housemaids had just left and Moll had arranged for Guinevere to

173

have an interview. It had not been easy. The buxom and formidable housekeeper, Mrs Williams, was frankly sceptical.

'How do you make a good polish for oak tables, then?' she challenged. 'How would you clean soot from a carpet?'

Who, thought Guinevere quite desperately at this stage, would ever have believed how complicated it was to be a maid? She had even modified her name to Gwen for the interview, feeling that her real name would only engender further prejudice.

Luckily, Sir John happened at that moment to come in through the kitchens from the stable and had stopped to overhear the interrogation. When Guinevere floundered under this rush of questions he'd stepped forward, a twinkle in his eye.

'Come now, Mrs Williams, give the girl a chance,' he said. 'You can teach her your tricks and it will be good to have a pretty face over the breakfast plates. Agatha was such a sour puss that she quite put me off my coffee some mornings.'

'Yes, sir.' Mrs Williams' lips folded into a flat line but he was oblivious to her disapproval.

Chucking Guinevere under the chin, Sir John added, 'We are short-staffed and I've two young blades fresh from the gold fields staying with us tonight. You'll help to make their stay an enjoyable one so put on your prettiest smile for them, eh.'

With difficulty Guinevere stifled a desire to slap his hand away and though she couldn't smile prettily right at this moment, gratitude made her at least nod obedience. 'Good. It's all settled then.'

The whole household, it turned out, was in a state of excitement. One of the young men was Sir John's godson and a great favourite of the family. A favourite too, with the staff.

'I owe me job to 'im,' Moll, the rotund little housemaid confided. ''E's ever so 'andsome. An' cheeky! 'E says the most cheeky things!' and she giggled, clearly hoping to hear more.

Mrs Williams said that he was nothing more than a disrespectful young scamp, but she could not prevent the hint of a smile from softening her stern features.

It had been a long afternoon; preparing the vegetables, ironing the linen, cleaning out two bedrooms and making beds up with fresh sheets. Hard to imagine miners appreciating this luxury, Guinevere thought, but they'd enjoy the fine meal being prepared downstairs in their honour.

She had to concede that Mrs Williams' reservations as to her efficacy as a housemaid were not entirely unjustified. She struggled with the plethora of unfamiliar tasks, though she proved herself of some worth by laying the table beautifully, and arranging freshly cut flowers and a few extra candles so cleverly that Moll exclaimed the dining room had never looked so well. In fact, it was because she'd been at the bottom of the garden selecting flowers with the gardener that Guinevere had missed the excitement of the miners' arrival.

The two young men had almost immediately been whisked upstairs to bathe which, judging by the state of the towels and the rings around the baths they'd left behind them for Guinevere to clear up, was not before time either. There was not much pause in her duties at the end of all this, however, as she was allowed only to slip up to her room to put on a clean apron and re-pin her mutinous hair.

'You watch yourself when you serve tonight, mind,' Mrs Williams warned her. 'Don't want no mistakes or else you're out on your ear no matter what Sir John says. I won't have useless maids on my staff, do you hear?'

Now Guinevere smoothed the apron down, noting ruefully that her hands were slightly shaking. Was she, Lady Guinevere, afraid of failing as a maid? Yes, she thought, terribly afraid. For if she failed at this, what on earth else could she do? Two failed positions already lay behind her in Christchurch.

Drawing in a deep breath and thanking her lucky stars that no one she knew would ever see her in this humiliating garb, she made her way down the several flights of back stairs to the kitchen. There she saw a young boy with jug ears sitting at the kitchen table enthusiastically tucking into a huge plate of food.

'Where did you spring from?' she asked.

The boy paused and bobbed his head. 'West Coast, ma'am.'

'That's no ma'am, that's Gwen. She's naught

but a maid,' said Mrs Williams, annoyed by the boy's instinctive deference to Guinevere.

'Ben 'ere came wiv Mr Elton's friend,' Moll explained.

Ben nodded vigorously. 'He bought me.'

'Brought you, you mean,' Mrs Williams corrected him.

'No, he paid real gold for me,' Ben declared with pride.

Moll and Guinevere exchanged looks but before they could question Ben further, Mrs Williams was chivvying them.

'There's no time for that, girls, and none of your business either. They're just going into the dining room so look lively and take out the oysters. Mercy, what a time for Agatha to go off and marry. Gwen, Moll's done table service before at big parties so you just follow her lead. Lord help me, the blind leading the lame.'

Moll, flushed with the importance of her new role, whispered behind Mrs Williams's back. 'I peeked in the drawing room when they came down and Mr Elton's friend's ever so 'andsome, too. 'E's got this lovely smile that goes up on one side.'

Then as Mrs Williams turned with a threatening expression, Moll added loudly, 'Grab some plates, Gwen and follow me. I'll do Sir John and Lady Whittering, you'd best do the visitors.'

Snatching up two plates, Guinevere followed Moll down the passage and into the dining room.

★   ★   ★

Quinn was surprised by how warmly he had been welcomed by Jack's godparents. In appearance they presented a curious couple; he short and rotund, with florid cheeks and a balding pate, she tall and wiry, with large, now yellowing teeth. But there was no mistaking the shrewdness in Lord Whittering's eyes, despite his ever-present good humour, nor the quick intelligence with which Lady Whittering summed up new acquaintances. They had come out to New Zealand some twenty years earlier, when the colony was in its infancy, and had doubled their already large fortune.

Their house, on the outskirts of Christchurch, would have been very acceptable in England or Ireland but here in New Zealand it was imposing. It was wooden and stood three storeys high, although the top storey contained only the servants' attic rooms. The windows were large and gracious, overlooking the well-tended gardens which, even in late summer, still brimmed with colour. The Avon River wove lazily through the grounds and willows were scattered along the banks.

Quinn had taken one look at this mansion and thought, 'This is what I will build!' He'd steeled himself to disregard any wariness his hosts might harbour towards their godson's Irish friend, but they proved well used to the New Zealand ways which measured a man's worth as much by his accomplishments as by his background. If he was Jack's partner in a lucrative gold find and a prospective trading business, then he was welcome in their home and both men had already been pressed into agreeing to stay for as long as they needed accommodation in Christchurch. The Whitterings had even accepted Ben's presence without a murmur, though tactfully suggesting the boy might be more comfortable eating in the kitchen and sleeping in a spare bed above the stables. Quinn, seeing Ben's saucer eyes, had agreed.

Quinn's bedroom was beautiful. Golden-sheened kauri wooden floors stretched to the tall sash windows overlooking the river. There was an elegant fireplace and a huge feather bed that Quinn eyed in amazement. It could easily accommodate an entire family. Not daring to move about in his dirty boots and dust-laden clothes, he stood in the middle of the room looking about him. Never in his life had he been inside such a home. He suppressed an urge to pinch himself and was glad he had as at that moment servants ushered in with a bath and pitchers of hot water.

'There you go, sir,' said a rosy, round maid as she emptied her ewer. 'Quick, get in while it's 'ot. Robert 'ere will bring some more water up directly.'

The smile she gave him was distinctly coquettish. Normally he would have been happy to respond to such an overture but in this room he felt wrong-footed. It was not his world and he did not know the rules. Instead he merely nodded his thanks.

As the door closed behind her he was quick to

strip off his clothes, dumping them on the cloth the maid had laid out alongside the bath and stepping into the hot water, which was pure bliss after so many months rough living.

Later, washed, shaved and dressed in a suit Jack had lent him, Quinn stood in front of the mirror. He had seldom seen his reflection and never full-length before and he scrutinised his image closely. Hair too long but combed back off his face, suit a little tight in the shoulders, a trifle short at the ankle but undoubtedly the finest suit he had ever worn. Clothes maketh the man. Was that true? He could only see Quinn O'Donnell in borrowed garb, but with luck his hosts would see him as the gentleman he posed to be.

Drawing in a deep breath he realised this was it, the first evening in his new life. If only Guin— the people he knew could see him now.

Going downstairs, he met his hosts in their drawing room where the men drank brandy and talked of the booming economy in the surrounding Canterbury region while Lady Whittering listened, though her occasional observations indicated she was following the discussions closely. Jack entertained them too with a few embellished tales of their exploits and had both godparents chuckling.

'It's as well your mother doesn't know what you are up to or she'd never sleep soundly again,' said Lady Whittering, with an admonishing shake of her head.

Then they moved into the dining room and

Quinn took in the white table linen, the silverware gleaming in the soft light of a few gas lamps. There were also clusters of candles, well placed to give not only illumination but also a warm softness to the atmosphere. The roses in the corner filled the room with a light scent.

This too I'll have one day, Quinn promised himself. He shook out his crisply laundered table napkin and heard the door open behind him. Jack had kept their spirits up over the arduous crossing of the Southern Alps with stories of the wonderful cook his godparents employed and Quinn was hungry enough for a banquet.

The first maid placed a plate in front of Lady Whittering then walked around the far side of the table from Quinn, past Jack. Quinn was amused to see her cast a roguish look under her lashes at his irrepressible friend but she was demure enough as she served Sir John. A plate appeared in front of Quinn and he turned to thank the maid only to find he was staring straight into golden-flecked eyes. Her hand jolted in shock, tipping the half dozen oysters into his lap.

'Jaysus!'

'Oh, you foolish girl! I do apologise, Mr O'Donnell,' cried Lady Whittering.

'No, 'tis I who must apologise!' said Quinn hastily, seeing Guinevere's cheeks flame. 'I bumped her arm inadvertently. My fault entirely.'

'No harm done, sir,' said Moll, coming to Guinevere's rescue and scooping the napkin off

Quinn's lap. 'See, it's all landed neatly on the napkin. We'll get a clean one, sir, and Gwen'll get you another plate too. Go Gwen.'

Grateful to leave the room, Guinevere fled. Outside the dining room she sagged against the wall, pressing the back of her hand to her mouth. If only she could die right at this moment, the ground swallow her up. Her knees shook and it was only with the sternest resolve that she didn't slither down the wall to collapse in a heap on the floor, throwing her apron over her head in order to disappear.

How on earth could she ever go back in there and face Quinn? What was he thinking right at this moment? Enjoying the sight of Lady Guinevere brought down at last to know what 'real' life was all about, no doubt. Well, she'd certainly learned a few lessons since they'd last met. Why, oh why, of all the houses in Christchurch – in New Zealand for goodness sake – would he fetch up here tonight of all nights?

But even as another wave of humiliation rolled over her, causing her to groan aloud, there was beneath, another vivid but unnamed emotion. Her heart was skittering and not purely in shame. A tremor of something akin to excitement rippled through her and she shivered. He was *here* in Christchurch and not on the wild West Coast. Here.

Then Moll came out, clutching the soiled napkin.

'Whatcha doin' standin' about 'ere?' she cried. 'We gotta meal to serve. Buck up.'

Errol of Hearthe had not flinched when Norman arrows whistled past his ear at Hastings and Guinevere would not shrink back now. Steeling herself, she followed Moll down to the kitchen.

The rest of the meal passed in a blur of mortification, which she held accountable for the otherwise inexplicable sharpening of all her senses. There were no more mishaps but she was vividly aware of Quinn's presence and even more aware of how he ignored her – just as maids should be ignored, she thought bitterly. She scarcely dared look at him, but as she leant over to pick up his plate she could feel the warmth of his body. Once he shifted just as she was clearing his dessert dish and their arms touched. No one else noticed but Guinevere cupped her elbow afterwards for a few seconds, her stomach both hollow and fluttering at the same time.

Lady Whittering retired and the port bottle and cigars were brought out. Quinn had heard all about this custom but had only participated in it at a few formal army dinners. The sense of male camaraderie it encouraged was strangely beguiling and with the departure of the maids, he was able to gain some control over his splintered thoughts.

Though he'd glanced covertly a number of times at Guinevere's face frozen into impassivity, still he found it impossible to believe that she was here, right here, under the same confounded roof. Why the devil hadn't the woman gone back to England?

What torture it was to sit there, maintaining a social facade, when all he wanted to do was grab her by the shoulders and shake her. What the hell was she up to, dressing in that damned ridiculous uniform? With some satisfaction he'd noted her wayward hair seeking to escape the absurd little cap, tendrils falling free from their confining pins. He imagined ripping the cap off and letting her hair fall heavy and free down her back . . .

'Quinn agrees, don't you Quinn?'

The Irishman looked up at Jack, a little startled.

'That we should be off south to the Otago plains before winter sets in,' Jack elaborated.

With an effort Quinn forced his mind back to the table.

'Definitely,' he said and joined in the discussion Jack and his godfather were having; talk of mining and business. No one would have guessed from his urbane manner that his thoughts were still flying in all directions.

As the level in the port bottle dropped, Sir John's mind moved to other matters.

'Apologies for the maid tonight,' he said. 'Shouldn't have happened. My fault. Insisted we hire the gel.'

'As I said, the fault was mine.'

'Pretty girl,' remarked Jack, refilling his glass. 'In an unusual way.'

His godfather nodded. 'Just what I thought when I saw her. But tell you what, there's a mystery about that gel.'

'Mystery?' asked Quinn.

'You didn't hear her speak but I tell you, that's no maid we've got out there.'

'Oh?'

'Talks like a lady. No clue about service either. Felt sorry for her when I heard her being interviewed so stuck my oar in.'

'That was chivalrous of you, Uncle John.' Jack grinned.

His godfather smiled back. 'None of your cheek, m'boy. Fact is, I have a theory about her.'

'Which is?'

'Think she must have got into trouble with some man. Family threw her out, he left her and now she's nowhere to go.'

'It's possible. So what'll you do with her?'

'She's welcome to stay as long as she likes. We'll give her a home if she needs one.'

'Always the philanthropist,' said Jack with a laugh, but there was something in his tone that made Quinn's fingers tighten on the stem of his glass.

'Ah, well,' said Lord Whittering. 'I'm happy to help a pretty girl and Moll has turned out most admirably, m'boy.'

The remainder of the evening was soured for Quinn and he was relieved when they could finally all turn in. However, having looked forward with longing for weeks to a soft bed with clean sheets, Quinn now found it impossible to sleep while Guinevere was somewhere in the house and a whole swathe of unfinished business between them.

The unfamiliar sounds of a large house seemed to go on for a long while; the muted clatter from the kitchen, the shuffle of his hosts' feet to and fro several times to the newly installed water closet. When the house had been very still for a long time, Quinn was on the verge of rising when he heard what he was sure was Jack's door opening very quietly and the sounds of steps creeping to the stairwell. Was Jack visiting the dark-haired maid? She had certainly seemed to invite him with those sidelong looks of hers. What on earth was he, Quinn O'Donnell, doing in this ridiculous set-up, playing the gentleman while a real lady waited upon him?

Finally he could not stand it any longer; if he bumped into Jack, so be it but he had to find out what the bloody hell Guinevere was doing here when by rights she should be almost returned to England by now.

Rising, Quinn pulled on a pair of trousers then tugged a shirt over his head not even thinking to tuck it in. He opened his door very slowly, wincing as it creaked. For a second he hovered, holding his breath but there was no sign of disturbance so very quietly he made his way down the main stairs, along the darkened hallway to the servants' staircase at the back of the house.

Taking these swiftly, two at a time, he was just rounding the corner of the top flight when he cannoned into someone who was running down. She gave a tiny scream while he muffled an oath, seizing the slight figure in front of him by the shoulders to steady them both.

'Idiot!' she whispered furiously. 'I nearly died of fright running into you like that.'

'Delighted to meet with you again too, Lady Guinevere,' he hissed back. 'Where the hell are you going at this time of night?'

'To find you, of course.'

Of course! In the darkness, he shook his head at her temerity. What the Whitterings would think if they found their maid . . . 'Quick, we must get to your room. We cannot be seen here.'

'I know that. Come with me.'

The skirts of her nightdress glowed ghostly in the darkness below the shawl she'd wrapped about her shoulders and he followed her up the remaining steps and through a door off a small landing.

'Who's in the other room?' he whispered.

'Moll. The other maid.'

Quinn stepped forward in the darkness and cracked his toe against something very hard. Swearing under his breath he hopped painfully.

'Ssh. Someone will hear. Don't move.'

How well he remembered that imperious tinge to her voice. There was the scratch of a match, a flare of light and then the flame of a candle danced, sending weird shadows about the walls of the tiny room. It also illuminated Guinevere's white face so that her eyes seemed huge and her cheeks thinner than he remembered.

'You've lost weight,' he commented. 'You haven't been looking after yourself as you ought.'

'And I see you haven't lost your Irish way with sweet words,' she retorted. 'What on earth are you doing here?'

'Here in Christchurch or here in your room?'

'Both!'

'I was going to ask you the same question. Why the hell aren't you on your way back to England?'

'If you remember, I distinctly said I had no wish to return to England.'

'And if you remember, I said you wouldn't survive in New Zealand if you didn't.'

'I'm surviving!'

'Barely!'

They glared at each other.

'And now, sneaking down to visit a man in his bedroom. Did you never learn even one vestige of propriety in your unconventional upbringing, m'lady?'

'You're a fine one to talk, sneaking up to the servants' quarters like that. Besides, I had to. I wanted to give you this.'

She thrust her hand out and crammed some notes into his.

Bewildered, he looked down. 'What's this?'

In the candlelight he could see her defiant look. 'The money you left when you abandoned me in that horrid town.'

'I didn't abandon you – you were packing to leave anyway. Don't tell me you continued with your bloody ridiculous plan to chase moa?'

'No, I didn't – though I probably would have, given the opportunity. Instead, I was robbed,' she said. 'Thieves took my money and smashed all my chemicals the evening you left.'

'Oh, Jaysus.' All fight went out of him and he sank down heavily onto the bed. 'I might have known you'd get into one scrape or another.'

'It wasn't my fault.' she remonstrated as she sat on the bed beside him.

'Oh, no?' Quinn asked. 'And where were you when I came to say goodbye?'

She was silent, her head down so that the curtain of her hair hid her face.

'Well?' he pressed.

'Walking on the beach,' she muttered.

'Oh God, you foolish, foolish girl! 'Twas those mongrels in the bar, I'll bet. No, 'tis my fault. I should have thought.'

Torn equally between anger at himself and at her, Quinn rubbed one hand down his face while the other still absently held the returned notes. What a damnable mess. Then he felt her shiver next to him and said, 'Look at you – bare feet on this cold floor, you'll be freezing. Go on, get into bed.'

He leaned past her to lift the blankets and the tension between them suddenly eased, his concern reminding them both of their days of friendship when he'd been her doctor.

Guinevere slid her chilly feet under the sheet. The candle on the stool beside her bed threw a faint, warm glow onto her face, emphasising her cheekbones and darkening her eyes. Her hair was as thick and curling as he remembered, but though her tone was lively, her face was tired and drawn.

Quinn could see how frightening, how hard, the past months had been for her but he knew too that she would sooner die than admit to that. The English sangfroid, he supposed.

More perplexed than angry now, he asked, 'I still don't understand. If your plans for the moa had fallen through, why did you not just return to England to marry that Ramsay fellow? I left enough money for you to purchase a berth.'

His question hung in the air as Guinevere paused, seeking a plausible answer while Quinn waited. She still could not tell him how distasteful she found the notion of marriage to Mr Ramsay. If he despised her for contemplating a marriage based on respect rather than regard, he would be disgusted if he knew she'd marry a man she loathed in order to save her home.

'I'd prefer to enter a marriage without a sense of obligation, if possible. To pay my father's debt as a son might,' she temporised. 'Can you understand that?'

Quinn looked at her for a minute. It was impossible to read his thoughts.

Finally he nodded. ''Twill do as an explanation for now, I suppose. So tell me, Lady Guinevere, having lost everything and having spurned my help, what did you land up doing instead?'

All anger had vanished from his face and instead he had that superior look that men assume when talking to women about their follies. She had a mischievous urge to rattle his composure.

'I became a dancing girl,' she said airily.

'*What?*'

His expression of horror was all that she'd hoped for.

'Oh, it was dreadful at the time but looking back on it now, it really was quite funny,' and she went on to relate how she'd borrowed a dress, slapped a miner and stormed out of the hall. She succeeded in making Quinn laugh, though he shook his head and groaned too.

'What were you thinking, Lady Guinevere, to even venture in such a place? 'Tis no place for a lady to be.'

'So I realised and that is when I came to Christchurch. I thought I'd get a better job here.'

'And is being a maid the promotion you sought?'

He shot her a sideways look designed to provoke and she retaliated by replying in grand style, 'Oh, no, I had my eyes set on something much higher to begin with, I can assure you. I managed to obtain a position of governess with one of the leading families in Christchurch, no less. I was exceedingly proud of myself and thought I was doing a wonderful job.'

'But?'

She grimaced. 'My charge, Elizabeth, was a sweet child but insipid. I thought if I could only infuse her with a little spirit, she would lead a happier life.'

Guinevere paused and heaved a theatrical sigh belied by the laughter, which now lit her eyes. 'Her mama caught me telling her dear daughter that one day women will have the vote, if only we all band together and fight for it.'

'Ah, a notion as scandalous as that of the Irish ruling themselves.'

'Worse, I believe. Anyway, I was strictly cautioned—'

'Let me guess,' Quinn interrupted, 'which you ignored.'

'Which I did not regard as seriously as perhaps I should have,' amended Guinevere. 'I continued to teach what I thought were ideas important to any young person's development. It was going well too until one dinnertime, when questioned as to what she had learned that day, Elizabeth informed her parents that we are all descended from apes. Alas, for me, the local minister was a guest at the table.'

Quinn grinned. 'Lord, I'd have loved to see his face. So what happened then?'

'Just as a certain insufferable Irishman had once predicted, I was turned out without a character.'

'I knew it!' Quinn was triumphant.

She sighed. 'My only consolation in this whole sorry affair is the knowledge that no gentleman would ever gloat over a woman's misfortunes.'

'Oh, unfair. Go on, then, seeing as I'm not to enjoy the told-you-so's.'

Quinn shifted so that the wall was at his back, his legs stretched out across the bottom of her bed and crossed at the ankle.

Guinevere settled back against her pillow. The barren attic room so bleak that afternoon, now seemed wondrously companionable.

'My next position was as a milliner's assistant.'

'Had you made hats before, m'lady?'

'No, but she wanted someone ladylike to make the sales.'

'Ah, well surely that was not difficult?'

Guinevere tossed her hair back over her shoulder. 'Not at all, if you want an assistant who will not venture an opinion and who would let a customer choose a hat entirely wrong for her complexion.'

'You couldn't keep your mouth shut, could you?'

She shook her head, rueful. 'My views on puce for women over the age of forty are best glossed over, as are my opinions of girls wanting ostrich feathers for a ball. But my greatest crime was when I helpfully pointed out to one fond mother that her daughter's freckles could be assisted by lemon juice for I knew an artist model who swore by it. If I had said prostitute, she could not have been more shocked. She gathered up her chick and positively scampered her out of the shop. I was scampered out shortly after. That was two days ago. You cannot know how relieved I was to get this job today.'

Then, as she became aware again of her present circumstances, she leaned forward to wrap her arms around her legs, her hair spilling about her as she rested her chin on her bent knees, suddenly serious.

'This is my final chance to redeem myself as a worker. I simply cannot afford to fail this time so I must thank you for covering up for me this evening. It just gave me such a shock to see you like that.'

'Me and all! For a second I thought I was looking at a ghost – but just for a second, mind. Soon as I felt my dinner fall into my lap – and me a starving man – I knew for sure it was you.'

'Beast. But you were so quick thinking. Thank you for not giving me away. I don't want anyone to know who I really am.'

'Ashamed?'

'No, it's not that. It's simply that it is hard enough to get a job sounding as I do. If they knew my background I suspect no one would employ me.'

'They might take pity on you and give you a home instead,' Quinn suggested.

'And wouldn't that be awful if they did! I told you, I will not accept charity.'

He looked down at the money still clutched in his hand and said, 'So, what is this then? I bought your drawings fair and square, m'lady.'

'You must get used to calling me Gwen now as that is who I am and you know you vastly overpaid me for those doodles. I kept and used the money for what they are worth and this is what is left over. I won't take charity from anyone. What's the matter? Haven't you forgiven me yet for being so high-handed?' Her voice was teasing but her eyes searched his face.

'I thought I hadn't but when I saw you in a maid's cap tonight, I saw you were justly punished for your pride.' His tone was severe but the concern in his eyes robbed the words of any sting. 'Will you not take this money as a loan at any rate, Lady Gu— Gwen. I have no need of it, you know.'

'No, thank you. It was my father's loan that got me into this pickle in the first place. Beside, I don't need it either. I've already earned enough for some chemicals,' Guinevere said proudly, 'and I intend to get back to my photography as soon as I can manage it.'

Quinn shook his head. ''Twon't be easy to find time to take photographs while being a maid.'

'I know,' she said, 'but I'll work something out.'

He smiled. 'Still so stubborn, m'lady,' but somehow these words sounded more like a compliment than a criticism.

Perhaps it was the candlelight but his eyes seemed unusually soft as they regarded her. Feeling her colour rise, she was quick to change the subject.

'And what about you? I thought you were a man determined to have no tethers in his life, but now I find you have a business partner – an Englishman

195

no less – and a child. Where on earth does the boy fit in? You didn't really buy him, did you?'

It was Quinn's turn to tell her of his unexpected reversal of fortune and his strange purchase.

'Damned if I know what I'll do with the lad,' he said, 'but I couldn't leave him with his brute of a father – especially when Ben fixed me with such a look. What else could I do?'

'You are not the only one burning with I-told-you-so's. Don't worry, you don't have to explain yourself to me, Mr O'Donnell. I know indeed just how hard it is hard to resist a pair of beseeching eyes.'

'You cannot be comparing a boy with a filthy nag,' Quinn protested, but a reluctant smile curled his mouth. 'Besides, if I'm to call you Gwen, you must call me Quinn.'

How well she remembered that crooked grin. At the sight, Guinevere's heart somersaulted, her unruly pulse sent fluttering. The past months had been the loneliest in her life – even worse than the ones following her father's death, but in the last thirty minutes the cold fear that had been so leaden in her heart since her arrival in Christchurch had miraculously dissolved. It was just so good to have someone to argue with and to laugh with again.

She felt glad too, that he'd come in search of her this night for she would never have slept until they'd talked again and he'd obviously felt the same. That unidentified emotion that had lashed her fury and humiliation into a passion had also made it imperative to see him again. But after the first minutes of his coming into her room, all animosity had evaporated, leaving only a bubbling, inexplicable joy. Absurd that one large, barely dressed Irishman could make such a difference, but he did.

As she breathed in, she could smell the faint wisp of brandy mingled with maleness that sent her senses leaping. She looked at his long, lean body lying relaxed along the bottom of her bed and it suddenly seemed too small for the two of them perched on it, her room too small to contain them both. A tingle went up her spine and to cover her shiver, she staged a yawn, which suddenly turned into a real one. Quinn leapt to his feet.

'Here's me blathering away and you've to be up crack of dawn tomorrow,' he said, contrite. 'I'll leave you now.'

'I'll see you tomorrow – over the breakfast dishes, no doubt. How would you like your eggs, sir, on a plate or in your lap?'

Quinn laughed but groaned too. 'I don't know if I can do this for long. It just doesn't seem right. An Irish farmer's son doesn't belong in the likes of a house such as this and you certainly don't belong in this attic. Everything has gone topsy-turvy.'

Guinevere laughed too but her voice was serious when she said, 'You must do this. You have everything in front of you, you cannot back off now. Who's to say you don't belong here? You are a doctor, for all you refuse to accept it. You are also a man with the makings of a fine business future. Don't pull yourself back after all that you've been through.'

'I just hate the thought of you waiting on me.'

'Why? I didn't have a qualm about you waiting on me four months ago.'

'But now?'

'Now?' She smiled but there was a quality of sadness in it. 'Now I know what it's like to be on the other side. It's been a good lesson for me. Now it can be a lesson for you.'

Impulsively Quinn took her hand in his and squeezed it. 'Stay brave, Lady Guinevere. Can I come and talk with you again?'

'Gwen, I told you. I'd like that – but we mustn't get caught.'

'Ah, so now you are a maid, you are finally concerned about your reputation.' Quinn couldn't help but grin.

She blushed but fought back. 'Insufferable man. Didn't I say those who point out when they are right are quite intolerable?'

'So you did. So I won't be mentioning the being turned out without a character either.'

'Go!' She threw her pillow at him and he caught it easily, tucking it behind her once more.

'No more talk, good night.'

★ ★ ★

Quinn stole out of the room, closing the door behind him, but as he was about to go down the stairs he caught a noise from the other maid's room. For a second he paused, trying to make sense of it then realised it was the muffled sounds of lovemaking. Jack had clearly not been able to resist womanising, despite being in the city of his adored Stella.

Quinn made his way swiftly down the stairs, his mind full of the conversations they had just had. It seemed incredible but fate had once more thrown the two of them together in a strange reversal of fortune. As he came into the hallway he heard the front door open and, stepping back into the shadows where he wouldn't be seen, he watched, curious to know who else was abroad tonight. There was no mistaking the lanky figure making its way to the main stairs and Quinn called his name out softly. Jack spun around with a stifled curse.

'Oh, it's only you!' he said, when Quinn came closer. 'You gave me the dickens of a fright.'

'Where have you been?'

He could see the gleam of Jack's smile in the gloom. 'The fair Stella, of course. I knew the performance would be over and couldn't resist popping out to see her. Can't let my godmother know, though. She would not approve.'

'I thought you were upstairs with that maid.'

'Moll?' Jack gave a soft laugh. 'She's a desperate flirt but my godfather's goods, you know. He's a generous fellow, but it don't go as far as sharing his maids. What made you think that anyway?'

For a second Quinn was tempted to tell him Guinevere's astonishing story but Jack, though well-meaning, might let something slip, landing her into new trouble.

'Heard a door open after we'd turned in. Assumed it was you, especially after the looks that maid – Moll? – was shooting you during dinner. Then I couldn't sleep. I've just been down to the kitchen for water.' It was a lame excuse for being in the hallway but Jack seemed not to notice.

'Probably was me slipping out, though it may well have been Uncle John, too. Don't be startled to see him padding around. He's a regular visitor of the upstairs.'

'And you sent Moll here, knowing that?'

Hearing the censure in his friend's voice, Jack shot him a look. 'It was the only solution I could think of on the spot. She was having the life beaten out of her in Hokitika. You can trust me that my godfather will treat her better than that. Ask her, if you like, and see where she is happier.'

Quinn remembered Sir John's comments about Gwen over the port. 'Is he likely to try something with that new maid?'

'Perhaps, I don't know. It's just something he does. My mother would warn our own maids to lock their doors when the old rogue used to come to visit.'

'What does Lady Whittering think of all this?'

'Lord knows. It's not something we speak of much – it's really not a big issue.' Jack gave an enormous yawn. 'Bed beckons. I'm completely worn out. Come on, let's see if we can make it back to our rooms without bumping into anyone else.'

CHAPTER 11

Over the following few weeks Guinevere, Quinn and Ben all adjusted to their new situations. For Ben the transition was easiest. He ate his meals in the kitchen where Moll and Gwen looked after him well; teasing him and feeding him up. During the day he worked in the gardens and stables. Quinn was happy for the boy to work for his keep for the moment, but he was determined to have Ben educated as soon as he could establish some sort of home for him.

Quinn was not finding it easy to be a – what? He simply did not know how to refer to the situation between himself and Ben. Clearly he was not the boy's father, but the term *guardian* sounded alarmingly formal. Having resolved not to become bogged down in untidy relationships, he had taken on a responsibility that could stay with him for a good few years to come. Not that he regretted buying Ben, but he was struck by his unsuitability to provide the boy with what he needed; namely a home and a family.

The worry of Ben's immediate future preyed on Quinn's mind as he and Jack made preparations to go into the gold fields of Otago. He liked the notion of leaving the boy with a kind family in Christchurch instead of dragging him through the mining tent cities, but had no idea how to go about finding one.

The best idea he could come up with was to buy a house and offer tenants free rent in exchange for looking after the boy, so Quinn began searching the town for a suitable cottage to buy. This was not easy as his wallet was becoming quickly depleted with the buying of supplies. It was not easy, either, to find the time, for their business preparations took most of their days and the evenings were filled with entertainments of various sorts.

The Whitterings were pleased to see the steadying influence Quinn seemed to have over their giddy godson and Lord Whittering introduced Jack and his partner to all the leading businessmen and estate owners in the area.

Lady Whittering, in the meantime, had her own brief. Jack's mother, her oldest, dearest friend, had implored her to find her son a suitable wife, one who might curb his libertine tendencies. Thus Lady Whittering was determined, while Jack remained under her roof, to acquaint him with every eligible girl in Christchurch. If abominable rumours were to be believed, he was already acquainted with the ineligible sorts! Her job was made considerably easier once word got around that she had not just one, but two very handsome, charming young men and invitations to social events quickly began amassing. If she found a wife for Quinn at the same time, so much the better.

Within a few days, Lady Whittering had conceived a fondness for the Irishman. He may have come from an impoverished background, but his education had been sound and what he lacked in polish was more than compensated for by a strong intellect, inherent good manners and a vast deal of common sense. She admired his quiet strength and composure, the hard-won rewards of a clearly arduous life. Though Quinn would not be drawn on his years in the American army, her father had fought in the Peninsular wars and her brothers in India, so she was adept at reading the pain and horror behind the silences. And though he might laugh and shake his head at Jack's colourful accounts of icy rivers, leaking tents, voracious sandflies, dwindling supplies and drenching rain, Lady Whittering was more inclined to accept Jack's tales than Quinn's denials. He deserved to have a wife who would provide him with all the comforts of a happy home and good connections.

As a result, despite his initial qualms, Quinn found adjusting to life as a gentleman easier than expected and very enjoyable, as he and Jack became quickly caught up in all the main social engagements of the town. The men accepted him readily for his shrewd good sense, while the women were divided into those who believed his slow, lopsided smile was his most charming asset and those who thought his soft Irish tones the more beguiling.

Indeed, his reception was so warm he began to forget that he hated the English and all they stood for. Perhaps what surprised him most, however, was how quickly this grand house began to feel like a home, the routines of family life more seducing than any of the fine furnishings. It was the inconsequential chatter over the breakfast table, the communal perusal of newspapers over a pot of tea in the afternoon, the late night billiards that he most enjoyed.

In fact, if it hadn't been for the constant presence of Gwen, he could have enjoyed this idyll with contentment. But, as he'd discovered before, when Gwen was around, she was impossible to ignore.

He steeled himself to cope with having her serve at mealtimes. This did have some advantages. At the first large dinner party thrown for their amusement, Quinn was reaching for one of a dizzying number of forks when Gwen, serving Lord Whittering, widened her eyes at him. His fingers hovered and very slightly he indicated to the fork beside. She gave the merest nod and he smoothly picked it up, grateful to avert social embarrassment. However, when she stood aside on the stairs or in the passages, he felt wrong-footed, and when she curtsied in response to Lady Whittering's commands, it was he who flushed. As for the thought of her doing his laundry – especially his undergarments – it caused him agonies of mortification.

One morning he returned to his bedroom to find her knelt on a sheet which was covered in soot, sweeping out his grate. He closed the door and advanced into the room.

'What the devil are you doing?' he hissed.

She rocked back on her heels, brushed the hair out of her eyes with the back of her hand and looked mischievously up at him. 'Please, sir, I was sent to clean the grate.'

Her damned maid's cap was askew. Flakes of ash clung to her apron, she had a smut on her cheek and looked, he thought inappropriately, utterly adorable. At that moment Quinn suddenly understood how it could be that masters might forget themselves so much with their maids. This unlooked-for discovery added fuel to his already intense discomfiture.

'But you can't . . . you shouldn't—'

'It's my job. It's fine.'

It wasn't fine. It wasn't fine at all. He did not know which was worse, to see her hands once so white and soft now so blackened, or the lamentable job she was doing. It was patently obvious she had not swept many fireplaces out.

'You're making an appalling mess.'

Awkwardness made him sound more censorious than he'd meant to.

Gwen, however, did not take offence. She looked about her and nodded.

'I know. Who would have thought how hard it could be. Moll and Mrs Williams even shake their heads over the way I mop. Mrs Williams said she's never seen anything so clumsy.' She shrugged philosophically. 'Still, practice will make perfect.'

'Practice be damned!' He spoke without thinking, then flushed and added with a rueful grin. 'Apologies, m'lady. I just hate to see the way you—'

'—are making a mess, I know,' she said, swiftly deflecting any sympathy. 'What are you doing here, anyway? I thought you were going into town.'

'I am. I've just popped up to get my hat.'

With this reminder he crossed the room to collect the item from the top of the wardrobe. When he turned around, he saw Gwen was looking at him.

'You look very smart.'

Her approval was strangely heartening for he still felt to be in a masquerade when dressed up in fine trousers, waistcoat and jacket, necktie knotted loosely at his throat. He retorted with false severity, 'I wish I could say the same about you.'

This made her smile. 'Oh, ungenerous!' She brandished her brush. 'Be off with you now before I remove lint from your sleeve.'

He laughed and went to the door but when his hand was on the handle, he turned.

'You know, I—'

'I know.' Once again she stopped his words. 'But don't worry about it.' She gave a twisted smile. 'Believe me, I never gave my maids much thought. Now go – don't keep the Whitterings waiting.'

He left without another word, but as he ran down the stairs the image of her looking mischievously up at him remained and he found his thoughts returning to her throughout the day, despite the gaieties around him.

That evening, he surprised his hosts greatly by asking not to have a fire in his room any more, explaining that after so many years in tents, he found it a trifle too warm.

Life for Gwen was, of course, very different. She belonged nowhere. Downstairs she was both too grand and too ignorant to fit in properly with the other servants, while upstairs, much of the time she might just as well have been invisible. Only Quinn ever seemed to be aware of her whenever she was in the room.

Lowering as it was, she could not help but feel she was learning far more about human nature than she ever had when a lady. For instance, Lord Whittering would pinch her chin if he found her alone in his library and call her a pretty little puss – although, in fairness, she had to admit he might well have done so even if he'd been staying at Maidenhurst. He had such an unabashed, indulgent air about him.

Lady Whittering must surely have guessed she was not the usual run of maid but if she did, she was clearly not willing to involve herself. She made no mention of it nor acknowledged Gwen in any way. Her requests were always issued crisply and imperiously.

Jack smiled but did not really see her, while guests to the house looked right through her as they handed over hats, gloves, capes and umbrellas on their arrival. Mostly she took no umbrage, only too aware of how little thought was spared to servants in general.

At one party, however, she felt the full force of humiliation any servant could have inflicted on them. Lady Whittering had invited a great many people – generally families with young, pretty daughters – so it was a bit of a crush but a cheerful one. Champagne flowed and the reception rooms hummed with conversation and laughter.

Gwen had been on her feet since dawn with all the preparations and now circulated the groups with trays of glasses and canapés. She could not help but notice how many young women gravitated towards Quinn, who was looking particularly striking; his dark evening dress sitting well on his broad shoulders, and giving elegance to his long, lean frame. One in particular, a Miss Smythe – admittedly a pretty girl, if you admired such obvious looks – seemed particularly taken with him. She laughed far too often and forgot herself so much as to touch his arm not once, but on several occasions causing Gwen to go quite stiff at this lapse in etiquette. The fact that Quinn seemed comfortable with this forwardness only showed what a naive fool he was, an easy target on the marriage mart and she made a mental note to warn him of preying women.

Gwen was just threading through guests with a particularly full tray of champagne flutes when Miss Smythe took an unexpected step backwards into her, upending the whole tray onto the floor with a fearful clatter. The chatter stopped instantly and everyone turned around just as Miss Smythe cried, 'You *foolish* girl! You were not paying attention at all.'

Stung by the injustice, Gwen replied, 'You stepped into me.'

Miss Smythe went rigid. 'What insolence!'

No doubt she would have gone on to say a lot more on the matter, but Lady Whittering stepped in, making all the right noises while directing Gwen, in a furious undertone, to clean up the mess immediately.

Quinn had watched it all, appalled. He made a move forward as though to help but Gwen checked him with a look. She was lucky, she knew, that she had not been dismissed – not for the glasses, but for her insubordination.

Clearing up the broken glassware, mopping up the champagne, aware of all the sideways or averted looks, had been a good lesson in mortification. Only her fury at hearing Miss Smythe telling everyone for the next half hour that she'd never encountered such a clumsy and ill-mannered maid kept Gwen's head high, her back straight.

Her one satisfaction was that she did not see Quinn speak again to Miss Smythe that night.

But despite all that she was learning, the days

seemed endless and she could not believe how hard the staff worked, even in this benign household. The Whitterings were not exacting but they did like to maintain standards, which Mrs Williams was excellent at ensuring. She continued to hold Gwen in deep suspicion and despairingly Gwen turned to Quinn for advice.

Despite his many engagements and her long working hours, it had become a regular occurrence for him to steal up to her attic late at night once the household was asleep. The bond they'd forged in Hokitika deepened as they shared the strangeness of their reversed roles, each helping the other in their new lives.

'How on earth can I win her over?' Guinevere was in bed, legs tucked under the covers for warmth while Quinn sat, as always, propped against the wall across the foot of her bed. Gwen found it strange that having had Quinn visit her every day in Hokitika when she wore nothing more than a nightdress, she now felt shy. With their changes in circumstances it now seemed somehow clandestine to receive her visitor thus clad. However, she could not bear the thought of greeting him in her maid's apparel and it would have been ridiculous to change into one of her few dresses. She compromised by wrapping a shawl about her shoulders for modesty's sake, but some nights it felt a thin defence against Quinn's maleness – not that there was the slightest hint that such a defence was needed. Which was just as well, she assured herself.

Now she leant forward to rest her forearms on her legs, her loosened hair billowing around her and he smiled.

'That's easy. She's a woman isn't she? Compliments.'

Gwen was surprised. 'What sort? Her hair, her dresses?'

'No, your ladyship. Her skills. She must do something – ragwork, perhaps?'

'Is that those awful rugs she makes out of scraps of material?'

'That'll be it.'

'I don't know what I can possibly find nice to say about them,' said Gwen doubtfully, 'and I'm a dreadful liar. Then she'll rightly pick me as toadying her.'

'Well, there must be other things she takes pride in,' he said. 'What does she nag you about?'

'Polishing the oak table!' Gwen kicked out and connected with Quinn's hipbone. 'Sorry. I just hate the thing.'

He patted the lump her feet made under the bedclothes.

'Learn to love it – it's your way to her heart. I'll bet she makes her own polish and won't tell anyone the ingredients.'

Gwen was impressed. 'How did you know?'

'All housekeepers hold the secrets of their trade very close to their heart. Say you've never used polish as fine as this one.'

'I've never used any other polish.'

'Then it won't be a lie.'

Changing the subject, he said, 'You did well tonight, m'lady, in restraining yourself over the dessert course.'

'You saw that?'

'I'm amazed no one else noticed. The look you sent Sir John was positively searing.'

Gwen laughed and blushed. 'I couldn't help it. When I heard him talking about the tin miners, it took all my self-control from leaping right into the conversation.'

Quinn was amused. 'And what, may I ask, do you know about mining?'

'Well, nothing until a few nights ago,' she admitted, 'but Robert – you know, the groom – is from Cornwall and he told us about his appalling childhood over dinner in the servants' hall. His family had other miners staying with them so there were twelve – and sometimes more – sleeping in a two-roomed cottage. He began working at the age of *seven*, and when he talked about the mines themselves – well!' She broke off and shuddered. 'So when I heard Sir John going on about the troubles his friend was having with his miners and knowing that these owners live in magnificent estates – Robert's told me all about them – I had to bite my tongue to stop myself from telling Sir John a few facts.'

Quinn looked curiously at her. 'I thought you'd be bored by talk at the servants' table.'

'To be honest, I was braced for tedium but you

know, I've learnt an amazing amount these past few weeks. I'd always considered myself to be well-educated, but there's so much I don't know – and not just about how to polish tables either. There's all the stuff Moll knows about growing vegetables and working in cotton mills. That's why she's here in New Zealand, to escape the mills. Her best friend's hair got caught in one of the machines and—' Gwen stopped, unable to continue with that particularly tragic story. She had never known such misery existed.

'Anyway,' she added, looking sideways at Quinn, 'it's been humbling to discover just how much I don't know.'

He smiled and nodded. 'It's been an education for me too.'

'Really? But you've lived so widely already. So much of what I'm learning you already knew. When I remember telling you off about the dignity of work—' she broke off and they both laughed. 'I think about that now when I'm dealing with slops and dirty hearths! So what are you learning?'

He hesitated, looking rueful. 'I'm learning just how easy it is to slip into being a gentleman and become accustomed to it. When I was at dinner at the Buckinghams the other night, I caught myself thinking the vegetables were a trifle overcooked. Me! The number of nights I've lain sleepless because of hunger, to suddenly turn fastidious, it gave me quite a shock.'

Again he and Gwen laughed companionably.

Then Quinn became serious. 'Worse. 'Twas only at the end of the evening that I realised I hadn't noticed the service once.'

'That just means the servants were doing their job well.'

'Maybe,' Quinn replied, 'but it's also a sign that I'm getting as short-sighted as all those I've derided these many years. 'Tis easier than I thought to make people invisible.'

'It's easier than I thought to become invisible,' she replied.

'Lady Guinevere, you will *never* be invisible.'

He spoke with certainty, his eyes meeting hers and for a moment something deeper than friendship lay between them. There was a look in the Irishman's eyes that made Gwen catch her breath and to cover the moment she said lightly, dropping her gaze, 'Well, thank you for telling me about the polish. I'll try that tomorrow.'

Gwen discovered that it was good advice, but the gradual easing of Mrs Williams bridling manner was also due to Gwen's willingness to work hard and her lack of superiority despite her ladylike ways.

Although Gwen never complained, she was exhausted at the end of each long day, and with sore muscles from polishing and scrubbing and carrying heavy loads of firewood and linen up and down the stairs. She had never understood the amount of work even a small family and a couple of guests entailed and felt humbled now to remember her myriad of careless commands, however smilingly issued. Her father, philanthropist as he was, had never really been aware of the plight of servants and now that she was intimately and achingly familiar with their lives, she wondered how she would ever adjust back to ordering them about at Maidenhurst.

She began to understand Quinn better too – his fierce defensiveness at the mere hint of condescension, his disapproval of the aristocratic class in general. He had spent his life under society's heel while she had only learnt of its full, humiliating weight over the past few months. She knew now why so many were desperate to seek gold or were driven to drink, to prostitution. Once down, it seemed almost impossible to ever rise. And yet Quinn, despite the odds, had succeeded thanks to his intelligence, his energy and his sheer Irish stubbornness in refusing ever to give up.

So Guinevere, too, fought on day after day, driven as much by a determination to keep up with the robust Moll as by the need to keep her employment, but at the end of the third week there was no soft, 'Come in,' when Quinn scratched on her door.

Peeping into her room, he saw that though the candle burned in readiness for his visit, Gwen was fast asleep, one arm trailing over the side of the bed. He tucked it under the blanket and she barely stirred. For a minute he stood looking down and then, feeling like a thief, he leaned forward to inhale her scent; pure and clean. His stomach clenched and for a moment he stayed there, eyes closed, allowing the riot of forbidden images to rampage, both easing and exacerbating his ache. Then, very softly, he brushed his lips against her hair before extinguishing the candle and slipping away.

The following morning, Gwen was scrubbing potatoes in the kitchen when through the window she saw Quinn returning from the stables. He had a loose-limbed way of moving and she paused in her work to watch him stride through the backyard. Perhaps he would pass through the kitchen, as he and Jack sometimes did, to beg a snack from Mrs Williams who, despite her formidable manner, seemed incapable of withstanding their smiles.

To Gwen's surprise, however, she saw Quinn suddenly stop by the outhouse door just as Moll was emerging with a hefty basket of washing. She leaned over the sink to see better as Quinn stepped up close to the maid and bent to speak into Moll's ear in a strangely intimate manner. Gwen frowned as she saw Moll fall back a pace. There was a little more discussion, their conversation both earnest and confidential judging by the way they looked around several times to check no one was watching.

The exchange ended with Quinn taking the basket from Moll and carrying it for her to the line strung up across the corner of the yard.

Whatever their discussion had been about, Moll had lost her first defensive stance and was now giggling and looking up at him in her most flirtatious manner.

Suddenly, Gwen experienced a kick of a quite unknown emotion; one that she did not like at all and for a second her fingers curled tight about the potato in her hand, fingernails biting into the brown skin. Though the day was warm, she felt strangely cold and there was a tightness in her throat that had not been there a minute earlier.

Moll, of all people! Well, men were like that, she thought as she resumed scrubbing with considerably more vigour, and why she might think Quinn would be any different from all the rest she really couldn't say. After all, a miner and a maid – what could be more fitting? And she gave a scornful laugh. Perhaps, on finding her asleep last night, Quinn had decided to visit Moll instead.

With a stab of the paring knife, Gwen gouged out an eye from the potato and tossed the offending vegetable into the pot with a splash. Not that it was any of her business what he chose to get up to.

Unfortunately for Gwen, Moll seemed determined to make it her business. She came in from the yard, positively glowing.

''E's ever so nice, that Mr O'Donnell,' she said with a happy sigh. 'A proper gentleman, that's what.'

Moll insisted on serving him at the midday meal

and when shoes were to be polished for dinner, she singled his out for an extra shine.

Gwen ignored this silly infatuation but in the early evening, as she came out from the library where she'd just lit the first fire, she saw Quinn halfway up the stairs taking from Moll the basket of wood that she was carrying up to the bedrooms. The maid giggled and, though she couldn't hear the actual words, Gwen could hear him teasingly scold her in a low voice.

Really, Gwen thought with a toss of her head, she hadn't thought he'd betray his common roots quite so blatantly.

That night when Quinn stole up to her room, Gwen was, as usual, in bed for warmth but she was not asleep this time. In fact, she was sitting bolt upright, her shawl pulled tight about her shoulders.

'Oh, I was not sure if you would come tonight,' she said offhandedly.

Quinn paused and looked warily from the set of her chin to her legs which stretched the length of the bed. Usually she curled up to make room for him. Forced to stand, he was reminded suddenly of being a flunkey and his eyes narrowed.

'And why should I not come tonight?' he asked. 'Am I not welcome? There was something in the way you slammed my plate down at dinner that made me think you were perhaps angry with me.'

She gave a dismissive laugh. 'Angry? I?'

'Angry, you!'

'What on earth would I be angry about?'

'That's the exact same question I'm asking myself.'

'Let me make it quite clear to you, Mr O'Donnell—'

'Oho! Mr O'Donnell again, am I?'

'Let me make it clear,' continued Guinevere grandly, holding up one finger to silence him, 'that what you do is of no consequence to me whatsoever. Is that understood?'

'It is,' he said, still wary.

'And just because we have had associations in the past,' this was a speech she'd rehearsed the whole afternoon while beating bed-sheets into submission with flat irons, 'that does not mean that any present cavorting you may choose to indulge in will have any bearing on our current relations. It is none of my business – nor interest I might add – what you choose to get up to, but I must warn you that such behaviour is not befitting of a gentleman. It is extremely unmannerly to conduct yourself in such a way under your host's roof.'

He blinked. 'Cavorting, is it? May I be so presumptuous, m'lady, to ask whom it is that I'm cavorting with?'

Again Gwen gave a brittle laugh and pulled the shawl even tighter about her shoulders. She flicked her hair back and shot him a disdainful glance.

'Oh, come, don't play the innocent with me. It's

been as plain as a pikestaff all day. You must be careful though. What you see as a dalliance, Moll might well interpret as something far more serious.'

'Moll?' Quinn echoed, astonished, and to Guinevere's fury, she saw a smile creep into his eyes. Abandoning his wary stance he sat down on her bed, squashing one of her legs and causing her to wriggle crossly to get free of him.

Turning his head sideways to survey her, he asked, 'Did you perhaps see me today giving young Moll a helping hand?'

'It's nothing to me, you understand, but Lady Whittering might find it strange to see her guest tripping over himself to oblige a housemaid.'

'Gwen, have you noticed that Moll is a little – round, shall we say?'

'She is what I believe you miners describe as "a comfortable armful",' she said, snipping each word.

'Lady Guinevere!' Quinn feigned shock. 'Now where would a well-bred young woman pick up such a cant expression?'

'Don't mock me.' Gwen swung a fist but he laughed and caught it, bearing it down onto the blanket where he held it prisoner in a loose but strong grasp.

Looking at her squarely, he said, 'Moll is increasing and she should not be carrying heavy loads.'

'What?' Gwen stared at him and then realisation dawned. 'Oh, heavens, do you mean she's . . .?'

'She'll be having a baby some months from now.'

Gwen pulled her fist free of his grasp and covered her face with her hands. 'Oh, I feel such a fool,' she moaned. 'I never even thought. How on earth did you know?'

'I knew it when I first saw her. There's a way a woman who is bearing carries herself. Not easy to explain.' He shrugged then he glanced at her sideways, a smile curling one corner of his mouth. 'But I appreciate the warnings to stay away from maids for my hosts' sake. 'Tis hard indeed being a gentleman and I'm grateful to have your guidance in these matters. Would it be best perhaps if I should go?'

'If you think for one minute that I will let you hold me hostage to my own words, you annoying man . . .'

Gwen let the threat hover but the suppressed fury that had been in her face had died away and now the golden lights in her eyes softened and became thoughtful. 'Poor Moll,' she said, returning to the main issue. 'Who is the father? Do you know? Will she marry him?'

Quinn watched the moods chase across her face. What an infuriating woman but still the thought that she might have been jealous – well, it gave him a little glow about the heart.

She leaned forward now, eyes fixed on his face. 'Well, do you know who the father is?'

He hesitated. 'I do, but there'll be no marriage. 'Tis Sir John's.'

'Sir John?' Guinevere was incredulous. 'Impossible. Why he's old and besides he's, he's—'

'He's a gentleman, if that is what you are trying to say. Guinevere, he's not so old that he cannot father children, you know. And as for his being a gentleman – well, there's many as finds their entertainment in different places.'

'But that is . . .' Gwen could not finish her sentence but revulsion was writ clear across her features.

Quinn wondered if it was the coupling of different classes that disgusted her so, or the age difference. He wasn't sure he wanted to know the answer.

'Does Lady Whittering know? What will become of Moll?'

Quinn shrugged. 'I don't know the answer to any of those questions. I never asked, Gwen. My interest was purely professional. Moll's begun to get a lot of colour in her cheeks and I was just warning her not to over-exert herself. Nothing more.'

He could see that Gwen was still concerned but there was nothing to be done about the situation, so to turn the subject he said, 'Now, I have need of your advice, your ladyship. Jack and I have been invited to a ball and I've never been to one save a few military affairs and I suspect they were rather different. What do I need to do to comport myself as a fine gentleman?'

With a conscious effort, Gwen shook off her thoughts and entered the spirit of the moment. 'Can you dance?'

'I can – with two left feet.'

This made her smile. 'Don't waltz then,' she advised. 'In fact, given the great many men in this town, your lack of participation on the dance floor might be appreciated. Make yourself charming over the dinner table, take a turn with a cigar outdoors, play a hand or two of cards and everyone will proclaim you a very fine fellow indeed. You will have a wonderful time.' She could not quite keep the wistful note creeping into her voice.

Without being conscious of it Quinn patted her hand. 'I feel like Cinderella's ugly sister going to the ball, leaving you home among the cinders. 'Tis not right.'

Gwen laughed. 'Oh, I'm not such a sad case as Cinderella. I always thought her a spiritless creature, drooping around the house, waiting for a fairy godmother to rescue her.'

'Rescue instead from a Prince Charming?'

'Of course not! I told you, I'm immune to love. No, Cinderella needed to pull herself together and do something positive, instead of sitting around feeling sorry for herself.'

Quinn shook his head. 'Oh, m'lady. Are you being quite honest with yourself? Is there not a secret part of you hoping to be rescued from this attic? I confess I'd like to get you away from this place myself.'

'Gracious, no. Don't talk like that. I'm not going to tempt fate. I know now how life can be beyond these walls and I've no desire to go back to the fear of wondering where the next meal and bed will come from. Do you realise it's been three weeks now and I still haven't been sacked. It's a miracle. I've finally found a job that I can do. I'm the paragon of a docile maid. And I haven't told you yet of all the wonderful ideas I've had for a photographic series based around the kitchen. You should have seen Mrs Williams's face this morning when I told her I'd love to photograph her rolling out pastry.'

Quinn smiled at her bantering tone and held his tongue. He knew she would hate it if he told her how much he loathed seeing her at the beck and call of masters – even nice ones. He hated to see her abundant hair tied so severely back, to watch her struggle to maintain impassive control of her expressive features as she served the meals. It was extraordinary that she appeared invisible to everyone save himself. Her qualities were so glaringly obvious but even Jack, with as roving an eye as any young man, seemed to see no more than a maid.

As it transpired they were both proved wrong the very next night: Gwen was neither so invisible nor so docile.

The servants were just clearing up the kitchen, getting ready to turn in when a whistle came down the speaking tube, a device of which Sir John was very proud. Gwen found the ability of her employers to literally whistle up a servant extremely annoying.

It was even more annoying to think how conven-
ient it would be to have one installed in Maidenhurst.
Now Sir John's voice floated ghostly down the
tube, requesting Gwen to bring up some hot milk
to his bed chamber.

'Did he say Gwen?' asked Moll.

'That's right,' said Mrs Williams, already filling
a pot with milk from the safe, in a tone that forbade
further comment.

Gwen did not notice Moll exchange looks with
Robert who was in the kitchen getting a late cup
of tea and saw nothing strange in the request as
she set the tray quickly with fine chinaware.

When she left the kitchen, Moll muttered with
a shrug to Robert, 'I'll be glad to 'ave a few nights
off, I will. 'E's been a right old goat lately. Don't
know how 'e'll go with Miss 'Igh an' Mighty,
though.'

Moll was not left wondering for long. Within
minutes the quiet of the household was shaken by
the sound of a ringing slap, breaking china and a
cry of pain from the master of the house. Quinn,
Jack and Lady Whittering – who was wearing an
enormous nightcap – raced to his chamber from
their different bedrooms in time to hear the maid
hiss, 'How *dare* you try that sort of thing with me,
sir. I am *not* some maid to be mauled at your
pleasure.'

A scene of devastation confronted them. Sir
John, looking sheepish and surrounded by broken
china, was shaking his hand, which appeared to

226

have been burnt by the hot milk. His cheek had a suspiciously red mark. The maid was standing defiantly; head high, fists clenched at her side.

'Well!' said Lady Whittering, taking the scene in at a glance. 'Gwen, you may pack your bags immediately.'

Her husband began to expostulate and Jack and Quinn added their protests, but she silenced them all with a lift from her hand. 'We cannot have the servants getting above themselves,' she said. 'Where would it end if we did? I'm sorry, my girl, but you must see you cannot stay.'

Strangely it seemed that Gwen was the only one who did. She nodded slowly at Lady Whittering who maintained her dignity despite the fearsome nightcap.

Quinn made a move towards Gwen but she froze him with a look. This was her battle. With stately deliberation she stepped over the broken china and swept from the chamber.

Once inside the sanctity of her small room, however, her precarious control deserted her. For a second she sank onto her bed. It seemed strangely hard to think, even to breathe. What had she done? Where on earth could she go at this late hour? The night seemed very black outside her uncurtained window and an icy wind beat against the panes.

But even as panic washed over her in nauseating waves, she was already gathering her wits, drawing on the courage and pride of her ancestors to give her strength. She could not, would not, succumb to these fears right now. First she must get away from this place. Not for all the money in the world would she stay in the house where she had been disgraced.

Rising from her bed, Gwen began to pack her meagre belongings but her shaking hands slowed her and her thoughts were still in turmoil. Just last night she had joked about this, her worst nightmare. Heavens, it had only been a kiss. Why had she made such a fuss? She should have maintained her dignity. But at the thought of him pawing her, using her as he had used Moll, the gorge rose in her throat. She, Lady Guinevere Stanhope, would never submit to such treatment. But at what cost? She groaned as she threw the last of her things into her holdall and looked around.

It was just a bare room but it had felt safe and she had enjoyed happy hours here – thanks to Quinn. She could never face him again now, not after he'd witnessed her humiliation. Tears rose in her eyes. Stupid! Stupid! It was just a kiss. This was exactly why the Molls of the world accepted their masters' advances.

A soft knock cut across these thoughts and too shocked still to even to wonder at it, Gwen opened the door to find Quinn standing there.

'Are you ready?' he asked. She found it hard to follow what he asked, simple as his words were.

'Yes.'

'Good. Jack says he has a friend who will put you up for the night.'

Gwen opened her mouth to protest but Quinn overrode her. 'Oh, I know, you'll be talking clap-trap about doing this alone, not needing anyone et cetera, et cetera, but we don't have time for that now. Jack's downstairs and waiting. For once in your life, Lady Guinevere, don't argue.'

Gwen closed her mouth and turned to pick up her bag but Quinn was ahead of her.

'I'll take that, you get your camera. I know you'll not let anyone but yourself carry it. Come on.'

She allowed herself to be led down the back stairs and through the deserted hall to where Jack was waiting outside the front door, holding the bridles of two horses. The late autumn night was cold and she shivered.

'I should say goodbye to the other servants,' she said. 'They were kind to me.'

'I'll say it for you,' Quinn promised. 'Best get you out of the house soon as possible. Jack, may I introduce you to Guinevere Stanhope.'

Jack grinned. 'Pleased to make your acquaintance, Lady Guinevere.'

She shot him a startled look.

'Quinn's been filling me in on some of the details – an extraordinary story, if you don't mind me saying. I'm taking you to meet my Stella. I've a feeling you two might just hit it off.'

While Jack was talking, Quinn had secured her belongings to one horse before mounting the second and reaching a hand down to Guinevere. 'We are using our own horses – it didn't seem tactful to use one of Sir John's. I hope you don't mind riding pillion.'

Jack helped Guinevere mount behind Quinn, then leapt into his own saddle and they set off down the long, dark driveway to the gates beyond. The city was some miles away and as Guinevere put her arms around Quinn and felt his supple strength, his body was suddenly a familiar haven to which she could cling. She did not trust her voice so remained silent and the two men, sensing her anguish, remained tactfully quiet. Over and over again, she replayed the scene in her mind, castigating herself for her stupidity.

She had in fact repulsed Sir John's first move, but he hadn't believed her and had pressed again. That was when she'd seen red and hit him as hard as she could. The force of the blow had given him such a fright that he'd jumped, knocking over the tray. She should have dealt with the situation rationally. What would she do? No job, only a small amount of savings. No one would ever employ her now. What a fool she had been.

Gwen leaned her cheek against the broad shoulders and, without realising it, tightened her hold around Quinn's waist. A large, warm hand came up to hold her fingers in a reassuring grip and a lump rose in her throat. Had she really said she wasn't looking for a Prince Charming to save her? Where would she be right now without this Irishman? She seemed to ricochet from one desperate situation to another and she knew now how desolate it was when Quinn was not around to help her. This back had already carried her to safety once and she rubbed her cheek against the rough cloth of his jacket, feeling briefly comforted.

They wound their way along a dirt track that widened into a road of sorts, which brought them eventually to the outskirts of Christchurch and they rode down the main street into the town itself.

The gaslit street was busy; thronged with diggers lurching from bar to bar, carriages carrying the well-to-do back to their homes, pickpockets lurking in the shadows and women in tattered dresses barely noticeable in dark corners.

Jack led them to the newly completed theatre and gave a grunt of satisfaction to see people pouring out of it, chattering excitedly. 'Perfect timing. Come on.'

They dismounted and Jack flipped a coin to an urchin standing in the shadows of the stage door. 'Take them to Gerry's,' he said to the boy, and it was clearly a well-established routine for the boy led the horses away without a murmur.

Jack took them through the door and down a narrow corridor into which heavily made up people in strange costumes seemed to overflow from small dressing rooms.

'Here she is, the star of the show.'

Jack threw open a door to a tiny room which was packed with people all saying, 'Glorious, darling Stella! Simply magnificent!'

When Gwen saw Stella, she blinked. The actress

really was magnificent; a tall woman with a mane of red curls tumbling down her Junoesque back. She had high cheekbones and the greenest eyes Gwen had ever seen.

'Stella,' said Jack, 'this is my business partner and friend, Quinn O'Donnell, and his friend, Guinevere Stanhope, who is in a spot of bother. I said she could stay with you.'

Stella looked at them with those glorious eyes and her voice poured over Guinevere in sympathetic, thrilling tones.

'Bother? Oh my dear, we've *all* been there. Of course you can stay with me.'

CHAPTER 12

Guinevere was woken early the next morning by a pressing call from nature. She lay on the narrow sofa on which she had spent the night and looked around the small room in hopes of spying a chamber pot, but there was none to be seen. The mound of blankets on the bed never stirred; clearly Stella was still fast asleep.

Gwen smiled as she remembered Stella's warmth in taking her in even though, as she explained, they had to be absolutely silent or her landlady would simply *murder* Stella for bringing a guest into her room. They had stolen up the stairs and had had to stifle almost hysterical giggles when Gwen stood on the hem of Stella's gown, nearly pulling the actress back on top of her.

Now Gwen sighed. There was nothing for it; she had to slip down the stairs to the privy at the bottom of the garden. It was still early judging from the chilly air and soft light, so with luck the landlady might still be asleep.

Silent as a ghost, Gwen slipped down the stairs. Thankfully there was nobody about. She unbolted the back door and hurried down the path through the overgrown garden, congratulating herself on her luck.

Unfortunately it did not hold for her return journey. Just as she was about to sneak back up the stairs a fierce voice behind her demanded, 'And who might you be?'

Spinning around, Gwen saw a large woman standing behind her, strong arms braced on broad hips. Caught off guard, she faltered. Who indeed? Lady Guinevere, Guinevere, Gwen?

'I'm Guinevere Stanhope.'

'And wot are you doin' in my house?'

Gwen did not know how to answer, unwilling to get Stella into trouble, unable to think of a plausible excuse. She was saved by a second voice, this one rich and low, floating down the stairs.

'Guinevere is a friend of mine, Mrs Staines.'

Stella stood on the landing looking stunning in a jade silk robe pulled over her nightdress, her hair flaming about her face. Gwen was slightly dazzled but Mrs Staines remained unimpressed.

'I told you you wasn't allowed no visitors.'

'It's my fault entirely,' interpolated Guinevere. 'I was in a desperate situation and Stella was most generous—'

Mrs Staines snorted. 'Generous with my house, that's wot!'

'I will of course pay you for your hospitality,' Guinevere assured her.

'You will and all. Then you can both pack your bags and get out.'

'You can't throw Stella out.' Guinevere was appalled by the consequences of her actions, but the redoubtable landlady cut through her protests.

'I can and just have. I'm sick to death of her creeping in all hours of the day and night, bringing back all sorts of riff-raff.'

'For tea, nothing more,' Stella pointed out.

'Sez you, madam, but I know your sort, my girl. I wasn't born yesterday and I've got eyes in my head. I see wot's really going on.'

Stella's head came up, her extraordinary eyes flashing green fire and her voice throbbed with passion. 'Nothing, *nothing* would induce me to stay a minute longer in this abode. You, Mrs Staines, have a sordid commonplace mind and I refuse to hear any more. Come, Guinevere, let us make haste to leave this dreary little establishment.'

Turning on her heel, Stella made a dramatic exit from the top of the stairs and Gwen looked about her, half expecting to hear a standing ovation but there was only herself and the stoically unmoved landlady.

'Good riddance!' she yelled up the stairwell and then turning to Gwen she snapped, 'Go on then, hop it. I want you out in ten minutes.'

Filled with remorse, Gwen went up to Stella's room. 'Oh, Stella, it's all my fault. I am so sorry—' she began, then stopped somewhat surprised for the actress was humming as she dragged dresses from the wardrobe and crammed them into battered bags. All signs of wounded indignation, so eloquent seconds earlier, had vanished.

'Don't be silly,' Stella said, flashing her smile that could dazzle a theatre full of men. 'It's not the first time I've been given my marching orders and it certainly won't be the last. Actresses are not desirable lodgers, you know. We keep irregular hours and have irregular friends. Come on, get cracking. I told Jack that we'd meet them at the Canterbury Tea Rooms. We'll have breakfast there. I'm simply *famished*, aren't you?'

It was not easy packing all Stella's belongings into a variety of bags and holdalls but eventually they were down in the street, surrounded by a small sea of her worldly goods plus Gwen's holdall. Gwen wondered how they could carry them all but Stella cast a look up the street, then down. Three men were ambling away from them, amicably wrangling. Instantly Stella became a damsel in distress, calling out in a voice that trembled woefully but still had the force to carry down the road.

'Excuse me, gentlemen.'

The three turned around and spied Stella dressed in peacock blue with a quite outrageous hat that had Gwen secretly both scandalised and envious. Within seconds they were beside the two women and Gwen had to smother a smile for their willing exuberance reminded her forcibly of Cerberus. She half-expected them to loll their tongues and pant.

'Can we be of assistance, ma'am?'

'Oh, yes, indeed, if you wouldn't mind helping my friend and myself,' exclaimed Stella, hypnotising each one in turn. 'We need our bags taken to the Garrick Theatre and wondered if you could *possibly* . . .'

'Absolutely our pleasure, delighted to be of service,' she was immediately assured as the three men scrambled to secure the bags, hatboxes and collection of umbrellas and parasols. Stella smiled at them.

'Can you manage all of it alone? How *strong* you all are. We are forever in your debt. If you come to the theatre tonight, I'll ensure tickets are left at the door for you.'

'Yes, ma'am! Wouldn't miss one of your shows for the world!'

'I saw you last week,' stammered the youngest. 'You were splendid, Miss Tyler, splendid.'

'Why, thank you. You are too kind. Now we simply must *fly* or we will be late. Enjoy the concert tonight, gentlemen.'

The men chorused their goodbyes, trying to touch their hats but not let go of their slippery cargo and Gwen laughed to see them stagger down the road, hung about with feminine paraphernalia.

'Stella, you've bewitched the poor fellows. Can you always get men to do as you wish as easily as that?'

'Always,' she said with a smile. 'Isn't it handy?

Come on, the tea rooms are just around the corner.'

Jack and Quinn were already waiting for them and rose as the two women entered the small shop. There was a ripple of interest as the other customers saw Stella, but Gwen felt a secret glow of pleasure when Quinn only smiled courteously at the actress before turning his full attention to her. Pulling out a chair for Gwen, he murmured, 'M'lady.'

Gwen settled her skirts and smiled. 'How kind you are, sir, to be so mannerly to a maid.'

'No longer a maid, thank God. I didn't think I could have taken much more of that set-up. How was your accommodation last night?'

'Very comfortable but I feel terrible. Stella has lost her lodging on my account.'

Jack laughed. 'Again, Stella? Why that's at least three times since I've known you.'

Stella sighed and shrugged helplessly, her woe seemed to fill the shop. 'I know. What *can* be done? Destitute again.' Her musical laughter quite undid the effect, however, and the way she began plying jam on the scones the men had ordered suggested she had not a care in the world.

Gwen saw Jack throw Quinn a questioning glance and Quinn, smiling, gave a small nod.

Jack leaned forward. 'Well, it's of no consequence as Quinn's got a business proposition for you ladies.'

Suddenly wary, Gwen looked at Quinn.

'That's right,' he said. 'This morning I bought a cottage that I've had my eye on. I've been wanting to provide Ben with a home so that I won't be traipsing him all about the country-side when he should by rights be in school. I wondered if you ladies would do me the very big favour of looking after the lad in exchange for accommodation.'

'What a *wonderful* idea!' Stella said approvingly, just as Gwen exclaimed, 'Impossible!'

'Why is it impossible?' asked Jack.

'She'll be thinking it charity, or some such nonsense,' said Quinn.

'Well, perhaps not charity – but I could never accept your *kindness*, shall we say.'

'Oh, Lady Guinevere. Homeless, jobless and still so proud,' murmured Quinn, casting her a provo-cative look through narrowed grey eyes.

'I'm not proud!' said Gwen, stung. 'It's simply – oh, thank you.' She took the cup of tea that Stella had poured for her, the domestic act punc-turing her indignation.

'Nothing could be simpler!' said Jack, who was buttering a scone. 'We don't need the boy holding us back and you need a home. Two problems solved. Quinn has stalled our leaving these past few days because of young Ben.'

'Sure, it makes sense, Gwen. I'm serious when I say you'd be doing us the favour. We need to be making tracks fast before winter really sets in. I don't know what else to do with Ben. He's a good boy and won't be giving you any trouble, if that's what's worrying you.'

'No, not at all. You know that I'm very fond of Ben. It's just that I've never had the responsibility of a child before.'

'Me neither,' said Quinn. 'But I remember once being told that 'tis a person's duty to be helping others.'

'Wretch. You can't use my words against me like that. Your proposal simply won't work, can't you see?'

Throughout this exchange, Stella had worked her way through several scones and two cups of tea. Now replete, she took charge of the situation, seeing a stalemate looming with Guinevere looking determined, Jack impatient and Quinn frustrated.

'Guinevere, *darling*, you simply *have* to accept the offer. Did you not hear Quinn? *I'm* to be included in this bargain. You take the child and provide us with free accommodation and my money will pay for food. Besides,' she held up an admonishing finger at Gwen who was about to protest, 'you haven't considered the *fun* we shall have. I'm sick to death of landladies and you'll *adore* the people I bring home.'

'What's that?' asked Jack looking annoyed. 'Don't want too many visitors traipsing through the place you know, Stella. Not good for the boy,' he added.

'Why, Jack,' she said with a dangerous smile. 'I assure you no harm will come to the boy at all. Have you any other objections?'

240

'Just don't fancy a bunch of chums hanging about you,' he muttered.

'Ah, well,' she said brightly, 'that's what you get when you tangle with an actress. Men do tend to crowd around, you know, if they believe a woman does not have commitments elsewhere. And I don't, do I, Jack?'

'No,' he said, sullen. 'I s'pose not.'

'Just as I thought,' she said in the same bright tone but which now was sharp as a shard. Then her manner softened as she turned back to Gwen. 'Well, what do you say? I think we will deal excellently together.'

'Say yes,' urged Quinn.

'Do agree to it, Lady Guinevere. Stella here needs a chaperone.'

'Darling, you simply *must*! It is all your fault after all that I am homeless.'

'But you yourself said that you were glad,' Guinevere began indignantly, then saw Stella was laughing at her. She looked around the table and felt three pairs of eyes – green, blue and smoky grey – upon her.

'All right,' she cried, holding her hands up in surrender. 'I give up. I'd be happy to accept your offer to mind Ben, but hear this – I do not want to be sacked for at least one full month this time.'

''Tis not much to look at,' said Quinn as he walked with the two women around to their new home,

241

while Jack went to the theatre to collect their belongings. 'But I'll fix it up when I return. 'Twas the best I could do for the present.'

It proved to be not far from the theatre much to Stella's delight; one of a terrace of small, double-storeyed buildings each with a bow window beside the front door. Several in the row had been turned into shop frontages. The windows of the cottage were dingy and the paintwork peeling. The door needed a nudge from the shoulder and opened with a creak into a passage with two rooms going off on one side. The kitchen was at the back of the house.

'This could be made lovely,' said Guinevere, looking around at the larger front room. 'See how the sun comes in.'

Quinn smiled to see her pleasure as she sized it up, oblivious of the spider webs festooning the corners. The room behind was linked with a door and had the same attractive ceilings as the front room. The kitchen was a good size with a generous hearth and windows overlooking a garden filled with straggling plants. The privy was at the far end and a shed abutted the back door.

Quinn grinned at Gwen. 'We'll come back to this,' he told her, 'but first you and Stella should see the upstairs while I take a look at that front door. We'll need to sort that out straight away if you are moving in.'

The stairs were narrow and the banister rocked under their hands, but there were three small rooms, each with a bedstead and some shelves. The larger room in the front also had a wardrobe.

'You should have this room,' Gwen said to Stella. 'You have so many clothes.'

'No,' cried Stella. 'You, after all, are the lady. Besides, as we are only getting this house because you can look after the boy, it is only right that you have the main room.'

'But I'd rather have one of the back ones,' said Gwen. 'They'll get the morning sun which would disturb you after your late nights, but which will wake me for work – for you must know I do intend finding another job. Anyway, I prefer looking out over the garden than the street.'

Stella rolled her eyes. 'Darling, Guinevere, you *cannot* call that wilderness a garden.'

'Not now, perhaps, but give me a few months,' Gwen assured her. 'Now, no more arguments, I'm taking that room.'

Smiling approvingly Stella said, '*Wonderful* lady-of-the manor tones, Guinevere. I cannot *wait* to study your ways more. You try to hide them but they do slip out when you aren't careful. No don't try quelling me with that look either – it won't work on me you know, but see if you can hold it a second longer so I can imitate it. There, what do you think?'

Gwen had to laugh to see the actress with her head tilted, looking aristocratically down her lovely nose.

Then Quinn called up the stairs. 'Are you finished up there? Stella, Jack's just arrived with

243

all your stuff and Gwen, there's something I want to show you.'

They trooped downstairs and while Jack and Stella began moving the various bags upstairs, Quinn led Gwen to the shed and threw the door open with a flourish.

'Ta da!'

Mystified, Gwen peeked inside. It was dark and decidedly musty. 'Mm,' she said.

'Do you know what this is?'

'A shed?' she hazarded.

'No, your ladyship, a darkroom. I have a carpenter coming to fix it up for you. Then you can use the front room as your photographic studio.'

'Oh, Quinn!' Without thinking Guinevere flung her arms about him. 'That's the most wonderful present I've ever had.'

Quinn laughed, reddened and, as if unable to help himself, he pulled her close against his body. His breath quickened and his arms tightened.

Then Gwen was pulling shyly away. 'I'm sorry, I wasn't thinking.'

'Don't apologise, I enjoyed it.'

He laughed but still there was a catch in his voice and Gwen caught a glimpse of something – an aching desire – before he turned his head and looked into the shed. 'So, you like the idea of setting up in business?'

'I love it.'

Her voice was light but the feel of his body against hers, the glimmer in his eyes had awoken something inside her. She wanted to see that look again, feel that tension hardening his body once more. It was as though they had been on the very edge of something she'd never known before. Sensing excitement, but also danger, she'd pulled back. Now she regretted it.

When Quinn turned back to face her, his eyes met hers and he must have seen something in her face that made him catch his breath. Stretching out his hand, he ran a finger slowly down from her eyebrow to her jaw. Gwen fought the strangest impulse to turn her face and catch that finger in her teeth, nip it just hard enough to make him catch his breath again. She had never felt like this before, heat kindling in the pit of her stomach, a yearning ache spreading through her body to be held again, and this time to be held very close and for a long time. She stood absolutely still, scarcely daring to breathe in case she disturbed this moment.

Looking into her wide eyes, Quinn saw no fear, just growing wonderment as the golden flecks darkened with some new emotion. She had never loved but she was not immune to passion as she proclaimed to be. He could see it flare even now, her pulses quickening for the first time to the touch of a man. And he, an Irish peasant, should not be the man to arouse a lady's senses. He would not make that mistake again.

Closing his eyes, he let his hand drop even as

every impulse in his body clamoured to kiss her lips, which were slightly parted as if waiting for his. There was a clatter of footsteps behind them and Quinn turned to see Jack and Stella coming through the kitchen.

'Well, what do you think of our new home?' Stella asked brightly.

'It's wonderful!' Gwen wondered if the others heard the strain in her voice. A pulse fluttered in the base of her throat and she wanted Quinn's fingers to feel it – his lips to kiss it. She blinked to clear her mind of such a shocking thought.

'What about your darkroom?' asked Jack. 'Quinn was pretty bucked with the notion.'

'I'm overwhelmed.'

And no one would ever know quite how much, she thought.

As the others began talking about mops and paint, she tried to marshal her scattered senses. Something had just shifted between Quinn and herself. Part of her longed to slip away so that she could turn it over and over in her mind. Another part wished they could go back five minutes so she could live that moment again, but have it last longer. Her cheek tingled where his finger had drawn a path down it, her every sense was humming.

And Quinn, just inches away, seemed to be vibrating with the same energy as though invisible cords still bound them to one another. He bent his head to look more closely at the state of the kitchen steps and it was all she could do not to burrow her fingers into his hair. She could almost feel the thickness of those dark locks, their texture.

'Gwen?' Stella was looking at her with a quizzical expression and Gwen gave herself a little shake.

'I'm sorry, I was miles away. What did you say?'

'I was asking if you would care to try out your skills as a maid and help me give the kitchen a jolly good clean while Jack goes off to get Ben and Quinn fixes up your darkroom.'

'Absolutely.'

The rest of the day passed in an exciting blur of cleaning and settling in, yet all of it felt slightly unreal to Gwen who still quivered at the memory of what had passed between her and Quinn. But there was no chance for any talk for as soon as Jack and Quinn had finished their last minute repairs, they bid the women and Ben farewell, keen to be gone early the following morning.

Ben clung to Quinn and Guinevere wished she too could throw her arms about him, feel his arms tighten around her again. He was leaving and she had never wished more for him to stay.

'Goodbye,' he said, offering her his hand. It was an absurdly formal gesture but the only way they could touch once more under the eyes of the others. His fingers tightened on hers and suddenly she knew that he too had been haunted by his thoughts all afternoon, unable to dismiss what had happened and that whatever lay between them was not resolved.

'I will be back,' he said softly.

'I'll be waiting,' she promised.

CHAPTER 13

'Do you realise that it has now been over four months since we first moved into this house,' Gwen announced, looking up from her sewing.

Winter, with icy blasts and thick morning frosts, was finally surrendering to spring. The days were still crisp, the wind nippy and the nights cold but the air seemed to tremble with the promise of new life. Flowers were appearing and even lambs, though freezing storms could still sweep in. New Zealand weather was legendary for its unpredictability.

Gwen, Stella and Ben were all in the kitchen, a snug room where they spent most of their time.

'No, *really*?' exclaimed Stella, swinging the pot of stew expertly from the heat of the flames in the centre of the fireplace to a hook on the slightly cooler sides. 'Doesn't time simply *fly* when you are having a good time. And we are, aren't we?'

She stepped back, her lovely face flushed, her glorious hair a loose mane down her back.

Sunday was Stella's day off, the day when

she washed her hair and dressed as plainly as possible for, as she said, even an actress must be allowed a day to be simply *hideous*. Secretly Guinevere thought on these days she was at her most luminous.

'I *definitely* am,' said Ben as he looked up from the model house he was constructing, unconsciously reflecting Stella's intonation patterns. The boy had mourned Quinn's departure for the first week but had soon been seduced by Stella's superb cooking and the generous amounts of freedom the two young women allowed him. He had of late discovered a talent for making things; small toys with moving parts and was particularly gratified that far from receiving a box about his ears for wasting time, Guinevere encouraged him. She'd bought him glue and a small knife so he could carve wood more skilfully, and hoarded her scraps of material and wools for his projects. The farmhouse he was building now was ambitious for he wanted everything to work. Doors opened, even on miniscule cupboards and his attention this evening was engaged by the sash windows, which were not only delicate, with gauze for window panes, but extremely fiddly.

'Dang and tarnation,' he exclaimed as once again the window refused to slide up.

'Ben,' Gwen reproved him, but without heat and she and Stella exchanged amused looks. They both knew the source of this new expression. Stella often brought friends back to the house either for a meal before the show or, on Saturday nights, afterwards and the small house resounded with laughter and chatter during this time.

Ben, used to the company of miners, first looked at these invasions with deep suspicion and not a little alarm but as the actors made a pet of him, he very soon thawed. Charles Eliot was an American actor with the most dashing moustache and exuberant manner and Ben watched in awe as the actor would describe what might have been for anyone else the most ordinary day, but which for Mr Eliot was always one of tragedy, triumph and adventure. His tales were liberally sewn with American idioms and oaths which Ben relished and used to great effect in the schoolyard.

'I *must* tell dear Charlie to modify his language in front of the child. It is *too* naughty of the man to teach Ben such things.' Stella sounded severe but Ben just grinned, seeing the twinkle in her eyes.

Guinevere, who had been watching Ben's struggles, laid aside the cushion she was sewing and said, 'Here, if I hold it in place, you could thread the sash better.'

They both bent over the model, their attention entirely focused on the intricate manoeuvres. 'There. Ben, you are so clever.'

The boy flushed at her praise. Stella was glorious fun but Guinevere was the one who encouraged all his enterprises, who delighted in the good reports she heard from his schoolteacher and who was teaching him how to be her assistant in her small, but already thriving, photography business. When she told him that she'd never met anyone so quick to learn, Ben thought he might burst with pride. His one dishonourable wish was that his father might see how well others thought of his son. That would show him.

'No one for dinner tonight?' Gwen asked, snipping her thread.

'No,' said Stella. 'So many of the company have sniffles and coughs, they are *not* in the mood to go out and I really do *not* fancy catching whatever they have. A red nose and sore throat is a *disaster* on stage.'

Gwen was a little sorry. She loved the flood of actors, singers, writers and poets that poured through their tiny house. The lively arguments and bright discussions were reminiscent of her youth. She'd discovered that the colonies not only attracted miners and farmers, but revolutionaries as well: people keen to establish a new philosophical and political framework that accommodated the ordinary person far more, rewarding enterprise over birthright. She often thought of how much her father would have enjoyed these gatherings.

As she threaded her needle now with white thread to mend a small tear in Ben's shirt, Gwen reflected on the acceptance she'd found amongst Stella's friends and their genuine interest in her profession. It was a new sensation to be taken seriously. Her father had only taught her photography so she might be a useful assistant to him, he'd never seen her as a practitioner in her own right. But then, he hadn't even taken Margaret Cameron seriously, though she had been made welcome in his house. His attention had always been caught up with the male artists. Strangely it was Quinn, so contemptuous of the photographs he had seen in Hokitika, who had nevertheless seen a darkroom in a shed, a studio in a dusty shop.

On the voyage out, Gwen had hoped that once she had her father entirely to herself, he might see her in a different light; a partner, not an assistant. An heir, not merely a daughter. He was often in her thoughts as she watched images slowly emerge as if by magic on the paper in the developing fluid. He would, of course, have been proud of her technical skills. He'd always acknowledged she was a clever little thing. Certainly he would have praised her portraits but would he have understood her deeper passion, growing daily, to record the unrecognised lives of workers?

Her time as governess, milliner and maid had changed the way she saw the things about her. Behind every glamorous bonnet, she knew now, were hours of finger-pricking, eye-straining work in back rooms with dull lighting. She was intimately aware of the unending hours of unremitting labour that supported the facade of gracious living.

She sometimes marvelled at her previous ignorance. Small wonder Quinn had been so frustrated by her glib naivety. She was now making a living by taking photographs of clients and their homes but in her own time she was consumed to record the unacknowledged, the humdrum, the unglamorous. She wondered if her father would have understood. She was not sure she fully understood herself.

Her musings were interrupted by a sudden knocking at the door and a voice crying out, 'Helloa in there! Bring out your dead!'

Ben leapt to his feet, knocking over his chair in his excitement. 'That's Jack! Quinn must be back!'

For a second, the breath stilled in her lungs. Then casting the shirt aside, Gwen followed Stella down the passageway in time to see Ben fling open the door. There on the doorstep, very begrimed and bearded, were Jack and Quinn.

'Quinn!' Ben threw himself at the tall Irishman. Quinn looked taken aback but then a grin broke through his dark beard. He gave the boy a hug and tousled his hair.

'You've filled out since I was gone,' he remarked.

'Stella is the most *wonderful* cook.'

Jack laughed. 'Is she, by Jove? Do you think we can wheedle a dinner out of her?'

'Looking like *that*, there is absolutely *no* chance in the world,' Stella said, stepping forward.

'Oh, but you are a sight for sore eyes,' exclaimed

Jack and he pulled her into an embrace, twirling her around. 'I've missed you, my fair beauty.'

'Put me *down*!' But there was nothing in Stella's tone that indicated anything but delight.

Jack acquiesced but only after planting a noisy kiss on her lips.

'Ugh!' said Ben.

Quinn smiled. 'You may like it better, Ben, when you are older.'

His eyes were on Guinevere and she blushed to see the expression in them. Though they did not touch, the air seemed to vibrate around them. Gwen had an urge to run a teasing hand down his bearded face, as Stella was doing with Jack. She wanted to reassure herself he was real; here and real at last after all the months of waiting.

'Come in, come in,' she urged and stretching out her hand, she caught one of his and tugged. 'Your hands are cold and inside we've an excellent fire.'

His fingers closed tight over hers for a second before letting them go and he shook his head.

''Tis a grand invitation and one we'd like to avail ourselves of in a short while. We are filthy and must go to the baths before we are fit to be in company – only Jack insisted we come by here first.' He did not add that he had been as keen, had thought only of seeing Guinevere and Ben again during the past six hours of hard riding.

'Quinn is right,' said Stella. 'We simply *cannot* have men in all their dirt sitting down to one of *my* dinners. Besides, I need to cook more potatoes,' she added. 'You have half an hour, otherwise the meat will be *ruined*. Not a minute later, mind.'

'Sweet Stella, it will be twenty-nine minutes, I'll lay my life on it,' Jack vowed.

'Quinn, can I come with you?' Ben was hanging onto his coat. 'I want to hear all about your adventures.'

Quinn looked down at the pleading face then up at Gwen who was watching the two of them with a smile. 'Impossible to resist those eyes, isn't it?' she said.

'If you crumble every time the boy begs, 'tis a spoilt child he must be these days.'

'Go on then,' Gwen challenged. 'Tell him no.'

Quinn looked down again at Ben and grinned. 'All right, but get a jacket. The wind bites something terrible down the street. Run – we can't keep the horses standing for long.'

'Yes!' Ben tore off inside and they could hear his feet clattering up the stairs.

'Weakling,' Gwen taunted.

'And I blame you if I am,' retorted Quinn. 'Never thought about pleading eyes at all, till you went blathering on about Pegasus and Cerberus. I'm surprised the boy has not been re-named Ulysses.'

'Ah, and here's the brat, now,' Jack said. 'Let's be going then.'

The men swung themselves back into the saddles of their weary horses whose flanks were dark with caked mud and Quinn pulled Ben up in front of him, snuggling him into his big coat.

'Twenty-nine minutes!' Jack promised and they were off.

Gwen and Stella retreated to the kitchen where Gwen began peeling a mound of extra potatoes, while Stella extracted a bone from the safe where the meat and butter were kept.

'There's not much meat left on it,' she said. 'I was going to keep it for soup but I'll add it to the stew and see if that helps. Those men will be *starved*. I'm sure Jack is thinner.'

Quinn was always lean but Gwen had seen lines around his eyes and mouth that bespoke exhaustion – yet still he had come straight to their house.

As she scrubbed, she noticed that her hands were trembling which was not surprising she thought wryly, considering the racing of her heart. A tumultuous excitement was brimming inside her which would not be suppressed, not now. She had been firm with her thoughts these past months, for whenever they'd turned to her Irishman – and they often had – she had been quick to quell them. Though there was still that unexplored moment between them when last they met, it was necessary to remember that she was immune to love, that Quinn thought it a most inconvenient emotion. She couldn't let herself be too excited at his return. There was no future in it for either of them. They were too different, their goals opposing. He wanted a farm out in the country far from people. Gwen could not survive without a flow of visitors passing through her home – through Maidenhurst.

The image of Mr Ramsay's face suddenly imposed itself over the memory of her house and she gave a little shiver. The size of the mortgage appalled her, especially knowing now how arduous it was to earn even a guinea, yet still she clung to her dream of saving Maidenhurst. Her savings, though, modest at present, were steadily growing and she was hopeful of increasing them still further in just a few weeks. If she could save a reasonable portion, she might be able to bargain, pay it back over a longer time with some interest.

But if Mr Ramsay refused, her duty was clear and no Irishman would make an already unattractive alternative positively detestable. Her father's greatest wish must be fulfilled. No matter how much she might love the way Quinn's eyes softened and crinkled at the corners when he looked at her, no matter how much she watched for his mouth to curl into his crooked smile, no matter how much his deep Irish voice played in her dreams, she was still Lady Guinevere Stanhope.

Her father had pointed out that he had been married to her mother for the betterment of both families, a capital arrangement until her mother had died in childbirth with Gwen. He had chosen to save the baby. It was what her mother would have wanted, he'd assured Gwen.

Stella interrupted these thoughts. 'How lucky an admirer sent us this basket of apples today. Gwen if you make the pastry, I'll prepare the apples and we can have apple pie.'

'Excellent notion,' said Gwen, passing the potatoes to Stella and drying her hands. 'Have we any flour?'

'Enough, I think. Your pastry always seems to turn out, no matter what quantities we have, anyway.'

Gwen flushed with pride. It was true! Lady Guinevere, they'd discovered, was a dab hand at pastry. She was slowly learning to cook from Stella and enjoying it – similar in many ways to photography. Mixing elements to create something new and wonderful. While she still lacked Stella's ingenuity at making a sumptuous meal out of a handful of dubious leftovers, Gwen had the lightest touch when it came to pastry and her pies were legendary among the theatre crew.

As she crumbled the flour into the butter, she threw a sidelong look at Stella who was humming as she peeled and cored the apples.

'You'll have to stop that when Jack comes or he may guess you are happier to see him than you care to let on,' Gwen told her.

Stella looked up and laughed. 'It's *dreadful*, isn't it? I simply *cannot* resist the rogue.'

'Would it be so bad if he knew how much you returned his regard?' Gwen asked curiously.

Stella paused a moment. 'Yes, it would,' she said and for once her voice was devoid of its usual inflections. It was soft and strangely cautious. 'I mean to marry, you see. An actress does not have a long career and I'm certainly not returning to the backstreets of St Giles when it's over. I haven't fought my way up from there just to go back. I want to be comfortable and respectable, but for Jack it's all just a game. I am his fair Stella and he can worship at my feet before disappearing back into the mountains where no doubt whisky and women drive all thoughts of me out of his mind.'

'Surely not. He's devoted to you.'

'Words are easy to say,' said Stella with a shrug, resuming her coring. 'It's the action I wait for. And I cannot wait forever. You know both Charles and Mr Worthing have proposed?'

'No!' Gwen looked up from her bowl in delighted surprise.

She loved this sharing of female confidences, never having had friends of her own age. The artists and their wives and lovers had been all far too involved in their own lives to befriend their patron's daughter. Over the months the two women had had many long conversations and Gwen had learnt of Stella's childhood in a London slum, until her mother had realised what an asset she had in her lovely daughter and had put her

260

on the stage at the age of ten. Since then, Stella's life had been one of touring from one draughty hall to another until she rose from being the adorable middle act, to star of the show. In turn, Stella had learnt of Gwen's privileged background and her current predicament with Maidenhurst and Mr Ramsay.

'What on earth did you say?'

'Well, of *course* I said no to Charlie straight away. Poor dear was in his cups, though I believe he was still sincere. He would be a *dreadful* husband, though. Like a child, he would want *all* the attention and you know I was *not* born to be an audience.'

'No, indeed,' agreed Gwen. 'But surely you can't be considering Mr Worthing?'

'Why not? He's rich and devoted. He would be the most attentive husband.'

'But he's – dull!'

Stella sighed and, with a mischievous little smile, said lightly, 'Well, one cannot have *everything* in a marriage. I daresay I would liven him up a trifle. And I would have a *lovely* carriage.'

'I'm sure you would but even so, you cannot marry a man for a carriage.'

'And a nice house,' Stella pointed out. 'Why not? After all, you may yet land up marrying Mr Ramsay for your house.'

'It's my home!' cried Gwen. 'It's not the same thing at all. Maidenhurst has been in the family for centuries. It's my duty to keep it for my children and my children's children. It's what my father expected of me.'

'Well, I never knew who my father was but perhaps he too would have wished a nice house for me and for my children,' said Stella, unmoved. 'Mr Worthing can provide one.'

'But Jack loves you and you love Jack.'

'But does he love me enough to marry me? I really don't know – he doesn't know himself.'

As if on cue, they heard the front door burst open and Ben came scampering down the passage shouting, 'Look, Gwen! Look what Quinn has brought me from Dunedin.' In his hands he cradled a toy train.

Behind him the men came into the kitchen, clean and shaven and looking, Gwen thought, like two of the handsomest men in the colony.

'Its wheels go around and the door opens, see.' Ben thrust the train up at Gwen.

'It's beautiful!' she exclaimed. 'The perfect toy for you.' Over his head, her eyes met Quinn's. 'You've made Ben very happy.'

'I have a present for you, too,' said Quinn looking mischievous. From behind his back he pulled a large book. Mystified, Gwen took it but Stella recognised the binding at a glance and went into a peal of laughter.

'It's Mrs Beeton!' she crowed. 'You will turn our lady into a housewife in no time with that.'

'I had a qualm about leaving my boy in the hands of a woman who has pitifully few domestic skills,'

Quinn explained. 'You see, I know for a fact that she does poorly when interviewed as a maid and as for her cooking – well, lamentable so she once assured me.'

Gwen cast him one of her haughtiest expressions and said, 'Repeat that, sir, if you dare, once you've tasted my apple pie.'

'It's true, Quinn,' said Ben, looking up from his train that he was running on the floor around their shoes. 'Gwen makes the best pies ever. Mr Eliot says when you eat one, you know what manna was to the Israelites.'

'Does he now?' said Quinn. 'And who is this Mr Eliot?' He glanced at Gwen but she was oblivious, having sunk down into one of the chairs to flip through her book.

'He's an actor and he has the most wonderful moustache. You'll meet him because he's always here.'

Quinn did not look excited at the prospect but his expression lightened when Ben went on, 'He wants to marry Stella.'

'*Ben*,' exclaimed Stella.

'Well, he does. I heard him ask you when I was out chopping wood.'

Quinn laughed and sauntered over to Gwen, supposedly to look over her shoulder at the recipes, but really just to be close to her. His boots brushed her skirts and though she did not look up he thought her fingers paused, just for a second.

'And what did my fair Stella reply?' asked Jack grimly.

'She laughed at him and said he would make a dreadful husband, but I don't know,' Ben added thoughtfully, 'he's very funny and kind.'

'But not,' Jack was firm, 'the man for Stella. What the devil are you doing receiving offers from men while I'm away?'

He took the pot from Stella, though she was quite capable of shifting it to simmer at the side of the fire. She threw him an innocent look. 'Why, Jack, I cannot stop them proposing. They know I am all alone in the world and—'

'Don't try that helpless woman routine on me. We both know that you are *never* alone. Especially not now that you've got Ben and Gwen.'

'And they are *wonderful*,' agreed Stella as she passed him the plates to set out. 'But our happy home has made me realise that one day, I would like one of my own.'

'Course you do,' Jack agreed.

'With a husband content to stay home with me.'

Caught off-guard, Jack froze, last plate still in hand, lost for words but Quinn came to his rescue.

'Sure, and you've turned my ugly house into the snuggest home a man could hope to return to. 'Tis amazing what you have done since I was away.'

Quinn looked around the room, his easy manner disguising the confusion of emotions he was suffering on seeing Guinevere and Ben again. Though he'd been as keen as Jack to return, he had been careful to minimise his anticipation. During their travels, he had persuaded himself that he'd imagined the flare of attraction he'd detected in Gwen, and had convinced himself that the best course of action would be to find a family for Ben at the earliest opportunity. Then the door had opened and Ben had launched himself like a cannonball and Quinn had been overwhelmed by a surge of affection and protectiveness towards the boy.

As for Guinevere, he had never seen her look lovelier, dressed in a jade dress, her hair caught in a long, loose plait over one shoulder. Tonight she was not a creature of the woods but a sprite from the oceans. He'd longed to snatch her up as Jack had done with Stella but seeing the queenly angle of her head, the set of her slim shoulders, he reminded himself that she was a lady and far out of his reach.

'You can thank Gwen for much of it,' said Stella. 'She's an absolute *tyrant*, isn't she Ben, when she has a notion in her head. We worked like *slaves* to get it to her liking. We were whitewashing until it was too late to see at night, and up at first light to begin the job again.'

'First light!' scoffed Gwen. 'You always sleep till midday.'

'And you hardly did any painting at all because you said you made too much of a mess,' Ben added.

'I begin to think,' said Stella, fixing him with a

265

stern eye, 'that you say altogether too much, young Ben.'

'Stella has been invaluable in procuring materials. All the cushions and drapes are thanks to her persuasive manner at the theatre. I'm amazed they've chairs left for the audience to sit on or costumes for the actors to wear.'

'But it's thanks to your needle that the tat I bring home turns into chair covers and cushions. Gwen has the most wonderful eye, you know. Have you seen her studio?'

'I noticed it as we walked through but didn't look closely, though I'd very much like to,' said Quinn.

'Come then,' said Stella, picking up a gas lamp. 'It will amaze you.'

They all went through to Gwen's studio in the front room, but she hung back feeling strangely shy. Stella, the lamp turning her red locks fiery, showed off her friend's genius.

'This curtain here is pulled across so that Gwen can take pictures as though in a fine country house. They are shockingly old and darned but she is cunning with the lighting and they look magnificent in the pictures. And then if you pull them back, *voila*. Scenery. You see, some like to have a picture of themselves as if in the countryside so in this corner we have the alps. Don't they look *wonderful*? And while this tree may look painted here, you'd be surprised at how *real* it looks in the photographs. Others prefer a more classical look so this is what we call the Grecian corner. I simply *adore* the way she has drawn the leaves twining up the column, don't you? And the grapes are positively *edible*!'

Jack gave a low whistle. 'This is remarkable.'

Quinn was silent but the expression in his eyes when he looked at Gwen in the flickering light caused her to catch her breath. He was seeing a new side of her, her true side, and she suddenly realised how much his opinion mattered.

'Lady Guinevere,' he said softly as he moved close to her, 'you never fail to amaze me.'

She gave a self-conscious laugh. 'Ben has helped me,' she said, deflecting the attention which suddenly seemed overpowering in the small room. She'd longed for his return but now having him here, in her studio, he seemed almost unbearably real. She wanted to reach out and touch him but with the others about, they had to maintain the facade of friendliness. When she looked into his eyes, however, she knew he too was waiting . . .

'Yes, she's been teaching me how to paint. And look, Quinn, this is the column we made for people to lean upon. It helps them stand still.' Ben gestured to a freestanding column which looked to be made of marble at first glance, but on closer inspection it was all done with paint.

'How on earth did you do this?' Jack demanded.

'It was an old fence post and Gwen and I did papier mâché up the sides. We had paste *everywhere*,' Ben said, laughing. 'Gwen looked so funny because her hair fell into the bucket when it came out of its bun and she had to wash it quickly before it set.'

The men laughed and Gwen made a lunge as though to throttle her charge. 'Wretch. That was supposed to stay a secret – remember?'

'And here is her office and exhibition space,' said Stella, leading them into the middle room.

Jack glanced at the pictures on the wall and said he'd never seen such beauties, but Quinn relieved Stella of the lamp and inspected each one. Several times he nodded and Gwen was aware that she was scarcely breathing. He sighed and shook his head at the classical poses but the ones in front of the Alps appeared to catch his fancy. Finally he turned around.

'It appears you are very good at your job,' he said. 'Business going well?'

She nodded. 'It's picking up more every month.'

'She is becoming *the* word in social portraits, you know. All the best families are coming to her. Somehow she manages to make even the most *frightful* hag look dignified.'

'I couldn't have done it without the house and darkroom,' Gwen said. 'I cannot tell you how grateful I am. I've even expanded as the shed became too small for all the work. I now develop the plates here, but I print the photographs off in a small lean-to at the back of Mr Orsmond's barn. It has also given me storage for all the plates.'

'Well, that is grand to hear. I'm grateful to you as well. It's good to see Ben look so fit and happy. Dreadfully fat, though,' he added, giving Ben a playful shove. 'If I go away too often, I'll return to a tub of lard.'

Ben laughed and stuck out his tummy. 'It's all the pies.'

'Now, you've been promising us a fine feed,' cried Jack, 'and I'm famished.'

'I'll second that. We've not eaten since breakfast,' said Quinn.

'Come this way, then,' Stella told them. 'You are in for *such* a treat.'

The meal was a lively affair and when done, both men had to push their chairs away from the table to recline more comfortably as they loosened belts a notch. Jack brimmed with their adventures in fording flooded rivers and crossing impossible passes.

'The places Quinn has forced me to go – well, I cannot tell you the very worst stories for fear of giving you the vapours. I had the vapours myself a few times. And at the end of every excruciating, death-defying trail was a bunch of starving, grateful miners who would have willingly traded their grandmothers for the supplies we carried. Stella, this Irishman is turning yours truly into quite a catch, I must tell you. Quinn's the canniest trader – fair but shrewd and willing to take risks, thereby trebling profits.'

'And what will you do with your wealth?' asked

Stella. Her voice was light but Gwen was not deceived.

Jack shrugged. 'Quinn is still looking for land. I don't know that I'm the farming sort. Don't know that he is either come to that, but in his stubborn Irish way, he's yet to see that.'

'Jack,' said Quinn warningly, but his irrepressible friend just laughed.

'You are born to be a doctor and you know it. Everywhere we went, if the man wasn't trading, he was stitching up wounds or setting bones. Wouldn't take any payment for it, but couldn't walk past an injured man anyway.'

'We should be going,' Quinn said, quelling Jack with a look. 'We've a long ride and your godparents are expecting us. We sent a message through to them,' he explained.

'They'll be happy to see you again,' Gwen said. 'They've missed you both.'

'And how would you be knowing that?' asked Quinn, surprised.

'They said so when I was visiting last week.'

'You are visiting my godparents? Good heavens! Isn't that a bit quaint? I know you are a lady and all that, Gwen, but dash it all, my godfather made a pass at you.'

She nodded, eyes dancing. 'And he was mortified when he first found out who I was, but Lady Whittering thought it very funny and told him that it served him right. We are all best of friends now.'

'But how did you come to be talking to them in the first place?' Quinn wanted to know.

'Photographs,' Stella said. 'Nothing gets between Gwen and her photographs. She had in mind a domestic series and so bowled up calmly as you please to the house that had turned her out but weeks before to ask if she might photograph the maid – what was her name? Moll? Yes, Moll and the redoubtable cook. They are *splendid* photographs. Go get them, Ben.'

Ben disappeared into the studio with a candle, returning minutes later with a sheaf of photographs. 'I've brought the ones of you backstage as well. Thought Jack might like to see them.'

The men pulled the gas lamp closer and bent over the black and white pictures. There was Moll, stouter than ever polishing shoes, hanging clothes. There were several of Mrs Williams rolling pastry with a grim expression that did not quite conceal the secret excitement she'd felt at being photographed. One lovely picture showed the two women sitting on the back steps of the kitchen with mugs of tea, the sunlight falling across them.

Gwen, watching Quinn, noted how closely he examined these images, nodding from time to time as though confirming something. He glanced up and the approval she saw in his eyes warmed her in a way she'd never felt before.

'Moll has left now,' Gwen said. 'Her baby is due very soon so she has been sent to a farm for the rest of her confinement. After that, she'll look for other employment.'

Quinn's lips tightened.

Jack saw this and said defensively, 'My godfather will make sure she has a nest egg to see her through.'

His words fell into a rather bleak silence.

The second pile contained images taken back-stage; actors putting on make-up, costumes being donned and one exceptional one of Stella collapsed after a performance, exhausted but radiant with success. Jack instantly offered five guineas for it.

'Pooh, five guineas is nothing!' Ben said. 'Mr Fortesque tried to buy it for ten pounds but Mr Worthing immediately said he would pay double. That was what started the idea of the auction.'

'First it was Mr Eliot, now there's a Mr Fortesque and Mr Worthing too,' groaned Jack. 'Quinn, you've got to teach this boy how to shoot a gun so that he might protect my fair Stella from all these lotharios cluttering the decks.'

But Quinn was not to be distracted. 'Auction?' He cocked an eyebrow at Gwen.

'It has been suggested that I have an auction of my works. These photographs, plus ones of the buildings around Christchurch. Everyone is taking such an interest in the growth of the city. I can also exhibit my social portraits as well, most of the clients have agreed to it.'

'Will you be having it here?'

'Oh, no. The rooms are far too small but I've been very lucky. Mr Orsmond – the farmer who lets me use his lean-to – has said I can also use the barn. He's just finished building a new one. I've only seen the outside as he has to clear it out a bit and he says it needs a bit of work, but I should be able to start setting things up in a few days' time. I can't wait.'

Ben butted in. 'And there's another man who has suggested that Gwen sell her pictures of buildings as postcards – a form of advertising for the colony he said, isn't that right?'

Gwen nodded, trying not to show how much the offer had meant to her. 'I'm hoping to raise a lot of money from the proceeds,' she said, looking meaningfully at Quinn who knew what she was really saying.

'That's grand news,' he said, though he did not sound as enthusiastic as before. 'Will it be enough?'

'I don't know but with luck it should give me a good start. By great good fortune, Mr Pilkington, one of London's most famous critics, is out in New Zealand for a visit and Alex – Stella's stage manager – is a good friend of his. He's promised to make sure he attends. If he likes my work . . .' she shrugged, a gesture of nonchalance that could not quite disguise her yearning hope, '. . . it may help me secure exhibitions back home where there is far more money to be made.'

Quinn nodded. 'So you are still intent on going back to England?'

'Of course.' She sounded, she knew, a little surprised, as though the question was impertinent. He could not guess the pang she felt when she said that. It would be so hard to leave Ben, Stella and . . . and everyone.

'I see,' said Quinn, pushing back his chair and rising. 'Well, I've been told I don't know much about art,' he said giving the word a humorously ironic inflection, 'but I like your pictures. Most especially I like these,' and he gestured to the photographs scattered across the table. 'They reveal the truth.'

Gwen was reminded of how he'd complimented her sketches before and now she better understood what he'd meant. She wanted to say something; to show she knew that he knew and she was so glad and, in some strange way, so relieved that he did. He was the only one who seemed to know why she was so intent on these domestic and backstage series. But before she could even begin to frame her thoughts, he'd continued.

'Congratulations, Lady Guinevere. You deserve wild success with them. Now, Jack, we really should be going. I've a fancy for your godfather's excellent port.'

He smiled but there was something in this impersonal cordiality that suddenly chilled Gwen. Hadn't he realised how much his words had meant to her? How could he now leave her so easily and still they had not talked – not really. There was so much that needed to be said, to be explored, didn't

274

he see that? But all she could read in his face was the polite mien of a guest taking his leave after a pleasant evening.

Stella, however, looking swiftly at him, thought what a good actor he was. *You may fool the others, you may even be fooling yourself,* she thought to herself, *but you don't fool me, Quinn O'Donnell.*

CHAPTER 14

Over the following week Quinn was about the house often; fixing the sash window in Stella's room, rehanging the kitchen door, mending a broken chair and a myriad of other small jobs. He whistled as he worked and Gwen loved seeing the faint frown of concentration, the way his hair fell over his forehead as he worked and, seeing how quick, how sure, how neat he was, she realised how skilled a surgeon he must have been. It was as though he had an inherent need to strengthen the weak and mend the broken.

When not at school, Ben followed Quinn everywhere and Gwen was touched to see how patient the man was with the boy, involving him in his many small projects, teaching Ben how to use the tools. An unaccountable lump would come into her throat to see their two heads bent together over a piece of woodwork and when she spied them fixing the fence on an unexpectedly warm morning, she had an idea.

Going out into her shed, she worked swiftly, preparing her solutions and polishing a square of glass till it gleamed. Then she surprised the menfolk mightily by arriving in the back garden gloved and with her tripod and camera.

'What on earth are you doing?' Quinn demanded as she began setting up her equipment.

'Are you going to photograph *us*?' cried Ben, his face bright with excitement.

'You see,' said Gwen to Quinn. 'Ben is far quicker than you.'

'But you cannot intend taking a photograph of us looking like – well, like this!' Quinn spread his arms to show the full glory of his scruffy shirt, open at the neck, sleeves rolled up to his elbows, his worn moleskins and battered boots.

Gwen laughed as she kicked the turf with her heel to provide a better surface for the tripod. 'That's exactly what I intend. Why, would you rather one of you all brushed and polished, posing in the studio?'

'No!' exclaimed Quinn, revolted. 'But I don't want a photograph at all.'

Gwen did not have to try to talk him around for Ben had caught him by the sleeve and was beseeching, '*Please*, Quinn.'

The Irishman smiled ruefully down at him and shrugged. He knew he was defeated.

Under Gwen's directions, they posed in front of the fence. Quinn's broad shoulder propped against one of the stronger posts to keep him still for the exposure while Ben leaned against him, a spade dug into the ground providing him with

277

further support. When she looked through the lens, she felt the tingle she always experienced when about to capture what she knew would be an excellent image. Though they appeared upside down, she could see how the sun lit the strong bones of Quinn's face, his expression, quizzical but steady while Ben's face was filled with suppressed excitement.

'Relax, but don't move too much. You are perfectly framed in the shot. I'll only be a few minutes.'

Back in her shed, she poured a small amount of the collodion solution onto the surface of the glass, tipping the plate very slightly one way, then the other so that every part, including the corners, was coated. After that she sensitised the plate in a bath of silver nitrate, then drained it, wiped it and loaded it into the plate holder which would protect it from the light. Time was now of the essence. She made her way quickly back to the camera, slid the holder into place under the shroud and checked them through the lens. Obedient to her instructions, Quinn and Ben did not appear to have moved a muscle.

'Ben, don't move even a fraction of an inch,' Gwen warned the boy.

Though he already knew this, having been an assistant for some of her photographs, still he couldn't help wriggling in his excitement. Quinn pulled him tighter to his side, exchanging a smile with Gwen as she emerged from the shroud. She pulled a timepiece out of her pocket and withdrew the dark slide, saying, 'This is it.'

She whipped off the lens cap and time hung in suspension. Focused entirely on the man and the boy, the rest of the world ceased to exist as she counted down the minutes. She did not hear Stella singing in the kitchen, nor the hens next door. She was oblivious to the slamming of the neighbour's door. Then, as much by instinct as by her counting, Gwen knew she had captured the moment. She replaced the lens cap and dark slide, then immediately removed the plate holder from the camera.

'There, I'm off to develop it now.'

'Can we watch?' Ben asked.

Gwen hesitated. 'Ben, you know it's not safe with all the chemicals.'

'I'll be good, I promise. Quinn can make sure I don't do anything wrong. Please.' He saw her waver and added with more intensity. 'Please, Gwen. You know I've never seen you develop the plate before.'

She looked at Quinn, who said, 'I'd like to watch too.'

'All right. But we have to be quick. And no noise. No distractions.'

At the doorway, however, Quinn recoiled, struck by the smell of ether coming from the shed. For a dizzying second he was transported back to hospital tents – blood, pus, gangrene, severed limbs and the cries of men.

'Quick,' said Gwen. 'Come in and close the door.'

Shaken, he forced himself into the tiny shed, shutting the door on the sunlit world outside. Then he tucked himself as far as possible into a corner from which he could watch the process, pulling Ben close in front of him, and slowly felt himself relax as he focused on the unlikely coincidence that ether was common to both their trades.

Watching Gwen work was strangely soothing. She had trays of solution ready, revealing another side of herself to him. Impetuous she might be in life, in her work she was orderly and neat. Her chemicals, pestle and mortar were all arranged neatly on a shelf.

She removed the plate from the holder and, working swiftly, dipped it into a tray then a few seconds later, into the second.

'This is developing and fixing the image,' she told Ben, who was peering over her shoulder but it was unlikely he heard, being transfixed by watching himself and Quinn slowly emerge – wraithlike at first but gathering in definition and clarity at every second.

Quinn was not surprised by the boy's absorption. It was the closest he'd ever come to witchcraft himself.

Gwen exhaled long and slow.

'There,' she said in a soft voice. 'It's going to be a beautiful photograph. You can see the strong contrasts of light and dark already and some of the detail is going to be particularly fine. Now we'll just rinse it like so and then I'll put it on a stand in the sun to dry it.'

Ben wriggled out of Quinn's hold to better peer at the image of himself. 'When will you print it? Today?'

Gwen stripped off her gloves in a workmanlike way. 'Yes, if you like. Now, if you put the plate against this black cloth, you'll get an idea of what it will look like. See.'

Leaning over her shoulder, Quinn looked at the plate and went still. The man and boy looked like father and son together in their own garden. It was both truth and subterfuge. Quinn had not consciously realised it but now, looking at the photograph, he realised that his affection for Ben had turned at some unmarked time and place into love.

This past week had confirmed it. He no longer had thoughts of finding a suitable family for Ben but of making a home for himself and Ben instead. His stance was proprietal, leaning against the fence as though he were in his own garden. Which, of course he was – but he had never lived in the house that had been bought in such haste. Then it had merely been a solution to several problems. But now, with Gwen's improvements and his own maintenance work, it was beginning to feel like home. It was as though in this image he was being given a tantalising glimpse into what he had been looking for all these years. The photograph, however, was incomplete. It did not show the house, for one thing. It also lacked – but he would not think on that.

'When it is printed off, you must enter it into the exhibition,' he said.

'No! It's a gift.'

He shook his head. 'Let me bid for it. After all, you are making Jack bid for Stella. Not,' he added with a smile, 'that the boy and I will create a bidding war. I doubt very much if anyone else will buy it so 'tis guaranteed I'll get it at a bargain price.'

Gwen laughed but she could hardly take her eyes off the plate. She had been right; Quinn's strongly defined features were accentuated in the photographic process. But it was more than that. She had been told that some native peoples did not like their image taken, believing it to steal their souls. Looking at the photograph of Quinn, she could almost believe it. He stood straight and strong, his broad shoulders standing out well against the lines of the wooden fence and his hand rested protectively on Ben's shoulder as he stared out steadily at the viewer. There was humour lurking in the lines about his mouth, resolve in the set of his chin. It was a photograph worthy of any that Margaret Cameron might take.

'Well, if you are sure,' she said.

After the exhibition she would make a second secret copy. A keepsake for when she returned home, though, she realised with a pang, it would look out of place on the walls of Maidenhurst. A wild interloper in a cultivated land.

The following night was bitter with a wild wind blasting at the windows and rattling the iron roofs, but Gwen and Ben were snug beside the kitchen hearth, she sewing and he painting his farmhouse. Stella was at the theatre and Quinn and Jack were meeting with some friends of Lord Whittering to discuss business propositions before attending Stella's performance later in the evening.

Suddenly the peace in the kitchen was shattered by a hammering on the door.

Gwen looked up at Ben, her eyebrows raised. 'Who on earth do you think that could be on such a freezing night?'

Ben shrugged and she put aside the sock that she was darning before lifting a small lamp to go and see. As she opened the door, it was snatched from her hands by an enormous gust slamming against the side of the house. Dumbfounded, she stared at the figure doubled over on the steps.

'Moll?'

'Oh, Gwen,' the maid gasped looking up, her face screwed up in agony, teeth chattering as she clasped her shawl closer. 'It's begun and I just know summat's wrong. I can't tell you 'ow bad the pain is and that Mr Jones and 'is wife I've been with said they couldn't 'elp, so 'e brought me into town but the one doctor ain't there and the other is drunk as a lord! I just couldn't go back to the farm so I said I could be dropped 'ere – you don't mind do you? Then, if the doctor does come back, 'e won't 'ave far to go. As for Mr Jones, 'e was only too 'appy to get shot of me, I tell you, 'e took off without even checking you was 'ome. Cheeky bastard! Scared I'd 'ave the baby with only 'im to catch probably. Oh, gawd, Gwen, I think I'm dying!'

As if to emphasise her point, the maid doubled up again with a gasping cry and her whole body shook but whether from pain or the cold, it was hard to tell.

'Oh, Moll.' Gwen pulled her into the house and through to the kitchen where Ben jumped to his feet, his eyes huge. Gwen turned to him. 'Ben, go and get Quinn immediately. He's at the White Horse Hotel. Run.'

Without a word the boy disappeared as Gwen stationed Moll in front of the fire, wrapping her own thick shawl over the maid's. The pain seemed to have subsided for a few minutes and Moll's breathing, though laboured, steadied. Gwen knelt and removed Moll's battered shoes to massage warmth back into her frozen feet and fought against the panic rising inside her.

'Can I get you anything to drink?' she asked.

Moll shook her head. 'I'll be sick if I do.' She suddenly arched and gave a small scream. 'Oh, gawd in 'eaven! I'm going to die for my wickedness.'

'Of course you won't. Quinn – Mr O'Donnell

– will be here any minute. He's back in town, did you know?'

Moll gave a glad cry.

Gwen nodded. 'Yes, that's right. He'll know what to do to help you but you have to stay calm. How long have you been like this?' It was hard to keep her voice calm.

'The pains began this afternoon but that farmer's wife, she don't know nothing and the baby just won't come. I've been feeling these pains and pushing but the damned 'ead is too big or sommat. In the end she said I was just wearing on 'er nerves and that 'er 'usband would take me to a doctor.'

'Can you climb stairs? We'll go up to my room if you can. It won't be as warm as it is down here but the bed is comfortable. Can you make it?'

'Oh, for a bed I'd climb the Alps themselves. The cart 'urt my back sommat terrible.'

Moll heaved herself up with a growl of pain and began plodding up the stairs, Gwen following close behind. As Moll lowered herself down to the bed, a fresh contraction caused her to arch and roll and she cried out again, 'I'm going to die, I know it.'

'Of course you won't,' Gwen said firmly but inside she quailed. What did she know about anything? But just as Moll screamed again, Gwen heard the door open below. Thank God.

'There's Quinn now,' she said. 'It's all going to be fine, Moll. He'll know exactly what to do.'

She ran downstairs but her bubbling words of relief died on her lips when she saw his face.

'I can't do it, Gwen,' he said.

'What do you mean? You've got to.'

'I've not much experience with babies and so much can go wrong. I daren't help here.'

'Moll's counting on you.' Gwen could hear her voice becoming shrill.

'I've sent Ben for a midwife.'

'When will she get here? Will she know what to do?'

Quinn shrugged. 'Far more than I do at any rate.'

'You must know something.'

'I did a lot of reading about it at one time because my mam died in childbirth but Gwen, there's not been much call for those skills on the battlefield.'

'Anything is better than nothing.'

Quinn ran his hands through his hair and rubbed his ears which were numb and reddened from the wind still howling outside. Then he looked at her, face haggard. 'Oh, Gwen, don't ask this of me! I swore I wasn't ever going to do any doctoring again. I can't do it, I just can't.'

'Why not? Give me one good reason.'

'I killed a patient.'

That made her pause. 'I . . . I don't understand.'

He gestured impatiently. 'That doesn't matter now. The simple truth is that I'll never put myself in that position again. I'll not have any more blood on my hands, d'you hear me?'

Gwen caught him by the arm. 'I don't know what you are talking about but Moll needs you. Think of all the good you've done – the bones you've set, the wounds you tended. Jack said you couldn't help yourself.'

'Those were easy. No one would die.'

'You saved me.'

Quinn smiled briefly. 'Well, that was just heroics. Besides, I couldn't say "told you so" to a corpse now, could I?'

Before Gwen had a chance to reply, Ben arrived at the door, panting heavily and shook his head. 'Couldn't find her. She's out at another birth. Left a message for her to come when she could, though.'

Quinn cursed and at that moment Moll gave a bloodcurdling cry. Gwen swung to face him, her eyes blazing entreaty. For a minute they stood locked in wordless combat and then with a gesture of defeat he said, 'Jaysus help me. All right, then. Listen. Get me hot water – towels and sheets – clean ones. Then get the hell out of here. Take Ben to the theatre to see Stella.'

Ben gave a happy exclamation and Quinn smiled down at him. 'You go put the water on and Gwen'll be there in a minute.'

When he was sure Ben was out of earshot, Quinn continued urgently, 'Go backstage after the show. Have a party, anything. If things go wrong here, I don't want Ben to hear a woman die.'

Gwen nodded, her eyes enormous. 'Shouldn't I come back and help you, leave Ben with Stella?'

'No.' His voice was sharp. 'This is something I'll do by myself.' Moll screamed again. 'Get me the stuff, then go.'

With that, Quinn ran up the stairs two at a time. His voice when he entered the bedroom however was warm and reassuring, stripped of all the desperation he'd shown just seconds earlier. 'Now then, Moll, don't fret yourself, I'm here now. Tell me what's happening with you. I must know when the pains started.'

Gwen didn't wait to hear more, racing instead to get the blankets and towels. Ben called to say the water was boiled and she took everything up to the room.

Quinn had cast his coat aside and was feeling Moll's stomach. Gwen's eyes met his.

''Tis a breech birth, and not some sort of monstrosity, which is what Moll was fearing,' he told her. 'No wonder poor Moll has been unable to push her baby out. I'm going to see if I can turn it.' Then he smiled at Moll. 'We'll be working together from now on, Moll, all right? We'll do it together.'

Moll nodded, her eyes blurred but fixed on Quinn's face.

He gave Gwen a brief smile. 'Go,' he said calmly, 'and mind what I told you.'

With a shiver, Gwen realised that he still felt the situation was indeed grave despite his reassuring manner.

'I'll be thinking of you both and Moll, you'll stay with us once the child is born. Understood?'

Moll nodded then screamed again, her hand crushing Quinn's in her agony.

Turning on her heel, Gwen ran downstairs saying lightly to Ben, 'Come on, let's go. Won't Stella be surprised and delighted!'

As they hurried to the theatre, Gwen felt like a traitor for abandoning both Quinn and Moll, no matter what Quinn had said. How could she sit through a performance while all the time her thoughts would be straying back to her small room? What if Quinn did need assistance after all?

'Look, there's Jack,' Ben cried out. He pointed to the lanky figure some way ahead, caught up in the press of eager patrons surging towards the theatre doors.

'Jack!' Gwen called out.

He spun around and immediately made his way to them, pushing against the crowd. 'Gwen, what's going on? Where's Quinn? What's happened about Moll?'

Quickly she explained the situation, being careful not to give Ben any inkling of how serious it was. 'I'd like to go back,' she said meaningfully, 'in case Quinn needs a hand. Can you take Ben?'

'Of course. You're in luck, m'boy,' Jack told Ben, who looked up with shining eyes. 'I've reserved seats right in the front row – you can have Quinn's.'

'Thank you!' Gwen's tones were heartfelt and Jack gave her a twisted smile.

'My role is the easy one. You take care.'

'I will. Don't hurry home.'

Jack winked at Ben. 'Now it's not often we are given permission like that, is it. Parties it is after the show then, what do you say?'

'Oh, yes!' Ben beamed and despite her anxiety, Gwen laughed and dropped a kiss on top of his head.

'Have fun.'

She watched for a minute as they moved back into the throng then began to make her way home, terror hollowing her stomach.

She could hear Moll's cries, hoarse and panting, even as she let herself into the house. Running up the stairs, Gwen stopped short at her bedroom door. Moll was bent over, hands pressed against the wall, her face slick with perspiration while Quinn rubbed her lower back, murmuring encouragement.

'Breathe through it. The pains will pass. They always do, eventually.'

'I'm awful afraid,' Moll gasped. 'I don't want to die.'

'Moll, I promise you, I'm going to do everything possible to keep you and your baby safe.' Quinn's voice was low and firm. It gave no indication of what his real feelings might be.

Gwen stepped into the room. 'Moll, I've come back to be with you. What can I do to help?'

Quinn whipped around. 'Where's Ben?'

'He's fine – at the theatre with Jack. I'm here to

help in whatever way I can. What should I do?'
Gwen moved forward and as the maid straightened, she took Moll's hand and squeezed it. 'I'm right here with you, Moll.'

Quinn bit his lip and shook his head. ''Tis no place for a la—'

'I'm a *woman*, Quinn,' Gwen interrupted him. 'Giving birth is woman's work.'

Moll's hand tightened fiercely on Gwen's, almost causing her to cry out in pain. 'Let 'er stay, Mr O'Donnell. I'm awful scared.'

Quinn was clearly unhappy but with a faint shrug, he accepted the situation.

'In that case, what would be really helpful would be if you could help me get rid of a lot of these damned clothes. I cannot be fighting petticoats at a time like this.'

Gwen thought for a second then inspiration struck. 'Stella's Lady Macbeth robe.'

Within minutes she and Quinn had managed to help relieve Moll of her clothes and to put on Stella's loose robe, which swamped the small maid but clearly gave her greater comfort. She couldn't stay still, however.

'Gotta walk!' she growled and paced back and forth, bending to lean her palms against the wall at intervals and groan.

'Could you turn the baby?' Gwen asked softly.

Quinn shook his head. 'Her waters broke on her way here. I don't think the baby can now.'

'So what do we do?'

He shrugged and answered in a low voice. 'I've no idea. We'll work that out when the time comes.' Then he spoke louder, 'Moll, I need to examine you, see how much you've dilated. Can you bear to lie on the bed again while I do?'

The following hours seemed endless. Gwen and Quinn eased the maid's pain as much as they could; massaging her lower back and bathing her sweating face. Moll could not find comfort in any position; leaning against the wall, leaning over the bedhead and even going down on all fours on the floor at one stage. This last amazed Gwen but Quinn was calm and reassuring throughout.

'You just choose the position you feel is best, Moll. We'll work around you.'

'There's no best,' Moll said, panting through gritted teeth, 'but I tell you doc, I think it's beginning to move. I've got this terrible urge to push again.'

'This is probably it, then,' said Quinn. 'Can I see once more?'

Gwen averted her gaze, staying at Moll's head and stroking the hair out of the maid's eyes as Quinn said with some satisfaction, 'I think you're right, Moll. It all looks fine down here. I'm right with you now. Anytime you like to push, you tell me. Do you want to move to another position?'

Moll shook her head, gulping air in spurts. 'Nah. It feels best like this, now.' She was leant awkwardly back at an angle, legs braced on the edge of the bed.

Gwen moved to settle herself behind the maid, her arms under Moll's armpits so that Moll could lean her weight back.

'There, how's that?'

The maid nodded, panting fast now. 'Better.' The pain ripping through her voice belied the word but clearly the support Gwen gave her was helping.

Quinn looked up and met Gwen's eyes and, with a tiny nod of approval, smiled. Then he turned all of his attention to the maid.

'This is it, Moll. I can just see the baby. Can you push?'

Moll, eyes screwed tightly shut, nodded. Gwen's mouth went dry and she braced herself as the maid spasmed against her hold.

'Oh, gawd!' Moll's scream rent the air, the most primitive cry Gwen had ever heard. A cry that gave her gooseflesh and for the first time in her life she thought about what it really was to be a woman. A woman who would herself one day undergo this same intense battle to give new life. A battlefield with death lurking in every shadow. Suddenly her mother, who had never been anything more than a portrait in her father's study, seemed real. In this ripping, rending way her mother had died. And in this way too, Quinn's mother had died. His words of warning for Ben echoed in her mind and Gwen went cold. What had she done? Was Quinn being forced to relive what must surely have been one of the worst times in his life? How was he feeling at this very moment? He didn't want any more blood on his hands but here he was, staying with Moll even knowing she might die.

Tears rose in Gwen's eyes and she looked down at him crouched on the floor, hands at the ready. Yet it seemed that Quinn had put everything from him for the moment. His face was intent, his thoughts entirely focused on mother and child.

Moll arched, screamed and Quinn said softly, but with great satisfaction, 'That was splendid, Moll. The baby's bottom is out. 'Tis a girl.'

Moll gave a hiccup, halfway between a cry and a laugh.

'Nearly there now,' Quinn said, his hands very gently cradling the tiny rump. 'You're doing grand, just grand, lass. I don't want to pull at it, though. I think it's best you do it yourself. Are you ready to try again?'

Moll nodded. Again a scream and Gwen was nearly rocked sideways as she struggled to hold the maid safe through her contraction.

'Grand, there's the belly and legs. I'm just helping to free the one that's a bit caught.' His voice was calm. 'Good. Now, there's just the head to come, Moll. I daren't do anything but hold the baby so the neck is safe. I've a finger on her chin to keep it down on her chest, that's all. You are still the one in control. Don't you worry, I won't let anything happen to your little girl. You just focus on what you must do. Final one. Ready?'

The words were barely out of his mouth when Moll screamed again and in a slithery bundle, the baby fell free into Quinn's waiting hands. Immediately he wrapped her and turned her so there was a tiny gasp and the first mewling cry of a new life.

'She's well, Moll. She's perfect.' Quinn's voice vibrated with joy. 'The grandest babe you ever did see!' and Moll burst into wracking tears.

At that very moment a woman's voice called up the stairs. 'Yoo-hoo. Is that a baby I just heard?'

Gwen dashed away her own tears with the heel of her hand. 'That must be the midwife.'

They heard the footsteps coming up.

'We're in here,' Gwen called.

The door swung open and in came the midwife; a trim, brisk woman well past her own childbearing years.

'I'm too late, I see.' She immediately crossed to Moll and put a hand on her forehead. 'How are you, deary? You just cry on. First baby is it? All over now.'

''Tis not quite over, there's still the placenta to come,' said Quinn.

'Do you need a hand?'

'I'd be grateful for your advice.'

The midwife gave a little snort. 'Looks like you are long past needing that, young man.' Nevertheless, she moved to assist him, taking the baby from him.

The room suddenly seemed overcrowded and Gwen knew her role was done.

'I'll go get water to wash the baby,' she said and the midwife nodded.

'That would be good. And I'd kill for a cuppa, dear. Came straight from another birth and haven't had a thing all night. The doctor here looks like he could do with something, too. Water's probably best for the mother?' Her voice rose in enquiry and Moll nodded wordlessly.

As Gwen slipped downstairs, she discovered she was trembling; awed by the miracle of birth. A happy ending, after all. Yet there was no time to assimilate what she'd just witnessed for at that moment the front door flew open once more and Stella and Ben tumbled in out of the wind. Quickly Gwen told them the news and Stella gave her a bone-crunching hug.

'Oh, darling, how splendid!'

It was as though real life had been suspended and now swung into motion again. Ben excitedly told Gwen all about the show and she gave an excellent semblance of listening as she put water on to boil, but it was a struggle to bring her thoughts back to earth and concentrate.

Stella was not deceived and very soon put an end to his chatter. 'Right, young Ben, you're sharing my bed tonight. But no snoring or kicking, or you'll be on the floor in no time.' She frowned in mock severity and with a dramatic finger pointed to the stairs. 'Up you go.'

Ben sighed. 'Do I have to? I want to see Quinn.'

'Tomorrow. Bed now, young man. See, you've just yawned wide enough for me to see down into your toes.'

Stella settled Ben as Gwen took basins and jugs of water to her bedroom, where Quinn and the midwife were busy cleaning up. Clearly not needed, she went back down to the kitchen where Stella joined her.

As they made the tea, Gwen told the actress she had offered Moll a home. Stella was not at all perturbed.

'We'll have our own little baby to play with. What fun we'll have! Ben can sleep in my bed for now.'

Gwen smiled. 'Stella, you are one of the nicest, most generous people I think I've ever met.'

Stella just laughed. 'Darling,' she pointed out, '*you* are the one losing your bedroom.'

Their conversation was interrupted by the arrival of the midwife in the kitchen. Her face was tired but tranquil.

'All's well upstairs but the doctor is just staying with the wee mite to make sure she falls asleep. Ah, is that cuppa for me?'

She wrapped her fingers around one generous cup and sank into one of the chairs.

'What a fine job that young man made of it tonight. Breech births are dangerous things and doctors always want to rush in and maul the mother about. The stories I could tell you.' She shook her head. 'No, that doctor's got a good head on his shoulders. Managed it all just fine. I want to recommend him to other women but he tells me he isn't a real doctor – is that so?' Her voice was curious.

'He was a surgeon in the American war.' Then honesty prompted Gwen to add shamefacedly, 'But he really doesn't want to practice medicine at all. I rather forced him into it tonight, I'm afraid.'

The midwife looked shrewdly over the rim of her cup. 'Don't look so guilty, girl. In all likelihood we'd have lost the baby without him. He's got excellent instincts. What a waste if he doesn't go back to it.' She shook her head. 'Now you go and bring him down. He looks tuckered out and no wonder. It's a stressful thing to bring your first baby into the world, especially when it's tricky like that one.'

Obediently Gwen stole up the stairs to her room and was glad to see Moll asleep, her hours of agony finally over.

Quinn turned at the sound of the door, a tiny bundle cradled in his arms. On seeing Gwen, his mouth curled up into the most wonderful smile she had ever seen and her heart leapt.

'Both asleep?' she whispered.

'They are.' Quinn's voice was soft. 'A long, exhausting road for both of them.'

Gwen tiptoed across the room and Quinn

lowered his arm so that she could look at the sleeping baby's face.

'Isn't she beautiful?' she said with a sigh.

He gave a low laugh. 'Now that all that muck's been washed off her, she's a champion little girl. A fighter and a survivor just like her mother.'

Gwen looked up at the Irishman and saw a tenderness in his face that she'd never seen before and she put her hand on his arm. 'You did so well, tonight. Thank you. I didn't know where else to turn. They owe their lives to you.'

He shrugged but his ears turned pink. 'In the end 'twas nothing. All I did was catch the babe.'

Gwen shook her head. 'That's not what the midwife says. But come, you look exhausted. Stella is downstairs making tea. Can you leave them?'

'I can. Both should sleep a long while now.' Gently he tucked the tiny baby into the crook of her mother's arm. Moll stirred, felt her baby and smiled, her arm tightening protectively before she drifted off again.

'Now, if you could only photograph that,' whispered Quinn.

The midwife had already left and Stella was washing the crockery, but there was still tea in the pot and Quinn downed two cups in quick succession.

'What'll she be called?' Stella wanted to know.

'Well, apparently 'tis the custom in Moll's family to name the baby after the midwife but in this case Quinn seemed uncommonly cruel for a little girl, so Moll came up with Jessica after her mother and Guinevere as the second name.'

Gwen, who'd picked up a towel and was now drying the cups, gave a happy exclamation. 'Me? But I did nothing.'

''Twas your bed she had the baby on, your clothes she was wearing.'

'Well, Stella's Lady Macbeth robe, actually.'

'*My* robe?' Stella pretended outrage. 'There ought to be a Stella in that line-up of names then!'

Quinn laughed. 'Talk to Moll about it on the morrow.'

'Today you mean. The hour is very late. I must go and get my beauty sleep. Goodnight you two.'

Stella exited for it was clear that despite looking exhausted, Gwen and Quinn still had things to say.

When they were alone, Gwen hung up the towel and pulled a chair alongside Quinn's in front of the fire. Turning to look into his face, she said in her impetuous way, 'Oh, Quinn! I'm so sorry. I forced you into an appalling situation, tonight. You coped marvellously, of course, but if it had gone wrong you'd have blamed yourself forever and it wouldn't have been your fault at all. It was only once we were up there and Moll was giving those horrendous cries that I realised she might die. I'll never forget the sound! And that's what you heard as a little boy, wasn't it, when your mother – when she . . .'

'When she died, yes. That was what got me interested in being a doctor in the first place. I felt so damnably helpless and my daddy was beside himself not knowing what to do. I swore then that I'd learn how to save people.' He gave a bitter laugh. 'Oh, I was full of fine dreams at that age.'

'But tonight you did just that! Three people now owe you their lives: Moll, Jessica and myself.'

'Hush. Don't talk such nonsense and don't go on about me saving you, either. All I did was pull you out of the water. Didn't need much brains for that!'

'Even so.'

A silence fell between them as they stared into the flames in the hearth.

'Tell me,' Gwen said softly.

'Tell you what?'

'Tell me of the patient you killed.'

Quinn sighed and shifted. 'I don't even like to think of it.'

'But you can't help it. I can tell it haunts you.'

For a long moment Quinn remained still. His face was set, his fine eyebrows drawn together. His mouth that she loved to watch was pressed in a thin line. The fire lit his cheekbones and cast shadows on his cheeks. His nose was strong in profile, his jaw firm.

He leaned forward, put another log on the fire then settled back and looked at Gwen. His guarded expression was back. 'I'll tell you but you won't like it and you won't like me for the telling of it.'

Gwen didn't know what to say so she took his hand and squeezed it.

The corner of his mouth lifted. 'Oh, Lady Guinevere, you are the strangest one,' he murmured, 'to hold the hand of a murderer as he makes his confession.'

Again he paused as if the words were too difficult to find but finally he began.

''Twas in the last days of the war. For years – decades it seemed – we'd done nothing but saw limbs off, stitch guts back into blasted stomachs and bandage the eyes of men gone blind. 'Tis hard, even in this kitchen, for me to remember fully the horror of it all. The smell of blood constantly in our nostrils, and the smell of festering.' His face contorted. 'The smell of festering seems to cling to everything. We'd not slept for weeks, not properly. Soldiers complained of boredom between battles but I tell you, for the doctors there never seemed to be any rest. We'd snatch a few hours here and there, even a ten-minute nap was heaven.

'Though the war was guttering, still the bodies kept arriving; men crying out in pain, boys some not much older than young Ben, with arms or legs blown off. You don't talk to them much – they just become so many body parts. You don't want to know of their lives or you could go mad with the senselessness of it. I used to stand there, sweat pouring down my face, sewing up wounds that had never been described in training, tending

302

burns that melted men's faces down and dream of being far away, all alone with high skies above and the clean smell of grass and heather.'

Quinn broke off but Gwen nodded. 'So that's why you want land so much,' she whispered.

He seemed not to hear, his eyes fixed on some distant place. ''Twas very late one night and I'd just sent the orderly off to bed. It seemed that for once we might have a quiet night but then they brought that final body in – a boy not out of his teens. I was relieved to see his injuries weren't too bad and he caught my arm as I leaned over him and said, "Am I going to die, doctor? I don't want to die."

'And I, arrogant fool that I was, assured him his injuries were not great and that he wouldn't die. He fell back against the stretcher and said, "I'm so glad! I'm to be married, you see."

'It made me smile for the boy was not much old enough to shave let alone plan his wedding but you know, 'tis dreams that keep a man alive.'

Here Quinn broke off and looked at Gwen. 'Dreams that keep a woman fighting on alone in a strange land.'

Despite the gravity of the story, she smiled. 'So that is why you gave me my darkroom. I cannot tell you how much – but not now. Go on with your story.'

'Well, it was a straightforward operation and I decided I could do it alone and not bother the orderly. I'd become quite skilled over the years you see, and proud of it too. There was no anaesthetic so I was working fast to lessen the shock to the body – too bloody fast.'

He stared unseeing into the fire. 'To this day I don't know how I did it. Somehow the scalpel slipped and I severed an artery. In seconds there was blood everywhere and the boy screaming and screaming. I was trying to tie a tourniquet but my fingers couldn't move fast enough, everything was slippery with blood. I shouted for help but by the time the orderly had dragged himself out of sleep, it was too late.'

'But it was an accident. You were probably too exhausted to think clearly.'

Quinn's face was a mask. 'There are no excuses. He wanted to live – should have lived – and I killed him. Through my arrogance.'

'Surely you weren't held accountable for his death?'

'I don't know what the authorities would have said – nothing probably. What is one death amongst so many thousands? But I didn't wait to find out. Something snapped inside me. I simply lay down my instruments, walked out of the hospital tent and kept walking. I never went back. Add desertion to my sins. I should have been court-martialled for abandoning my post but it was easy enough to disappear into the chaos of the war. I didn't stop till I reached California. Mined for a bit, caught a boat and landed here.'

His hand was cold in hers, his eyes dark with

shadows. Without thinking Gwen rose and wrapped her arms around him, hugging him as though he were Ben with a scraped knee.

His hands came up to clasp her arms and then somehow she was in his lap and his arms were tight around her and he was kissing her with desperate intent as though to block out the memories.

She wound her arms around his neck and kissed him back. To begin with she was gentle and unsure, even shy – but his hunger for her ignited something within her and Gwen's kisses quickly became as fierce as his.

His lips moved to her neck, causing her to moan in a sensation she'd never known before and his hands came up to her bodice. Then as if suddenly wakening from a dream he pulled back, his breath jagged and he groaned.

'I cannot do this all again.'

'What do you mean? What are you talking about?'

'I'm sorry,' he said. 'I shouldn't have kissed you.'

'Don't apologise.'

'I took advantage of you.'

'Oh, Quinn!' Frustration made her voice sharp. 'I'm not a child! I wanted to kiss you, you fool.'

But he had set her on her feet and was already rising.

''Tisn't right, 'tisn't right at all. I shouldn't have taken advantage of you. I'm nothing but an Irish peasant. Believe me, there is no future in any of this – only pain. You'll be regretting it all first thing in the morning, you'll see.'

'I'll regret nothing – except your Irish pig-headedness.'

The corner of his mouth lifted slightly but still he made his way to the door where he stopped and looked back over his shoulder. 'Good night, Lady Guinevere,' he said, then paused before adding softly, 'and thank you.'

CHAPTER 15

The following afternoon Jack and Quinn arrived at the house at the same moment as a well-dressed young man was rapping at the door. The men nodded civilly to each other, though there was a speculative glitter in Jack's eye. The door swung open and there, like a goddess in a dark yellow dress that set her hair on fire, was Stella.

'Mr *Worthing*, how good to see you today. I trust you enjoyed last night's performance. Oh, are those flowers for me? How *sweet* of you. Jack, Quinn. Have you come to see the baby? Such *fun*, Mr Worthing, we have new additions to our household – the *prettiest* baby you ever saw. Gwen and I have been playing with her all day. *Do* come in out of the cold gentlemen and be prepared to fall quite in love.'

Stella led the way through the studio. Jack, who had been in high spirits until just a few minutes earlier, followed on her heels with a thunderous face. As the men filed into the kitchen, Gwen was just wrapping the baby up in warm blankets and Quinn was struck by how lovely she looked. She was wearing dark green, her hair caught in a careless knot on top of her head and the spring sun that shone in through the window caught red lights in the glossy chestnut.

She smiled as she snuggled the baby into her shoulder.

'How lovely to see you all. Have you come to make your acquaintance with Jessica? I fear that poor Stella will be quite cast in the shade by this little lady.'

Stella, looking undismayed, peppered kisses on the tiny head. 'She's just the *sweetest* little darling, I could gobble her up. My turn to hold her, Gwen. You've been hogging her this past half hour.'

Laughing, Gwen relinquished her bundle and turned to Quinn. 'We've been fighting over Jess all day so don't go thinking you can claim a doctor's rights and steal a cuddle for yourself.'

Her eyes were teasing but there was something else; a warmth, an intimacy that Quinn noted with a pang. It was not right. He had to quash all of this before it went any further. 'I came by to see how Moll is doing,' he lied.

Moll was, of course, important but Quinn, having been awake since before dawn, had not been able to last the day without seeing Gwen. Though he knew there could only be pain in visiting and not touching her, still he could not help himself. Now, looking into those gold-flecked eyes, he knew it was a mistake to have come. He had behaved appallingly last night, taking advantage of her innocence, which was all the more despicable given that she was alone and undefended in the world. In a moment's weakness he had given into desires suppressed for months and she, so unsuspecting, had only meant to give comfort. She did not understand that she was playing with fire while he – oh, what a fool he was. Had he learnt nothing over the years?

He loved her. He'd finally, bitterly admitted to himself, had loved her all these past months. He loved her spirit, her warmth, her capacity for making a hovel into a home, her undaunted courage in the face of so many adversities. But a common Irishman would never figure in the future she had so clearly fixed in her mind. He well knew how tenaciously the English aristocracy clung to their fine homes, their lands, their unassailable place in society and Guinevere, for all her impetuosity and courage, was still just one of them. And as he'd lain in the darkness, acknowledging the truth of this, his anger – so hot against himself – had boiled over against her too.

He had felt her quickening pulse during their kisses, had felt the flare of her passion. She was a creature of impulse and would certainly follow her desires, a lady not used to being denied. But these were dangerous games, all the more dangerous because now she owned his heart. He was determined, however, she would not break it. She must never guess the extent of his feelings towards her. He could not bear to see contempt or, worse, pity in those eyes so he met her smile now with an expression of cool, professional interest.

'How is my patient this morning?'

Gwen's eyes narrowed as they searched his face and her face lost its warmth though she replied evenly enough, 'Moll's asleep. She was in excellent spirits this morning, though weak as a kitten. If you would care to stay for a cup of tea, I daresay she will waken soon.'

As Quinn took a seat at the table with the other two men, Guinevere, spine very straight, moved to the fire where she put a pot on to boil. She had been sleepless much of the night, reliving over and over the glorious memory of his kisses that had fired her senses in a way she'd never dreamed possible. Yet always she came back to that wrenching moment when he had pulled away. Why? What reason did he have? How could she make sense of her own tangle of emotions until she understood him better? And now, when she most needed to talk, to find answers, he was back to being the intractable, infuriating Irishman she'd first met.

What was this cold distance he was putting between them? Men trifled with women, she knew that, but surely Quinn wouldn't play games with her? She felt suddenly humiliated to remember her fervent response to his caresses and her cheeks burned as she leaned over the fire. Did he think her common? Wanton? Did he have the temerity – the cruelty – to be judging her? How dare he.

Stella, who had been chatting brightly to her two swains as she rocked the baby in her arms, now exclaimed, 'There! The little darling is falling asleep. I'll just take her upstairs.'

'And I'll check on Moll,' said Gwen, snatching at the opportunity to escape and as the women walked out, silence fell on the visitors.

Jack eyed Mr Worthing, noting the immaculately cut suit, the gleaming shoes and the shining hair. Dashed fellow was as spruce as a new pin and suddenly Jack was aware of his own careless clothes, his muddied boots. Stella could not possibly fancy such a dull dog, yet the smile she bestowed upon the man was one of particular sweetness. Unable to look at Mr Worthing's natty attire a moment longer, Jack glowered down at his hands clenched tight between his knees.

Mr Worthing picked an imaginary piece of fluff from his jacket and cleared his throat.

Quinn stretched his legs out and shoved his hands deep into his pockets, cursing himself for coming today, cursing Gwen for not having caught the bloody boat to England when she could.

All three men looked up in relief when they heard Stella clattering down the stairs again.

'Moll's just woken and Gwen's having a word with her. Now, tea, gentlemen?'

She filled the silence with chatter and Mr Worthing rose gallantly to the occasion. The ease with which he and Stella talked of mutual acquaintances caused Jack to grow ever more sullen and it was left to Quinn to supply a few commonplaces so they did not appear wholly graceless. He was glad, however, when Gwen slipped down to say that Moll was keen to see him.

Quinn immediately rose and followed Gwen up the stairs, remembering how she'd been wearing a green dress the first time they'd met. He should have just left her in the forest then and there.

Outside the door they heard Moll's exclamation. 'Oh, Jessica! Pooh!'

Despite the cold restraint between them, their eyes met and the corner of Quinn's mouth lifted. 'Now I most certainly do intend claiming the rights of a doctor. I am here to tend the mother only, seeing as the daughter is clearly thriving.'

Gwen shot him a withering look but her smile was rueful. 'She's such a darling little thing but that'll be the sixth today! Why is it that everything wonderful must always have a miserable downside?'

Why indeed, Quinn wondered, following her into the room.

Downstairs, Mr Worthing rose. 'I regret I must now take my leave, Miss Tyler.'

Jack bounded to his feet and put out his hand. 'Good to have met you, Worthing. No doubt we'll see each other around town.'

Stella frowned at Jack's evident desire to be shot of her admirer and bestowed one of her blinding smiles upon the natty young man who blinked, dazzled. 'I'll see you to the door, Mr Worthing.'

Having bid Jack farewell in the most proper way, Mr Worthing followed Stella to the door where he engaged her in conversation in a low voice. Jack strained to hear the words but though he could not catch them, there could be no mistaking the urgent warmth of the other man's tone. Stella's replies were gentler than he'd have liked. There was none of the teasing laughter she usually employed to set her swains at a distance.

When Stella returned to the kitchen, she was in time to see Jack fiercely kick a log deeper into the flames, sending sparks flying up the chimney. She eyed him thoughtfully and settled herself next to the table, where she picked up some knitting. She and Gwen were on a mission to make baby clothes as swiftly as possible.

Jack dropped into the chair next to her. 'You surely don't mean to have that dull dog?' he asked belligerently.

'I haven't decided,' said Stella, counting stitches. 'Oh, I've dropped one. What a nuisance.'

'What do you mean, haven't decided? You cannot be serious. What has he to offer you?'

'Marriage, a home, children.'

Stella lifted her beautiful green eyes and in them there was an expression Jack had never seen before. Usually they danced with mischief but now they were serious, even a little sad.

'Jack, I cannot be playing forever,' she said. 'I'm tired of it. I don't want to be Stella Tyler the actress any more. This house has been my only home since

I was ten years old and in a few months I'll have to leave it again when the troupe moves up to Wellington and later back to Melbourne. I'm tired of travelling, of being adored but never loved. And seeing Jessica has made me yearn for a baby of my own. I just want to settle down – I know that sounds dull to you, but to me it sounds like heaven.'

Jack stared at her. 'But dash it, Stella, I thought that we – that is, that I – you know. I thought what was between us was a bit different to what you have with all the other fellows.'

'If you mean, do I like you more – yes, I do. But not enough to give up an offer of a secure and comfortable future.'

'Damn it! I can give you those.'

'You've never offered them.'

'Do you mean you want me to offer for you?'

'Not if you don't want to.'

Jack looked at her. 'I'd always thought that one day – but not right now – we'd, you know.'

Stella laid down her knitting and looked frankly back at him. 'No, I don't know. You come from a fine family, they won't welcome an actress as a daughter but I will *not* be your mistress, Jack.'

He gave a low whistle. 'You were always one to talk straight, Stella. Doesn't matter a damn what my family thinks, to be honest. Always been the black sheep, you know. Just never thought of myself as the marrying sort.'

'That's fine,' said Stella, resuming her knitting. 'We are clear on that, then.'

'No, dash it, we are not! I love you, Stella.'

'Love isn't enough for me.'

He laughed suddenly. 'Then marry me, for God's sake. I don't want to live without you and if I saw you marrying that dreary man, I think I'd blow my brains out.'

'What are you offering me, Jack?'

Now he became as serious as she. 'I'll buy you a home. Quinn and I have made a packet these past few months. My uncle has proposed several business ventures and I'll take one of those. We can have as many brats as you like.'

'But is this what *you* want?'

'I just want you,' he said simply. 'Any way, any how. Even if it means becoming a respectable family man.'

'Oh, Jack!' And Stella, who had not cried since she was fourteen years old, found to her astonishment that tears were sliding down her cheeks.

Jack caught one on his finger. 'Silly, Stella. Didn't mean to make you cry,' and taking the knitting out of her hands, he pulled her into his arms.

When Quinn and Gwen joined them ten minutes later, Stella was rosy and dishevelled and Jack boisterous in his delight.

'Congratulate me! I'm the happiest man alive.'

Gwen clasped her hands together and her face lit up. 'You mean you and Stella—?'

'Yes, she forced me to it! Damned if I was going to see that dreary cove make off with my fair Stella.'

Gwen threw her arms first around Stella, then around Jack, exclaiming her delight.

Quinn was taken aback but disguised his amazement as he shook hands with Jack and kissed Stella on the cheek, saying all the right things. Jack was clearly cock-a-hoop and Stella glowed with a new radiance.

'We're off out of here to go buy a ring before she changes her mind! Get your cloak, Stella and let's make haste. Tonight we'll all celebrate – our engagement and Quinn's land.'

'Quinn's land?' Gwen's eyes flew to Quinn's face, which was inscrutable.

'He clinched the deal last night just before young Ben came in looking for him. A magnificent tract, a couple of days' ride from here. Got it at an excellent price too – my godfather was most put out over the breakfast table to hear that Quinn stole a march on him. He's had his ear open for similar land for the past six months and didn't hear of this deal at all till we told him this morning.'

Gwen's heart faltered but she put on a brave face. 'So, will you be leaving us?'

Quinn nodded. 'Ben and I'll go and check it out tomorrow. There's a cottage of sorts that we can live in until a house can be built.'

'How *splendid*!' cried Stella.

'That's wonderful.' Gwen forced herself to sound happy. 'I'll miss Ben terribly though.'

Quinn looked uncomfortable. 'You can stay in

this house as long as you are in New Zealand, of course. You're an excellent tenant.'

How cold that sounded. She nodded. 'Thank you. Yes, I'll have to think. This will be just the motivation I need to decide my next move.'

'Plenty of time to discuss details. Quinn can't throw my bride out of her home before our wedding. We'll see you tonight. I'll bring the champagne.'

The newly engaged couple disappeared in a clatter of excitement and joy, leaving the kitchen feeling strangely desolate. Quinn and Gwen looked at each other awkwardly.

'Congratulations on your land,' said Gwen again. Quinn nodded his thanks. 'I know it has always been your dream.'

He did not look as rapt as one might expect from a man who had achieved his heart's desire.

'And isn't it wonderful about the engagement,' Gwen blundered on to fill the silence. 'I thought Jack would never get round to it. I couldn't have borne it if Stella had married Mr Worthing. He couldn't have been more wrong for her. But you look dubious. Why?'

Quinn shrugged. 'Jack's a gentleman even though he's a scamp and Stella – well sure, she's just an actress when all's said and done. His godfather is Lord Whittering, for goodness sake. How will he present her to them?'

Gwen was indignant. 'Stella will conduct herself beautifully and they will have to accept her.

317

Besides,' she added with scorn, 'Lord Whittering himself is no gentleman – not deep down.'

'Oh, Gwen. Because of Moll?'

'Don't sound so dismissive. It's appalling that he should get away with such behaviour.'

'But that's exactly what English gentlemen do. It doesn't alter their position. Why, even your own father—' Quinn caught himself up, but Gwen pounced on his words.

'What about my father?'

Quinn looked away. ''Tis nothing.'

In her haughtiest voice she said, 'If you mean to imply that my father could ever have behaved in such a way—'

Quinn, stung by the tones he loathed so much, interrupted, 'Don't be so blind, Guinevere! Your father was not the bleeding saint you make him out to be. Jaysus, you had three governesses, all young and pretty. Think Gwen! Why did they leave?'

She hesitated. 'I don't know.' Then more confidently she added, 'Eccy was ill.'

'What sort of illness?'

Gwen shrugged. 'Something with her stomach – she vomited a lot.'

'In the morning?'

'Ye-es.' Gwen faltered and sank down into a chair. 'That is a sign, isn't it?' she whispered.

Quinn nodded.

'You think . . .?' but she couldn't finish the sentence.

'Think that out there somewhere you have a

younger brother or sister. Yes, I think it.' Quinn's tone was brutal. 'That's what fine English folk do. They take their pleasure where they find it and the consequences be damned.'

Gwen shook her head, still defiant. 'But Father never once said anything.'

'What could he say? Guinevere, you've a brother but I cannot recognise him for what will the neighbours say?'

Then seeing her stricken face, Quinn squatted down next to her chair and began chafing her cold hands, his voice harsh with remorse. 'There, I shouldn't have said anything. 'Tis all old history. I may well be wrong. Forget it.'

It did not seem she would as her fingers closed over his, nails digging in like claws, to leave crescent welts in his skin. 'I'm so naive!' she whispered. 'Why didn't I guess?'

'You thought the world of your daddy. It wouldn't have crossed your mind to think anything bad of him. And from his point of view, it probably didn't seem so terrible. I expect he supported them – he sounds a generous man.'

Gwen pulled her hands away from his, her eyes blazing. 'Why then, if you have so little respect for the English gentry, do you find it so hard to contemplate a love match between Jack and Stella?'

Quinn rose, retreating a few paces to lean a shoulder against the mantle. ''Tisn't right. They are from different worlds. In this case it isn't quite so bad because Jack will pull Stella up into his world, but if it had been the other way round . . .' He shook his head. 'It wouldn't have done at all.' His tone was very final.

'Yet Stella is the one who will make him respectable.'

Quinn's sombre expression lifted for a second as he grinned. 'I confess I'm looking forward to the sight of Jack as a spruce husband and father.'

Shakily, Gwen laughed too and the air between them cleared a little. 'For my part,' she stated, 'I couldn't be more delighted. I think Stella is exactly the sort of wife Jack needs to keep him in order. Any young woman his parents might approve of would not be able to manage him at all. They were meant to be together.'

Quinn shot her a look through narrowed eyes. 'So you believe in love matches?' he asked.

'Absolutely.'

He threw up his hands, only just stopping himself from grabbing her by the arms and giving her a good shaking. 'Then how in the name of all that's holy can you even contemplate marrying a man you do not care for?'

Her head went up, her chin jutted. 'That is entirely different.'

'How so?'

'Maidenhurst has been in the family for centuries. I'm the last one left. My father didn't have a son so it's my responsibility – and I'm proud of it! Would you have condemned Stella for marrying Mr Worthing?'

'Not at all, I would have understood.'

'Then why can you not understand this? It was my father's dying wish. I cannot – will not – fail my father. I'll buy it back if I can, but otherwise—' she broke off.

'Oh, you don't have to explain! I know exactly how it is with you English girls. I've seen it all before.'

The bitterness in his voice goaded her. 'What do you mean?' she demanded.

'I lost everything in the world so an English witch could keep her fine house. She took it all and never cared a damn.'

'Is that why you hate the English so much?'

He met her eyes and said with deliberate cruelty, 'It's why I hate English women.'

Gwen flinched but held her ground. 'Who was she, then? Where did you meet?'

He shook his head. 'It's all in the past. No point raking it over.'

'Quinn!' Frustration boiled over. 'This is about last night, isn't it? You have to tell me. I cannot take your veiled comments any longer, do you hear me! Who was she and how did you meet her?'

Her imperious tone jarred but also made him smile just a little. With a shrug, but not looking at her, he began.

'Her name was Louise and her daddy had lands in Ireland that I worked on when I wasn't studying. They came over each summer. She was a pretty young piece and we lads in the village watched her grow up, becoming lovelier every year. But she was always out of reach, see – an English princess we'd never dare even think about.

'Then when she was eighteen, I caught her eye and became her personal groom. Each day she took me for wild rides around the countryside; a grand little rider. I'll say that much for her.' Quinn paused and laughed in self-disparagement. 'I thought I was in love. One night, when they were having a ball, I even crept up to the window to watch her dance in one man's arms, then another's. She was laughing, and flirting but what none of them knew was that her kisses were kept for me. In the forest, where no one could see us.'

He stopped again and reddened. 'I cannot say more. 'Tis not for a lady to hear.'

Gwen sliced the air in a frustrated gesture. 'Quinn, I shall scream if you insist on treating me like a porcelain doll. You've shattered my illusions about my father and now you are blenching at this?'

For a second he debated then sighed and sat down at the table. Gwen drew up a chair on the far side.

This time Quinn looked at her, his face expressionless. 'Well, as I said, I was young and stupid. I used to talk of our future together, drawing her pretty pictures of how it would be – me a doctor and us with a house in Dublin – but she'd just stop my nonsense with a laugh and a kiss. As always she went away for the London season and when she came back, she was engaged to some English lord.'

Gwen made a small sound but Quinn disregarded it. 'The family was very pleased and the whole village buzzed about the fine match she'd made. I was once again her groom but now I resented it – how I resented it. Then on our first ride out, she stopped where we always stopped and kissed me. Said she was not marrying for love and that the man she was marrying was old. Then she kissed me again. I wanted to resist her but I couldn't.'

Unable to remain sitting, Quinn shoved back his chair and strode across to the hearth where he leaned both hands on the mantle, staring into the flames. Silence filled the kitchen. Outside a bird landed on the windowsill and pecked at the seed Ben had put out earlier in the day. Then Quinn turned to look at Guinevere.

'She had planned it all. Oh, I knew that I was being used but it made no difference to how I felt, 'twas a madness we shared. We met often. I think she enjoyed the danger and I was well past caring about consequences I was that in love with her.' He broke off and shook his head at the memory. 'Of course we were finally caught one day – by her brother. She immediately cried rape, calling me an Irish peasant.'

Gwen's hand went to her throat.

Quinn noted the gesture and the harshness in his voice eased. 'I don't think her brother believed her but he had to do something. He told me to leave Ireland immediately or he'd have me arrested and I would hang.' Quinn shrugged. 'In a way I was glad to go. I couldn't bear to stay. Not after that.'

He threw Gwen a grim, sideways look. 'Well, now you know everything.'

She nodded. It was all so much to absorb. She looked into her palm, which was scored by her fingernails. It amazed her just how much searing jealousy she could feel for a woman she had never met. But it explained a lot.

'And you think I am like her?'

He would not look at her. Gwen crossed the floor to him.

'I am not her.' Her voice was hard, insistent.

Still he did not reply.

She repeated, 'I am *not* her. This isn't about her, any more. This is about us, this is about *me*, damn you Quinn O'Donnell.'

Stepping forward, Gwen reached up and twined her fingers into his hair, pulling his mouth down to hers. There was nothing gentle in her kiss. It was fierce and urgent as though to scorch away all memory of the other woman and Quinn responded with equal ferocity. He backed her up against the wall, his lips bruising hers. She crushed herself against him, feeling the hardness of his body, as he pulled the pins from her hair. Her bun came loose and he wound his hands into her curls as though to bind himself to her.

Then just as suddenly he pulled back, breathing heavily. His eyes were almost black. 'Why did you kiss me?' he demanded, voice hoarse.

Gwen slumped against the wall, knees weak to be so suddenly released. 'I don't know,' she faltered. 'To comfort you. To prove I am not her.' Looking up at him she added, 'Because you awaken sensations I have never experienced before.'

'It feels good, doesn't it?' His voice was harsh and though she nodded, she was suddenly wary. 'Good enough to throw away your silly dreams of Maidenhurst for?'

'No!' The answer was out before she even thought about it.

He nodded, unsurprised. 'Why not? Go on,' he challenged her, 'tell me why the hell not.'

Drawing herself up off the wall Gwen faced him, chin tilted. 'Because Maidenhurst is who I am and well you know it! I am a Stanhope; it is my birthright. I will not give it up for anything, for anyone.'

'Ah, and there we have it!' His voice was dark with bitter satisfaction. 'Thank you, Lady Guinevere, for your honesty. So what on earth makes you so sure you are not as cold and libertine as the rest of your kind – Louise and even your own beloved father?'

'But this is different,' Gwen cried. 'I'm not just marrying for any fine house – it's to save my home.'

'All houses are nothing more than bricks and mortar in the end. 'Tis the privilege you cling to, your position that really counts.'

Furious, she swung her hand to hit him but he

caught her wrist and bore it down. 'Go back to your home then, Lady Guinevere. Your time in New Zealand is nothing more than play acting while you wait to pick up your real life. None of us – Stella, Ben, myself – mean anything to you, not deep down.'

Now a sense of outrage, of hurt, joined forces with her fury. 'That's not true! I love Stella and Ben. How can you say such horrible things?' she cried, as she fought to free her wrist. 'How can you kiss me like that and still believe I'm so heartless?'

He dropped her arm and turned away, his voice was jagged with anger. 'Because when you get your money you plan to sail away and leave us all. Because you'll marry without love to hold a house. And because,' he added, his voice suddenly very soft, 'in all the reasons you gave for kissing me, not one of them was for love.'

CHAPTER 16

'Now mind you dress warmly, especially at night. And watch how you cross those rivers. You'll freeze before you drown if you fall in at this time of year.' Gwen tucked two extra apples into Ben's bag.

'Gwen, I came over the Alps with Quinn. I'll be fine.' His voice was full of ten-year-old exasperation but he looked pleased at having a fuss made of him all the same.

'Yes, but that was before I knew you to worry about you,' said Gwen.

'I'll take good care of the boy,' Quinn said.

'Of course. It's just that I feel so—' Gwen broke off. Furious? Hurt? Abandoned? Bereft?

For Ben's sake they were both being cordial but Quinn's eyes were bleak as a winter's sky while Gwen knew that she was far too brittle and bright. It had been another sleepless night but she took some comfort in that Quinn was looking as haggard. Was that a hint of remorse she saw when he noted her bruised lips? And so it should be! Yet the anger that had fuelled her first hours of sleeplessness when she'd argued in her head with the intolerable Irishman, pointing out the innumerable ways in which he was wrong, had almost burnt out. Her tempers were always vivid but short-lived. Dawn had brought the cold discomfort of thinking that perhaps, despite all her self-justifications, not all he had said was entirely wrong. But still, she reminded herself, it wasn't all right either. He was wrong about Ben, for instance. She loved the boy.

'You mustn't worry, Gwen,' he assured her. 'Quinn said we'll be back in time for your exhibition. We're just going to check out the land and then we'll turn right around again.'

Making an effort Gwen smiled into the bright face and stroked his hair. He was brimming with excitement now at the adventure in front of them, though before Quinn's arrival that morning he'd expressed some wistfulness at missing school.

'I'll be counting the days till you return.'

She kept her eyes on the boy but the words were meant for Quinn too. She could not bear to leave matters unresolved and besides, no matter how bitterly they had fought, her treacherous heart still leapt at the sound of his voice.

The house felt desolate after they'd gone for Moll was still in bed and Stella had slipped out uncharacteristically early.

'Right,' she told herself. 'There'll be no languishing today, Guinevere Stanhope. The barn awaits you.'

Word had come to her that Mr Orsmond had cleared out his barn and she was now welcome to start setting up. Shivering in the frosty morning air, Gwen made her way down to the river, which ran clean and cold and was feathered by willows beneath the vast dome of a brilliant blue Christchurch sky. The barn was easy to locate on the fringe of town and Gwen paused for a minute outside its large doors. This really was it; the setting for her first ever exhibition. Drawing in a deep breath, she pushed open the door and stopped short.

A spot of work needed was what Mr Orsmond had said. Slowly she took in the filthy floors, the dank boards of the walls through which outside light squeezed, smelt the rot and spied the cobwebs which liberally festooned the high roof and corners.

Gwen closed her eyes for a minute and reminded herself of Harolde who, family legend had it, had risen up at dawn every day for three years with axe in hand to clear his newly-gained land of forest to establish the fields which she, six hundred years later, had grown up admiring. She could do this – she could.

At that moment she heard Jack's cheery voice call out, 'Helloa!'

Spinning around, Gwen saw to her astonishment not only Jack but what seemed to be a small army of volunteers, led by Stella who could still look glamorous in a patched dress and with a cloth tied around her head. All the theatre folk had forsaken their habitual late risings to come to Gwen's aid and tears rose in her eyes as she laughed to see the motley collection of brooms, brushes and pails they'd brought.

'I can't believe it. This is wonderfully kind of you all,' she exclaimed. 'But of course you shouldn't have.'

'Good golly, Lady G, after enjoying so many evenings in your kitchen, you surely didn't think we'd leave you to slave away on your own sweet lonesome now, did you?' Charlie asked, bestowing a kiss on her cheek and tickling her with his extraordinary moustache.

'First time I've been up before noon in *years*,' said Percy the pianist. 'Rather lovely, isn't it.'

Not surprisingly, Alex, the stage manager, and his assistants took charge of operations. Used to transforming the bleakest of halls into makeshift theatres in a matter of hours, they set to work with gusto and the rest of the cast performed their parts if not always with the best of efficiency, certainly with enormous good humour and heart, especially when Percy brought out his accordion and provided them with lively tunes to keep them all going for the last few hours. Finally, at the end of the long day, they stood back to admire their handiwork.

'Not bad,' said Alex. 'The wind howls in through the gaps over there but I'll bring some planks tomorrow to cover them up. Bill and I'll whitewash the whole thing and while it won't be quite up to London galleries, it'll look credible at the very least. I've a paste chandelier which will set it all off very nicely.'

Gwen stood in the middle of the floor, hands clasped, mentally placing her pictures along the walls.

'It will be wonderful!' she cried. 'I simply don't know how to thank you all.'

'That's easy,' said Bob, Stella's impossibly handsome lead. 'Apple pie and lots of it – but only *after* the exhibition. You've your work cut out for you until then.'

'But what a head start you've given me.'

They all trooped back to the tiny house and though it was a crush, somehow everyone found a nook as they flowed not only into the studio and kitchen but perched up the stairs as well. Moll, her colour now returned, had made an enormous pot of vegetable soup and several loaves of bread and the meal was quickly demolished. There was much chatter and laughter and then quite suddenly the house emptied as the cast raced back to the theatre and Gwen was left alone, Moll having gone back to bed with little Jessie.

Gwen stoked the fire then sat before its warmth, feeling guilty to think of her friends priming up to a performance while she collapsed wearily. How wonderful it was to have friends of her own; people who liked her for her own sake. She knew that only genuine regard would have dug them out of bed for the frosty start. How much her father would have enjoyed the day.

His image rose up in front of her; his laughing eyes, bushy beard and high forehead. Could Quinn really be right about the governesses? She remembered her revulsion when Sir John had tried to kiss her and the idea of her father behaving in such a manner sickened her. He would never have used force of course, but would they have felt in a position to be able to refuse his advances without fearing for their jobs, without feeling compromised? There had been no Quinn to rescue them.

Now, having felt the urgency of Quinn's passion, Gwen wondered if he'd wanted to kiss her all those many nights they'd met in her room. He had never once tried to take advantage of a situation which, she now realised, most men would have been unable to resist. How grateful she was to him that he hadn't. Physical intimacy shifted things – see what chaos it had already caused between them. Then she'd been in desperate need of a friend and he seemed to understand that. But now the situation was different, she was different, that which she sought from him was . . .

She pulled her thoughts back to her father. With Eccy, at least, Gwen was sure the feelings had been mutual. Yet if Quinn were right, in the end her father had refused to cross the divide of class. Eccy would have been set aside just as Moll had been. The child would be about ten now. Wild thoughts of tracking them down and bringing them back to Maidenhurst crossed her mind but she realised she could only do that if she were mistress of her house. Mr Ramsay would never countenance such an arrangement. Unlike Quinn.

He'd be the first to agree to give Eccy a home. Not that she was thinking of him.

Deliberately, she forced herself to think instead of Maidenhurst. Strange, she had not thought specifically of her home for a while now. The nightly walk through the rooms when she'd both comforted and tortured herself with her memories had fallen away, although she couldn't quite remember when. While her resolve to regain the house was as strong as ever, she did not feel the same aching need for it that she had before. But even when she did not think consciously of it, Maidenhurst was always there, a part of her. Quinn was wrong; it wasn't just bricks and mortar.

Her father had married her mother for her dowry to save the home for another generation and he had assured Gwen it had been a satisfactory union. In Gwen's world, marriages like this happened all the time. Quinn just didn't understand. A son of a farmer could have no idea how it was for people . . . and here Gwen suddenly broke off. She'd been about to say 'people of her station'. She could well picture his lip curling at that!

Leaning back in the chair she closed her eyes and despite all her resolutions, her thoughts strayed again to Quinn and Ben camped under the stars and as she pictured them rolled up in blankets beside a dying fire, a great loneliness welled up. Hard physical labour all day had driven the last of her fury away, leaving a myriad of confused emotions.

Why had she kissed him? The answers she'd given were honest enough but had they told the whole truth? Was there a part of her that had been driven purely by the unbridled passion he'd aroused in her? Was she – and here the thought made her groan and cover her face with her hands – was she indeed more like her father than she cared to admit? She must be for her whole body ached to be taken by him again. What did Quinn want from her? He seemed to burn for her as much as she did for him, but he'd also talked of love. Well, she cared, that must surely be obvious. He had not said whether he loved her either. They both surely knew there was no point.

What if she did love him? What if, by some miracle, she found the money and could buy Maidenhurst back. Would he accompany her back to England? She tried to imagine him in her world; drinking tea and discussing the drapery in a painting or the nature of the noble savage. The mere image made her smile. He was a man who forded flooded rivers, explored virgin forests. He could never be contained within the hedgerows and well-ordered English villages. Worst of all, the soft Irish tones she loved would provoke contempt, condescension. Some would cut them, others would be nice to their faces but behind their backs there would be comments, knowing laughter. It did not bear thinking about. She would never ask him to expose himself to ridicule. He belonged to this landscape; the mountains, the wide skies.

She pictured them again, asleep on the plains. Quinn was certainly wrong about her feelings for Ben. She missed the boy greatly and ached to think of him isolated on a sprawling farm. He was doing so well at school and though Quinn would ensure the boy continued with his studies, it looked to be a lonely life. Ben loved companionship. Perhaps Quinn would marry and have other children. Her stomach curdled at the thought. Yet it was very likely, for though the colony teemed with men, still Quinn stood out; tall and handsome, already financially sound and with a good livelihood ahead of him. He might be out of place in England but in New Zealand he was already becoming known and respected. His family's security would never be in jeopardy for he would ensure that they would always be provided for. They would never be left alone and penniless as she'd—

But even as this thought slipped into her head, Gwen snapped upright and her eyes flew open. She had come within a hairsbreadth of disloyalty to her father's memory. Determined to keep any further introspection at bay, she rose and began getting out the apples and flour to make a thank-you supper for the cast.

The rest of the week rushed by at a giddy speed and fortunately for Gwen she had time for no other thoughts than her exhibition. The white-washing worked wonders and Alex found yards of very coarse sacking which, when dyed deep crimson, came up splendidly and were draped to dramatic effect against the white walls. Jack proved handy with a hammer and knocked up a number of frames and Alex taught Gwen how to paint them so they looked like old gold-leaf.

Gwen was up at dawn each day and worked by gas lamp into the night but finally, unbelievably, everything was in place. There was nothing left to be done for the opening that evening. The Whitterings had insisted they would attend to the catering. As the artist, Guinevere was to make herself charming to everyone, Lady Whittering explained, to ensure her photographs sold for high prices at the auction the following day.

Gwen suddenly found she had the house to herself save for the pleasure of baby Jessie's company. Stella was out with Jack, and Moll, who was making a remarkable recovery, had asked if Gwen would mind if she went down to the park to get some fresh air.

'I've been that cooped up this week, I'm nearly going mad with boredom, what wiv you and Miss Stella out most of the days. And then I 'ad all that time on the farm when I never saw another blessed soul. I've a right yen to get out and see people and shops again but that wind nips cruel and I daren't take the baby out. Would you mind keeping an eye on Jess for me? She'll no doubt sleep all afternoon.'

In fact Jess woke unexpectedly soon after her

mother's departure but Gwen was delighted to have the distraction for she was jumpy and restless. Nerves about the exhibition she told herself, but deep down she knew that it was because she was listening out for horses' hooves in the street; waiting, waiting. They'd promised to be back for the opening. She was a fool for all the while as she was siting there and playing with Jessica, her ears were straining, nerves on edge for a man who despised her. But she couldn't help it. She yearned to see him again, hear his Irish voice.

Finally, late in the afternoon, just as she was giving up hope, there was a rap at the door. Gwen's heart somersaulted. The baby on her shoulder, face alight with happiness, Gwen flung open the door. To her astonishment there stood a man, immaculate in black city clothes more appropriate for a London bank than a Christchurch street. Gwen stared at him disbelievingly.

'Mr Ramsay? Good lord, what on *earth* are you doing here?'

CHAPTER 17

It was not the greeting Mr Ramsay had anticipated these past three months. Upon receiving a letter telling of her father's death and learning that Lady Guinevere would be virtually penniless until the will could be settled, he had set off across the world forthwith. He had always been reasonably confident that she would be his bride – her father would never have managed to repay the loan – but now it would be with her heartfelt thanks at being rescued from the uncivilised world in which she'd been stranded.

This confidence had strengthened when he arrived at Hokitika and saw just how crude and raw a town it was. He shuddered to think of his gently-bred Guinevere living here all alone. However, it was with mixed feelings that he learned she had in fact moved on to Christchurch. Not only did it lengthen his journey considerably, it rather took the bloom of his chivalrous dash to the end of the world.

Nor had locating her in Christchurch been immediately easy – no one at the post office nor any of the reputable hotels seemed to know a Lady

Guinevere, but just when the man was beginning to despair a chance, disbelieving glimpse at a billet tied to a tree announcing the opening of a photographic exhibition of one Gwen Stanhope had led swiftly to this humble door. His consternation at finding his bride in such a wretched cottage was, however, immediately overpowered by the sight of the baby.

Ramsay paled and stammered, 'Is that yours?'

For a second Gwen was stunned but then she laughed. 'Baby Jessica? By no means though I wish she were. She's the dearest little thing. But you haven't answered my question, Mr Ramsay. What brings you all the way here?'

'You, of course.'

She stared blankly at him. 'Why?'

This was not how he'd envisaged it. He had expected cries of profound gratitude; his secret hope was that she'd forget herself so far as to fling herself on his chest. He had not anticipated such a cool reception, and a baby had certainly never featured in any of the scenarios he had conjured up on the tediously long hours of the voyage.

'We need to talk,' was all he could think to say.

'Well, you'd better come in, I suppose,' said Gwen grudgingly. 'I don't want the baby to get cold.'

He followed her into the kitchen which, though warm and cheery, was hardly a setting fit for a lady. Gwen, however, seemed at home as she swung a pot expertly over the flames with one hand, the other still holding the baby.

'I expect you would like a cup of tea. Now, tell me why you came all this way for me?'

'The lawyers contacted me to tell me of your father's death.'

'Why should they do that?' Gwen asked sharply.

'To inform me of my ownership of Maidenhurst.'

'*What*?' Now, at last he had cracked her calm. 'That simply cannot be. I don't believe that. There are still some months to go on the mortgage.'

'Not in the case of death. If you would like to look at the contract your father signed,' and here he pulled out from his inside jacket pocket a document which he handed to her, 'you will see that if the debt remained unpaid at the time of his death, all would pass to me.'

Gwen sank onto a chair, cradling little Jess and staring unseeingly at the papers in her left hand.

'I can't believe it,' she said dazed. 'Naturally, I thought it would all come to me and that I still had a year to find the money.'

Mr Ramsay shook his head. 'I'm afraid not. These are the conditions your father agreed to. Of course neither of us at the time ever believed – it was just a precaution on my behalf. I never thought – but there you are, that is what precautions are for, the unexpected. It should have come into effect within two days of your father's death,' he continued, 'but your lawyers and I agreed that the time frame should only begin once you'd been notified of the terms of the contract. They fancied your father may not have divulged the whole to you. As you can see here,' and his finger pointed to the relevant line, 'unless you can provide the money in the next forty-eight hours, the house and all its contents pass to me.'

Seeing that Guinevere was unable to bear looking at the contract right at that moment, Mr Ramsay took it from her limp fingers and restored it to the pocket over his heart.

'I took it upon myself to come and tell you in person, rather than have you hear of it through a letter.' He paused and smiled as though to deflect any thanks but none, it appeared, were forthcoming so he pressed on, determined to demonstrate his magnanimity. 'My actions were further prompted by the real desire I had to rescue you from the unfortunate circumstances in which you were left. You do not have the money, I take it.'

She shook her head slowly. 'I have some savings, but not enough. Not yet. Then Maidenhurst is yours?' Still she could not quite comprehend it.

'I prefer to think that it is *ours*, Lady Guinevere,' he said, leaning forward in his chair and looking at her earnestly. 'I have come to take you home. It is a match you know your father desired. What could be more fitting than for you to take your rightful place as the lady of the manor? I know how much it means to you and it's there waiting for you. You are the heart of the manor, you must

341

know that. Without you, it is nothing but a shell awaiting its mistress.'

These words, it has to be said, though uttered sincerely, did not come on the spur of the moment. They had been carefully honed over the months and Mr Ramsay sat back well pleased with their delivery. This was where Guinevere would raise her beautiful eyes to his and say, 'Yes, yes, take me home.'

But alas for carefully cherished plans. Just as he had not anticipated the baby, nor had he made allowance for the door crashing open at this tender moment and a boy's voice crying out joyously, 'Gwen, we're home!'

She leapt to her feet and handed her bemused suitor the baby just in time to catch in her arms and swing around a small boy with jug ears.

'Oh, Ben, I have *missed* you,' she cried, relief and joy flooding her face and she squeezed the boy in a tight embrace as though clutching at some small anchor.

Mr Ramsay felt aggrieved. He'd travelled all this way to rescue her and here she was behaving as if he'd threatened her in some way.

'I missed you too,' Ben said, his voice muffled by her dress. Then he squirmed to be free, as though remembering suddenly his dignity. 'We've had such adventures.'

We? wondered Mr Ramsay but the question was answered as a tall figure filled the doorway of the kitchen.

'There now, I said we'd be back in time,' said a low Irish voice with a lilt of laughter. 'Ben was anxious I might misjudge the distance, distrustful young scamp.'

There was no mistaking the softness in those grey eyes, nor the answering glow in the gold-flecked ones and it suddenly seemed to Mr Ramsay that a cold wind had swept in with these arrivals. He shivered and looked from the man to the woman again. Though they did not touch, there was in their first looks an intimacy as blatant as a kiss. Revulsion welled up inside the Englishman's breast. Surely Lady Guinevere could not have, could not have – he could not utter the thought. Not with an Irishman. Mr Ramsay took in the mud-splattered boots, the battered mole-skins, the patched jacket, the rough, unshaven face and wondered what other coarse company his bride-to-be had been forced to endure these past months.

When he looked into the grey eyes, however, he was taken aback to discover that he was being surveyed quite as critically. The impudence of the fellow was extraordinary. An eyebrow cocked enquiringly and a long, lean hand was extended.

'Good day to you, sir. My name's Quinn O'Donnell.'

'Oh, my manners have gone begging,' said Gwen, who'd been brushing Ben's hair back from his eyes before smothering him in a hug again. 'I do apologise. Quinn, this is Mr Rupert Ramsay. He has just arrived from England.'

'England? I see. And did you enjoy an easy voyage out?' The voice betrayed nothing but casual interest but the eyes narrowed and Mr Ramsay had the uncomfortable feeling this Irishman knew of him and he felt strangely at a disadvantage. He was hard put too, to be able to place the relationship between Guinevere and this tall interpolator and he wondered if he had imagined that first look they'd exchanged. There seemed now to be a reservation between them as neither looked directly at the other again. As if, thought Mr Ramsay illogically, it was too dangerous. Then he realised they were both waiting for his answer.

He gathered his wits and said, 'Tolerable.'

He couldn't help but feel that he would appear to greater advantage if he weren't holding this infernal infant but was disconcerted to discover he liked it less when Guinevere took the baby from his hold and passed it to the Irishman.

'See how she's grown and it's only been a week.'

The sight of the two faces bent over the baby made him feel squeamish.

'She's gained a few ounces and looking well with it. Where's Moll?'

'Out walking.'

O'Donnell seemed surprised. 'She's making a swift recovery then?'

'Yes, it's amazing. But she couldn't stand being inside any longer. She said she needed to see people out and about again.'

'No doubt eyeing up all the young chums.'

The comment in itself was made lightly but again O'Donnell and Guinevere exchanged glances that, for a second, seemed to exclude everything else in the world.

'No doubt.'

Then as if recalling her guest, Guinevere turned back to Mr Ramsay and said with a smile that looked forced, 'You have arrived at an exciting time, Mr Ramsay. This evening I have an opening for my exhibition, which I trust you will attend. However, I would also very much like to give you a preview now, if I may.'

So that billet on the tree hadn't been a hoax. Controlling his disbelief with some difficulty, Mr Ramsay maintained his composure and bowed. 'I would be honoured.'

He could not show how sordid he found the notion of her having an exhibition but was pleased to see her second smile seemed more natural as she thanked him. However, this pleasure died almost instantly as she turned back to the Irishman, looking up into his face as if to convey more than just the words she uttered. 'Quinn, will you stay with Ben and Jessica?'

'I can do that. I'm here for whatever you need.'

O'Donnell spoke with such quiet intensity that again Ramsay had the feeling that there was more behind these words than he could know and he suddenly desired nothing more than to escape the cottage and its stifling domesticity.

'Then shall we proceed, Lady Guinevere?'

'Can we come too?' Ben asked eagerly.

Guinevere hugged the boy to her side. 'Oh, Ben, I'd love to show you but we cannot take Jess out into that cold air.'

His face fell for a second but lit up again. 'Can we come when Moll returns?'

It seemed Guinevere's expression was almost maternal as she replied, 'If she's back in time, of course.'

What on earth had transpired with his intended over these past long months? Mr Ramsay was not sure he recognised her any more.

Guinevere's thoughts raced as they walked down to the barn in the bright spring's sun. The day was glorious with high blue skies sweeping down to the sharp spine of the Southern Alps on the horizon, magnificent now in their mantle of snow. The wind was bracing and clean and carried on it the scent of grass as they came to the river-bank.

Gwen usually gloried in these crisp Christchurch days but now she wanted nothing so much as to scream and shake her fists at the empty sky. The taste of betrayal was bitter in her mouth. How *could* her father have willed everything to Mr Ramsay? He had signed away her entire future without even consulting her. Of course he had not expected to die and of course he would never have thought his daughter might rise to the challenge of repaying the debt, but with this contract he had removed any hope of independent thought or action. She was, in effect, destitute and entirely at the mercy of Mr Ramsay. Her one forlorn hope was that she could somehow persuade him to give her a chance to recover that which her father had thrown away. Begging was not in her nature but she knew she was fighting from a very weakened position and she drew in a deep breath.

'Mr Ramsay, I am keen to pay my father's debts,' she said and was relieved to note that her voice remained steady.

'You have just told me you do not have the money.'

'I don't. Not yet. But I hope to. I am taking you to look at my exhibition for tomorrow all my works will be auctioned off. I am hoping to raise a reasonable sum from it. I have also built up a good business which generates an income. An illustrious critic from London happens to be in Christchurch and if he likes my work, there is every chance I can begin to make it as an artist in my own right. One of the local businessmen is also keen to use some of my shots as postcards. These will all bring in revenue. If you would accept a down payment, I believe I could repay most of the debt in five years.'

Mr Ramsay shook his head at this absurd offer. 'It is not the money I want, it is the manor and your hand in marriage.'

'I realise that. But surely you would not take my home from me?'

'I am offering you your home.' Her silence wounded him. 'I would not be a bad husband to you, I can assure you. I have loved you these past three years. Your father approved the match.' Chagrin made his tone harsher than he might have wished but when he saw her chin come up, he realised this was no way to win her affection. Willy-nilly, he would have her hand in marriage, but he would like to have her heart too so he added more gently, as though talking to a recalcitrant child. 'Of course, I will look at your pictures, Lady Guinevere, although I am sure you can see that it is nothing more than a hopeless dream. It will never pay its way properly, you know. You cannot seriously plan to stay in this rough country another five years in hopes of recouping all that your father lost. It is a madcap notion – you are very much your father's daughter in that regard.'

'Don't talk of my father like that!'

'Lady Guinevere, you mistake me. I held your father in highest esteem. He was a visionary, a great thinker but he was not practical and I see that you need someone practical in your life. Let that someone be me. This is no place for you,' and his hand gestured dismissively at the wide sky, the river running clear and the mountains far beyond. 'You belong back in England, among your own type. I cannot tell you how much it hurts to see you consort with such rough people.'

Biting the inside of her lip till she tasted blood,

Gwen was only just able to keep her fury – and her desperation – under control. Now was certainly not the time to tell Mr Ramsay exactly what she thought. He held all the cards and they both knew it. Instead she said as levelly as she could, 'All I ask is for the chance. Take a look at my exhibition, please. Look, it is in this barn, right here.'

She threw open the door and led the way inside. There was nothing about the set of her head and shoulders that suggested in any way that her heart was thudding wildly. It was intolerable that this man whom she could not admire should land up being judge of her enterprises, her whole future depending on his verdict. She stood back and watched as Mr Ramsay dutifully walked about the room. He admired the cityscapes and enquired as to who the various people in the portraits were. Like every man, he stopped short in front of the photograph of Stella but passed swiftly over the other ones taken in the theatre and scarcely looked at the kitchen scenes at all.

'An eclectic range,' he said in his dry, measuring way. 'Your technique is much improved. I'm sure your father would have been proud.'

Gwen wished she could believe he spoke sincerely. He was the only one in New Zealand who could have reassured her of her father's approval but there was something perfunctory in the way that he said it that belied his words. Still, she had to take what she could out of the situation.

'Thank you,' she said. 'Does that mean you will allow me time until after the auction?' She would not plead so her voice carried a slight hauteur.

Mr Ramsay looked at Guinevere standing there head held high, spine straight and supple as a wand, and was pleased. This was the Guinevere he remembered and he ached to be married to a lady with such inborn pride and dignity. This is what his money could buy. The future would go better if he showed generosity now, however. Having seen her work, he knew that he was in no danger of her ever being able to pay her father's debts. She would be his no matter how the auction went. And as it was at the bottom of the world, no harm would be done. No one in England need know that she had ever indulged in unladylike forays into the masculine world of commerce.

'Have your auction,' he said indulgently. 'If you can raise twenty per cent of the mortgage, we can talk again.'

But once again his moment of munificence was spoilt by that infernal child bursting in, red-faced from running.

'Moll's back,' he panted. 'Gwen, it all looks amazing!'

''Tis a miracle,' Quinn agreed, arriving close on the boy's heels. He looked around him. 'You must have worked like a galley slave to do all this.'

Gwen blushed and it seemed to Ramsay that her whole face had lit up at this praise. 'Oh, I had lots of help from the theatre folk. I owe apple pies from now until Christmas I believe.'

The Irishman's mouth lifted in a crooked smile and he too walked around the room, looking at all the photographs. Unlike Mr Ramsay, he passed over the portraits to a large extent but paused at the others, particularly at the domestic scenes which, Mr Ramsay thought, was typical of one of his breeding. His statement showed how little he understood of art when he turned to Guinevere and said, 'These look particularly good, framed up like this. You have done an incredible job here.'

'Thank you,' she said. Was her voice far warmer in accepting a compliment from this man than from her own father's closest friend? 'I've been very excited by how they've turned out, I must confess. And Quinn, I've had a new idea for a series.'

The Irishman raised his eyebrow. 'What is it?' he asked with humorous resignation.

'Mining.'

Mr Ramsay spluttered at this. 'My dear Lady Guinevere! You cannot be serious. A lady amongst all those men.'

Quinn laughed. 'A wild notion but one step up, I have to admit, from moa hunting.'

The teasing glance he cast at Mr Ramsay's bride was more than the Englishman could bear.

351

'Well, thank you, Lady Guinevere, for showing me your pictures,' he said, turning his back on the Irishman. 'I will be most happy to attend tonight's festivities. May I escort you home now, for I am sure you have much to do beforehand?'

He proffered his arm but O'Donnell cut in cheerfully, 'Oh, I can take Miss Stanhope home. I need to settle Ben back into the house.'

Mr Ramsay stood completely undone. He could not even begin to frame questions of why Ben appeared to be living with Lady Guinevere or why this Irishman seemed to have the run of the place. All he knew was the sooner he could remove his bride from her current situation, the better it would be for all concerned.

With great dignity, he enquired as to the time the opening would begin and again expressed his felicitations on all her work before turning on his heels and making his departure.

Quinn and Gwen watched his retreating back.

'He doesn't like me,' Quinn said with amusement, but a trace of sympathy too. 'I fancy he did not expect to find you up to your elbows in children and coarse sorts.'

'He's always been unbearably stiff,' said Gwen, winding an arm around Ben and giving him a squeeze. 'He was horrid to poor Gabriel Rossetti and Will Morris too. He doesn't like arty sorts which is strange when you think about it because he fancies himself as an art connoisseur.'

'I'm not arty, just common – and Irish.'

'And very dirty,' Gwen added. 'I must get this boy scrubbed down. You both look like you've slept in mud for a week.' She was relieved that Quinn's anger also seemed to have disappeared during his absence. They were back to their easy way of talking to one another and she thought how very good it was to have them both back again.

Ben laughed. 'We have. It was freezing and wet up in the mountains.'

'And the land?'

'It's nice.' Ben's voice suddenly lacked its usual enthusiasm.

Gwen looked up at Quinn who had a slight frown of consternation as he looked down at the boy.

''Tis good land but it took us the devil of a time getting there because of the flooding. I've told Ben it won't seem so far away come summer and things dry out some.'

'I don't want to be so far away from you and Stella,' Ben explained. 'Or school.'

Gwen tousled his hair. 'Oh, Ben, I'll miss you too but you'll love it there; room to ride and fish and have a dog. And just look – there are Stella and Jack right now.'

Ben tore off to greet them and Gwen turned to Quinn. 'Was it wonderful to see the land? Have you great plans for it?'

''Tis all I ever hoped and dreamed of,' Quinn said but his voice was curiously flat. 'But that's not what I want to talk about now. What's that fellow come to New Zealand for?'

'Me,' said Gwen.

CHAPTER 18

There had been no time to talk for Gwen had to get ready for the opening. Quinn bore Ben away, saying the boy needed smart clothes for the occasion. Gwen knew it was also to keep the boy out of her hair and though she appreciated the thought, she felt a little slighted. It seemed Quinn was weaning Ben away from her – which was understandable because they would be leaving her to live on the land. And, as Mr Ramsay's appearance reminded her poignantly, she too would soon be leaving. Yet, seeing them set off together, she could not help but feel excluded.

In fact, thought Gwen as she fumbled over her dressing, it was impossible to marshal the jumble of her emotions; the horror of Mr Ramsay's appearance and the delight in Quinn and Ben's return were almost overshadowing her terror and excitement of the coming evening. Mr Ramsay's arrival also rekindled memories. The last time she had seen him had been at her father's side when Mr Ramsay had called to bid them bon voyage. Her father had been in enormous good humour, buoyed by his ebullient optimism in the success of their venture.

After Mr Ramsay had left and her father had disappeared into his library, she had taken her last, tearful tour of her beloved Maidenhurst. Now, as she dressed and did her hair, she recalled the laughter of past dinner parties, the joy of long summers and the many, many hours she and her father had spent together on his photography. How proud he would have been of her this evening. He seemed almost unbearably close and the pain of her loss struck her anew. Though she could hear Moll singing lullabies off-key in the next door room, she felt most horribly alone – something she hadn't felt since, well, since Quinn had shown up at the Whitterings.

However, when Gwen came down the stairs into the kitchen she found Stella humming as she toasted bread over the fire. Always radiant, her newly-found happiness lit the kitchen but as she turned, she caught sight of Gwen's face.

'Gwen, dear, what has happened? You look more like you are facing an execution than an exhibition. Do come and sit down. I'm just making some tea and toast for you must have something before the opening. Only fancy how *devastating* it would be to have a rumbling stomach. Don't look so *wretched*, my dear. This is to be *your* night!'

As she spoke, Stella bustled Gwen into a chair at the table and set a steaming cup of tea in front of her. Stella's voice remained light but there was an underlying concern that warmed Gwen's heart as she realised she'd never had a friend to lean on before. Apart, of course, from Quinn. And so soon she would lose them both.

She felt tears prickle but at that moment the smell of burning bread caused Stella to rush back to the fireplace. It was too late and Stella was loud in her lamentations over the scorched toast. This minor domestic tragedy made Gwen laugh, releasing the knot in her stomach and as Stella made more toast, Gwen could tell her all about the afternoon's drama.

'Mr Ramsay's arrival is most terribly timed,' she concluded. 'I have a dread of failing spectacularly in front of him.'

'If he loves you, he will not let it affect his feelings for you.'

'No, you don't understand. It is not his regard I fear losing. If I fail, he will grow more powerful – don't you see?'

Stella did not make an immediate reply as she turned the fresh slices over the fire. When she spoke, it was with unusual solemnity.

'Gwen, it is one thing to contemplate marriage with a man whom one does not love but who is of an amiable disposition. I could consider Mr Worthing because I knew his qualities would make him a kind and caring husband. Love might well have grown under careful attention. But nothing you have told me of Mr Ramsay assures me that he would make you a good husband.'

'Oh, he is very considerate. Only fancy, he has sailed across the world to come to my aid.'

'A gesture,' Stella noted, 'that has brought you neither gratitude nor pleasure.'

'I was simply taken aback. His arrival was a surprise, that's all.'

Gwen knew her words did not sound convincing but she did not like the direction Stella's observations were taking her. Surely Stella ought to be alleviating her anxieties rather than adding to them.

'What does Quinn say?'

'It matters not one jot,' Gwen retorted. 'After all, he will soon be gone from Christchurch – and taking Ben with him.'

Stella sighed. 'Truly, it is harder to know which one of you is the more stubborn or foolish. And don't glare at me just for telling the truth. The fact is—'

But whatever Stella was about to say was lost as the front door banged open and Ben came running down the passage calling, 'Gwen. Stella. Are you ready? We are come to escort you to the opening.'

He burst into the kitchen and Gwen exclaimed, 'Why, Ben, you look perfectly splendid.'

'Quinn bought me a whole new outfit. He says we mustn't do anything tonight to put you to shame.'

'Ben, you *never* put me to shame,' Gwen said as she stood up and dropped a kiss on the boy's cheek. 'I cannot tell you how glad I am to have you home again.'

Ben scrubbed the kiss off with the back of his hand but went pink with gratification.

'Quick, we must go. And just when the toast is perfect,' said Stella. 'Here, Ben, you can have it.' She rose, shaking out her skirts. 'As for you, Gwen, banish all bothersome thoughts for now. This evening will be your greatest performance. Take the stage with conviction and the audience will *adore* you.'

Gwen laughed and embraced the actress. 'Sound advice, indeed. Stella, you are the best friend any woman could want.'

Stella's voice was unusually soft as she said. 'I will miss you when you go.' Then briskly she added, 'Come, Ben, stop shovelling the toast down like that or you will choke. Gwen, here's your shawl. Have you got your gloves? Good. Your cape is in the hall. Right, let us depart.'

Quinn and Jack were on the doorstep, stamping their feet and blowing on their fingers for the early spring night carried the sting of snow from the mountains. The stars were brilliant in the clear black sky.

Quinn turned at the sound of their footsteps and as he looked at her, there was something in his expression, in those far-seeing grey eyes, that caught at her heart.

'Lady Guinevere,' said Quinn in his funning tone as he took her hand and kissed it. His breath was warm on her fingers. 'You look beautiful.'

As he straightened, he looked into her eyes with

that faint smile she loved so much. Gwen flushed but before she could reply, an all too familiar voice was calling from just down the road.

'Lady Guinevere.'

Mr Ramsay arrived, slightly breathless and immaculately turned out. He visibly started when he saw one of the men was Quinn and any other time Gwen would have been amused by his fleeting expression of disbelief and chagrin. She was used now to Quinn's ability to transform himself within an hour from dishevelled adventurer to gentleman but Mr Ramsay had clearly not expected any such event. His eyes swept the Irishman from his thick, newly cut hair down to his well-polished boots. It cannot be said that he took any pleasure in noting the elegance of the suit nor the quality of Quinn's coat.

'Mr O'Donnell. I scarce recognised you.'

The chill in Mr Ramsay's voice and smile made the night air seem warm in contrast.

Introductions were speedily made. Mr Ramsay blinked at the full force of Stella's beauty, but was summary in his acknowledgement of Jack. Gwen was clearly his quarry for he turned immediately to her.

'Lady Guinevere, I am come especially to accompany you to the opening.'

'Twas a thoughtful notion,' said Quinn. 'But as you can see, *Miss Stanhope* already has an escort party.'

Their exchanged looks of dislike clashed like rapiers.

'Yes, indeed,' said Gwen, hastily taking Ben's arm. 'As you can see, I have my protector right here.'

The boy straightened up with a gratified beam and there was the slightest check in hostilities as both men were left nonplussed. Then Stella stepped forward in a rustle of skirts and placed a hand on Mr Ramsay's sleeve.

'Now, Mr Ramsay, I want to hear *all* about your adventures on your travels to New Zealand. Were you *hideously* seasick? I can assure you I was. And do tell me about London. How is it? I am *agog* to hear what is in the theatres at the moment,' and she bore Mr Ramsay off down the street.

Quinn and Jack were left to follow in the two women's wake, neither amused by the presence of Mr Ramsay but both determined nothing should spoil the evening for Gwen.

And what an evening it was. There are some times in life – all too few – when expectations and hopes are not only met but exceeded. This was one of those times. All of Christchurch it seemed turned out to view the exhibition and from the moment the doors of the barn opened, Gwen was barraged by many kind words and fulsome compliments. Over the months she had known her popularity as a photographer had been growing but this evening was the culmination of all her hard work. There were many friendly faces for all the theatre folk were there, as were the Whitterings and past clients, but there were also introductions to others who urgently pressed for a sitting at her earliest convenience.

As the evening wore on the warmth of the responses accelerated and she found herself being addressed, much to her surprise and discomfort, as Lady Guinevere rather than as Miss Stanhope. She could not account for this until she saw Mr Ramsay in a group and came close in time to hear him say, 'Of course, I have had the pleasure of knowing Lady Guinevere for a number of years. Her father was a dear friend.'

'*Lady* Guinevere?' asked Mr Johnson, one of her clients. 'Really? I had no idea.'

Mr Ramsay smiled. 'She is an eccentric – they often are, these artists. Her father was equally whimsical.'

It was too late for her to retract what he was saying. Word flew around and the awestruck whispers did nothing to lessen her appeal. It was too late but Gwen wished he had not made so much of her title. She wanted to succeed on her own merits, not as her father's daughter. Mr Ramsay would never understand.

Stella was right – it was like a performance. Gwen smiled and chatted and accepted compliments graciously but a part of her was always to one side, looking at the numbers of people actually viewing the photographs, looking to see that glasses were filled. Looking for Quinn.

He seemed to be everywhere at once, engaging people in discussions about her works, pointing out the finer features of the individual photographs. It seemed to Gwen an unusual number of women laughed flirtatiously when he spoke to them and she noticed how men were happy to include him into their conversations. Quinn had become, she realised, a most popular and respected member within the community. It was hard to see now, the filthy, antagonistic miner in the confident businessman and she experienced a small pang. This man was no longer in need of late night conversations in a tiny maid's bedroom. But when she saw him also straighten one photograph and unobtrusively re-attach a curtain coming loose from its mooring, she felt a warm glow deep within.

Gwen was talking with one group of people when she felt a touch on her arm and turning, she found Quinn before her, mischief lurking in his eyes. 'Lady Guinevere,' he said in very formal tones. 'May I introduce you to Miss Smythe. She is most desirous to make your acquaintance.'

In disbelief, Gwen stared straight into the pretty, petulant face of Miss Symthe. It was clear she had no memory of the maid whom she had embarrassed so greatly just months earlier.

'Lady Guinevere, I am so delighted to meet you. I am a great admirer of your work and wondered if I might sit for you. It would be an honour.' She babbled on for several minutes in this vein, while Gwen fought to school her expression though she could not help exchanging glances with Quinn and saw his lopsided smile grow wider, until he finally bore Miss Smythe away after Gwen had promised she would indeed be delighted to take the woman's photograph. An unprofessional part of her was tempted, though, to set the lighting at just the right angle to enhance the shadow of the double chin Miss Smythe was developing.

Quinn did enjoy the encounter but he found the evening overall bittersweet. Gwen had never looked lovelier, her eyes bright, her manner animated as she parried the compliments and flattering attention with charm and modesty. Her exhibition was unquestionably a success which augured well for the auction the following day. He had been near her when she was introduced to an agent from London who had been extremely complimentary and had pressed her to contact him when she was returned to England. This she promised to do – a promise that cut Quinn to the quick. This success that she had worked so hard for was going to be her ticket back to her home and to a future in which he had no part at all. Ramsay's presence was a constant reminder.

All evening Quinn would have sworn Ramsay was as conscious of him as he was of that English worm. They circulated in different directions but the barn was not that large and each time they passed, their smiles were as ferocious as snarls. His skin crawled to hear those well-modulated tones and it took all his will power not to punch the man when he heard him behaving in such a confident and proprietal manner towards Gwen. Interest had certainly swelled with Ramsay's disclosure of Gwen's title but if he'd thought this was a way to her heart, Ramsay had much mistaken the matter. There was a distinct glint in Gwen's eyes when people began addressing her as Lady Guinevere; a glint that heartened Quinn though he could not – or would not – say why.

Quinn had no proper understanding of why Ramsay had turned up in New Zealand but the look of anguished relief that Gwen had given him on his arrival in the afternoon had brought out his every protective instinct. Until he learnt exactly what was going on, Quinn was damned if he would leave Ramsay alone with Gwen. Thus it was that when the crowds had left, he made his way over to where she stood, Ben pulled close into her side, chatting to the Whitterings and Ramsay.

He arrived in time to hear Ramsay say, 'I would be honoured if you would dine with me tonight, Lady Guinevere.'

'I am so sorry,' said Gwen, 'but I must take young Ben here off to bed as Stella has already left for the theatre. He is exhausted after all his travels.'

Ben began to protest but under the combined attack of a warning look from Quinn and the force of Gwen's fingers on his shoulder, he quickly fell silent.

'Indeed,' said Quinn, 'we travelled a long way

today. I will be happy to accompany you both home for our ways lie together.'

Lady Whittering cast a shrewd glance in his direction and said, 'Mr Ramsay, you must allow us to offer you a place in our carriage.'

'No, no,' said Mr Ramsay, looking at Gwen. 'I would not put you to any bother on my account.'

'No bother at all for your hotel is on our way.' She ignored her husband's outraged stare for she was adding several miles to their journey and added, 'We would be delighted to have your company.'

Unable to refuse, Ramsay accepted with as much grace as he could muster but the flat line of his lips as he was led away showed his displeasure at leaving his fiancée-to-be in such deplorable company.

'Thank you,' said Gwen as Quinn wrapped her cape around her shoulders. 'It seems you are forever rescuing me.'

'That may be,' said Quinn, 'but I don't think I've ever seen you face such a damnable situation as this one. Once Ben is in bed, you are going to tell me what the hell is going on.'

CHAPTER 19

Mr Ramsay spent the rest of his evening in gentlemanly solitude at his hotel. He ate alone and he drank alone. He drank far more than he was used to but the day's events had brought out angry feelings of misusage. He had travelled around the world in great discomfort to discover the woman for whom he had cherished tender feelings these past three years had sadly changed. She had always had an impulsively friendly manner with her father's protégés but in New Zealand, apart from some fine people like the Whitterings, she had been forced into company with those vastly below her station. That Irishman was nothing but a jumped up commoner and though Miss Tyler was indeed very lovely, she was, after all, merely an actress. As for that dreadful boy with his jug ears, Mr Ramsay shuddered to think where he fitted into the story.

More disquieting still was all this nonsense about her photography. In England it had been a modest hobby which her father had encouraged. Now she was *exhibiting*. Really, it was all too vulgar, especially this nonsense of wanting to earn the money to pay her father's debt. It showed a sad want of proper feeling. That afternoon, the notion of an auction had seemed as ludicrous as her father's scheme to find the moa but after this evening's opening, Mr Ramsay was not quite so sure. Indeed, from the moment he had first stood on her front door in Christchurch, Mr Ramsay had had the curious sensation that the world was indeed upside down. Nothing was as it ought to be – the Irishman, most especially.

Mr Ramsay threw back another glass of wine. His head was spinning but it was better than being sober and prey to his thoughts. Unsteadily he rose from the table and wove his way from the dining room and out into the night. The bite of the night was invigorating after the claustrophobic hotel and the sky was very black and liberally strewn with stars. Digging his hands into his pockets he drifted through the streets which were thinning fast of all people save for numerous groups of young wastrels who were boisterously loud as they bounced from one bar to the next. Their exuberance seemed somehow to mock his own very different feelings.

He meandered away from the gaslit streets and down darkened roads until he came to the river, which flowed as slippery and black as his thoughts. Idly he followed its course until quite without design he came upon the barn housing the exhibition. Mr Ramsay stopped and stared at it with loathing.

From his inside jacket pocket, he took out his

evening cigar and lit it. The strong scent of the smoke helped to steady him and he flicked the match into the river while leaning back against a tree beside the barn. He tried to smile sardonically at the thought of Guinevere's vain dreams of success from the auction but it died on his lips. He thought about the London dealer, the warmth of his praise and remembered Guinevere's avid expression. It would not be easy to curb this passion but he would put his foot down – gently of course, but firmly. It appalled him that the future Mrs Ramsay could even consider selling merchandise like some sort of trader.

Conveniently, he forgot that he and his father had amassed a fortune through buying and selling. He was a gentleman and Guinevere was to elevate their family even higher. What could be better than have his children aligned with such a fine genealogy? If Guinevere discovered she could not raise the funds, she would be grateful to him, see in him finally both her rescue and her refuge. She would come to him willingly and over time she would learn to love him. She would. Yet even as he reassured himself, the face of the Irishman ghosted through Mr Ramsay's thoughts and taking a last angry pull on the cigar, he tossed it into the dry grass beside the barn. As he strode away, he thought he heard a faint crackle. He did not look back but rather quickened his steps and disappeared into the dark.

★　★　★

Mr Ramsay might have found some consolation in the knowledge that there was little happiness in the cottage either that evening. Ben and Moll had gone to bed; Stella and Jack were at the theatre.

Quinn and Gwen were alone and though they sat seemingly companionably on either side of the fire, the atmosphere quickly became cold as she told him of the conditions of the contract. Quinn heard her out in silence with eyes like flint but when Gwen fell silent at the end, he swore softly and fluently.

'It wasn't my father's fault,' she cried as much to convince herself as Quinn. 'He never expected to die. Besides, it was a match he thought would be most suitable.'

'For yourself or for him?' Quinn asked brutally.

Gwen's chin lifted. 'He admired Mr Ramsay's qualities.'

'You are evading the question.'

'He believed he would make a good husband.'

'Did he not talk to you about this contract at all?'

'No, not the details and when I learned of the original agreement, I didn't say how I felt so how could he know?'

'He might have asked you. For such a progressive man, it seems to me he was as happy to marry you off as the most conservative father.'

'I don't want to talk about it.'

'Gwen, you cannot be refusing to face the facts

all your life. Sure, you're running out of time, you must see that. Your daddy was not a saint and yet you are still thinking that you will marry this man whom you do not love to protect your father's name.'

'And my *home*. Don't forget that Maidenhurst is my home.'

'Is it? Is it really? Have you thought how it will be to return, even if you do raise the money and don't marry Ramsay? Your father is dead. All will be different. 'Tis the house you grew up in, to be sure, but what is this?' and Quinn gestured to the kitchen. 'Everywhere I look, I see you. These are your cushions, your chairs. You have turned a squalid cottage into a home. Life moves on but you are burying yourself in your past, you stubborn bloody Englishwoman. 'Tis nothing but moa you'll be chasing by going back to England.'

Gwen's head went up, her manner glacial. 'What about you? You are chasing your own moa, Quinn O'Donnell. You can buy all the fine lands that you like, yes and build a grand house and farm till your back breaks but they will never satisfy you. Deep down you are a doctor. I have never once seen you turn your head to admire pastureland yet I see your concern when we walk past a child with a bloodied knee. Don't you talk to me about burying myself in the past and being stubborn. You hoard your *aloneness*, your hurt and your self-disgust. Yes, you made a mistake and a boy died.

Yet how many lives have you saved? How many more could you have saved if you'd been practising medicine these past few years? We all make mistakes and must live with them. But can you? Oh, no, not Quinn O'Donnell. You are determined to remain closed off rather than risk rejection or loss ever again. Can't you see that in doing so you will lose everything worth living for?'

Quinn's temper ignited and he leapt to his feet. 'Don't talk of that which you can never understand,' he shouted.

'Don't understand what? That you can talk piously of my father selling my life away for a house and lands while I can see you doing exactly the same thing to one who loves you.'

'Who the devil are you talking about?'

'Ben!' cried Gwen, springing to her feet too. 'You'll bury him alive out there. The lands are your dream – misplaced as it may be – but anyone with half an eye can see Ben doesn't want to go. He's happy here. For the first time in his life he has friends and he's good at school – oh, very good at school. You'll take all that away from him so you can leave as you always do when things get difficult.'

'I do not always leave.'

'You do. You left Ireland and your job and Hokitika and now you are leaving here! Go away then, go hide in the mountains and nurse your broken Irish heart and your stupid Irish pride.'

They were standing almost nose to nose, fists

clenched glowering at each other but at that moment they heard indistinct shouting in the streets, the sound of running feet and then a faint cry. 'Fire!'

All thoughts of argument fled as they rushed outside to see how close it was. Fire was a constant terror in this town of wooden houses.

'I can't see anything,' said Gwen, turning around and looking upwards for smoke.

Quinn pointed. 'The sky is lit up over there – yes, there's the smoke. The fire's down by the river.'

Guinevere's face paled. 'My exhibition.'

Quinn had misgivings too but forced his voice to sound calm. 'Gwen, don't fret. I'll go down to help put the flames out and I'll check it's all right.'

'I'm coming with you,' said Gwen, and taking one look at the set of her face, Quinn knew not to waste his breath trying to persuade her otherwise.

'Get your shawl then,' he said. 'We must hurry so it doesn't take hold.'

They ran down the streets that were thick with people; some wanting to watch the drama but most intent on getting the fire under control as soon as possible.

'Hell and damnation,' Quinn muttered as they grew nearer. Without doubt the fire was coming from the vicinity of the barn and Gwen gave a sob.

'Don't cry,' he said, grabbing her hand to help her. 'Run!'

As they got down to the riverbank, however, it was clear that though the flames were already being brought under control by the newly formed fire brigade, the barn was past saving.

'No!' shrieked Gwen. She shook herself free of Quinn's hand and began rushing towards the conflagration, shoving a fireman out of her way in her haste. Quinn bounded after her but caught his toe on a root. He stumbled and that was enough to put her out of his reach. Jaysus but she was fast. Despair lent her speed and it was only the heat of the flames that checked her – but just for a second. She swerved away from the main doors, heading for the back and suddenly he realised she was after her plates. They were her last hope.

He put on a spurt and they rounded the corner together. It was too late. There was a whoosh and the entire lean-to went up in a fireball, fuelled by her chemicals. Gwen gave a cry of anguish and began to dart forward, but Quinn caught her about the waist, swinging them both around so that his back was to the flames, his body protecting her from the sight. The heat of the fire beat against his spine and they were both coughing from the stench of the smoke but still she fought against him.

'I have to get my plates. I have to.'

''Tis too late, you can see that. Oh, Gwen, I am so sorry.'

'There has to be something we can save!' Her voice was high-pitched as she shrieked to make herself heard over the fury of the fire. 'I never made a copy of the photograph of you and Ben.'

'That doesn't matter now, Gwen,' Quinn spoke into her ear. 'It's gone. There's nothing you can do.'

He turned her around in the circle of his arms that she might see for herself. She gave a moan, and sagged, her last hope extinguished.

'Let me take you home.'

But she shook her head, leaning back against his chest to watch with wide, dry eyes the barn burn to the ground. When the final wall fell, she shivered convulsively and his arms tightened.

'Shall we go now?' he asked and she nodded.

Though there were excited people shouting all about them, Gwen moved as if in a dream, conscious of nothing but an enormous emptiness and helplessness. Quinn led her back home and took her into the kitchen where he wrapped a blanket about her shoulders. Her eyes were huge with disbelief.

'How on earth could a fire start there?'

Quinn shrugged. 'Vagrants?' he suggested. 'Perhaps a fellow lit a fire hoping to warm himself.'

'It's all gone.'

'It has.'

'Everything.'

'Not everything. Your beautiful photographs, yes. But not everything.'

'But my last hope of saving Maidenhurst. I must marry Mr Ramsay after all.' She began to laugh hysterically.

Quinn grabbed her by the shoulders and shook her. 'Stop that. Take hold of yourself.'

Her laughter broke into wild sobs and he pulled her into an embrace, rocking her and saying, 'Hush, this too will pass.'

He kissed the top of her head where the smell of smoke still clung to her curls. Gwen raised her face and he began softly kissing away her tears. His mouth found hers and though he began gently, she was suddenly kissing him desperately as though she could draw all his strength into her.

'Marry me,' he murmured as his lips moved to her ear. 'Marry me! I cannot bear to see you married to a man like that. What a waste.'

Her arms twined around his neck and her fingers wound into his hair pulled him closer.

More urgently, holding her tightly as though he'd never let her go, he said again, 'Marry me, Gwen. Forget your manor.'

But at these fateful words, her arms went limp as all life seemed to drain out of her. She stepped back away from him, freeing herself from his embrace, her face averted.

'I cannot,' she said. 'I cannot forget the duty I owe my father. You must go.'

Quinn tried to pull her close again but she put her hands to his chest, resisting him. He dropped his arms.

'You cannot go through with the marriage,' he

said, and it was hard to tell whether he demanded or implored.

She shook her head and said in a dull voice, 'There really is no other choice to save Maidenhurst now. I will see Mr Ramsay in the morning.'

CHAPTER 20

The following day Gwen rose early and stole down to the site of the fire. The area was scorched black and drenched in dew which sparkled in the rising sun's rays. Twisted pieces of wood were all that was left of the walls and the corrugated iron from the roof was blackened and bent. Tiny shards of glass glinted in the grass. All her precious, precious plates. It was hard to remember that only yesterday she had thought this day, this place, would bring her greatest success – had been her only hope.

Feeling numb, she walked amongst the charred remains, disregarding her skirts which soon became coated with a tide of ashes at the hemline. Now she really had lost everything. She could not bear the idea of picking up her camera and starting again. Not after having lost all those many, many hours of hard work. All for nothing.

She remembered the argument with Quinn the night before when she had taunted him with wallowing in his losses. Now at last, standing in the blackened ruins of her life, she understood how he must have felt. He'd lost his family, the woman he'd loved, his homeland and finally his sense of worth as a doctor. And she had told him he should risk all again. How trite her words seemed now.

Slowly she made her way back to the house and was surprised to find Quinn there with Ben, both sitting at the table looking very serious. Then she saw that Ben had his small holdall beside the chair.

Quinn rose and as he glanced at her blackened skirts, his face softened. 'We've been waiting for you these past twenty minutes,' he said. 'We didn't want to leave without saying goodbye.'

'You're leaving?' She found it hard to comprehend.

'I am but I've something for you.'

He handed her an envelope and inside was a banker's note covering the sum of the mortgage.

'What's this?' she whispered.

''Tis the money to buy Maidenhurst. Give it to Ramsay today and the place is yours. You'll not have to marry that English worm.'

Gwen sat abruptly down in a chair at the table, her knees suddenly weak. 'Where did it come from?'

'Quinn sold his land to Lord Whittering this morning.' Ben told her. 'He says we're off to Dunedin.'

'Your land!' Gwen's eyes flew to his face. 'But it's your dream. You cannot sell it for me.'

She pushed the note back across the table to

Quinn who had sat down again, but he didn't take it.

'I don't want it,' he said. 'Be careful what you dream of as the old saying goes. Gwen, I've had a long, sleepless night of it. There were that many thoughts going around and around my head. It just didn't feel right when we were up there, did it Ben?'

The boy shook his head vigorously and Quinn gave a twisted smile. ''Tis no place for a child alone.'

He looked at Gwen. 'You were right about that for Ben, but it was more than that. You made me look at myself, and it didn't make for pretty looking, I can tell you. All my talk of land – 'twas really just to play lord of the manor, so that people might see something more than an Irish peasant when they looked at me. I wanted to prove I was the equal of any Englishman.' He smiled ruefully and looked down at his strong hands clasped on the table and shook his head. 'I realised, Gwen, that as long as I thought like that, I was making myself prisoner to the English forever, giving them the power to direct my life, my decisions. What a fool I was.'

Gwen nodded but could find no words.

Ben sat still, head cocked to one side, eyes bright as a sparrow's.

She looked up at Quinn and their eyes met. With surprise she realised that the wariness that so often cloaked his expression was quite gone. He looked, she thought, like a man who was finally at peace with himself.

He smiled at her. 'And then, when I was thinking of the English, it suddenly occurred to me – daft, stupid Irishman that I am – that all the people I care for most are English. Ben here,' and he smiled down at the boy as he ruffled his hair, 'Jack, Stella – and you.' His voice dropped softly on the last two words. He pushed the note back across the table to her. 'Take the money, Gwen.'

She shook her head. It was hard to think clearly. 'I can't! If I do, you will have nothing.'

'No, you forget I still own this cottage. Ben and I will return one day, but for now we'll go to Dunedin.'

'With nothing?'

'With Ben,' he corrected her. 'Sure, I've started from scratch before, don't look so appalled. We'll be fine.'

'Quinn thought he might go work in the hospital in Dunedin,' Ben informed her.

Despite the pain of the moment, her heart leapt. 'Quinn! Are you really returning to medicine? But that's wonderful.'

'Well, a person whose opinion I respect told me most severely that I was a doctor, not a farmer and it seemed to me last night that she was right. I'd allowed my hatred and my silly pride to lose sight of my real dream. All I've ever wanted to be was a doctor – since the day my mam died. I'd betrayed her memory, quitting it so. 'Twas also pointed out to me that I've wasted enough years so I thought the sooner I got back to my proper profession, the better.'

Quinn planted his hands against the tabletop and pushed back his chair, rising and looking down at Gwen who was still sitting, bewildered by the speed of events.

'We must go, Lady Guinevere. Our boat sails on the tide tonight and so we must catch the coach to Lyttleton.'

'Why do you always want to leave?' she cried. 'Christchurch has a hospital too. Why can't you stay here?'

Ben looked from one to the other, but Quinn just said, 'Sure, but you're the one who'll be leaving us soon enough. I cannot stay here to be haunted by memories, Gwen. This must be the day of new beginnings for both of us. You've always said you were only here to get the money for your home. You have it now. Take it as a loan if you prefer. I know a good business investment when I see one. I just hope – I truly hope – that you will be happy.' His voice started firm but cracked at the end.

Gwen caught him by the arm 'But now I am free. We could marry – can't you see. I have a home, I have land. Marry me and come to live at Maidenhurst. You could be a doctor in the village.'

Quinn smiled sadly at her. 'Oh, Lady Guinevere, I love you with every part of me but it would kill my soul to live in England and you know it.'

Of course she did. Everything was gained – and

lost. She wrapped her arms around Ben, hugging him tightly and felt his thin arms squeezing back. 'You find a school in Dunedin, do you hear? And one day you must come to England to visit, promise?'

'I promise.' His eyes were swimming with tears.

Quinn laid a hand on his shoulder. 'Come, boyo. I've told you before that life is about leave-takings. Lady Guinevere, safe sailing and I hope very much one day to hear you are a famous photographer with exhibitions in London and Paris.'

She tried to laugh but it broke halfway and all she could do was nod. 'Thank you,' she whispered. 'I cannot find the words—'

''Tis not for you that I did it, 'twas for myself. It would have eaten my heart to imagine you married to one such as him. I like to think of you as lady of your own manor.'

He bent his head and she raised her face, her heart quickening but his lips fell chastely on her forehead.

'Godspeed, m'lady.'

Rooted to her chair, unable to believe this was really the end, Gwen watched them disappear down the hallway. Quinn had his arm around Ben who was crying. The door opened and a blast of chilly air whooshed down into the kitchen. Then it closed. And that was that.

Gwen stared blindly at the banker's note lying on the table. It was impossible to comprehend that after all those months of hardship and fears, she was mistress of her own house at last. Her father's name was saved. Her children would inherit the family home. It was all that she had ever wished for. Yet the desolation that welled up in her now as she saw in her mind's eye the tall man and the boy with jug ears on their journey to Lyttleton, was even greater than the loss she'd believed unbearable just half an hour earlier.

She tried to focus on Maidenhurst. The gardens would be alight with late autumn colour and the artists would be boating on the lake – or they would when she returned. Then she wondered if they would come around again now that her father was not there. Mr Ramsay was wrong; she was not the heart of the manor, her father was. It would be an entirely different house with her at the head.

She looked around the cottage. And Quinn was right; it was stamped with her personality. Though it was not a grand home, in this room she had laughed and talked as much as she ever had at Maidenhurst. Within these walls she had also loved as she never had before.

She could start her photography business in England. It would be easy to pick up portraits, she had many connections – through her father. She wondered suddenly how long it would be until she was seen as Lady Guinevere and not Lord Stanhope's daughter. Her mind roamed back to a year ago, how grateful she had been to her father for allowing her to be his assistant. Everyone had been kind to her but Quinn had been the first person to truly encourage her to be an artist. The first person to buy her work. She smiled, remembering the blissful hours she'd spent in her tiny shed, developing photographs. How well he understood her.

She had told Quinn defiantly that Maidenhurst was who she was but what really defined a person? Background? Quinn always called himself an Irish peasant but who, in fact, was the real gentleman – Quinn or Lord Whittering? And she was a lady. What did that mean? Who had she been a year ago? Her father's daughter, her father's assistant, an audience for artists.

Gwen shook her head to clear it of unwanted thoughts. Resolutely she picked up the banker's note and looked at it. Lady of her own manor. She tried to picture it. The dinners, the balls. But now, every gorgeous image was overlaid by the knowledge of the human cost of these extravagances. How could she take photographs documenting such lives in the morning, and then perpetuate them in the evening? How could she ever live with herself, knowing what she knew now?

She turned the bank note over, as though seeking answers on its back but the paper was white and blank. Society portraits. Depictions of myths. Grand houses. Her series of gold-mining would not happen now. She remembered the approval warming Quinn's eyes when he'd looked at her domestic series. Maidenhurst was an extension of herself. Within its walls, her ancestors going back

385

many generations had fought and lived and loved. But as Gwen thought back over the centuries she remembered that Maidenhurst had not always been there and that the first home, on the site of the manor, had not been grand. In fact Nanette, a young Norman girl newly arrived on uncivilised English soil and on her way to marry a Norman lord, might not have noticed it at all if her carriage hadn't lost a wheel on the excruciating English roads. While her driver and guard cursed as they struggled to re-attach the wheel to the axle, she'd wandered over to the edge of some fields to watch the strange Anglo-Saxon men at work and to better see the humble cottage beyond. One man spied the beautiful young girl and, shouldering his pick, stepped forward to talk to her in a strange tongue. She did not know what he said but there was no mistaking the message in his mischievous brown eyes and her own golden-flecked eyes began to dance in response.

Be careful what you wish for – suddenly Gwen knew exactly what it was that she wished for. But was she too late? With a cry she sprang to her feet, thrusting the banker's note into the deep pocket of her skirt and winding a shawl about her shoulders. They had probably already caught the coach but if she ran, she could intercept them at the far crossroads. But just as she was reaching the door, Stella came down the stairs. Her beautiful face was filled with sympathy.

'Gwen, my dear, how *are* you? I was devastated

when I heard. I did knock on your door last night but you were asleep – or not in the mood to talk. But where are you going – and in such a state?'

'Quinn has taken Ben. They are going to Lyttleton to catch a ship to Dunedin. I have to stop them. I can't let them get away.'

Stella gave a crow of delight, bounded down the last two steps and threw her arms around Gwen. 'You'll stay? Oh my dear, that's the most sense I've heard from you in a long time. I'm thrilled but don't let me keep you. Go!'

With a strangled laugh, Gwen broke free of the embrace, pulled open the door and very nearly tripped over Mr Ramsay who was standing, his hand raised ready to knock.

'Lady Guinevere,' he began portentously. 'Please allow me to offer you my condolences—' but the long, practised speech of properly phrased sentiment was cut rudely short.

'Yes, yes, but not now. You may have Maidenhurst, Mr Ramsay. I have come to realise that it does not play any part in my future.'

'What? You would stay? With him!' cried Mr Ramsay, revolted.

'Yes, but I must find him first. I cannot stay. Please get out of my way and bon voyage for your return.'

The last glimpse Mr Ramsay ever had of Lady Guinevere confirmed all his deepest suspicions. She was racing down the road, her skirt bunched in both hands, hair tumbling down for all the world like some sort of – commoner! Not one word of gratitude after all that he had done for her. One day, she would of course come to her senses and realise what an opportunity she had thrown away but it was already too late. He would return forthwith to England, to Maidenhurst and as Mr Ramsay began making his way back to the hotel, he was already planning how to arrange his furniture in Lord Stanhope's library.

Gwen ran as she had never run before towards the Port Hills. The streets were crowded and she dodged around some people and pushed at others in her need to get past. She darted in front of horses and was very nearly run over twice causing people to shout and gesticulate, but she didn't care and didn't break pace as she wove through the centre of the small town to the roads beyond.

Her breath came in gasps but still she vowed she wouldn't miss them. Another, more rational part of her brain said even if she did, she'd just catch the next boat down to Dunedin. She would hunt the length and breadth of New Zealand if necessary – why, she'd once contemplated tracking down moa – a man and a boy were simple in comparison.

Urgency spurred her ever faster, however, and when she saw the crossroads up ahead she put on an extra spurt, her heart wildly racing and her lungs in agony. Then, with only five hundred yards to go she heard the clatter of horses' hooves and the rumble of the coach as it shot past in a whirl of dust – too far away to notice her.

'No,' she screamed. 'Quinn! Ben!'

But she was too late. It had gone. She collapsed onto the road, despair washing over her as she drew in a shuddering breath, then another. 'I will find them,' said that angry, determined part of her. 'They will not leave me.' Her hands clutched at her blackened skirts as she fought to control her breath and her despair but still the tears would not be stopped. She pressed the heels of her palms hard into her eyes, inadvertently streaking her cheek with soot.

Then a shadow fell over her and strong arms lifted her.

'Gwen, what the devil are you doing here?' asked a warm, dearly familiar voice trembling with laughter and hope.

'Chasing moas,' she said, clinging to his jacket. 'Oh, Quinn, I thought you'd gone and left me.'

'Young Ben was sure he heard a cry – I didn't dare believe but the boy was so insistent that we stopped the coach. Then I saw you – I knew it had to be you. Who else would be collapsed in the road in such a hoydenish manner but you, m'lady?'

He cupped her face with his large warm hands and gently rubbed at the smudge on her cheek with his thumb. She chuckled and though her breathing was steadying, she still shook and her heart still raced.

'I have something for you,' she said, fishing in her pocket and pulling out the cheque. 'I cannot take it. I cannot let you lose everything you worked for because my father – though I love him dearly – was a fool where money is concerned. I will not save his name at the expense of your life.'

The tenderness faded and he shook her roughly by the shoulders. 'Oh Jaysus, don't be telling me you intend marrying then after everything?'

'Yes, I hope to, very much.'

Quinn growled and dropped his hands from her shoulders, turning away from her.

'I have been thinking of what I wish for,' she continued, 'and now I know it is not the past I want, but the here, the now and the future. Quinn O'Donnell, for once in your life will you stay? Stay and marry me?'

Whirling about on his heel, his face alight with disbelieving joy, Quinn snatched her up in his arms with a shout of laughter, and there in the middle of the dusty road he swung her around and around and around.

'Will I?' he cried. 'Just try and stop me! Lady Guinevere, you never fail to amaze me.'